CRUEL DEFLECTIONS

Geoff Brown

TSL Publications

First published in Great Britain in 2022
By TSL Publications, Rickmansworth

Copyright © 2022 Geoff Brown

ISBN / 978-1-914245-57-2

cover image: https://www.pexels.com/photo/man-standing-facing-body-of-water-1106406/

ABOUT GEOFF

Geoff Brown was born in Lancaster. After graduating with an MA in Modern History from Sidney Sussex College, Cambridge he had a management career in three large UK companies. He then spent thirteen years as a partner in Heidrick and Struggles, a leading global executive search firm. Geoff is widely travelled with a particular love of Italy which he has visited dozens of times. He is a member of Watford Writers, is married and lives with his Danish wife in Hertfordshire.

ACKNOWLEDGEMENTS

I shared my manuscript with many friends and family members and I'm grateful for their positive feedback and encouragement.

I'm particularly indebted to several fellow members of the Watford Writers group whose input has, I think, improved the style and structure of the book. Brian Bold and Mike Lansdown offered detailed forensic critiques which were enormously helpful. Chris McDermott provided the introduction to my publisher, Anne Samson at TSL Publications.

When I got stuck with a plot line towards the end of the novel, my friend and ex-business partner David Peters came to the rescue with a creative suggestion which spurred me on to the finish line.

15 AUGUST 1974
LECCE, PUGLIA, ITALY

Luca woke drenched in sweat after his third nightmare in as many nights. He had snapped awake as he was about to be engulfed by a massive avalanche. Pursued by dark hooded figures, he was emitting a high pitched scream of pure terror. This had probably set off the avalanche thundering towards him. It had also disturbed old *Signora* Martucci in the flat above who was banging her stick energetically on her floor to make him stop.

It was the first morning of Luca Vento's twenty-sixth year on earth. Even at 6 a.m., Thursday 15 August promised to be another sweltering, energy sapping day. It was *Ferragosto*, a national holiday since Roman times. He was in his small apartment off Viale Otranto in the Puglian city of Lecce. The first stirrings of his cohabitants in this crumbling block of flats incongruously called a *palazzo* filtered through the partition walls and mingled with the insistent buzzing of the scooters outside.

He rose from the sodden bed sheets and sat at his tiny desk pouring a whole litre of water down his parched throat. He thought about the momentous events of the past few weeks and wondered what the future held for him. President Nixon had finally announced his resignation the previous Thursday. An idealistic young man, Luca had felt repulsed by the endemic corruption and abuse of power exposed by Watergate. This had somehow strengthened his resolve to do the right thing in his own birthplace in the heel of Italy.

The right thing was to blow the whistle on the widespread corrupt collusion between local government officials and the Camorra, the Neapolitan branch of the mafia with tentacles reaching into Puglia.

The day before the Nixon announcement, Luca's beloved grandmother, *nonna* Valentina, had died suddenly at the age of seventy-five. Her old friend Adriana had sent for Luca when she discovered Valentina lying dead in her vegetable garden.

"She died of a broken heart you know Luca," she said. "She never got over the death of her lovely daughter."

Adriana was referring to the horrific car accident in January on the newly opened Bologna to Bari southern extension of the A16 *Autostrada* which had claimed the lives of Luca's parents. They were casualties of the apparent collective death wish of Puglian drivers who habitually drove at maximum speed a metre from the car in front. Luca was devastated and he and his *nonna* had grown exceptionally close through supporting each other in their shared grief. In the past several months he had spent more time in his *nonna's* fisherman's cottage in nearby San Cataldo than in his own apartment.

Since graduating with a degree in Jurisprudence from the University of Perugia two years previously, Luca had been working in the *Avvocatura* of the *Giunta Regionale*, the Puglian regional administration. The *Avvocatura* was responsible for providing legal services to all local government departments in the region. Luca dealt with the legal side of commercial contracts involving both local and national government and Puglian and external industrial and agricultural businesses.

After the Second World War the Italian government had created an agency, *Cassa per il Mezzogiorno* (*Casmez*), to direct more investment to the south of the country. Big companies were required to allocate a certain percentage of their capital spend to industrial and agricultural initiatives in the southern regions including Puglia. This large funding stream predictably attracted the attention of the local mafia, the Camorra. In early August, Luca had inadvertently come across evidence of the siphoning off of some of this funding into Camorra coffers. Where he worked in this small satellite office in Lecce most of his colleagues, including his boss, Giuseppe Moscatelli, were on holiday. As the most junior lawyer on the team Luca had been "asked" to hold the fort until the whole office closed mid-month for *Ferragosto*.

He was working on a contract for a local refuse collection service and needed to check some figures on previous contracts that he believed were in his boss's filing cabinet. Although his boss had locked his cabinet, Luca knew where he hid the key. He had seen him put it in a plant pot in his secretary's office one evening when Moscatelli had rushed out. Luca was being pressed to conclude his work on the contract by the obnoxious head of regional environmental services so he decided to unlock the cabinet when the office was deserted one evening.

He immediately found the relevant file but when he was lifting it out of its hanging pocket, a thin plastic wallet came out with it. It had a label "Consulting Services", which he saw was the same as the tag on the adjacent file. Realising it had been filed in the wrong pocket, he was about to rectify the error. But something made him stop and slide the folded papers out for a quick look. He was in fact intrigued because he had never heard of any consulting work done by his department.

The first thing he saw was a postcard with a striking picture of Vesuvius and a Naples postmark. It was addressed to *Signor* Moscatelli and said, *"Thanks for your help with the Primitivo project."* It was unsigned. Luca knew that the previous year there had been a well-publicised investment in a producer of the local Primitivo red wine. Various companies had bid for the building and equipping of a new, modern storage and bottling plant and the contract was finally awarded to a company based in Naples. Luca's family had extensive vineyards in the region and produced one of the best Primitivo di Manduria wines so this news story naturally aroused his interest. On the day the local paper announced the name of the company which had won this prestigious contract, Luca was having dinner with his parents. When he arrived, they were in the huge kitchen of their *masseria*, a rambling, old fortified farmhouse outside Sava near the town of Manduria. This was one of hundreds that dotted the Puglian landscape. The region had for centuries been subject to wave after wave of invaders and predatory Saracen pirates. The local estate owners had made their main houses as impregnable as possible with thick walls and substantial outer perimeters. The *Masseria Vicenzi* had been in the Vento family for centuries and Luca loved its weathered immutability.

His father Gianni looked away from his local paper and his whole face lit up when he saw his son. Luca kissed both his *mamma* and *papà* and immediately grabbed a *bruschetta* his mother, Paola, had prepared as an antipasto. This was his favourite; toasted bread topped with tomatoes, garlic, olive oil, basil and a sprinkling of chilli. His mother slapped his hand as he went for a second, but smiled indulgently at her only child.

"I don't know how you stay so skinny," she laughed. *"Va bene*, take another one but don't spoil your appetite as I've made all your favourite dishes tonight."

Whilst both parents idolised him, Luca had not been spoiled like many only children. He looked at his mother and not for the first time thought of how often she showed she loved him. He smiled to himself recalling that this did not mean she allowed any tantrums or impoliteness. "She was not averse to smacking my legs if I was naughty. But she instilled in me a strong sense of right and wrong and also my duty of care to those less fortunate. She made sure I worked in the vineyards and olive groves during my school holidays and I was expected to pull my weight."

After the first course of small ear-shaped pasta shells with courgettes and mussels, Gianni went to retrieve his newspaper. He pointed to the headline. "Have you seen this garbage?"

"Not now Gianni," Paola said. "Can't you wait till we've finished our meal?"

"Sorry *carissima* but this is an absolute disgrace and I want to know if Luca has heard about it."

"I don't know what you are so het up about *papà*," Luca said.

"It's this bloody big investment in the old Graziani winery the other side of Manduria. It says here that the total modernisation project has been awarded by the *Giunta Regionale* to a company in Naples. My friends in the Wine Growers Association are convinced that this is a front company for the mafia. They are muttering that there must have been a lot of back handers to officials to push this through. There are loads of local companies who could easily handle this type of thing. Why bring in a bunch of Neapolitans?"

"I know absolutely nothing about it," Luca said, "and I don't think you should listen to those old fogies in the Association. It may be that the firm from Naples has a particularly strong track record in building modern wineries. God knows Puglia needs some fresh thinking to drag it out of the dark ages."

The Vento family loved nothing better than a good robust argument and the spark Luca's comment provided ignited a spirited discussion that continued through the next course of a herby lamb stew which had been Luca's best loved dish since he was a small boy.

The debate went on through the dessert course of Almond Tart until Paola decided enough was enough. "*Basta!*" she said with a steely look in her eye. "Let's talk about something else…Luca when are we going to meet that girl you've been seeing…?"

Driving back to Lecce that evening, Luca tried to put his father's suspicions out of his mind. His *papà* did have a very excitable nature and was prone to extravagant statements. But this time he had made a pretty compelling case and there certainly did seem to be Puglian companies well qualified to execute this big contract. Eventually Luca convinced himself it was a storm in a teacup and that people often saw the black hand of the mafia where altogether more prosaic factors were at play. This conversation over a year earlier came back to him like a blow to the face when he found the postcard from Naples in his boss's files. He could not resist having a detailed look at the file contents. Over the next few evening hours in the quiet, empty office, Luca pieced together the chicanery behind the awarding of the Graziani winery contract.

It was an elaborate scam.

The principal investor was a large wine producer, Marzoni Vini, based in Tuscany, supported by the government agency, *Casmez*. The latter provided state subsidised finance and attractive tax breaks, massively reducing Marzoni's capital investment. But, the granting of these financial incentives was conditional on a vetting process conducted by local government officials in the *Giunta Regionale*. Luca's boss was responsible for scrutinising the seven bids that had been submitted – six from Puglian firms and one from a Neapolitan firm, Vizzari Costruzioni S.p.A. When all the bids were in, Moscatelli had contacted someone in Vizzari to give them the contract prices submitted by the local firms. Vizzari then re-jigged their price to undercut substantially the other bid tenders. At first Luca couldn't see how this would benefit Vizzari as it could not make a profit from the deal.

Then he had a bit of luck. He found some scribbled notes in Moscatelli's handwriting headed *"Vizzari – goes bankrupt?"* dated shortly after the contract had been awarded. "Why," Luca pondered, "would he be asking if a company for which he had just secured a big project was going under?" He looked again at Vizzari's tender document and the stage payments proposed. There was an advance payment of four hundred million lire covering the purchase of construction materials and a second payment of nine hundred million after completion of the building work – for wine production, bottling and packaging equipment. There was a much smaller third and final payment on handover of the finished facility.

Luca dug further and found a sheet with two columns. The first was headed "Estimated phase 1 building costs" and the second "Estimated phase 2 equipment costs". Comparing these to the stage payments in the approved tender document, he immediately saw that the phase 1 estimate represented about 20 per cent of the advance payment and the estimate for phase 2 was only about five per cent of the second stage payment. Luca knew there was a consolidated file with copies of all invoices received. He found it and saw that the first and second stage payments to Vizzari Costruzioni had been paid in full.

It was close to midnight when he locked up the office. He got home just as various church clocks struck the hour. He sat on his tiny balcony with a glass of beer listening to the strangely soothing night sounds of a city centre on a sultry summer holiday night – snatches of radio music, raised voices, baby cries and the ubiquitous, unmistakeable, echoing sounds of scooters weaving through the narrow streets. None of this distracted him. He was in his own thought bubble and he spent the next fifteen minutes piecing together what he knew or suspected.

Vizzari had indeed gone bankrupt three months earlier leaving its creditors high and dry – particularly a Puglian building products firm which had not received a penny from Vizzari for the cement, bricks and steelwork it supplied. That spring, Luca's boss had bought a flashy new Alfa Romeo letting it be known that he'd been a lucky beneficiary in the will of a recently deceased aunt. Just after Vizzari Costruzioni had been declared bankrupt, there was a massive fire at the Graziani Winery which reduced the whole complex to a shambles of charred remains and twisted metal. The *Gazetta* reported that the police suspected arson but had made no progress in identifying the perpetrator.

A fully fledged hypothesis took shape in Luca's mind.

The Tuscan wine company, Marzoni, had put up a limited amount of funding for the project but would probably not incur much of a write-off after claiming on its insurance for the losses incurred when the whole plant went up in smoke.

The construction firm Vizzari ostensibly spent only 20 per cent or eighty million of the money they received as an advance payment – actually much less as they did not pay their suppliers – at Stage 2 they spent forty-five million, a fraction of what they were paid.

Luca's boss was in cahoots with this probably Camorra-backed firm feeding them information to ensure they won the contract. He approved full payment of their obviously fraudulent invoices. He knew of their planned declaration of bankruptcy.

It was highly likely that the work done on the winery project was just for external cosmetic purposes – maybe tarting up the building and access roads. It was equally unlikely that any new equipment had been purchased – hence the miniscule cost estimates. They had probably just put in a load of old scrap metal.

"I bet the insurance loss adjuster was on the mafia's payroll," thought Luca. "He probably recommended that his company settle in full the claim submitted by Marzoni Vini. "

The balance of the first and second payments, after the very modest initial outlay, must somehow have been squirreled out of Vizzari before it was declared bankrupt.

The Camorra had therefore netted well over a cool billion lire less the *bustarelle* or kickbacks, they had to pay to their various corrupt cohorts along the way.

"I bet Vizzari Costruzioni and Marzoni Vini colluded in the whole scheme and split the proceeds but I haven't found any evidence to corroborate this," was Luca's final thought.

He reflected angrily on the entrenched corruption gnawing at the very heart of his beloved Puglia. Everyone knew there was an undercover network embracing business, politics and crime which "re-distributed" much of the money flowing into the South. Luca had read somewhere that as much as one third of the central government's *Casmez* funds were completely subverted by corruption of one form or another. A further large slice of funding was misallocated for political reasons. Dams were built but not connected to irrigation projects. There were half-finished factories and public works and ill-conceived capital intensive industrial developments. These all became known as "cathedrals in the desert".

The next evening, the first Friday in August, Luca spent on his own in the *Avvocatura* office digging through a lot more files in Moscatelli's cabinets. He also devoted most of that weekend to intensive research in the quiet, deserted building. He uncovered a plethora of examples of bribery and corruption. As well as the prevalent practice of awarding contracts to mafia controlled companies, his forensic investigation discovered falsified inspections leading to the approval of sub-standard construction work on a major road building project. The actual "selling" of building permits and also civil service jobs was rife. His boss also seemed to be used by the Camorra as their paymaster to local police and politicians for services rendered. These included fabrication of police evidence leading to the acquittal of a mafia hitman; turning a blind eye to drug smuggling and prostitution and not stamping down on the payment of *pizzo* (protection money) by hundreds of restaurants and bars.

Luca identified more than a dozen senior people in the *Giunta Regionale's* finance, transport, refuse disposal and building departments who were on the take. To this list he was able to add a similar number of policemen of all ranks who were in the pay of the Camorra. He made copious notes of the relevant cases and took photocopies of the most incriminating documents. He could hardly credit the sheer stupidity of his boss in leaving so much information in his filing system. He had learned the hard way that Moscatelli was an obsessive pedant who wanted so much detail on every issue that the work of his department crawled along at a snail's pace. This anal retentiveness was so deeply embedded that Moscatelli had to record everything no matter how sensitive. Luca actually found a ledger with every monthly payment made to senior policemen over a period of five years.

Most of the payments to individuals were for the same amount but every so often there was a spike when a much higher sum was recorded. Against a number of these payments there were cryptic notes in Moscatelli's tiny, precise handwriting. Two in particular caught Luca's eye. One was marked "Witness/Santoro". Luca recalled a high profile court case a couple of years earlier when a vital prosecution witness had suddenly changed his mind about seeing Arturo Santoro, the accused, beat a man to death with a hammer. He said that, on reflection it had been too dark to make an accurate identification and he felt he had been badgered into fingering the suspect by over-zealous policemen bent on making an arrest. The judge threw the case out but made it plain in his summation that he felt the witness had been got at.

The other shorthand note, "Trial/Larusso" related to a more recent trial of a notorious drug baron who was arrested when three kilos of cocaine were found hidden in the boot well of his car. Larusso's lawyer claimed the police had planted the so-called drugs and when the case came to trial the evidence had sensationally "disappeared" from the police secure storage facility. Luca was convinced that his boss's notes summarised the specific services these particular policemen had provided in intimidating a witness and removing vital evidence to guarantee a criminal's acquittal. He photocopied the entire ledger. He was sure that a detailed investigation into all the entries would highlight other specific examples of delinquent police behaviour.

His boss's flagrant disregard of the need to be ultra-careful in recording these transactions also spoke volumes about their accepted normality and ubiquity. This specific group of people he had highlighted probably represented only a fraction of those involved in this network of corruption in Puglia. Why should his boss be particularly concerned about secrecy when he was one of hundreds, probably thousands of people operating in a highly effective alternative society? In effect, Moscatelli shared in a collective arrogance that this illicit fraternity was so powerful and so pervasive as to be untouchable.

EARLY AUGUST 1974

LECCE

During the early part of the week commencing 5 August, Luca consolidated all the data he had assembled into a clear, concise report supported by the one hundred or so photocopies he had made and ran off a second copy of the whole dossier for himself. Then on the Wednesday morning he got the tearful call from his *nonna's* friend Adriana telling him that Valentina had died suddenly. Luca spent the next two days in a flurry of activity arranging the funeral in the parish church in San Cataldo, dealing with the legalities associated with her death and trying to contact relatives to invite them to the burial ceremony set for the following Monday.

Luca was amazed at the number of people who turned out to follow the horse-drawn hearse. The procession from her cottage to the church must have been half a kilometre long. The church in Via Valona was packed. *Nonna* Valentina was a hugely popular local figure because of her efferves-cent personality and kindness of heart. Anyone in trouble in San Cataldo always found a sympathetic ear and wise counsel in her cottage. She had also helped dozens of local people in more material ways when they had fallen on hard times – a few thousand lire here, a large basket of fruit and vegetables there. She had even shared her cottage with families evicted from their own homes.

Early on the morning of the funeral, dozens of people had come to her house as tradition demanded bearing food and drink. After the funeral ceremony Adriana had laid all this out in the cottage and garden. There was so much food and wine it would have taken an army to consume it. At least eighty people had come from the church and they made hardly a dent in the food mountain. Luca was drained by the constant repetition of condolences and was glad finally to show the last mourners out. On his way back to Lecce early that summer evening he had time to reflect on what he now knew was a recent premonitory conversation with his *nonna*.

At the end of July, when Luca was having lunch at her cottage she said she had something very important to tell him. She sat facing him in her tiny, dark, shuttered parlour and took both his hands in her own. He looked down at her strong, sunburned hands thinking how much he loved this old woman who was like a rock in his life.

"Luca I want you to know that I love you beyond words and I'm so proud of the man you have become. Your *mamma*, God rest her, and your *papà* will be looking down from heaven and blessing the day they made such a wonderful son." The power of her expression of love brought a gush of tears to Luca's eyes and *nonna* also wept quietly. She composed herself and said, "*Carissimo*, I am old and I may not be here much longer…"

"Nonsense *nonna*," cried an alarmed Luca, "you've got many years to go yet."

"Maybe so, but I want to tell you a little secret just in case. I don't trust banks as you know so I've always kept my money here at home. Your *nonno* was not a rich man but he inherited quite a lot of money from his brother who died childless…come with me. I want to show you where I keep it."

Nonna Valentina took him to an outhouse on her large vegetable plot and moved a big plant pot in one corner to reveal just bare earth as far as Luca could see. She scraped away some soil and underneath was a thin stone slab.

"Push that to one side," she said. He did and in a shallow recess underneath was a battered leather wallet.

"*Va bene*, now put it back…and the slab and brush that soil over it again. There's quite a bit of cash in there so when I pass away I want you to have it."

"*Nonna* I don't really like to hear you talk like this…it makes me sad."

"Luca, we all have to go sometime and I'd be kicking myself all the way up to heaven if I hadn't told you where that money was."

His *nonna* must have known she was going to die soon. He thought she may even have willed it to hasten her longed-for reunion with his dead mother, her only child. He had certainly heard of people who had simply decided to die. The previous day, whilst he was sorting out her effects in the cottage, he had retrieved the wallet from its hiding place in the outhouse. He sat at her kitchen table and got a shock when he counted the money inside it which was all in high denomination notes.

"Wow, forty-five million lire," he gasped out loud. This was many times more than his annual salary as an "apprentice" lawyer. He realised that suddenly arriving at his bank to deposit such a large amount of cash was bound to raise questions. So he locked it in the bottom drawer of his desk until he could think more clearly about what to do with it.

The evening of the funeral he spent in a stunned, half drunk state, hoping that alcohol would deaden the pain. It didn't…It simply made him more maudlin as he reflected on his now pure orphan status, without parents, grandparents or siblings. He also thought of what a very good, much-loved person his *nonna* had been and how he had come to rely on her after his parents died. He wanted to do something that would honour her memory and this pressing demand finally pushed him into making the decision he had been agonising over since completing his dossier on local corruption several days earlier.

Just after dawn on Tuesday 13 August, he left his apartment and drove up to Brindisi. He had decided to deliver his report to Corrado Fontana, a crusading anti-mafia magistrate. Luca had spent a few months' internship in this investigating magistrate's office as part of his university law degree. He had seen at first hand how this highly pro-active role in the Italian judicial system worked. And he had observed how fearless and full of integrity Fontana was in fighting the widespread interconnected criminal and political corruption in the region. Luca felt he was the only person he could trust to act on the potentially explosive information he had assembled.

Having checked that Fontana was expected in the office that day, Luca gave the security guard on duty at the central magistracy a securely sealed envelope. It was addressed to *Doctor Fontana* and marked *"Urgent"* and *"Personal/Addressee Only."* He had worried about whether to put his name to the report. In the end he did sign the covering letter as he thought it was the courageous thing to do and would have made his *nonna* proud. He also knew that Doctor Fontana had formed a good impression of him during his internship. His tutor had shown him the glowing testimonial Fontana had sent on the conclusion of his placement. The latter's receipt of such allegations from a trusted source would hopefully make him treat them very seriously.

For the next twenty-four hours Luca was on tenterhooks, but Tuesday and then Wednesday passed without any message from the magistrate's office. After waking from his horrible nightmare on *Ferragosto* morning, a long cool shower did little to lessen his residual sense of foreboding. He decided to go for a run to clear his head before it got too oppressively hot. He had been a serious distance runner at school and university and he still ran ten kilometres three or four times a week. In the dark vestibule of his apartment building there were open pigeon holes for the residents' post. Luca glanced at his and was surprised there had been a delivery on a national holiday. He plucked out a folded note. When he opened the single sheet of folded paper he read these scrawled, frightening words containing a couple of misspellings which bizarrely caught Luca's eye first.

"*Buon compleanno. Devi andartene oggi dall'Italia. Sanno che hai fatto una sofiata su di loro. Ti ucideranno domani. Hanno un bagno di acido pronto per te*

Buona fortuna

Un amico

(Happy birthday. You must get out of Italy today. They know you grassed on them. They will kill you tomorrow. They have an acid bath ready for you. Good luck.

A friend.)

He slumped down on the cold stone steps leading up to his apartment. It took him a few minutes to gather his thoughts and get his breathing and heart rate back to near normality. He had no doubt the warning was genuine. He realised that he had half-expected something awful to happen given the ominous silence since dropping off the dossier in Brindisi.

So what had happened? Either his report had been intercepted before reaching the magistrate or someone in his office had seen it and informed either Luca's boss or the Camorra. The *amico* who had sent the warning note was clearly a Camorra member and was in the know about their plans to kill him. One of Luca's best friends at secondary school was Alessandro Rizzo who was a bit of a tearaway. The youngest son of an agricultural labourer with a large family, Alessandro had learnt to fend for himself from an early age as his father's wage did not go far. His petty thieving had inexorably developed into more advanced criminality. Luca had once taken the blame for some explicit graffiti Alessandro had left on the blackboard of the most unpopular teacher at the *Liceo*. Luca knew that Alessandro was already in very hot water over two other misdemeanours and that this third transgression might just be enough to have him expelled. Luca himself was a model student who never got into trouble so the school authorities treated his offence as a one-off adolescent aberration by their star pupil.

Alessandro had never forgotten this and when Luca was home from university he would occasionally invite him out for a drink. He genuinely liked Alessandro who had a cheeky charm, although he suspected that he was getting more deeply embroiled with the criminal fraternity. Luca guessed that he had already been recruited by the Camorra. So it must have been Alessandro who had tipped him off – as repayment of a debt of honour. Certainly the spelling was characteristically inaccurate. The words *sofiata* and *ucideranno* needed an extra consonant each and there was something really familiar about the upward slant to the note's crossed letter t-s. That clinched it – the t-s were identical to the blackboard graffiti of a decade ago which was understandably burned into his memory. The teacher was called an ugly *bastardo* among other far more graphic insults. Luca had to write out one thousand times, "I must not use these obscene and insulting words again."

He went slowly back up to his apartment sat down at his desk and worked out a plan of action. There were a number of imperatives. He clearly had to leave Puglia by that evening at the latest. Even if his dossier had reached magistrate Fontana, he knew that his life was forfeit. Against the long arm and even longer memory of the mafia there was no absolutely guaranteed protection. The only absolute certainty was that they would eventually kill him. There were indeed well documented cases of bodies being dissolved in acid.

With the enormous reach of the mafia, he probably needed to get out of Italy altogether to stand any chance of survival. Given the *Ferragosto* holiday, all the banks were closed so he could not withdraw any of the substantial funds at his disposal. What he had inherited following the untimely deaths of his parents had made him a very wealthy young man. Particularly as he had sold *Masseria Vicenzi* because he could no longer face being there. It brought back too many painful memories.

He could only use the money his *nonna* had bequeathed him plus the spending money he had drawn out for the holiday period. If he needed help, this must come from someone he could trust implicitly – literally with his life. When the Camorra found out that he had disappeared they would pull out all the stops to find him. He had to lay a false trail to buy some time. A plan began to take shape in Luca's fertile and logical mind. He decided he would make for the UK which was the only foreign country he knew well and where he had at least some language capability. But, he would leave a few not too obvious clues suggesting he was, in fact, headed for Argentina where there was a big Italian community.

The previous summer, he had been on holiday to Malta with some friends from university and he knew he could get from there to the UK reasonably easily. But how to get to Malta under the mafia's radar screen? The best idea was to enlist the help of Bernardo, a friend since childhood. Bernardo Colangelo came from one of the wealthiest families in Puglia. He and Luca were both only children and had "adopted" each other as brothers whilst at primary school. They were inseparable through their teens and even spent time together in London. Bernardo was sent there to work in an Italian bank whilst Luca was working in various restaurants which were customers of his father's wine business.

They actually looked like brothers. Both were tall with slim athletic builds, brown eyes, dark tousled hair and handsome open faces.

Bernardo was now running one of his family's businesses but when not working his passion was sailing. He had a boat moored at Gallipoli to the west of Lecce and Luca often joined him on weekend sailing trips. He had seen Bernardo at his *nonna's* funeral and knew he was going to Gallipoli the following day to spend a couple of weeks on his boat. If Bernardo was still in port he could take him to Catania on Sicily's west coast from where Luca knew he could get a ferry to Malta on the second leg of his escape.

First things first. He had to go to Gallipoli and find his friend. If he was not there, Luca's contingency plan was simply to drive through Italy to the French or Swiss border and then on to England. By 9.30 a.m. he had packed a couple of bags, retrieved his passport and *nonna's* wallet and checked the oil, water and tyres on his fairly new Fiat. He had also left a loosely torn up piece of paper in his waste paper basket with a calculation of the exchange rate for lire into Argentinian pesos. Just as he was about to leave the apartment he remembered to pick up a bunch of personal papers including his high school diploma and university Master's Degree certificate. He put these in a folder together with the copy he had kept of the report he had sent to Magistrate Fontana…which had caused his life to implode in such spectacular fashion.

On the way to his car, parked a block away from his apartment, he had put an envelope through the letterbox of the *Banca Popolare di Bari* on Viale Otranto. He knew the bank would not open again until the following Monday but he had written to his Bank Manager to let him know he had left on urgent family business. He said this would take him to Spain first and then Argentina to deal with some complex property issues which had emerged following the death of his *nonna*. He told the banker that he would probably need, in due course, to transfer substantial funds to a foreign account. He said that this matter was extremely confidential and he hoped he could rely on the manager's discretion. He got to Gallipoli an hour later and, driving across the causeway towards the harbour in the old town on its small island, was mightily relieved to see Bernardo's boat at its usual berth close to the Castello. *Il Delfino* was a gift to Bernardo from his parents the previous Christmas. It was a brand new Pierrot, 30 foot, five berth sailing boat with a powerful Lombardini engine.

Once he had embraced his friend, Luca quickly outlined his dangerous predicament. Bernardo did not try to dissuade him from his escape plan. Through his own family's business dealings he had first hand knowledge of the Camorra's ruthlessness in disposing of people who would not play ball with them.

"Luca, you are lucky to find me still here. When I took the boat out a couple of days ago the engine started missing and I had to sail back to port. The local marine mechanic figured out that I had run the diesel level far too low prior to my last fill-up. When I filled it up the next time, water had got in and contaminated the fuel...so the tanks had to be completely voided and the air and fuel lines checked. This has now been done and *Il Delfino* is fully seaworthy."

"Fantastic; but Bernardo I need to get my car back to Lecce. If I leave it here, it's too risky. They may put two and two together and realise I've left with you. Also, I've a couple more things to do to try to cover my tracks."

"*Va bene*, I'll follow you in my car so you can drop yours off and we can then get back here in under a couple of hours."

Luca insisted that Bernardo park on the outskirts of town rather than follow him into the centre and they agreed to rendezvous at one o'clock. Luca first drove to the railway station and purchased a single ticket to Rome via Brindisi on the night train leaving that evening. He then parked his Fiat in its usual spot and went back to his apartment *palazzo*. He trotted up to *Signora* Martucci's apartment and told her that he had to go to Spain on urgent family business and didn't know when he would be back. When the Camorra came looking for him the next day, she might just help to put them on the wrong track. She was the biggest gossip in the building.

Jumping into Bernardo's car around 12:45 they were back in Gallipoli by 1:30. His friend dropped him off before the causeway as they did not want anyone to see him board *Il Delfino*. There was a very popular beach which was only about half an hour's walk away on the road towards Sannicola. The friends agreed to meet there at 3:30 after Bernardo had checked his boat in preparation for a lengthy voyage and made sure his inflatable dinghy was securely lashed to the stern. He would also inform the *Capitano di Porto* that he was headed for the Greek islands and would probably be away a week to ten days. Bernardo would moor about a hundred yards out from the beach and Luca, who was now very lightly dressed in shorts and T-shirt, would swim out to the boat.

When Luca arrived at the beach it was absolutely packed with people and there were a fair number of boats either moored or tacking up and down. No one paid him any attention and as soon as he spotted *Il Delfino* approaching he swam out to the vessel in a fast crawl and Bernardo hauled him aboard. It was only about an hour later when he was sipping a strong coffee that the enormity of what he had done hit him. Things had moved so quickly since he had found the warning note at dawn that he had been operating on automatic pilot. Was there really no other option but to cut and run? Surely he could have made contact with magistrate Fontana and asked for protection. But, in the end, Luca kept coming back to the inescapable conclusion that the only person who could guarantee his safety was himself. He had to make sure that no one except Bernardo had any inkling of his plans – and even with his friend he had to limit disclosure to a minimum. This was motivated by the need to protect Bernardo rather than by any apprehension that he would betray him.

That was why he had only told him that he was making for Malta where he had made some friends whilst on holiday the previous year. He said he needed some time before he decided where to go from there and would then get in touch. They agreed to sail the 200 or so nautical miles to Catania in easy stages. They would not stop at any intermediate ports but moor up off isolated coves and do some fishing to supplement the limited extra provisions Bernardo had managed to forage on what was a national holiday. They would aim to arrive in Catania the following Wednesday or Thursday hoping that the Camorra would not be looking for them there. Luca then had a brainwave. He knew he would need to show his passport when boarding the ferry to Valletta. What if he borrowed Bernardo's passport?

"Do you have your passport with you?"

"Sure, I always take it when I'm on the boat and this time I was thinking of heading for Corfu so made sure I packed it."

They looked at the photo in his passport and typically it was not a particularly good likeness. Unless a border guard scrutinised it very closely, it could easily pass for Luca. They agreed that he would post it back to Bernardo as soon as he reached Malta.

They took *Il Delfino* across the Gulf of Taranto and that first night moored her close to the *Isola di Capo Rizzuto*. They stayed there the whole of Friday and then dawdled their way along the southern Calabrian coast and stopped for a couple of days off *Rocella Ionica*. On the Sunday evening as dusk fell they could hear the sound of music and laughter as it reached them from some sort of *festa* in the village. A wave of melancholy washed over Luca as he had the stark presentiment that he would never set foot in his native land again. He must burn his boats and invent a brand new life for himself.

The next morning they agreed that Bernardo should go ashore to pick up some supplies so he attached the outboard motor to the inflatable and chugged to shore. He was away about an hour and Luca used the quiet time to pull himself together. He began to see some positive sides to his situation. He had no close family ties in Italy. He was young and resourceful. Thanks to his *nonna's* legacy he had enough money to live on for a few years. He might also be able to figure out how to get additional funds out of Italy without leaving footprints for the Camorra to track. He had always wanted to travel and experience different cultures and he really liked the British way of life in all respects except the weather.

By the time Bernardo hove to in the dinghy, he had stopped feeling sorry for himself and started planning what he would do when he arrived in the UK. The next few days were uneventful. The two friends fished, swam, sun bathed and talked incessantly. It was as if they knew this might be their last opportunity to do so. They put *Il Delfino* under sail and only used her engines on the approach to Catania. The plan was to land south of the town in the early morning of the twenty-first of August. Luca would then get a bus or a taxi to the ferry port. He did not know the ferry timetable but if he was unable to get to Malta that way, he was sure he could pay for a cabin on a cargo ship bound for Valletta.

He said an emotional goodbye to Bernardo. They were both in tears as they embraced and Luca stepped onto the quay of the small marina where they had berthed *Il Delfino*. The girl in the tiny office of the *Capitano di Porto* was very helpful in ringing for a taxi and in no time at all Luca was on his way to Catania. At the ferry terminal he discovered there was a ferry leaving for Malta that day. He booked a cabin in Bernardo's name and spent the rest of the day buying clothes and a couple of suitcases in preparation for his new life.

At embarkation there was an extremely cursory glance at Bernardo's passport and Luca breathed a huge sigh of relief. Nor had he spotted any people taking a particular interest in the queue of passengers. He found his cabin and decided not to venture into the public areas of the ship and risk anyone engaging him in conversation. He arrived in Malta about eight hours later and disembarked without incident. He checked in to a small nonde-script hotel a short walk from the port and the next morning was at the Tourist Office as soon as it opened. He found to his relief that Air Malta had just started regular services to several UK cities. He decided on Manchester and took a taxi out to the Airport at Luqa having first changed some of his lire into both Maltese liri and pounds sterling. At the Air Malta sales desk he managed to get a seat on a flight the following day and this time he used his own name rather than risk an eagle-eyed immigration officer in Manchester spotting that he was travelling on the wrong passport. Back in Valletta he found a Post Office and sent Bernardo's passport back with a brief unsigned note saying, "*En route* for Argentina. Thanks for everything. Have a good life."

On Friday 23rd he arrived in Manchester, where the sun was shining but much more weakly than in Malta. The pilot had said it was nineteen degrees but it felt like the middle of winter to Luca. He checked into the Excelsior hotel a short walk from the airport and when he got to his room rummaged in his luggage to find a sweater.

He needed to determine his next move. He had used the days sailing in *Il Delfino* to sketch out a few possibilities. He knew he needed another career because he couldn't practise law in the UK. He also wanted to find somewhere to live and work that was a bit off the beaten track. On one of his teenage summer stints in the UK his father had arranged for him to spend a fortnight in Leith, near Edinburgh. He stayed with Paolo Biagi and family. Paolo owned a big, bustling Italian trattoria in the town and had recently opened a delicatessen which was proving very popular with the locals and the growing Italian community in the Edinburgh area.

He and Luca's father had been great friends and served together in the Italian army. Paolo had been captured in North Africa in 1941 and was a POW in Orkney until the end of the war. He had then decided to stay in Scotland and, through a family connection, managed to get a job in Edinburgh with the food and wine distributor Valvona and Crolla. In the late forties he married a Scots/Italian girl who shortly afterwards inherited a tidy sum from a maiden aunt. This enabled Paolo and his wife Maria to open their first small restaurant in Leith on the coast a few miles from the capital city. They called it Ristorante Zia Lucia in memory of the aunt benefactress. By the mid-sixties with a rapidly growing clientele they had tripled the size of the restaurant by buying adjacent properties and adding an upstairs bar and dining room to the enlarged ground floor restaurant.

Luca's father became one of his key wine suppliers and they kept in regular contact. Luca had last seen Paolo at his parents' funeral in January. Paolo had found a quiet moment to take him to one side.

"Your *papà* was a very loyal and generous friend to me and helped us out during some tough times when we were struggling to make a go of the restaurant. He even sent me two large consignments of wine and refused any payment. You should know, Luca, that I will do everything in my power to help you if you ever need it."

Luca had been too overcome with grief to pay much heed at the time. But, one very early morning sitting on the deck of *Il Delfino* as the Calabrian coast gradually emerged in the dawn light, Paolo's genuine heartfelt words came back to him. He resolved to travel to Edinburgh to see him and enlist his help in forging a new life. Luca had always been interested in food and wine. From his involvement in the family business and his vacation work in restaurants he already had a useful reservoir of experience and knowledge. Also to the great amusement of his father who had never been near an oven in his life, he had spent hours in the kitchen. Under his mother's expert eye, he learnt to cook increasingly complex dishes which his father ate with great relish along with his earlier dismissive words.

He rang the Biagis from his room and Mrs Biagi answered. He said he would be in Edinburgh the following day and would love to pop in for a chat.

"Paolo is out at the moment visiting one of his suppliers, Luca, but he will be so pleased if you come to see us. The best time would be around 3:30 in the afternoon when there is a lull between the lunch and dinner trade."

Luca walked across to the airport and hired a car for the next morning. He had an early dinner and back in his room switched on the TV. He watched with a mixture of amusement and bemusement a heat of *Jeux Sans Frontieres* from Switzerland. England was represented by a place called Farnham. The sheer exuberant childishness of the competition made him laugh out loud for the first time since he had fled Italy. He switched off after the nine o'clock news and read a couple of newspapers to test his English comprehension. He was pleased that he understood most of what he read but depressed by the continuing reportage of the economic recession. He noted that leading shares on the London Stock Exchange had lost about 70 per cent of their value since the start of the global downturn the previous year. Extensive coverage of the troubles in Northern Ireland did not make for more cheerful reading and he reflected that things were bleak all over. In Italy before he left, the media coverage had been dominated by the latest terrorist attacks, particularly the bombing of the Roma-Brennero express earlier that month.

He slept fitfully and picked up the rental car around seven the next morning. He drove in a leisurely fashion to Edinburgh arriving at lunchtime and strolled around the city centre. He was amazed at how busy the city was, not having realised it was Festival time. He drove the five miles or so to Leith and presented himself at Ristorante Zia Lucia at exactly 3:30. He was greeted by a stunning, tall young woman with jet-black hair and a smile that immediately dispelled the butterflies fluttering in his stomach.

"Hi, you must be Luca. I'm Rosalba Biagi. I'm sorry but my dad had to sort out some problem with a meat supplier. He said he'd be back in about half an hour."

"Ah, so you are the famous Rosalba. I remember when I was here that summer you were travelling in Europe before starting college."

"That's right; I went to Strathclyde University to do a degree in business with modern languages. After I graduated, I decided to stay on in the academic world and I'm now working on my PhD thesis on an aspect of international business finance. This autumn, I'm starting to earn some money – which my dad is very pleased about – in my first real job as a researcher and lecturer at Napier College…Oh heck, Luca, I'm so sorry to have blurted out my life story in one burst. Mum said I was to take you next door as soon as you arrived."

Luca was mesmerised by the sheer vibrancy of this animated and beautiful girl and would have been happy to just stay there listening to her talk for hours. Rosalba locked up the restaurant and pointed to an adjacent terraced house.

"That's where we live now…look there's Mum."

"Rosalba…what have you been doing with Luca? I saw him arrive ages ago."

"*Mamma,* don't exaggerate, it's only been a few minutes."

Maria Biagi greeted Luca like a long lost relative and said she was so sorry she could not accompany her husband to the funeral in January but she had to stay to look after the business. She had set out coffee and cakes in the large kitchen and when they sat down she explained proudly, "Since your visit in the mid-sixties we have substantially enlarged both the restaurant and our living accommodation by acquiring and knocking together two neigh-bouring terraced houses. This gave us a house with four bedrooms but we are only using two at the moment as Rosalba's younger sister Claudia is now working in London…"

At that moment the front door slammed. Paolo burst in and enveloped Luca in a bear hug in his characteristically extravagant way.

"What a wonderful surprise. I was so thrilled when Maria told me you were coming."

"It was a spur of the moment thing," Luca said. "My *nonna* died a couple of weeks ago and after the funeral I felt I needed to get away from Puglia for a while."

He continued quickly, "But *Signor* Biagi, I also need to talk to you about a serious problem I have. When would be a good time?"

"Luca, call me Paolo please...right now is fine. Why don't we pop upstairs to my office?"

Maria and her daughter were a little taken aback by this sudden turn of events and speculated about what Luca's problem might be as they cleared the table. Up in the attic space that had been converted into a small office, Luca perched on a stool in front of Paolo's incredibly cluttered desk and spent the next twenty minutes relating the strange history of his recent past. The words poured out in an unstoppable stream and Luca felt a cathartic release in finally being able to unburden himself. He saw a range of emotions passing across Paolo's large, kindly, expressive face – incredulity, anxiety, sadness and finally pride at Luca's courageous stand.

When Luca had finished, Paolo grabbed him again in a rib-crushing hug. He said, "I have always been interested in reading philosophy and it seems to me that you have taken to heart the famous observation by Edmund Burke...'All that is necessary for the triumph of evil is for good men to do nothing.' I'm sure your *papà* would have been enormously proud of you. You will stay with us for as long as you like. Tonight, you can eat here with Maria and Rosalba. Tomorrow is Sunday and the restaurant is closed all day so we can discuss in detail what to do next. Luca, I don't like keeping anything from my girls. Is it OK with you if they hear the whole story too? We are a very close family and we could then all pull together to help you. My girls are very smart and will, I'm sure, come up with lots of good ideas."

Luca was rather apprehensive about extending the broadcast of his troubles but he did not feel that he could refuse this large, good-natured man who had opened his house and his heart to him. He was also realistic enough to know that if Maria was anything like his own mother, she would quickly prise the full story out of Paolo. Luca nodded his assent and Paolo went downstairs to tell them Luca would be staying for a while. Maria bustled upstairs and showed Luca to a guest bedroom.

"This was Claudia's room but she now has a place of her own in London, so we use it for guests."

Luca retrieved his suitcases from the hire car and when he had stowed away his clothes, Maria said, "Why don't you and Rosalba have a walk around Leith while I prepare dinner? I'm going to make our version of *Fritto Misto di Mare* because I remember you loved that when you were here that summer."

Luca smiled. "It was without doubt the best thing I have ever eaten."

Maria spontaneously pecked him on the cheek and shooed them out. After a leisurely stroll along the seafront and a drink in one of the pubs by the harbour, they all sat down to dinner. Both Maria and Rosalba looked at him with a wide-eyed expectancy that was almost comical.

"We can't wait to hear your story. Before he went to the restaurant Paolo told me you had something to tell us but we'll let you eat first."

With that Maria brought in the first dish – ravioli filled with pheasant meat. Luca attacked this with real relish suddenly realising he was absolutely ravenous. Then came the famous *Fritto Misto* which was even better than he remembered it, with feather-light batter encasing an array of ultra fresh local seafood. The langoustine in particular were melt-in-the-mouth delectable. Whether it was because she knew he was nervous or just an example of her naturally hospitable nature, Maria kept topping up Luca's glass with a delicious Gavi di Gavi which she said came from a vineyard next to her grandparents' home in Piedmont. The meal came to a triumphant conclusion with the lightest *zabaglione* Luca had ever tasted.

"That was easily the most superb meal I have ever had," said Luca bringing a pink glow of pride to Maria's face. He helped the two women clear the table and wash up which seemed to surprise and please them. They both laughed and said it was a unique experience for them, as all the men in their circle had never seen the business end of a kitchen.

At last, they sat around the cleared dinner table, again sipping a glass of Strega with their coffee. Luca retold his story. He was so captivated by Rosalba that he could not resist embellishing it at several points to make his escape sound more daring in retrospect than in reality. It seemed to work. As he told them how he had sat on the deck of *Il Delfino* in the summer twilight and felt such an unutterable sadness, Rosalba reached over and put both her hands over his. She looked so pretty and admiring that his heart melted. He decided at that exact moment, he told her later, that she was the girl for him.

A wave of utter exhaustion suddenly swept over Luca. He had an unconquerable urge to close his eyes and sleep. He had slept only fitfully during his escape and for the first time was able to relax in the shelter of this supportive household. He thanked Maria again for her wonderful cooking, staggered zombie-like upstairs and collapsed into bed. He was asleep almost instantly but before he drifted off he had the most delightful feeling that he had found a second family.

He slept for twelve hours straight. He was greeted with a round of good-natured ribbing when he finally emerged in the kitchen come family room at eleven o'clock where Paolo, Maria and Rosalba were drinking coffee.

"Luca we have been talking about your incredible tale. We have some ideas we want to share with you. *Va bene?*"

Luca nodded at Paolo and sipped his coffee.

"When you were here several summers ago you showed a real interest in the restaurant business. I said to Maria at the time that I thought you were a natural. You were certainly great with the customers; you surprised us all with your cooking skills and you clearly knew a great deal about wine…"

Luca smiled and held up his hand to stop the word flow.

"I think we have come to the same conclusion Paolo. If I have to forge a new career it seems that the restaurant business is a good fit. As you say, I have a basic platform to build on but I don't want to delude myself that I've done more than skim the surface. I have a proposal to put to you. What I think I need to do is spend a few years educating myself both in theory and practice and improving my English. With Rosalba's help maybe I can find a suitable college course. I can pay for this with *nonna's* legacy. I could also work for you during the evenings, weekends and vacations. I know I would learn a tremendous amount from you and I'd be happy to work for no pay."

The family Biagi looked at each other and engaged in a spontaneous round of synchronised nodding. Maria said, "That sounds like a splendid plan but we wouldn't hear of you working for nothing, would we Paolo?"

"No, of course not. We will pay you the same rate as our other staff."

Luca was adamant that he did not want to be paid. Paolo could see he was unlikely to budge and looked a little stumped until Rosalba came to his rescue.

"Why don't we have Luca stay here with us? He can then work in exchange for full bed and board."

This broke the deadlock and honour was satisfied on both sides. So began the second phase of Luca Vento's life. The next day he returned his hire car to Edinburgh airport and over the next few weeks he and Rosalba became inseparable. They researched all possible college courses for him. They also borrowed Paolo's pride and joy, a nearly new, red Spider *Veloce* to explore the Scottish coast and mountains. They were immediately attracted to each other and it took only ten days for Luca to tell her he loved her. She said nothing but clasping his head between her slender hands she kissed him so hard that any verbal response was rendered redundant.

It was clear to Maria and Paolo that they were destined for each other. It was with great joy tinged with sadness that they accepted the match. Maria had lost her firstborn, a boy named Lorenzo, only six weeks after his birth because of a botched forceps delivery. He would have been a couple of years younger than Luca had he survived. On the mid-September night when the young couple told them they wanted to get engaged, Paolo and Maria were talking in bed.

"Perhaps God has blessed us with another son," Maria said with a catch in her voice.

"No one can replace our Lorenzo," Paolo said quietly, "but if he had lived I hope he would have turned out to be as good a man as Luca. He will certainly be more like a son than a son-in-law to us and it is wonderful to see Rosalba so happy."

36 YEARS LATER, 7 DECEMBER 2010

VERONA

She thought she was being followed. Since arriving in Verona the previous early December morning, Gina Biagi had on several occasions sensed someone tracking her. She was a well-grounded woman emotionally and certainly not plagued by an over-active imagination. But, she was an omnivorous reader of quality spy fiction since being hooked at school on the early John Le Carré novels. In fact, she had just bought his latest offering, *Our Kind of Spy* at Heathrow to read on the plane. She had tried to flush out her follower by one or two manoeuvres she recalled from her reading. She had stopped suddenly and doubled back on herself as if she had lost her way or forgotten something. In Via Mazzini, a pedestrianised up-market shopping street, she had turned as if to look in a shop window and scanned the street behind through the corner of her eye. Each time she tried these expedients she saw a man falter in his stride or stop suddenly to window shop. The only problem was that it was a different man each time.

On this second afternoon on the way back to her hotel near Piazza Erbe, one of the bustling hubs of this ancient city, she told herself not to be so paranoid. Unless her followers were using a sophisticated relay system which was stretching credulity to breaking point, she should snap out of it and put it down to exhaustion following the most demanding episode in her career to date.

Gina was a headhunter; a partner in Buckman Collins, a leading international firm and the top performer in their London office. In the current 2010 year, even in very testing economic conditions, she had won close to two million pounds worth of business. She preferred the explicitly evocative term "headhunter" to "executive search consultant". This fancy title was often used by her colleagues in an attempt to add a more professional lustre to their activities. She had come to Verona this December, a city she knew very well, to interview four potential candidates for an assignment she had won. It also gave her the chance to escape the snow and ice that had settled on the UK in what was to become one of the coldest months on record.

She recalled the somewhat unusual background to this job. Three weeks earlier she had seen in the business press that Simon Ramsay, the Group Chief Executive of Mondo Foods Group had left suddenly "for personal reasons." Ever alert to a business opportunity, Gina contacted the Chairman, Sir Roger Simmons, for whom she had worked previously. To her surprise his secretary put her straight through.

"Gina, are you able to meet this afternoon?"

"Absolutely," she replied thinking about how to limit the collateral fallout from the three scheduled meetings already in her diary.

She arrived at the Head Office of Mondo Foods at three o'clock. It was in a quiet Mews in the heart of Mayfair. The office was unostentatious, but there was an expensive price tag on the décor and furnishings to achieve its understated style. A man in his mid-fifties, of medium height and stocky athletic build, Sir Roger exuded that air of confident competence characteristic of many businessmen at the top of the corporate heap. The body language said "...I'm in this job because I'm bloody good and I don't have to prove anything to anyone..."

When she was seated in his office, he got straight down to business. Sir Roger didn't do pleasantries. "Gina, I know you would like to have a crack at finding us a new Group CEO but I'm sorry, we've already asked one of your competitors to take this on". Gina thought, 'Why on earth have you wrecked my busy day to give me the brush off personally.'

"But I have another assignment for you," Sir Roger went on, "to get us a Managing Director or rather *Direttore Generale* for one of our Italian subsidiaries. The company is called Sapore Senza Pari or SSP. It's based near Modena and is a leading producer of balsamic vinegar and infused olive oils."

Gina immediately clicked into focused consultant mode. Although not the plum top job, the Italian role would give her a chance to show what she could do and open up further opportunities within this large, successful international food group. Her company had been badly hit by the worldwide recession triggered in 2008 and needed new clients very badly. She had never worked for Mondo Foods before. Her previous involvement with Sir Roger, who was a "serial" chairman, had been with another of his companies in the fast moving consumer goods field.

"I remembered the great job you did for us at Spirex and when you rang this morning I was pondering what to do about this Italian post so your call was serendipitous. Your Italian background and language fluency make you an ideal person to take this on, so here we are…"

"I'm flattered Sir Roger, but before I agree, we need to resolve one or two issues. Firstly, I'm sure you appreciate that any candidate worth their salt will want to know exactly why the Group CEO left so suddenly."

"Can't tell you that I'm afraid," Sir Roger cut in, "because we have a confidentiality agreement in force, binding on both sides." He looked her straight in the eye and continued. "You'll have to take my word for it that there is nothing sinister about this and the Group is in rude health and will continue to thrive under a new man."

"Or woman?" Gina said a bit abruptly. "Maybe," smiled Sir Roger rather indulgently, "but as the search for a replacement is now at an advanced stage it looks probable that it will be a man." Gina digested this and knew that if the recruitment process was nearing completion, the Chairman must have set the ball rolling months before Simon Ramsay's recent exit. It was not at all uncommon to start a confidential search for a replacement for someone about to get the chop. This meant that the new incumbent could be slotted in quickly with minimum loss of business continuity.

In her ten years as a headhunter, Gina had learned that executives approached about a new career move tended to walk away when the top management of the business was in a state of flux. She knew that disclosing that the client was Mondo Foods to potential candidates, before a new Group CEO was in place, would be a big deterrent to top quality people. She therefore proposed a halfway house approach to Sir Roger.

"I think the best thing would be for us to start quietly to identify individuals who might be contenders for the Italian *Direttore Generale* rôle and make discreet approaches to those we think are possibilities, without telling them we are working for your Group. This way we can assess whether these individuals are prepared to consider other opportunities. We will at least have some of our ducks in a row when you announce who the new Group CEO is going to be. I can then quickly interview the apparent front runners and confirm a shortlist for you to see."

Sir Roger was an experienced corporate animal and appreciated the logic of Gina's proposal. "OK, let's proceed on that basis but I need you to get your skates on as we hope to have our man in the net in the next few weeks."

Sir Roger's intercom buzzed. "Your next appointment is here," was the message in the cut glass accent of his formidable secretary.

"OK Gina, we'll have to leave it there for now I'm afraid."

Gina stood. "Fine, but we need to get together for a more detailed briefing on the Italian rôle so that I know exactly what I'm looking for."

As Sir Roger showed her out, he said to his secretary, "Margaret, get Gina in the diary asap – top priority and get Charles to join us." Margaret e-mailed later to confirm an early evening meeting the following day and that Charles Williamson, the Group Human Resources Director, would be joining them. Gina replied that she would be bringing her researcher Tom Nyholm with her. Gina and Tom then spent the rest of the afternoon and following morning looking into the Mondo Group, trying to find out why Simon Ramsay had left so suddenly. Tom did most of the probing. He was a young Dane with an international business degree and a command of the English language which equalled Gina's own, delivered in an almost perfect Home Counties accent. He had come to London from the Copenhagen office of her firm Buckman Collins on a two year secondment to increase his exposure to a much bigger marketplace. He was seen as a rising star and for once the advance publicity actually understated the case. He was absolutely brilliant and Gina thanked her lucky stars that, because she had a reputation as a good coach, he had been allocated to her.

As well as plugging into the obvious business information services, Tom talked to several industry insiders – competitors, past employees of Mondo and even one of their Divisional Finance Directors. These were all people known to Buckman Collins because they had been candidates or clients in the past. This extensive network of contacts was one of the prime assets of a headhunting firm. "The Crown Jewels" as one of Gina's partners called them.

Tom popped his head round Gina's office door at lunchtime on the day of the meeting. "Sorry but I've come up with absolutely zilch after lots of phone calls. No one seems to know a thing." If Tom couldn't dig up anything there was nothing to be dug, thought Gina. She was a bit disturbed as in her previous experience of similar cases there were always rumours or more substantial sound bites floating around. Here, the Board seemed to have closed ranks and there was not even a sniff of a leak. She was mollified by the fact that Tom's homework had corroborated Sir Roger's assertion that Mondo was in very good shape indeed. Market leader in most of its specialist food brand categories, it was highly profitable and with little debt. In fact, it had a cash pile from a recent disposal and had signalled its clear intent to launch an extensive international programme of acquisitions. He had also done a quick check on the Italian subsidiary – Sapore Senza Pari – and discovered that its English translation of "Flavour without equal" suited it perfectly. It was a long established luxury condiment producer in Emilia Romagna with a fantastic reputation. Tom had also discovered that the reason why the CEO job was vacant was the death of the previous incumbent in a car accident in Tuscany.

All this was useful input, but Gina couldn't shake off a nagging concern about embarking on a search without all the cards on the table.

Still, at 6 p.m she and Tom pitched up to Mondo's HQ and were shown immediately into Sir Roger's office. With him was Charles Williamson, a slight, pinched faced man with an oleaginous style that Gina had heard outdid Euriah Heap. When she knew he was to attend the briefing she had immediately called a long standing friendly contact of hers who attended a professional forum for senior human resources people, of which Williamson was also a member. Gina was known for her meticulous preparation and she never went into a new situation without checking out the other protagonists.

"He's an unpleasant little shit," was the immediate reaction. "He has a reputation for being a complete sycophant to his superiors and an awful bully to lesser mortals. He loves himself to bits and almost has an orgasm when he delivers what he considers his pearls of wisdom in our forum. He always does Sir Roger's bidding without question and he doesn't seem to have a moral compass. I know of several instances when Sir Roger has used him as his hatchet man so that he himself can stay aloof from any nastiness."

This was going through Gina's mind when Sir Roger started the briefing. "Over to you Gina; ask whatever you want to get a solid base for this job." Gina had a comprehensive, well-thumbed checklist of probing questions to get under the skin of any senior management search assignment. She and Tom ran through their list of questions about the job, the history and culture of the company, its forward strategy and the specific mix of skills and experience Mondo was looking for in the new appointee. Sir Roger monopolised the discussion on all these items. It was only when they got to the question of compensation that Charles Williamson stepped in.

"We can pay whatever it takes to attract the right person," he said emphatically.

Gina had been caught out by this *carte blanche* approach before. Although it appeared to give a headhunter complete flexibility, the open chequebook had a nasty habit of snapping shut when a company was faced with an expensive candidate who needed a big inducement to make a career move. As she always did, she asked what Carlo had been paid and almost fell off her chair when Williamson said, "His salary was 250,000 euros and he could double that if he met his profit target."

For a business with a turnover of a little over 40 million euros this was way above the market rate. Seeing Gina's raised eyebrows, Sir Roger interjected, "Gina, you need to appreciate that this is a business for which we have very ambitious plans. We are going to add substantially to its product portfolio using the strength of the SSP brand to the hilt. That's why when we recruited Carlo a couple of years ago we went for a man who was much bigger than the current size of the company demanded."

The upside of this for Gina was that her fee was based on a third of the first year's cash compensation of the executive hired. She did some quick mental arithmetic and said to the two clients.

"I propose a fee of 120,000 euros representing one third of estimated salary and one third of half the possible bonus. This will be billed in three equal instalments over three months. If the actual estimated compensation exceeds 375,000 euros, I will charge you a further fee of one third of the additional sum."

Gina sat back expecting a tough negotiation but Sir Roger waved his hand airily and said, "Good people don't come cheap and I know you'll do a first class job for us. Charles will be your main point of contact from now on. I'll only be involved again when you have a shortlist of candidates for me to see."

Gina and Tom walked a couple of hundred yards towards their own West End office through the Mayfair back streets. It was about eight o'clock and there was a chill November wind cutting into them. Gina needed a drink and to get out of the cold so they detoured into a lively wine bar off Berkeley Square. Gina had her usual gin and tonic and Tom settled for a "designer" beer from Africa which she had never heard of.

"You trendy young devil," she teased, "I thought you Danes only drank Carlsberg and that firewater *Akvavit.*"

"You forget," Tom shot back, "that I am a citizen of the world and cannot be stereotyped as crudely as that." He clinked glasses with her and said, "As we say in God's own country *'Skol!'* or bottoms up if you prefer your quaint old English expression." Gina had to laugh. Tom talked like this all the time.

Concise he was not. Why use only one word when you could use three. But he was very amusing. Gina had discovered that the Danes and the Brits seemed to have an identical sense of humour, including a strong ironic streak. She had been surprised to learn that Tom was an expert on all the British TV comedy classics from *Python* through *FawltyTowers* to *Little Britain*. Apparently on some evenings Danish State Television's output was monopolised by BBC 1 and 2 productions. This to some extent explained why so many Danes spoke such excellent English.

Gina and Tom made a strong team. She was a veteran of a decade in the headhunting business. She had been promoted very quickly from researcher to consultant and had made partner by the age of 31, seven years after joining the firm. She now had over a hundred and fifty search assignments under her belt and this wealth of experience plus her acknowledged skill in building relationships with clients and candidates made her an excellent mentor for Tom. However, she knew that Tom had a more incisive intellect than her. The cocktail of her instinctive empathy and nous and Tom's king size brain had a real kick to it. They had whistled through half a dozen jobs much more efficiently and quickly than she had managed with previous research assistants. She dreaded the day when he would be recalled to Copenhagen.

"What's your take on this Mondo job," she asked.

"It's not going to be a cakewalk," he said. "The biggest problem is going to be how to convince a person of the stature they say they want to join such a small company. We will need to have chapter and verse on the Group's growth strategy for Sapore Senza Pari to have any chance of attracting a big fish. Also, I agree with you that we can only make serious approaches to possible candidates when we can tell them who the new Group Chief Executive is going to be."

As usual, thought Gina, Tom had homed in on the critical issues. They had another round of drinks before Gina headed for the Green Park Tube and Tom for their office to make a few calls. One of their other assignments was for a California-based client and Tom had set up some calls to candidates on the West Coast for early afternoon their time. Gina got into the office as usual at seven thirty the next day. She had just sat down at her desk with a cup of restorative coffee when her private line started ringing.

She pressed the receive button.

"Charles Williamson here. I didn't expect to reach you. I thought you headhunters only started mid-morning and then took an early lunch." Gina didn't rise to the bait but she thought, "What an idiot!"

"I want to get a few things straight," Williamson said in what he intended as his master to servant voice. "I'm now running this assignment and I want you to call me every Monday morning with a full progress update. I have not had a good experience with headhunters. I think all you guys do is contact people already on your books and recycle them to different clients. For this Italian assignment I want clear evidence that you have gone out into the market to identify from scratch a full list of suitable candidates."

Gina had to bite her tongue and in as measured a tone as she could muster, she replied, "Mr Williamson that is how we approach every assignment and our client feedback is that our rigorous approach to research is second to none."

"I'll believe that when I see it," he snapped. "Call me next Monday." And without another word he slammed the phone down.

"This is all I need," thought Gina. She was already juggling seven assignments, a couple of which were deep in the mire due to the late withdrawal of prime candidates. She needed this arrogant, nasty little man like a hole in the head. She had to fly to Frankfurt the next day to try to placate a key client who was incandescent with rage at the lack of progress on his search for a Finance Director. Although he was Gina's client, whenever a search was to be done for a company based outside the UK it was Buckman Collin's policy to nominate a co-responsible consultant in the country concerned. In this case Gina had asked the Stuttgart-based Hans Bloch to conduct the search within Germany. Hans had monumentally failed to understand the type of person her client Holger Foerster was looking for. Consequently he had presented a string of candidates who were way off the mark and two evenings previously Holger had called Gina at home to express his extreme dissatisfaction and say he wanted Hans to be taken off the assignment. Gina rang Hans who refused to accept this so in the end Gina had to ring her Managing Partner to get his help. He in turn called the German Managing Partner and said that as Foerster's company, Hausholt Produkte, was one of the firm's biggest clients in Europe they could not risk alienating him. He insisted that as Gina had built the relationship from scratch, they needed to sideline Hans and get whoever was their best consultant in the finance field to take over. Leopold Kaufmann, a young, ambitious consultant from the Dortmund office was duly nominated. She was due to see him at a Frankfurt airport hotel in the morning before the two of them met Foerster in the afternoon at his office in the Frankfurt business district.

Gina had heard good things about Leopold and she was pleased with the initial impression when he came into the meeting room they had booked.

Exceptionally tall and slim, he had one of the most open and immediately likeable faces she had ever seen topped with a shock of unruly blond hair and a boyish, infectious enthusiasm.

"Hi, I'm Leo," he beamed.

She was even more taken with him when he showed he had done his homework in the twenty-four hours since she had spoken to him.

"This is, as we Germans say, *eine katastrophe*. I have been through the computer files very thoroughly. The notes on the client's reactions are clear. He wants an international operator not, an insular German. Preferably someone who has spent some time in a big non-German company. He also needs a person with substantial acquisition experience."

"Bingo," said Gina.

"*Bitte?*"

"Sorry…an English expression meaning you have grasped the key factors."

"That's good, because I've already identified a few people who look right for this. I've just finished a big Finance Director search and our extensive research trawl produced some very useful fish. This is a correct expression?"

"Absolutely spot on," Gina confirmed.

"*Bitte?*"

"Sorry, I meant it was very appropriate."

Gina's spirits lifted by several notches. To be able to talk to her client about concrete possibilities later that day was way beyond her expectations. When she had scanned the candidate CVs Leo had brought, she held out her hand to him. A bit startled he shook it and went a bit red when she said, "I'm really impressed and ever so grateful. You've probably saved my bacon."

"*Bitte?*"

"Sorry, just another expression. The bottom line is you've given me a chance to keep a very important client sweet."

"*Bitte?* What means sweet?"

Gina resolved to restrict her use of English idiom to a minimum otherwise their discussion would take all day. She and Leo then talked about tactics for the meeting with Herr Foerster before grabbing a bite to eat in the hotel bar.

The meeting went spectacularly well. Gina immediately apologised and said, "Herr Foerster, I know we are at fault here but I hope you will remember the good work I've done for you in the past and give us a chance to put things right. I promise that we will give this top priority and get qualified candidates in front of you as quickly as possible. To this end, I'd like to introduce my colleague Leopold who has already started work on your assignment."

Holger Foerster was a Gert Fröbe lookalike. Same substantial girth and stand up gingery hair as the man who had played Auric Goldfinger in the Bond film. The resemblance was almost uncanny and when they had first met a couple of years earlier Gina had to resist the temptation to ask him if there was a familial connection to the famous actor. She resisted because you could never be sure whether someone would be flattered or annoyed by the assumption of similarity.

After Leo had run through the career profile of the first putative new candidate he paused as suggested by Gina and said, "Herr Foerster, what do you think of this person's profile?"

To both Gina and Leo's amusement he replied, "I think it is 'spot on' as the English say."

Gina knew the next three possible candidates were even better.

"Never start with your best person," her first boss and mentor at Buckman Collins had told her. "If your client doesn't rate him or her you have backed yourself into a corner. You can't then show him profiles of less good people."

Gina always started with a credible candidate but typically kept her best bet until last as the *coup de grâce* when the client was already well and truly hooked. This usual ploy worked brilliantly with Holger Foerster who almost drooled when Leo ran through the CV of Konrad Baer, a thirty-eight year old Swiss-German with a wealth of international finance experience in both German and non-German owned companies. He had an MBA from INSEAD, the top European Business School, and had just played a leading role for his current American multinational employer in making several sizeable acquisitions.

Leo said he was sure he could persuade Baer and the other two candidates of particular interest to Herr Foerster to meet him within the next week or so. They parted with him on the best of terms after Herr Foerster had taken Gina to one side and said to her quietly. "Your colleague Bloch did a really bad job initially but I am very impressed with the speed and quality of your response. We all make mistakes but I think the real test of a professional is how you set about putting things right. You have passed this test completely. I think Leopold is excellent and look forward to working with him."

Gina and Leo walked across to the Airport terminal where he had parked his car, having driven down from Dortmund.

"Leo, thanks for pulling out all the stops."

"*Bitte?*"

"Sorry…I mean you've done brilliantly and I'm sure you will get more work from Herr Foerster in the future."

Impulsively, she stood on her tiptoes and gave him a peck on the cheek.

"It was a real pleasure meeting you," he said colouring slightly. "*Auf Wiedersehen.*"

Sitting in business class on her return flight to London, Gina consumed with relish two large gin and tonics and a couple of glasses of wine with the in-flight meal which was a surprisingly appetising Bouef Stroganoff.

Over-imbibing was a reaction of sheer relief that she had managed to pull a key client back from the brink. Once again, she reflected on the precarious nature of the business she was in. You were only as good as your last job.

8 DECEMBER 2010

VERONA

On her final day in Verona Gina got back to her hotel around five, after a late afternoon drink in the magical Piazza Erbe. This was elegantly decorated with pulsing Christmas lights strung across the whole square and she sat outside on the heated terrace of one of its many bars enjoying the buzz of conversation and watching the often animated passers by. As this was way outside the tourist season she was delighted to hear not a single non Italian voice. This was pure Verona for the Veronese. She then window shopped again down Via Mazzini. It was when she stopped abruptly to admire an impossibly expensive pair of boots that she sensed she was still being followed.

She finally shook off this apprehension and cut across to Via Adua. She stepped into the Hotel Victoria's tiny, cramped lift and, not for the first time, thought of contacting *The Guinness Book of Records*. She was sure the lift would be a dead cert to qualify as the slowest such contraption in the world. As it creaked and juddered its way upwards, she reflected on the people she had interviewed that morning and the previous evening. She had booked a meeting room in the Best Western Hotel Firenze on Corso Porta Nuova as it was only about 500 metres from the main railway station and outside the old town with its narrow streets and parking problems. She had, though, booked her own overnight accommodation at the Hotel Victoria as she loved being in the old city with its intoxicating ambience and wonderful array of shops, restaurants and bars.

In the three weeks since her meeting with Sir Roger Simmons and her least favourite person, Charles Williamson, she and Tom had been very busy and productive. With the help of their colleagues in the Milan office they had unearthed a highly credible "long list" of candidates for the Sapore Senza Pari job. As instructed, she had called Williamson on his direct line at eight o'clock on the first Monday to give him a progress update. There was no answer. She tried several times and finally, at just after nine, his secretary picked up the phone.

"Sorry, Mr Williamson usually gets in about 9:30; I'll get him to call you."

"What a moron," thought Gina recalling his snide comments of a few days earlier. "He must have called me from home just to try to catch me out. Obnoxious little twerp." She made a mental note to watch her back even more carefully when dealing with him.

The first and successive Monday reports were relatively painless. Williamson was hard pushed to find any fault with the impressively qualified people on their target list. Only two weeks into the assignment Gina got a call from Sir Roger.

"You'll be pleased to hear," he said without preamble, "that we've netted our new CEO for Mondo Foods. There'll be a press release in the morning before the Stock Market opens but I wanted to give you prior notice. I know you've only been testing the temperature of the water with prospective candidates for the SSP job but you can now tell them who we are and that the new Chief Executive is Adam Palfrey."

Gina was impressed and relieved in equal measure. Palfrey was a terrific catch. A product of the famous Unilever graduate trainee scheme, Palfrey was a marketing star who had developed into a highly successful Managing Director. His most recent assignment had been to turn round a real lame duck of an international toy company. Having restored it to robust health, he masterminded its sale to the industry leader Mattel. He left with a very big pay-off. Palfrey had a high profile in the business press and there had been all sorts of rumours about what he might do next. He was still only in his mid-forties. Without doubt he was a real coup for Mondo and Gina expected the Stock Market to react very positively to the news of his appointment.

By lunchtime the following day Gina had spoken to the three front-running candidates for the SSP position. She told them Mondo was her client and they were looking for a top quality person to head up a very important Italian subsidiary. She encouraged them to check out Adam Palfrey who was one of the brightest stars in the European consumer products sphere. What she did not disclose was the identity of Sapore Senza Pari because she wanted to tell them when they met why Mondo was looking for a big fish for this relatively modest operation. She thought that SSP's size and highly specialised niche would be a deterrent unless presented within the detailed context of Mondo's ambitious growth strategy for the business. Gina knew that a telephone conversation with someone with whom she had not previously established a personal rapport was a poor substitute for an extended face-to-face discussion. She could then deploy her well-honed persuasive skills to best effect.

All three possible contenders agreed to meet her and she staggered the interviews over two days in Verona the following week as all were based in Northern Italy. She rang Charles Williamson to confirm this and he said,

"Another candidate has surfaced from our own network who we want you also to see. He's been highly recommended to the Chairman by one of our key suppliers. His name is Vittore Santoro and I'll email his details to you."

Gina was not particularly surprised. Clients quite often suggested possible candidates thrown up by their own extensive business networks. What did surprise her when she looked at this man's CV was how lightweight he was compared to the other candidates. Santoro was a thirty-five year old businessman from Brindisi with a limited track record in smallish food companies in Southern Italy. Compared to the other three candidates she had shortlisted he seemed to be a non-starter. However she did not want to risk souring the relationship with Mondo by dismissing him out of hand. Far better, she thought, to interview him and then give them evidence based feedback on his unsuitability.

Santoro was the last of the four people she interviewed and her initial reaction to his career profile proved to be correct. He was a tall, handsome, exceptionally well-groomed man with a full head of grey flecked black hair and the whitest teeth she had ever seen. There was something very familiar about him and Gina felt that she had seen him somewhere before although she couldn't think where. He shook her hand and asked if they could speak Italian as his English was not very good.

"Certainly, I'm bilingual," she replied.

He annoyed Gina immediately by then saying in a highly supercilious tone,

"I'm not sure why I needed to come all this way to see you. The Mondo people know me very well so why did they ask an outside consultant to get involved?"

"Because, *Signor* Santoro, I am the only one who can calibrate you against the other people who are possibles for this job."

She was also annoyed because he said that Mondo had already told him that the company was SSP and that he was a serious contender for the *Direttore Generale* position. Things didn't get any better as she embarked on her normal probing questioning. His answers were either monosyllabic or flippantly superficial as if he was thoroughly bored by the whole process. After about twenty minutes when she had barely scratched the surface, he glanced at his watch and said, "I have to leave now as I have an important business meeting in Milan this evening."

Gina noticed that he stressed the word "important" as if to underline the difference between this commitment and spending any more time with her. That tipped her over the edge and she decided to call his bluff.

"*Signor* Santoro, as I indicated when we set up this meeting, you needed to allow about two hours for a full review of your career. I'm afraid I can't consider you as a candidate until we have had a more detailed discussion."

Santoro glared at her as if she had just insulted his manhood and there was a noticeable tightening of his jaw muscles as he looked at his watch again and said, "I can give you another hour now but I need to leave no later than three o'clock."

The next hour was without doubt the most difficult interview she had ever done. Santoro was obviously extremely uncomfortable and seemed to be on edge as he answered her questions. He might have been a big fish in Puglia but his experience was parochial and he was no strategist. He looked at her with such antagonism that she felt more than a little threatened. It was if he was having to exercise rigid control over his real desire to jump up and charge out. She felt a visceral sense of relief when he finally exited the hotel meeting room after predictably slamming the door behind him.

She thanked her lucky stars that the other candidates had turned out to be very credible. She smiled when she recalled the one she regarded as the front runner – Corrado Gori. He had literally interviewed himself for a full thirty minutes after she had asked him to tell her about himself.

"*Va bene*," he said, "I was born in Torino but my family moved to Bologna when I was five. Why? Because my father got a better job. I went to university in Milano. Why? Because they had the best business course. I accepted my first job with Parmalat. Why? Because they had a great reputation. I moved into marketing. Why? Because I thought it was the best route to eventual general management..." He went on making statements and then asking himself the reason behind them like an unstoppable train. It was only when he paused in his staccato delivery to take a sip of coffee that she was able to break in and regain control of proceedings. She then discovered that he was a real talent with an impressive track record in blue-chip consumer goods companies and whilst he was extraordinarily fast talking he could also listen and had a really winning personality. She thought he was the one and looked forward to getting him in front of her clients at Mondo.

The Hotel Victoria's lift finally reached Gina's floor and as she walked into her room she saw the message light blinking insistently on the bedside phone. She rang Reception and was told a *Maggiore* Bruno Canepa of the *Guardia di Finanza* would like to see her.

"Did he say what he wants?"

"No *Signora*, only that it was a confidential personal matter."

Gina was nonplussed. Why a Major in some kind of special police branch wanted to see her was a mystery.

"I'll come down in a few minutes. Do you have somewhere private where we can talk?"

"*Si Signora*, you can use the bar which is closed at this time of year."

In the large, marbled central atrium, Gina saw a solitary figure dressed in a very smart lounge suit, sober tie and expensive classic brogues polished to a military sheen. Gina smiled to herself recalling one of her mother's favourite sayings that you could tell a lot about a man from the quality and state of his footwear.

He rose as she approached and said "*Signora* Biagi...?"

She nodded and he bowed slightly. "I am Major Canepa of the *Guardia di Finanza.*" He said, holding up a small open wallet for her to inspect. "Can we talk privately?" Gina looked at the impressive badge and photo and pointed the way down the stairs to the bar. It was shuttered and deserted.

"Can we speak Italian please? My English is how you say a little rusted."

"No problem – go ahead."

"*Signora*, do you know what the role of the *Guardia di Finanza* is?"

"I've absolutely no idea."

"OK then, briefly, we are a militarized police force. Like the *Carabinieri*, we are part of the Italian Armed forces but we report to the Finance Minister. Our job is essentially to deal with financial crime, smuggling and drug trafficking which, as you will appreciate, usually involves cross-border activities. We liaise very closely with pan-European and international law enforcement agencies like Europol and Eurojust."

"Thanks for that Major but I'm at a loss to understand why you want to talk to me."

"*Signora* Biagi, please tell me why you met Vittore Santoro this afternoon."

"I'm a headhunter and I was interviewing him for a very important job," said Gina rather taken aback. "Why do you want to know?"

"*Signora*, I must ask you to keep what I now tell you completely confidential. It is for you own safety. I head up a special commando unit of the *Guardia*. I report directly to the *Comandante Generale* who in turn reports to the Finance Minister. With support from police forces in several European countries we are closing in on a huge interlocking criminal organisation with a finger in just about every type of crime you can imagine. What's unusual about it is that it embraces many separate criminal groups in Europe and beyond. Several Italian mafia branches including the Camorra in Naples, the 'Ndrangheta in Calabria, the Sacra Corona Unita in Puglia and the Sicilian mafia are involved. Also equivalent organisations in Albania, Romania, Colombia and Nigeria are implicated. The extent of their activities is mind boggling. The money they make equates to the GDP of a decent sized country."

"That's amazing," said Gina a little tartly, "but I still don't see where I come in."

"We believe Santoro is a senior member of the Puglian mafia, the Sacra Corona Unita, which spun off from the Camorra some time ago. He has been groomed by his father to appear to be an educated businessman but make no mistake he is a dangerous criminal."

Gina swallowed nervously, remembering the disturbing encounter with Santoro earlier that day. Major Canepa continued, "We have checked you out with SOCA in the UK and confirmed that you are a high flying professional with an unblemished record."

"I'm not sure, Major, that I like the idea of you checking up on me and what on earth is SOCA anyway?"

"It's the Serious and Organised Crime Agency that your Home Office set up in 2006...please understand *Signora* Biagi, we had to make sure of your *bona fides* before we involved you in this highly dangerous affair."

"*Va bene*," Gina said, partially mollified, "but I need to know a lot more about this before I commit to anything."

"*Signora*, there is a lot to tell you and if you agree I suggest perhaps we meet for dinner later when I have finished a scheduled meeting with members of my team."

"Oh yes, my followers this afternoon," said Gina provocatively.

Major Canepa did not rise to the bait but did look a little sheepish she thought.

He carried on regardless. "I've taken the liberty of booking a quiet table at my favourite restaurant, the *Dodici Apostoli* for eight o'clock. Is that OK?"

Gina thought, "Why not?" She had in fact been thinking of eating at the same place herself. The Twelve Apostles was also her first choice restaurant in Verona so she smiled and nodded her assent.

"I'll pick you up a few minutes before eight then. Goodbye until then."

She took a lot of time over her make-up and clothes. She did not have a great deal of choice having only brought an overnight bag, but she was quite happy with the result. She wore a very well cut black Armani trouser suit which showcased her slim but curvy figure to perfection. To soften the effect she used an elegant Ferragamo scarf like a cravat tucked into a crisp white shirt.

"Not bad," she said to herself as she posed by the mirror near the door of her room, partly wondering why she had gone the extra mile for a meeting with the Major.

She grinned and thought, 'It's because I'm going to the Secret Policeman's Ball.'

She was pleased to see the admiring look on his face as she emerged from the lift and they set off to walk the few hundred yards to the famous old restaurant. The *Dodici Apostoli* got its name from a group of twelve trades-men who used to lunch there in the mid-eighteenth century. It had a perfectly preserved *Belle Époque* interior with beautifully polished tile floors, wonderful wall frescoes and ornately decorated windows.

Entering the restaurant had always given Gina a sense of well-being. It was as if she had stepped back in time and was immediately cocooned from the frenetic pace of the modern world.

In true continental fashion Major Canepa asked if they could eat first and then talk about his mission afterwards. In her international business dealings Gina had often been amused by this marked difference between her Ameri-can and UK clients and those from France and Italy.

Whereas a business lunch was just that to Byron from Chicago, it was a contradiction in terms to Michel from Paris. "We have lunch and then we do business, *d'accord?*"

Gina much preferred the more civilised European approach, so readily nodded agreement to the Major's suggestion. Although she had been to the restaurant a few times before, he was obviously a regular and highly prized customer. After an effusive greeting from a member of the owning family they were immediately shown to the most secluded corner table in the almost empty restaurant. They wasted no time at all ordering and laughed as they realised they had picked exactly the same dishes as starter and main course – gnocchi followed by lamb chops on a base of crispy potatoes. From the voluminous wine list they chose a bottle of the lightish red Bardolino from nearby Lake Garda and Captain Canepa ordered a couple of glasses of Prosecco as an *aperitivo*.

Gina then quizzed him about his background.

"I live in Rome but I'm originally from Santa Margherita Ligure, near Genoa. I'm afraid I followed the family tradition of joining the military but chose a different branch from my father who was an officer in the regular army. After completing my secondary education I started my officer training with the *Guardia di Finanza*. This lasted five years concluding with an undergraduate course at the *Guardia's* academy attached to the University of Bergamo. They run a special degree in Economic and Financial Security Science which I completed in 1997." Gina did a quick mental calculation and, assuming he was around 23 when he graduated, he was now 36, a couple of years older than her.

Gina was extremely sensitive to other people's moods and she had felt that there was a kind of residual sadness behind Major Canepa's eyes. The reason then became clear as he told her that he had been married but had lost his wife three years previously to an ultra aggressive form of bone cancer. She was truly saddened by this revelation and the utterly genuine nature of her quietly expressed condolences seemed to touch him.

"OK, let's talk of something a bit more cheerful – ah, here comes the gnocchi…"

As they ate the unctuous pasta in its delicate sauce with great relish, the mood lightened, helped also by the exceptionally smooth Bardolino. He then started to tell her in an amusing and thoroughly self-deprecating way about some of the cases he had dealt with in the *Guardia*.

On his most recent case he had been jointly responsible for an investigation into a group carrying out skimming of many thousands of payment cards in the EU yielding a haul of millions of euros. An Albanian organised crime group operating from Greece and Italy was the architect of the scheme. He had led a coordinated European operation culminating in about forty arrests in seven countries. Another case resulted in the seizure of 400 kilos of cocaine being smuggled into France and Italy from Colombia.

"We arrested fifty suspects around Europe and I got this little present as a bonus," he said, pointing to the still livid inch long scar just above his collar. "I thought women were supposed to be the gentler sex but the

Romanian girl who gave me this with a tiny knife she'd hidden in her boot disabused me of that romantic notion."

He had none of the macho bombast of many of his compatriots and she warmed to him as the meal progressed. She also found him very attractive. He was a couple of inches north of six feet with an athletic build that spoke of a rigorous fitness regime. He admitted he was an exercise junkie; a fanatical squash and tennis player, he also tried to have a serious gym workout twice a week. He had a strong square face with a near perfect aquiline nose and ice-blue eyes. He had short cropped nearly blond hair and she commented on the fact that he looked more Scandinavian than Italian. He laughed.

"That's probably due to marauding Viking ancestors who left their genes in many parts of coastal Italy."

Their main courses arrived. In Gina's view, lamb chops in Italy tasted better than anywhere else in the world. They tended to be done *scottadito* – flattened to about half their normal thickness and then scorched on a very hot grill with rosemary and olive oil. These were fine examples of this culinary convention and she attacked them with an evident gusto that made Major Canepa smile.

"Now what about you Gina?" said Bruno after they had ordered dessert from the huge array on the three trolleys wheeled out to them in a famous display manoeuvre of the 12 Apostles. They had decided to switch to first names halfway through the main course when they also confirmed that, "Yes," they would have a second bottle of the excellent Bardolino, the first having disappeared very quickly.

"I'm from Italian stock as you know Bruno. My parents met in the seventies when my dad came to the UK from Puglia. He was in his mid-twenties and had tragically just lost both his parents and his *nonna*. He told me he also had a run in with the local mafia and all this made it necessary for him to make a fresh start. He trained as a lawyer originally but made a successful career as a restaurateur in the UK. He now owns four restaurants in the Lake District in the north of England and recently opened a fifth in Manchester. My mother was a second generation Scots Italian from Edinburgh and is now a university professor. My father was obviously traumatised by his multiple bereavements and this maybe explains why he has not been back to Italy for nearly forty years. My mum often visits her extended family in Torino but my dad has never been with her. I was born in Scotland but we moved to a place called Silverdale in Lancashire when I was a little girl. Both my younger sister and I went to local schools and then she went to Oxford to study economics and I got a place at Cambridge to do Modern Languages."

"Brainy family," said Bruno, "I'm very impressed."

"Yes Mum and Dad were thrilled that we were both successful academically. I had a fantastic time at Cambridge and also spent a year in Milan as part of my degree course. Like you, I'm hooked on exercise and was lucky enough to represent the university both at volleyball and karate. I still play volleyball in a London league and try to run a few times a week. I've let the karate lapse but I did get up to brown belt level. After college I spent a year travelling round the world doing all sorts of jobs to pay my way. When I got back to the UK I was 23 years old and I still didn't have a clue about what to do in terms of career. I then had a lucky break. On a trip to London I was having a drink with a university friend and discovered he had joined a firm of headhunters and was loving it. The company was called Buckman Collins and he said with my languages and family business background I'd be a good fit with them. I met a couple of the partners and a few days later accepted their offer to join as a researcher. I'm still with the firm and was lucky enough to make partner a couple of years ago."

Gina realised she had been talking non-stop for several minutes and when she glanced at her watch she was startled to see it was already after ten o'clock.

"Bruno that was a lovely meal and I've enjoyed your company very much but don't you think you ought to brief me on the Santoro issue before they throw us out of here?"

Bruno smiled rather ruefully and immediately clicked back into a more serious mode.

"OK. The vast criminal network I mentioned when we met earlier is involved in drug smuggling, people trafficking, prostitution, money laundering, protection racketeering, financial fraud and sophisticated cybercrime. It has bought or extorted support from an unbelievable range of top political, business and judicial people in many countries…Oh yes, one other horrific string to their bow is the systematic dumping of radioactive waste off the Italian coast and also in places like Somalia.

"I am co-responsible with a Commander from the Serious and Organised Crime Agency in the UK for a big pan-European task force – Operation Achilles – focused on dismantling this truly 'evil empire'. Because of the risk of leakage from such a large body of officers, we operate on a strict need to know basis. In each jurisdiction that country's task force members follow very tramlined avenues of enquiry relating to specific crimes and suspects. There are only six people who know the whole picture – me, Commander

Gibbs, my *Comandante Generale*, our Finance Minister, the Metropolitan Police Commissioner and your Home Secretary.

We are close to gathering the final pieces of evidence to nail this very nasty criminal fraternity and that's where you come in."

Gina swallowed nervously and the pleasant ambience of a few minutes previously disappeared in a flash.

"We believe that your client, Sir Roger Simmons, is one of the top people in this criminal organisation."

"What!" exclaimed Gina taking in this bombshell, "that can't be right."

"I'm afraid it is and several Mondo companies have been used as vehicles for drug and people trafficking and washing dirty money. We strongly suspect that the death of the last MD of Sapore Senza Pari was no accident. We believe Carlo Giordano had discovered that his company trucks were being used to smuggle drugs from outside the EU into the UK, Germany and Scandinavia. We know that the company's Operations Director is certainly a mafia member. We also know from a tapped phone call that the day before he was killed in what was probably a staged car accident, Giordano had called Sir Roger Simmons to say he had evidence of criminality in his logistics department. Sir Roger told him to hold fire and not call the police until they had reviewed his evidence together and decided on how best to minimise any adverse publicity.

"The next day when Giordano was on his way to Pisa airport to fly to London he was shunted off the road by a juggernaut and his car with his mangled body ended up in a ravine 200 metres below the highway."

"I find it hard to believe that Sir Roger is involved in this…and that he sanctioned a contract killing," Gina said shaking her head vigorously.

Bruno nodded firmly.

"We believe his initial involvement was secured when he was shown some very graphic photos of him sexually assaulting a rent boy. Once he had taken the first step into criminality he appears to have found his true calling. He quickly demonstrated to his criminal bosses a usefulness that elevated him from pressed man to equal partner in no time at all. We also believe that his Personnel Director is complicit in this criminal activity."

"Now that doesn't surprise me," Gina said grimly.

"Right, let's get to the key point. We're sure Mondo is using your search for a new *Direttore Generale* for SSP as camouflage for their plan to put Santoro into the job. They need to convince their Board that they are going through a proper process to fill the post. What better way to demonstrate that than by hiring one of the top headhunting firms."

"THE top firm in the world," said Gina with a half smile, although she was feeling far from cheerful about having been pitched into this nest of vipers.

"Is Santoro a valid candidate for this job, Gina?"

"Absolutely no way. He's a real lightweight compared to several other people I've found."

"Good; then if they insist on appointing him it's clear confirmation that they are using your work as a smokescreen." Bruno paused, leant forward and looked her straight in the eyes.

"We need your help Gina to put this particular piece of the jigsaw into place. We want to record your conversations with Sir Charles and his colleagues so we have firm evidence of this sham recruitment."

"So you want me to wear a wire?" Gina said, reddening as she realised she sounded like a character from an American cop show.

"Yes and we'll also put an intercept on your phone calls."

"OK, I'll do it."

"Just like that?" said Bruno.

"My dad drummed into me the need for all of us to stand up for decent values. He has an acute sense of right and wrong. I've always tried to live up to his standards and I know he would be disappointed if I said 'no' to this."

"Gina, you know there is an element of risk in this for you – small but no less there. I'll do everything in my power to keep you safe. When you get back to London I'll arrange a private meeting with Commander Gibbs to progress things. He'll be the only one who knows that you are working with us. We'll be tapping the Mondo people's phones so you will just be one of a wide range of folk they talk to."

He paused and looked a touch uncomfortable. "I have seen that you are not wearing a wedding or engagement ring. I have to ask if you currently with someone who we need to consider regarding this assignment."

"No, I'm not. I was 'in a relationship' as they say but we split six months ago when he took a job in San Francisco."

Gina thought the look of relief on Bruno's face was probably a reflection of his personal rather than professional concern for her. She was secretly pleased because she realised that, even after just a few hours with him, she liked him enormously.

They were by then the only people left in the restaurant. In fact, there had only been two other tables occupied the whole evening. Bruno insisted on paying the bill and they strolled back to her hotel on a cold but beautifully clear night. At the hotel they exchanged phone numbers. Bruno said that she should only call him on a certain secure number and not give her name until he answered in person.

"Gina; I wish we had met under different circumstances but I can't tell you how much I've enjoyed your company this evening."

"Me too Bruno and I look forward to seeing you again; next time on a purely social basis maybe."

She realised that she was giving him a clear signal she wanted to spend more time with him but she knew she would regret it later if she didn't say so directly.

"I'd very much like to do that` and I'll be in London just before Christmas for a meeting with George Gibbs so perhaps we could have dinner then…"

As they parted he took her hand and kissed it. It was done so tenderly and without affectation that it touched her deeply. In the ancient hotel lift she said to herself, "Gina, you're smitten," and she was still smiling when she drifted off to sleep after the oddest day of her life.

11 SEPTEMBER 1974

LECCE, PUGLIA

Bernardo Colangelo was at his desk when his secretary buzzed him.

"*Signor* Colangelo there is a young lady on the line, Antonella Perugini. She says you know her. Will you take the call?"

"Yes of course. Please put her through."

"Bernardo, do you remember me? We met at Federico's summer party in Bari."

"Of course…how are you Antonella?"

"Not so good," came the halting reply and it was obvious Antonella was very distressed even before she started sobbing.

"What on earth's the matter?"

"Do you know where Luca is? I need to speak to him urgently and he's disappeared. I know you are his best friend and I thought if anyone knows where he is, it would be you…"

"Sorry Antonella he just went off about a month ago on what I think was some urgent family business. It may have had something to do with the sad death of his *nonna* but he left in such a hurry he didn't have time to contact me…I was down in Gallipoli on my boat…There was a rumour that he'd gone to Argentina but no one has heard from him since."

"Please Bernardo can you see if you can find out more as I'm at my wit's end…please help me…oh my God…" She was weeping uncontrollably at the other end of the line.

"Where are you now?"

"I'm in Brindisi but I'm coming to Lecce this afternoon to see my aunt…why?"

"Well I was thinking that we could meet for a cup of coffee and you could tell me why you are so upset. In the meantime I'll do a bit of digging to see if anyone has heard from Luca."

"OK," sniffed Antonella, "let's say four o'clock in Bar Pepino."

Bernardo put the phone down and wondered whether Antonella had been caught up in the dangerous situation in which Luca had found himself. Obviously he could not help Antonella with any concrete information on Luca's whereabouts as he had absolutely no idea where he was except probably Argentina. But at least he could find out why she was so agitated. He recalled that she and Luca had dated several times that summer and he thought she was a really nice girl.

He turned up at Bar Pepino a few minutes early and got a shock when he spotted Antonella. She looked haggard with dark rings under her eyes and the air of a hunted animal.

"Oh Bernardo thanks ever so much for coming. I didn't know who to turn to now that Luca's not here. Any news of him?" This last question was such a desperate plea that when Bernardo shook his head she dissolved into tears again. Bernardo put his hand over hers and said gently.

"Tell me what's up and I'll help in any way I can."

"I'm pregnant," she blurted out.

"What…how…?" stammered Bernardo.

"Luca is the father…he's the only man I've ever slept with. Actually it happened only once at the end of June when we were a little tipsy."

Bernardo knew instinctively that she was telling the truth. Luca had confided in him that he had had a fling with Antonella and although she was a sweet girl, he didn't think it would last as they did not have much in common.

"What are you going to do Antonella? How far gone are you?"

"About two and a half months," she whispered. "What can I do?"

"Have you told your parents yet?"

"Oh my God no! They would be so ashamed. My mother in particular is so religious she could not face the social disgrace of a pregnant unmarried daughter."

"Have you thought of abortion?...I can help with the money if you need it."

Antonella started sobbing again in a truly heartrending way.

"I couldn't go through with it...it's a mortal sin. Whatever happens, I have to have the baby."

"OK, then you must tell your parents as soon as possible. I'm sure that once they get over the shock, they'll stand by you."

"I think *papà* will," Antonella said, "but I don't think they will let me keep the baby. They'll probably do what Anna's folks did when she got pregnant. Do you remember?"

Bernardo shook his head. "I don't know Anna."

"She was one of my best friends and she had a steady boyfriend. He got her pregnant a couple of years ago. Her parents packed her off to a relative up north to have the baby which was immediately taken away for adoption...I couldn't bear it if they made me give up my baby."

"Antonella, you need to think very carefully about that. You are a young woman with your whole life ahead of you...marriage, kids the whole thing. If you don't want an abortion it may be that the best option is to have the child adopted."

"I know," she said quietly, "but it will break my heart...Oh why isn't Luca here to share this with me? Are you sure there's no sign of him?"

"No, none...I'm really sorry but he's just vanished which I'm very worried about. It's so unlike him but something pretty traumatic must have happened. You know he lost both his parents and his *nonna* this year and I have a feeling that this unhinged him. He may have decided to take a complete break away from Puglia until he's back on an even keel."

Bernardo felt more than a twinge of guilt at his duplicity but he felt the most important thing was to convince Antonella that Luca was out of the picture and she had to act unilaterally. He continued, "We've got to assume that Luca is not going to turn up soon and therefore you need to act now. If you leave it much longer you'll start to show. Better to get things out in the open now so that you and your family can decide what to do."

Antonella seemed to grow calmer as Bernardo spoke or maybe it was just a resigned acceptance of the reality of her position which stemmed her tears. She straightened her back, looked him squarely in the eye and said, "Thankyou...I just needed to talk to someone. I think I already knew what

I had to do but found it difficult to accept. I'll tell my father tonight when my mum is visiting my *nonno* so he'll have time to take it in before my mum's predictable hysterics."

"Let me know how it goes. You must believe me when I say I'll do anything I can to help you. Obviously I'm not Luca but I know he would want me to be a true friend to you in your time of trouble."

Antonella reached across the table and brushed his cheek in a light caress before gathering her things and leaving the bar. The next day, a much calmer young woman called to tell him that breaking the news to her parents had been every bit as traumatic as she had feared. Her father was visibly shaken when his favourite daughter had disclosed her condition. Then his essentially pragmatic nature cut in and, without angry recriminations, he began to focus on the necessary practical steps. He said he would use his contacts in the police and elsewhere to initiate an intensive search for Luca. As an influential local businessman he had an extensive network to tap but he set a deadline of two weeks for this effort. If the manhunt was fruitless, Antonella would have to stay with her aunt near Urbino for the remaining six months of her confinement. The baby would be removed at birth and a good adoptive home found for it.

If he could have done, Bernardo would have spared Antonella's father the time and trouble of arriving at what he knew would be a dead end. Sure enough, a fortnight later she rang to tell him what he already knew. He was though very buoyed to hear that her father's sources had confirmed that a month earlier, Luca had boarded a train to Rome where the trail ended. However, from information obtained from his bank it looked as though Argentina was his eventual destination.

"Well done Luca," he thought, "It appears your hasty attempts to cover your tracks worked very well."

He heard nothing more from Antonella until the middle of the following year. Out of the blue, one lovely day in June, he received a letter from her which read:

"Dear Bernardo,

I did have my baby in the spring – a healthy and beautiful boy as it happens. I spent a few precious hours with him before he was taken away. Since then I've been so low that I have to confess once or twice I've contemplated committing the mortal sin of taking my own life.

I'm feeling a little better now but I've decided that I cannot bear the thought of returning to Puglia and resuming what would be a pretend life as if nothing has happened. I've been offered a job in Australia, working for an Italian bank in Melbourne and I've decided to give it a go. I'll be leaving in the autumn and I'm not sure if I will ever come back.

I just wanted to say a heartfelt thank you for giving me your shoulder to cry on when I was in a very dark and lonely place. I hear that Luca has still not reappeared. If he ever does I need you to promise me not to tell him about any of this. I'm certain he would have stood by me but now it's all over what purpose would be served by telling him? It would only make him sad or guilty or perhaps bereft at the loss of a son he never had an opportunity to know. I don't want that because I think he is a good man who deserves a good life.

Please keep this our secret.

Antonella"

Bernardo was very touched by the letter which was redolent of the absolute pain and despair Antonella must have felt when her baby was wrenched from her. In a strange way he felt that he had also lost something precious. If Luca had stayed and acknowledged the baby as his own then Bernardo knew he would have inevitably become an honorary uncle and grown close to his best friend's son. This was not to be and he would honour Antonella's wishes if he and Luca were to meet again.

AUGUST 1974 TO SUMMER 1982

EDINBURGH

The few years following his arrival at the Biagi's door were both happy and productive for Luca. He enrolled as an overseas student on a two year Higher National Diploma in Business Studies at Napier College. He thought that this, plus the practical experience he would gain working with Paolo, would give him a solid base for a career in the hospitality sector. Although he was very late in applying, Paolo managed to pull a few strings to get him accepted on the course. One of his regular customers in the restaurant was a senior faculty member at the college and was happy to facilitate Luca's application given his outstanding academic record in Italy.

Rosalba started her research post at Heriot-Watt University and exactly one year from the day they met, Luca Vento and Rosalba Biagi got married. In their initial discussions about Luca's future plans, they had all been concerned about advertising his presence in Scotland too widely given its large Italian community. Clearly, he would need to confirm his identity when he enrolled at Napier. However, no one on Ristorante Zia Lucia's current staff roll had been employed when Luca was there eight years' previously. So it was agreed that he would be introduced to the new staff brigade as Luca Biagi. They would say he came from Umbria and was a distant relative of Paolo's. At college he would have to use his real name but they all felt that the risk of anything filtering back from there to the heel of Italy was minimal. At a later date, Rosalba suggested, he could change his name by Deed Poll to close off this avenue of risk.

The need for extreme caution was chillingly reinforced by a phone call Luca made a week after arriving in Leith. He rang the office of Magistrate Fontana in Brindisi.

"I'm very sorry," said the switchboard girl, "Doctor Fontana was killed in a car crash on the *autostrada* a couple of weeks ago…"

In shock, Luca replaced the phone in its cradle and sat staring into space for several minutes. He had no doubts that the magistrate had been murdered. Whether it had anything to do with his own dossier on local corruption was an unknown. What was for sure was the fact that Magistrate Fontana had made many dangerous enemies because of his anti-mafia crusading work. He had told Luca one evening during his internship over a glass of wine that he knew he was a marked man. There had already been two failed attempts to silence him and he said he was glad he did not have a family to worry about.

Because of this need for secrecy, they had a Registry Office wedding with only Paolo and Maria in attendance. The young couple honeymooned in the English Lake district, borrowing Paolo's Spider again for an idyllic week in a cottage near Grasmere. They both fell in love with this uniquely beautiful corner of England and resolved to return as often as they could.

The phone call to Brindisi also confirmed Luca's worst fears about the impossibility of extracting his considerable assets from his bank in southern Italy. Trying to get his money out could leave a clear trail for the mafia to follow. Given that they had penetrated all echelons of Puglian society, he could not be one hundred per cent certain that the banking sector was whiter than white. He still had his *nonna's* legacy. He had checked the current exchange rate of over 1,500 lire to the pound and discovered it was worth around £27,000. This in itself presented another problem. He could not walk into a UK bank and exchange such a large sum in one go. Paolo came up with a solution. He told Luca rather shamefacedly that he paid several of his regular suppliers in Italy off-the-books in cash so they could avoid some tax. He said he could use some of Luca's notes for these under the counter payments and pay Luca in sterling instalments over two or three years. He said Luca could keep this in the office safe he had just had installed after a spate of local burglaries. Luca could then exchange the balance of his lire over an extended time period in dribs and drabs.

After their marriage, Luca and Rosalba moved into a small furnished flat in central Edinburgh which was roughly equidistant from their colleges and Ristorante Zia Lucia. Until the wedding, Luca worked at the weekends, during his vacations and one or two evenings a week in the restaurant. Afterwards he continued with the weekend and vacation work but dropped the evening shifts. He covered every aspect of the business – front of house, waiting on, food preparation and cooking, menu planning, supplier management and financial matters. During his first Easter vacation he completely overhauled Paolo's chaotic office procedures. He persuaded him to hire a good accountant to provide more professional input than he was getting from the part-time bookkeeper he had used for years. He amazed his prospective father-in-law by working with Dougal the accountant to identify very substantial cost savings through off-setting many more business expenses against tax, amending his payment terms to suppliers and drastically pruning his far too extensive supplier base.

"This boy is a genius," Paolo said repeatedly to Maria and Rosalba. "He is going to be a stellar success in this business."

Luca really enjoyed his Diploma course. He majored in accounting and marketing which he thought would be the twin pillars on which to build a successful restaurant operation. His English improved rapidly through the heavy reading programme and the constant interaction with his classmates. Because he was several years older and much better qualified than the other course members, he became a mentor to many of them. Whenever they were stuck on some difficult issue they beat a path to his door. Although he was busier than most with the heavy combination of course and restaurant work, he was unstintingly helpful. Rosalba nagged him a little about spending so much time supporting his fellow students but she was quietly pleased that his natural kindness and generosity was so evidently on display.

"He'll make a wonderful father," she thought to herself.

Rosalba worked hard on her post-doctoral research at Heriot-Watt having been awarded her PhD in May 1975. As she took on more lecturing and tutoring, she found that she was a natural teacher. She loved the intellectual stimulation of dealing with bright, challenging undergraduates. Her seniors in the Faculty quickly recognised her potential and made sure she was given responsibility beyond her years.

Luca finished his course in mid-1976 and gained the only distinction awarded in his class of fifty. Even though he had married a UK citizen this did not confer residency rights once his course was over. He discovered that these were only given to women who married British men. Fortunately, Paolo had experience of applying for work permits for several of his Italian restaurant workers. He applied for the necessary permit the Easter before Luca's graduation. He cited Luca's unique contribution to the restaurant operation given his fluency in Italian, knowledge of Italian wine and his business qualifications. Luca's work permit was approved without demur and he settled in to a hectic routine taking more and more responsibility for the running of Ristorante Zia Lucia. Not that Paolo was looking for an easy life. Far from it. Although in his late fifties, he was as vigorous as a man half his age. He had a robust constitution and was immensely proud that he had never had a day off sick since arriving in Edinburgh. As both the restaurant and delicatessen business were now very profitable, he decided that he wanted to push on with a new venture that he'd been thinking about for some time – a combined deli and café in the centre of Edinburgh. He and Luca had looked at dozens of sites and eventually opted for dilapidated shop premises on two floors with a large basement just off the Royal Mile. These were ideally suited to their plan for a food shop and sandwich bar on the ground floor and a café upstairs offering a limited menu mainly targeting the lunch trade.

Characteristically, Paolo threw himself into this venture like an excited schoolboy at the start of the holidays. Fortunately Luca was on hand to curb some of the excessively extravagant ideas which tumbled out of Paolo's head in a constant flow. The upshot was that Café Bar Mariarosa was launched with a fighting chance of success and without a big debt burden around its neck. Luca and Dougal had convinced Paolo to invite some of his suppliers and other contacts to invest in the business with a guaranteed payback with a decent return after three years. The working capital this provided enabled

Paolo and Luca to move ahead more quickly with an ancillary project to supply local offices and businesses with a customised sandwich and snack menu. Orders phoned through by eleven would be delivered in specially designed boxes with cutlery, napkins and condiments.

Luca's marketing skills ensured that the research, promotion and communication of this de-luxe service were all highly professional. A free trial offer of up to six sandwiches or panini secured an immediate clientele which continued to grow rapidly. Luca found he had a natural aptitude for business and loved the frenetic pace of life zipping between Leith and Edinburgh, dealing with suppliers and most of all acting as a charming host to old and new customers alike. But he was ambitious and although he loved Paolo as a second father, he wanted to stand on his own two feet. He wanted his own restaurant, reflecting his own style. He wanted the freedom to inject contemporary thinking without having to battle against Paolo's ultra-traditionalist attitudes every step of the way.

But their first daughter, Gina, arrived at the end of 1977 and her sister Maurizia followed eighteen months later. Juggling the demands of a thriving business with those of a loving father muted Luca's ambitions for a few years but in the spring of 1982 Paolo came with some news that lit his fuse again. In Grange-over-Sands on the coastal fringe to the south of the Lake District, a friend of Paolo had opened a restaurant after the war. He had called Paolo to tell him he was heading back to Italy to take up a substantial inheritance following the death of his wealthy father. He said he was looking for a buyer for the restaurant and could offer an attractive price to someone who could complete quickly. Paolo knew how much Rosalba and Luca loved the Lake District and as he had predicted, they were extremely keen to consider this opportunity to develop a business there.

Luca and Rosalba travelled to Grange a few days after Paolo had received the call from the restaurateur, Andrea Carlotti. They fell in love with the place and managed to do a very good deal with *Signor* Carlotti who was clearly anxious to get back to Italy without delay. With the still substantial residue of his *nonna's* bequest plus his share of the profits from the highly successful business venture in Edinburgh, Luca contributed about a third of the agreed purchase price. Rosalba had a trust fund set up by her parents which chipped in another third and the balance was made up by loans from Paolo and the local Bank manager in Leith. He had been greatly impressed by Luca's business acumen when he had approved a small loan to support the new catering venture in Edinburgh.

Within weeks of moving to a lovely stone built house in the village of Silverdale a few miles from Grange, Rosalba had secured a senior lecturer post in the business faculty at the relatively recently established University of Lancaster. Gina went to the village primary school and the Biagis hired a very sweet local girl as a part time nanny for Maurizia. Luca had successfully applied for British citizenship in 1980 and later changed his name to Biagi by Deed Poll. The girls had both been given the Biagi surname on their birth certificates as Rosalba had discovered that this was the mother's prerogative under UK law so there was no need to make any other changes in the family group.

So began a very tranquil and successful period in the life of the Biagi family.

14 DECEMBER 2010

LONDON

Gina's meeting at Mondo's HQ was a bruising affair. If she had not been briefed on what to expect by Commander Gibbs at Scotland Yard the day before she would have walked out after five minutes. The meeting was to discuss progress on the Sapore Senza Pari assignment. Gibbs had forewarned her that they would probably try to discredit her negative input on Vittore Santoro and find spurious reasons to discount the better qualified candidates she had found.

As soon as she walked into Sir Charles' office that freezing cold and miserable mid-December morning she knew she was in for a torrid time. The usually urbane Sir Roger Simmons did not look up from the document he was reading but merely pointed peremptorily to indicate she should take a seat at the table near the window where the loathsome Charles Williamson was seated. He smirked at her as Sir Roger put his reading glasses down and said, "Your progress report was not what I was expecting Gina. Your main candidates are far too senior for this small company and you have summarily dismissed Vittore Santoro. Our Italian advisers tell us he is a brilliant operator and he is the right size for the job."

Gina sat back and paused for a few seconds before responding in a very measured way.

"Sir Roger, you pay me for my judgement which in the past you have been kind enough to say is excellent. The three candidates I presented are indeed senior and well-qualified executives and they conform exactly to the original brief you gave me. I confirmed this in my proposal letter of November 11th which Mr Williamson signed off. You wanted someone with the proven credentials to drive your ambitious growth strategy for SSP...I stand by my assessment that Santoro does not meet any of the criteria you gave me. Also, he is supremely arrogant and would alienate everyone he works with. He would be a disaster if appointed."

Sir Roger's jaw line tautened visibly as he said very coldly, "Thankfully that's not your call Gina. You don't know this but you have already upset some of our key associates in Italy. Vittore rang me personally immediately after your meeting in Verona. He was furious and said he had never been treated so appallingly in his life. Particularly by a lightweight, blonde personnel officer who knew nothing about business...that's a cleaned up version of what he said but you get my drift."

Gina was fuming but as a good poker player she managed to stay calm.

"Unfortunately Sir Roger you were not at the meeting or you would see that Santoro's bluster is a smokescreen. He was totally dismissive of me from the outset and was initially only prepared to give me a few minutes of his precious time. He seemed to think he already had the job in the bag and gave me the impression that he had been given assurances by someone at your end."

She was pleased to see that this last point had hit home as Sir Roger and Williamson exchanged furtive glances.

"That's your side of things but we've had feedback from several of our key suppliers in Italy that Vittore is a clever guy who has a lot of potential."

"I bet you have," thought Gina recalling Bruno Canepa's highly disturbing revelations about Santoro's position in the Sacra Corona Unita.

She said, "We obviously have a major divergence of view about him so what happens next?"

Williamson who had been mute until then chipped in in a somewhat condescending way. "The three people you have shortlisted seem to be of reasonable quality although not right for this job. We are prepared to see them as we may have other opportunities in our rapidly growing European operation. Fix that for early January here in London," he said high-handedly.

"Yes, I can do that but what about Santoro?"

"Leave him to us," Sir Roger said abruptly. "Your relationship with him is irretrievably fractured so we'll take it from here. But, if we do decide to offer him the SSP job we'll need you to send us a modified report on him we can share with our Board colleagues."

"What exactly does 'modified' mean?" Gina asked icily.

"It means that if you want the remaining unpaid two thirds of your large fee you need to soften your extreme criticisms and acknowledge that Santoro is a valid contender for the job. Actually, I've asked Charles to draft an amended report for you to approve…he's already e-mailed it to you."

The sheer arrogant effrontery of Sir Roger's demand took Gina's breath away. Her natural reaction would have been to refuse point blank and walk away rather than compromise her professional integrity. But, she knew that if she did so her usefulness to Bruno and Commander Gibbs would be at an end. She decided to eat humble pie although it very nearly choked her.

"It's an unusual request Sir Roger but if it helps you out of an awkward situation and you guarantee to pay our full fee, I'll consider submitting a more positive report. Maybe I did get off on the wrong foot with *Signor* Santoro. If you've had excellent feedback on him from your respected Italian contacts perhaps I got it wrong."

She almost gagged at this point but continued, "You agreed to such a good fee for this project that I would be very unpopular with my partners if I put this at risk by being stubborn."

She could see from the fleeting but satisfied smiles that passed across the faces of the two men that she had hit bull's-eye with her last statement. She knew that in their shared warped assessment of people, they believed that everyone had their price.

An hour later Gina was in Commander Gibb's office at Scotland Yard. He was smallish in stature and must have only just squeezed past the Met's minimum height requirement. But he had a very alert manner and a natural authority. He made Gina think of the famous Lloyd George quote, "In Wales we measure someone from the chin upwards," as he was clearly very astute. Bruno had told her he was also an accomplished linguist, having joined the Met after completing a degree in Modern Romance Languages. Bruno had laughed as he ruefully admitted, "He speaks better Italian than I do which I guess is why he was picked for this job."

Commander Gibbs said, "Amazing. We picked up every word of your conversation with them and it confirms our hypothesis that they want to insert Santoro as MD of Sapore Senza Pari and square it with the Mondo

Board by saying he was the best of a very good crop of candidates identified by a top headhunter."

"What I don't understand though," said Gina, "is how they will maintain the fiction that he is any good. As soon as other Mondo people meet him they'll realise he is a thoroughly nasty piece of work with limited ability and business nous. The new Group CEO, Adam Palfrey, is a very smart guy and it won't take him more than a couple of seconds to realise Santoro is the wrong person for the job."

"I can probably answer that. We know that in another Mondo subsidiary in Hungary which we suspect has been infiltrated by the mafia, Sir Roger has ring-fenced the business. The MD reports directly to him and is not part of the normal divisional structure reporting to the Group CEO...Incidentally, another thing that may be connected with all this is the sudden removal of the previous CEO, Simon Ramsay. He has remained tight-lipped about his abrupt departure but we suspect he may have found out something about the mafia's involvement. If so, the only reason he is still alive is likely to be that they have something on him which is so potentially damaging that it guarantees his silence. That's how they operate and, as Bruno probably told you, that's how they netted Sir Roger in the first place. At some point we may have to lean on Ramsay to find out what he knows but we can't risk hauling him in at the moment in case he tips off Sir Roger and they abort their plans for SSP."

Gina digested this and said, "I have the best researcher in the business and if you want he could do some more intensive digging on Ramsay's exit from Mondo."

"OK...any help gratefully received," nodded the Commander, "But you must tell him to be extremely circumspect as the stakes are very high."

"I understand that Commander, but Tom is used to operating in very delicate and confidential situations and if anyone can dig up the dirt on this, he can."

In the taxi on the way back to her office she checked her phone messages and was thrilled that Bruno had called. Since meeting the previous week he had phoned her a couple of times and on the last occasion they'd chatted for over an hour and were very much in tune with each other. She called back and he responded immediately.

"Gina, lovely to hear your voice again...I'm coming to London on Friday to see George Gibbs and I'm staying until Sunday afternoon...I've booked a room at the Sherlock Holmes Hotel on Baker Street. Any chance we could spend some time together?"

"Bruno…that's great…the hotel is just round the corner from my flat…"
"I know, that's why I chose it," he said with a smile in his voice.

They agreed that Gina would meet him at the Hotel and they would have dinner together somewhere and plan what to do on the Saturday. He said he didn't know London very well and was really looking forward to exploring it with her. Gina had three days to think about how to showcase a city she had fallen in love with since moving down from Lancashire a decade before.

She decided that on Friday evening she would take him for a cocktail at the Tsar bar in the Langham Hilton in Portland Place, opposite the BBC. She thought that having a couple of drinks from the huge list of vodkas on offer would get the evening off to a flying start. They would have dinner in Ozer, her favourite Turkish restaurant which was just across the road. She knew how much he liked lamb and in her view, Ozer had the softest, most succulent lamb in town. On Saturday, they could spend some time in Borough Market near London Bridge. She had already discovered that he was a real foodie like her and she knew he would be impressed by the quality and international variety of the foodstuffs on display and the lovely, lively market feel of the place. They could also buy food for a tapas style supper at her place that evening. Since Verona she had simply not been able to get him out of her mind. As a realist, love at first sight was not a concept she would have recognised until their dinner together. But when he called her a couple of days later she knew beyond any doubt that she had fallen for him in a big way. She thought he felt the same way and that if they were alone in the privacy of her flat it would be easier for nature to take its course. If they fell into bed after an enjoyable dinner, so be it.

"You are a bad, bad girl," she thought to herself, but her mock self-censure did not weaken her resolve to show him how much she wanted him.

She sketched out the rest of a tentative plan for Saturday. After the market, they could spend some time wandering round the Inns of Court. She loved the Oxbridge college feel of this old, sequestered enclave smack in the middle of a manic modern city. They could have lunch in Covent Garden and then walk round either Hyde Park or Regent's Park. If he wanted some culture they could finish off with a look at the National Gallery or maybe the smaller, charming Wallace Collection which was a stone's throw from her flat.

She left Sunday open as she wasn't sure what time he had to leave for Heathrow. She knew he wanted to do some shopping and she had half promised her sister Maurizia that they would also hit the shops together to look for Christmas presents for their mum and dad. She and Maurizia were extremely close and she wanted her sister to meet Bruno as she'd already told her how much she was attracted to him. The next few days seemed to pass agonisingly slowly but finally Friday evening arrived and she walked into the foyer of his hotel with mounting excitement. When he came out of the lift and saw her his smile was so warm that she had no hesitation in hugging him tightly and pressing her cheek against his.

"That's a nice welcome…it's so good to see you…I've been thinking about you a lot…"

"Me too," said Gina, "I've been so looking forward to this weekend."

"So…what's on the agenda…?"

Gina filled him on her tentative plans and Bruno seemed delighted with the programme. That first evening went by in a flash. "We are so natural with each other", she thought, "it's as if we have known each other all our lives." The pepper vodkas in the Langham Hilton's bar were really redundant as ice-breakers but they bolstered their mellow mood as they walked across the road to the buzzy atmosphere of Ozer. As usual, the flamboyant restaurateur Huseyin Ozer who had developed the Sofra chain of Turkish eateries in London was on hand to greet them. He welcomed Gina with the warmth befitting a regular customer and once they had been shown to their table, sent over two complimentary glasses of champagne.

"This evening gets better and better," Bruno said raising his glass to her, "but I'd be just as happy wherever we were so long as you were with me."

He said this without pretence and she reached across the table and put her hand over his to show she felt exactly the same. As at their first dinner in Verona they both wanted exactly the same starter and main course. They laughed and wondered whether they were telepathic or just inveterate carnivores. They shared a mixed platter of tabbouleh, falafel, hummus and spinach and feta pastries with wonderful fresh baked Turkish bread. They followed with Ozer's special mixed grill of three kebabs of lamb, chicken and beef kofta.

"This is as succulent as any lamb I have ever tasted," Bruno said, "and this Yakut Turkish wine is a revelation. I'll have to revise my misguided preconceptions about Turkish food…this meal is simple and unpretentious but absolutely delicious."

"So far so very good," thought Gina.

After dinner, as it was still relatively early, Bruno wanted to take a walk in the crisp, refreshing air.

"I love the lively, cosmopolitan flavour of London," he said. "Whenever I come here I feel like an excited child."

"I know exactly what you mean," she replied. "I think it's because originally we both came from places a bit off the beaten track...I still get a real buzz from the city even though I've lived here for a good few years."

They set off down Regent Street with the Christmas lights winking down at them. Gina said she thought the seasonal decorations in Verona were more elegant but anglophile Bruno would have none of it. Gina slipped her arm through his and they chattered about everything and nothing. Before they realised it they were in Trafalgar Square where lots of people were still milling about. They continued down The Mall to Buckingham Palace and then cut through Green Park towards Piccadilly.

"Do you fancy a nightcap?" Gina asked.

"Absolutely," was the enthusiastic response.

"I know a lovely tapas place near Hyde Park Corner called El Pirata. I've eaten there loads of times and Fernando the manager has become a friend...they have a nice bar...let's go there."

Fernando was his usual bubbly self and the pre-Christmas atmosphere in the restaurant was very lively. Fernando found them a couple of stools at the bar and served them two gargantuan brandies. They continued chatting until they realised the hubbub around them had abated and they were virtually alone in the place.

As they left, Gina suggested they take a cab to drop Bruno at his hotel and then take her on to her flat. In the taxi Bruno took both her hands in his.

"Gina, this has been one of the most magical evenings in my life. I know it is ridiculously early in our relationship, but I must tell you that I have not been able to think of anything except you since we met in Verona. I have fallen in love with you and I hope you have some feelings for me."

Gina didn't say a word but kissed him with such spontaneous passion that it took a while to register that the cabby was tapping on the glass partition, saying, with a huge grin on his face, "Here we are...I didn't want to let the meter run on any more but we've been here a few minutes already."

Gina and Bruno disengaged slowly from their embrace with their eyes still locked on each other.

"I'll come for you at around nine o'clock tomorrow," Gina said softly.

In a bit of a daze Bruno disembarked, said "*a domani*" and climbed the steps to his hotel.

"Seems like a really nice bloke," said the cabby cheerily. "Where to now love?"

A few minutes after the cabbie dropped her, Gina went straight to bed but couldn't sleep. Her mind raced around the multiple strands of their conversation. She was amazed at the symmetry of their tastes. It became something of a game for them as the evening progressed to calibrate their preferences across a wide spectrum of social and cultural activities. It started when they both nominated Queen as their favourite group and Don Maclean's *Vincent* as one of their all time best pop songs. They found they both loved cinema and particularly well crafted non-blockbuster type films such as the recent Argentinian film, *The Secret in their Eyes*. Favourites they shared in the acting world included Yves Montand from a previous generation and Colin Farell and Kate Winslet as current practitioners. Their favourite places in Italy were the smaller, more intimate cities like Urbino in Umbria, Verona and Bolzano in the Dolomites. They each preferred lighter red wines like Bardolino and Brouilly and dry, steely white wines such as Pouilly Fumé. They had both recently discovered the wonderful music of the composer Carl Jenkins and absolutely loved the haunting *The Armed Man*.

They were intensely family orientated. Bruno was as close to his brother Marco as Gina was to her sister Maurizia. He clearly adored his mother and had idolised his father who had been tragically killed in a helicopter crash when Bruno was twenty-five.

"OK, we know we like many of the same things," said Bruno "but let's turn things round and see if our pet hates are similar." Again, there was an astonishing homogeneity. They hated tattoos, discourteousness, stinginess, pretentious French films and strident nationalism. Finally, with something akin to relief they agreed to disagree on one thing. Bruno insisted that Italian drivers were better than their British counterparts and Gina exploded into laughter at this ludicrous assertion.

Before she finally drifted off to sleep Gina kept thinking to herself, 'He loves me, he actually said he loves me and like an idiot I didn't tell him I feel the same.' But she consoled herself that the prolonged, brandy infused passionate kiss had surely served as an adequate proxy for her unspoken declaration.

When she went to pick him up at his hotel the next morning she immediately rectified her omission. She flung her arms round his neck and whispered in his ear, "I love you too."

They spent a couple of hours wandering around Borough Market and returned to her flat in Marylebone weighed down with their rich selection of food purchases. As she had predicted, Bruno loved the bohemian feel of the famous market and was surprised at how eclectic was the selection of foodstuffs on show. They foraged for their "picnic" for that evening and ended up with an international mix of Argentinian empanadas, Morecambe Bay shrimps, hand carved *jamon iberico*, German *bratwurst* and French cheeses. They changed their lunch plans as Maurizia could not meet them on Sunday. They arranged to see her for lunch at L'Autre Pied on Blandford Street, near Gina's flat. She took to Bruno immediately and when he went to the loo after lunch she grabbed her sister. "Wow," she exclaimed, "you've won the jackpot with him…he's absolutely gorgeous and is clearly totally besotted with you."

"Maurizia, I've fallen head over heels for him and he's already told me he feels the same…I'm so happy I can't tell you." Maurizia was very curious about how they had met and they had decided to say that it was a chance encounter in Verona in *Dodici Apostoli* where they had struck up a conversation in the near deserted restaurant. Maurizia was still inquisitive about Bruno's trip to London but he said firmly that he was engaged in a highly confidential cross-border project that he was not at liberty to discuss. Maurizia looked quizzically at him but didn't press the matter. Gina knew that being the excellent investigative journalist she was, Maurizia would try to get it out of her later when they were on their own. Since joining the *Financial Times* Maurizia had specialised in uncovering corruption in the corporate world. She had recently completed a lengthy investigation into a major Belgian holding company which had set up a network of fictitious subsidiaries and bogus financial transactions in the Dutch Antilles, the Bahamas and Switzerland to hide the ownership of assets. She had calculated that the company was guilty of massive tax evasion to the tune of around two billion euros. She had passed on her detailed dossier to Eurojust, the EU's cross-border judicial cooperation unit who were now finalising a case against the Board members responsible.

She had told Bruno about this over lunch. He was impressed and had already heard about this major fraud from a colleague in Switzerland who had been granted a European Arrest Warrant for a prominent Swiss banker who was implicated.

Maurizia had to work so Bruno and Gina spent the rest of the afternoon shopping, sightseeing around Covent Garden and finally spending an hour in her favourite art gallery, The Wallace Collection. They got back to her flat around six and she asked Bruno if he minded having dinner in front of the TV as she wanted to watch the final of *Strictly Come Dancing* at seven. They opened a bottle of Taittinger whilst they heated up the empanadas and spread out their Borough Market feast on her large coffee table. Gina asked Bruno to select a bottle of red from her wine "cellar" – otherwise known as her spare bedroom- and he came back beaming, brandishing a bottle of Gattinara from Piedmont which was one of his all-time favourite wines.

They watched the dancing and agreed that Kara Tointon and her professional dance partner, Artem, were worthy winners. Things then progressed naturally as she had hoped towards her bedroom. *"Carissima,"* Bruno whispered as they started to undress each other, "I'm a bit nervous as I have not made love for a very long time."

"Caro," she said softly, "this is the first time but we have the rest of our lives to perfect things…and I'm a great believer that practice makes perfect." In the event it was if they were synchronised and knew instinctively how to please each other.

In the early hours as she was dozing off Bruno leapt out of bed and moved round to her side. Kneeling down he took her face in his hands and said with quiet tenderness, "Will you marry me?"

In the morning Gina woke around seven-thirty and spent a good twenty minutes just gazing at Bruno as he slept on peacefully. She knew she had found someone very special and couldn't wait to tell her family that she had accepted his proposal.

They stayed in bed until mid-morning, reading the Sunday papers and indulging in leisurely love making in contrast to the urgent passion of the night before. He had to be at the airport by mid-afternoon and she decided to go out to Heathrow with him extend their time together to the maximum. They agreed he would come back for the New Year holiday when she would take him to meet her parents.

Before going through the departure gate at Heathrow he embraced her so tightly she could hardly breathe.

"I now believe in *amore a prima vista,"* were his final whispered words.

15 DECEMBER 2010

LECCE, PUGLIA

"Is it done?" Arturo Santoro asked brusquely as Enrico Pozzi entered his inner sanctum and virtually stood to attention before his boss.

"*Si capo*, it is done," he replied and quickly turned on his heel as Santoro dismissed him with a casual wave of his hand.

Santoro then placed both hands on his desk and heaved his huge bulk upright. A combination of his obesity and the inherited family curse of rheumatism had virtually locked his knee joints into a constant, mind-numbing, bottomless pit of pain. As boss of the largest of the clans operating in the Puglian mafia federation of the Sacra Corona Unita he was feeling increasingly embattled. The physical discomfort his gigantic body was experiencing in its seventy-third year was compounded by an unprecedented level of anxiety about the concerted attack on the SCU's plethora of activities by anti-mafia forces.

Pozzi was simply an assassin – a member of a death squad, *la Squadra della Morte*, which was directed by Santoro and the other seven members of the *Società Segretissima*, the most senior decision-making body of the SCU. Santoro was urgently covering his tracks as one of his informants, a senior officer in the *Carabinieri*, had forewarned him that the anti-mafia crusade was closing in for a massive cull of SCU members. Pozzi had been despatched to dispose of a local politician. He was about to spill the beans to the Anti-Mafia Directorate on how he had helped Santoro secure numerous contracts in exchange for very large "sweeteners". The politician had been guaranteed immunity from prosecution in exchange for chapter and verse on Santoro's extensive illicit activities. Unfortunately, this man did not know that Santoro had arranged for his phone to be tapped and so knew he intended to make a full statement the following day, the sixteenth of December.

So this particular evening, Pozzi had waited outside the politician's house near Brindisi for the man to return from work and had used a butcher's knife to slash his throat and then cut out his tongue as an unambiguous message to other potential waverers to keep quiet.

In July of that year a huge police and army operation in neighbouring Calabria, involving three thousand officers, had resulted in the arrest of three hundred members of the 'Ndrangheta, including the head of this mafia branch, eighty-year-old Domenico Oppedisano.

The 'Ndrangheta had grown its revenues to an estimated €44 billion, equal to the combined GDP of Slovenia and Estonia and equivalent to over three per cent of Italy's GDP. It had been particularly successful in transplanting its operations, via Calabrian migrants, to around 20 countries in Europe and beyond, including Australia, Canada and the US. Key centres in the north of Italy included Genoa, Turin and Milan. The development of this extensive network had been greatly assisted by the forced resettlement of mafiosi initiated by the Italian Government in 1956, under a scheme called *Soggiorno Obbligato*. This policy was based on the naive assumption that the mafia was the product of a backward society. Moving mafia members away from their home areas like Calabria to more "civilised", law-abiding places like Turin, would encourage them to abandon their old ways. So it was hypothesised. But it was a massive miscalculation as it simply enabled the 'Ndrangheta and other mafia units to establish themselves outside their traditional spheres of influence whilst maintaining their links with the "mothership".

Santoro's SCU clan had been in collaboration with the 'Ndrangheta since the early eighties. The links had been cemented by the marriage of Arturo's son, Vittore, to the daughter of a senior member of the Bellocco family, one of the major 'Ndrangheta clans. It looked as though this long-term, highly lucrative partnership was severely threatened by the intensifying efforts of the integrated anti-mafia operations of the judiciary, police and specialist units of the *Carabinieri* and *Guardia di Finanza*.

As further evidence of the net closing in on him, a few months earlier his close friend and partner in crime Albino Prudentino had been arrested in Tirana, Albania where he ran two casinos. Both gambling resorts were seized by Italian anti-mafia police in conjunction with the Albanian authorities. The previous year another SCU boss, Pietro Bassi, had been arrested in Amsterdam.

Even more worrying was the grass-roots opposition to the mafia spreading inexorably across the whole of southern Italy. Movements such as *Addiopizzo* – "goodbye extortion payments" which mobilised whole communities to refuse to pay protection money and *Ammazzateci Tutti* – "Kill us all", threatened the very essence of mafia power – the collusion of a cowed and accepting citizenry. Santoro was most worried by the latter movement, started a few years earlier by young people in the wake of the mafia assassination of Calabria's Regional Vice President, Fortugno. This had since spread across to Puglia and to other parts of Italy with what seemed like an irresistible momentum.

Santoro hobbled over to his favourite armchair poured himself a glass of red wine and sank into a gloomy, reflective state. He remembered as clearly as if it were yesterday that Christmas day nearly thirty years ago in the early 1980s, when Giuseppe Rogoli had beckoned him into his cell in Trani prison, north of Bari.

"Arturo, I'm pissed off with the way these Camorra bastards lord it over us. What do these back street sons of Neapolitan whores know about

Puglia? Why should we bend the knee to them? Enough I say, *basta!* I want to set up our own operation in Puglia, free from their grasping mitts. I need you with me because your drugs business is very well organised and you take no shit from anybody. I want you to work with my pal Antonio Antonica who's already done some of the groundwork."

"Yeah, count me in," Santoro said enthusiastically. "I'm fed up to the back teeth with those pimps too."

Santoro was doing a four year stretch for possession of a sizeable stash of heroin. He did not succeed in having his case dismissed as he had been able to do in the early seventies. This was due to the fact that he was tried in front of the same judge who had expressed his dismay at having to throw out the earlier murder case when the key prosecution witness refused to testify.

Santoro was coming to the end of his sentence and would be freed before Rogoli. He agreed to act as Rogoli's "enforcer" in persuading Puglian members of the Camorra to switch allegiance to the new operation which would become the Sacra Corona Unita. Santoro was certainly the right choice for the job. A huge man weighing close to 130 kilos, he had a fearsome reputation for psychopathic violence of extreme unpredictability. It was widely known that he had killed a restaurant owner in Lecce who had the temerity to ask him to pay for two bottles of very expensive wine. Santoro paid but waited outside until the man closed the establishment and then beat him literally to a pulp. He rammed a wine glass into the dead man's mouth and poured several bottles of wine over his body. At the mortuary his wife was only able to identify her husband by his wedding ring with her name engraved inside. The police pathologist confirmed that the face and body had been smashed only with fists, but over eighty times. It was a frenzy of violence she had never seen before. The power of the code of *omerta* had guaranteed that Santoro was not charged. He was merely interviewed in a desultory fashion by local police who accepted his corroborated alibi that he had been playing cards with friends into the early hours.

This was only one in a long catalogue of extreme acts of violence perpetrated by Santoro throughout his life. But he was feared more for the random nature of his eruptions into violence than his brutality which was by no means a unique attribute in his criminal brotherhood.

Santoro was born in a village outside Lecce to reasonably well-off middle class parents. However, the values of these upright members of the *borghesia* held no attraction for him and from an early age he showed violent criminal tendencies. As early as six years old he caught and tortured small birds and animals and by the age of nine he was leader of a gang of feral children who terrorised their neighbourhood. In his early teens he deserted the "upper world" of civil society for the Puglian underworld, severing all ties with his family and dropping out of school. His immense physical presence was accompanied by a cunning mind and he quickly rose through the ranks of the Camorra and later the Sacra Corona Unita. His speciality was smuggling contraband drugs and cigarettes from the Balkans via links with the Albanian mafia. He was among the first to use ultra fast speedboats as safe transport for the merchandise. He gradually extended his range to embrace a wide spectrum of criminal activities including extortion, kidnapping and people and arms trafficking. His links with other organised crime groups grew commensurately and he built firm alliances with, *inter alia*, the Vary V Zakone or Russian mafia, the Mexican drug cartels, and the mafia equivalents in Turkey and Nigeria. His closest ties were with the neighbouring Calabrian 'Ndrangheta.

For the past few years, Santoro had also forged a highly lucrative connection with the Hezbollah who supplied him with top quality hashish from Southern Lebanon and the Bekaá valley near the Lebanese/Syrian border. Through his Russian mafia connections Santoro supplied small arms and more destructive military ordnance to various militias and resistance groups in the Middle East.

As he did increasingly these days, Santoro found himself slipping into a nostalgic reverie. He liked to recall happier times when he had been undisputed master of all he surveyed. He congratulated himself on how he had won and kept his top position in Sacra Corona Unita. He was a living example of Machiavelli's dictum that it is better to be feared than loved. Any perceived threats to his standing were responded to with such ferocity during his climb to power that for the past fifteen years he had been unchallenged. He chose methods of execution as gruesome signals to potential enemies and dissidents within SCU ranks not to risk opposing him. He drew on both current practices in other parts of the world and from his fascination with forms of torture historically. He had two main methods, "Necklacing", which a friend who had been in South Africa told him about. This involved forcing a rubber tyre filled with petrol around a victim's chest and arms and setting it on fire. His absolute favourite was the so-called "Colombian Necktie" where the victim's throat is slashed and then the tongue is pulled through the gaping wound.

He relished these executions and made sure as many people as possible witnessed the horrendous results of his sadistic efforts. He was not exactly sure how many people he had killed, but the grand total executed and eliminated by more traditional shootings, knifings and beatings topped thirty. Once the killing spree had abated, he had concentrated his formidable planning and organisational skills on building alliances with other criminal organisations to secure channels for the ever-growing markets for narcotics and contraband goods. He was also at the forefront of the push to enter legitimate business sectors in an attempt to reduce the impact of increasingly effective, concerted attacks by law enforcement agencies on overtly illicit activities.

A key plank in this strategy was the grooming of his adopted son, Vittore, as a genuine businessman. He kept him away from the overtly criminal side of his many activities. He wanted Vittore to have a clean record so that he could act as the legitimate face of the genuine businesses he intended to acquire. He had sent Vittore to the prestigious *Università di Roma, La Sapienza*, to do a degree in business management. On graduating, he had been given a management job in one of the growing number of legitimate enterprises funded by SCU. This was a large, federated network of funeral directors. Here, Vittore was able to combine a genuine business role with more traditional intimidatory tactics. To increase the flow of cadavers to his company, he used strong-arm tactics to "persuade" the owners of nursing homes to direct all their funeral needs his way. After a year or so cutting his teeth on this operation, he moved on to a range of other businesses in the construction, waste management and tourism sectors.

For the past three years he had been running a mini-conglomerate food company with interests in olive oil, vegetables, fruit juice, wine and pet food. Whilst this was a legitimate business, it was also a front for a large scale smuggling operation. Drugs imported from Colombia and Afghanistan were sneaked past customs in Germany, France and the UK in consignments of pickled vegetables, dog food and wine. It was a hugely lucrative activity and Santoro senior had been extending it by adding other distribution conduits such as the Sapore Senza Pari company in Modena, which provided access to the important Spanish market.

After disposing of the last *Direttore Generale*, Carlo Giordano, Santoro senior had arranged with Sir Roger Simmons at Mondo Foods to shoehorn Vittore into the top job there to provide a totally secure umbrella for the smuggling operation. Arturo had established the "vacancy" personally. He had arranged for a trusted cousin in Genoa to kill Giordano – making it look like an accident. Sir Roger had told him that on 15 October Giordano was due to drive down to Tuscany to see customers in Poggibonsi and then Volterra. After this he was going to Pisa airport to fly to London to tell Sir

Roger about his discovery of illegal activity in SSP. Santoro's man waited in a large stolen truck in a lay-by on the hill road from Poggibonsi. The high vantage point he had chosen gave him a clear view of the oncoming traffic upto a kilometre away. By mid-afternoon that clear autumn day there had only been a trickle of cars on the road and through his binoculars he easily picked out Giordano's distinctive black Audi A8 on the chicane below. He had selected the spot where he intended to force the car off the road into a deep ravine and the plan worked perfectly with the added bonus of no witnesses. He dumped the stolen truck on the outskirts of Pisa and walked to the car park in the centre where he had left his car. As if it was the end of a completely normal working day, he bought his youngest daughter the latest Barbie doll before driving back to Genoa.

21 DECEMBER 2010

LONDON

"Happy birthday Gina darling." A little groggily Gina glanced at the bedside clock as she held the receiver a few inches away from her ear in an attempt to muffle the loud, unfailingly cheerful voice of her father. It was 06:00 on Tuesday 21 December and her dad, always an early riser, refused to acknowledge that anyone else might have a different body clock. In her teenage years if she ever tried to have a lie-in he would admonish her in the time honoured way telling her she was "sleeping her life away."

"Oh hi *papà*; thanks for leaving it so late in the morning to call…"

"Gina, you know your mother always says that sarcasm is the lowest form of wit."

Sorry *papà*…it's great that you are always the first to call on my birthday…I love you."

"I love you too *carissima* and I just wanted to say that I have to come down to London tomorrow to sign some papers to do with our new restaurant venture. Can we have lunch?"

"That would be good…do you want to go to my favourite place again? Remember, last time I took you to Patterson's off Regent Street and you said it was one of the best meals you had eaten for ages."

"Great – let me know what time. My meeting in the City will be over by 12:30."

"OK...will call you later...love to *mamma*."

Gina had been fretting about whether to tell her dad about the murky waters in which she was paddling. She had finally decided to put him in the picture and thought it would be so much easier to talk face-to-face than over the phone. She had always confided in her dad – probably more than her mother who was very loving but a lot more judgemental.

Gina really wanted to tap his brain on the Puglian mafia connection given his local knowledge and personal experience. During her teenage years he had often talked about his happy childhood and youth in Puglia but she knew there was something very distressing about his departure that he never disclosed. He came close one mid-August evening when she was about eighteen. They were on holiday in Brittany and he had imbibed a little too much Muscadet during an idyllic dinner in Auray on his forty-seventh birthday. After dinner when Rosalba and Maurizia returned to the hotel, Luca and Gina took a post prandial stroll down to the river port where he became very quiet and melancholic.

"What's up *papà*? You seem a bit low."

"I am rather sad tonight, *cara*, because today it is twenty-one years to the day that I had to leave Italy."

"Had to leave *papà*?...I don't understand...*mamma* always told us you left because of the tragic bereavements you suffered that year..."

"That was the cover story we concocted to satisfy people's idle curiosity but I'm afraid the real truth is more sinister. I had a run-in with the local mafia which made it too risky to stay in Italy. I had to get out fast with the help of my closest friend. I made my way to Scotland where I met your *mamma* and the rest, as they say, is history."

Gina had a million questions but her dad seemed to collect himself and got up from the river wall they had perched on.

"Sorry Gina, I shouldn't have told you and I don't want to go into detail. All you need to know is that the path I was forced to take has given me the most wonderful family a man could wish for. It is only very occasionally that my nostalgia for Puglia gets the better of me. But I wouldn't swap my life now for anything."

Try as she might, Gina could prise no more out of him and as he kissed her goodnight he made her promise not to tell her sister about it.

She was remembering this when her father breezed in to Patterson's restaurant and gave her a hug.

"Sweetheart, what have you been up to lately? It seems ages since I saw you last."

"*Papà* I've been so busy it's not true. I've just been to Germany and Italy on business…and I've met someone I want to tell you about. His name is Bruno Canepa and he's an officer in the *Guardia di Finanza.*"

"Really? And how did you meet him?"

"Well I need to tell you something but it is very confidential…and I don't want you to tell *mamma* about it."

Gina then ran through the whole saga of her assignment for Mondo Foods and her discovery of its mafia connections. She couldn't help but register the look of alarm which flashed across her father's handsome face when she mentioned the Sacra Corona Unita and the names of Arturo and Vittore Santoro. When she told him she had agreed to help the police her father reached across the table and grabbed both her hands in his.

"Gina, I don't want you involved in this. It's too risky and you have no idea of the kind of vicious animals you are dealing with. Please stop now… I couldn't bear it if anything happened to you."

"But *papà* you've always impressed on me the need to stand up for what is right and anyway I've given my word to Bruno and Commander Gibbs and I can't back out now."

"Please listen to me Gina. I'll now tell you the full story about my escape from Puglia in the mid-seventies. I was a young lawyer and had unearthed a web of corruption. Many local politicians, businessmen and police officers were in the pocket of the mafia and I made a chance discovery of a number of scams. I prepared a full dossier and delivered it to the offices of a crusading local magistrate I knew. Somehow the report was intercepted and I got a warning to get out or be killed. That's when I came to the UK, met your mother and started a new life here. It's a cruel irony that you have now been dragged into this same evil world. Please tell Bruno you can't do what he wants you to do."

"*Papà*, I can't. It wouldn't be right and besides I think I'm in love with him so I simply can't let him down. If it's OK with you and *mamma* I want to invite Bruno to stay with us for the New Year celebrations…so you'll get a chance to meet him then."

Luca was not really ready to let it drop but he knew his daughter had inherited a very determined streak from her mother. He realised that if he tried to press the issue it would only serve to lock Gina even more firmly into her decision. The next day on his way back to his home near Lancaster he hatched a plan. He would contact his old friend Bernardo Colangelo to get detailed up-to-date intelligence on what was happening in Puglia. If he couldn't dissuade Gina from her planned involvement with the police operation he wanted to see if there was any way he could help her.

As soon as he got home he fired up his computer. Google directed him to a mass of information on Bernardo who was now a big wheel in the business world. Twenty years earlier he had taken over the already sizeable family business interests. By some shrewd acquisitions and the accelerated growth of several key companies he was now at the helm of Transmeridionale, one of the biggest diversified groups in the whole of southern Italy. Whilst retaining and developing his family's traditional operations in food processing and clothing and footwear manufacturing, Bernardo had built two important new legs to the business in the hospitality field and container shipping.

After an hour's research Luca sat back and pondered his decision to contact his friend after so long. Although more than thirty-five years had passed since his self-imposed exile, he could not be one hundred per cent certain that re-introducing himself to his oldest friend was risk free. In the end his strong paternal instincts took over and he realised he had to do everything he could to help Gina.

The next day with some residual trepidation he picked up the phone and dialled the number of Transmeridionale's head office in Brindisi. Within seconds he was speaking to Bernardo's somewhat officious secretary.

"I know this is a bit unusual but would you simply give *Signor* Colangelo the following message…say it's from his only stowaway on *Il Delfino*…and ask him to ring me on this cellular phone number 07902 225345."

A few minutes later his phone rang and a breathless voice blurted out, "Luca? It is you isn't it…?"

"Yes it's me. I can't tell you how pleased I am to hear your voice after all these years."

"Me too…but where are you now Luca? You said you were heading for Argentina…"

"I didn't go that far. I actually moved to another European country and carved out a new life. I've re-invented myself and now own a few restaurants…best that I don't tell you where on an open line…but I hope we can meet up somewhere. I'll then be able to say more and also ask for your help with something that's worrying me. Tell me, do you travel much outside Italy now that you are such a bigshot?"

"Oh, I'm not really a major league player…just a sizeable fish in a relatively small pond…but, yes, I do spend a lot of time in aeroplanes nowadays. In fact, I'll be in Paris and then Frankfurt on business early next month."

"OK, how about meeting up then in either country if your schedule permits?"

"To hell with my schedule…I'll meet you anywhere you wish. I can't wait to hear what you've been up to for the past thirty odd years."

"That's great Bernardo…so how about Paris then?"

"I'll be there on 12 and 13 January staying at The Baltimore Hotel near the Trocadéro. Why don't you book a room there for the night of the 12th? We can have dinner and catch up for a few hours."

"I'll do that, but please don't tell anyone we are going to meet. I'm still a bit paranoid about you know who."

"*Va bene*…and I can't wait to see you in the flesh. *Buon Natale, amico mio.*"

Luca put the phone down and sat quietly at his desk, barely noticing that tears were coursing down his cheeks. The emotional jolt of hearing his best friend's voice after more than three decades had affected him greatly. He realised that the loss of Bernardo's companionship for more than half his lifetime was by far the worst deprivation he had suffered as a result of his enforced flight from Puglia.

1 JANUARY 2011

SILVERDALE, LANCASHIRE

"*Papà*…this is Bruno." Gina and Bruno had decided to take the train up to Lancaster on New Year's Day and Luca was waiting for them as they came through the barrier. Bruno and Luca shook hands and Gina gave her father a big hug.

"Well *cara* I must say you look fantastic and so happy. Bruno, you are obviously having a positive effect on my darling daughter."

"*Signor* Biagi, I am so pleased to meet you. Gina has told me a lot about you…"

"No…Call me Luca please…we are very pleased you can spend a few days with us…My wife can't wait to meet you, so let's go. Maurizia is waiting for us in the car. She needed to make masses of phone calls as usual."

Before telling her father about her involvement with the Mondo investigation, Gina had first discussed it with Bruno. She told him about her father's escape from Puglia and that he might be able to provide some useful input on the local mafia scene. Her father had told her that he still had a copy of the dossier he had compiled and sent to Magistrate Fontana all those years ago. Bruno was worried about this further extension of the group of "in the know" people, but he acceded to Gina's request.

"I have always been very open with my dad," Gina had said. "He is the most honourable man I know and I just wouldn't feel right keeping something like this from him."

It was agreed that Luca would take Bruno down to Manchester on 3 January, ostensibly to show him the large Trattoria Biagi which had recently been opened. Bruno could spend some time looking through Luca's old dossier to see if there were any useful linkages to the on-going probe into Sacra Corona Unita's relationship with Mondo Foods. In this way their conversation would be completely private with no risk of Gina's mother or professionally inquisitive sister getting wind of it.

As soon as they were seated in his Alfa Romeo, Luca handed Bruno a large envelope containing his findings and the dozens of photocopies of incriminating documents which he had assembled in the mid-seventies. Bruno was thoroughly absorbed in the intricate chronicle of events and they were approaching the outskirts of Manchester when he shuffled the papers together and said, "Brilliant forensic analysis Luca…any detective would be proud to put his name on such a report. I've made a few notes on some possible actions we can take even after such a time lag. We can talk about this when we get to your place."

Trattoria Biagi was in the city centre, just off King Street. They walked in and were greeted by the young, enthusiastic restaurant manager. "Bruno, this is Matteo Conti who has been instrumental in getting this place off the ground in the past year or so. Matteo used to manage one of my other restaurants in The Lake District and jumped at the chance to come to the big city to manage my biggest investment to date."

Bruno saw immediately that the Trattoria was the antithesis of a traditional Italian restaurant. No chequered tablecloths, pictures of the Bay of Naples or Chianti wicker flasks. Instead, a high-ceilinged room with oiled wooden floors, Scandinavian hanging lights and a combination of banquettes and tables with crisp white linen and elegant bentwood chairs. On one side of the restaurant was a long bar with a line of bar stools for customers to eat there or just have a drink. The very large room was made more intimate by the addition of a mezzanine floor two-thirds of the way in and by the discerning placement of ferns and other green plants to break up the massive interior space. Even at twelve noon, half the bar stools were occupied and people were trickling in for an early lunch.

"Very impressive Luca. You must be delighted with the decor and ambience…it's really stylish."

"*Grazie*…yes, for a place with a seating capacity of 160 I think we have created a pretty 'clubbable environment' as our designers called it…and I must tell you the food is terrific with the accent on light, modern Italian dishes…you'll see when we have lunch a bit later."

Off the main body of the restaurant were two private dining rooms and once settled in one of these Luca said, "So Bruno, do you think my ancient dossier may still be of some use to you?"

"Yes, I think there is a distinct possibility we can still benefit from your courageous work all those years ago. Last year I was involved in a huge police operation resulting in the arrest of hundreds of 'Ndrangheta members in Calabria. We picked up lots of valuable intelligence on the links between them and the neighbouring Sacra Corona Unita. I'm pretty sure that among the officials thought to have been collaborating with SCU was your old boss Moscatelli. I don't think we were able to assemble enough concrete evidence to nail him and, because he was in his mid-seventies and had retired a few years earlier, it was decided to focus on nabbing those officials still actively involved with the mob. However, armed with your irrefutable evidence I'm sure my friends in the regional anti-mafia unit would be only too happy to lean on him to see what he can cough up about the SCU's activities. Even though he might elude prosecution because of the Statute of Limitations, I'm sure the threat of his graft being leaked to the media would be enough to make him cooperate. I bet you, Luca, that being the pedant you described, he will have neatly documented a lot of his dealings with his mafia cronies."

Luca couldn't help smiling wryly at Bruno's affirmation that the report which had utterly deflected him from his life's path in Puglia might still have a part to play in eradicating the mafia stain on his native region.

3 JANUARY 2011

LONDON

Maurizia Biagi was staring intently at her computer screen in the *Financial Times* building in Southwark. Since meeting Bruno Canepa the previous month she had been unable to resist tapping into her paper's extensive databases to find out more about her prospective brother-in-law. Her curiosity was fuelled by the extremely straight bat Bruno had deployed when they were all at her parents' house over the New Year and she had tried to get him to open up about the assignment he was working on. His totally noncommittal response was a challenge to her journalistic pride.

On her screen was a photo of Major Canepa receiving the highest bravery award of the *Guardia di Finanza* – the *Medaglia d'Oro al Valore*. The accompanying text explained that the Gold Medal was awarded to those who had demonstrated *spiccato coraggio e singolare perizia e l'esposizione della vita a manifesto pericolo* – in other words notable courage and skill whilst ignoring the palpable risk to their own life.

In Bruno's case the medal was awarded for his outstanding bravery in a joint action against a large band of Albanian drug traffickers. At great risk to himself Bruno had crossed open terrain under automatic fire to rescue a Greek Coastguard Officer who was trapped in a cleft in the rocks. He had carried the injured officer back to the position occupied by his own men before leading an assault on the Albanian gang. After a furious fire-fight, three Albanians were killed and a further ten gang members had surrendered, with Bruno's team only suffering light casualties.

"So, not only good looking and charming but a real, live hero...lucky Gina," she thought to herself. Maurizia's research was not solely motivated by idle curiosity. Her finely tuned journalistic instincts were insisting that Bruno was involved in some big operation which could produce a great story for her... maybe a real scoop. For much of the previous year she had been one of the key members of a *Financial Times* team working with the Bureau for Investigative Journalism at London's City University. Over a nine-month period they had conducted a huge research project tracing how every penny of the European Union's Structural Fund had been distributed – a whopping €347 billion in the current budget period. A product of this mammoth exercise was the creation of a database covering over 600,000 recipients across all member states during the current spending round. The *FT* reported the main findings over five days from 30 November 2010 and lifted the curtain on a trail of undetected waste, misdirected investment and outright fraud.

One of Maurizia's principal areas of interest had been exploring how Italy's most dangerous mafia, the 'Ndrangheta had become expert at getting its hands on these funds. Brussels had been alarmingly willing to hand over vast sums to mafia infested regions like Calabria despite the almost inevitable consequence of European taxpayers' money ending up in criminal hands. During this major exercise she had developed mutually beneficial relationships with senior officials of both *l'Office de Lutte Antifraude* or OLAF, the EU's antifraud office in Brussels and Eurojust, the judicial cooperation unit based in The Hague. She had made several visits to both agencies and she was currently flavour of the month with them. Her work uncovering the major fraud in a Belgian multinational had led to many arrests, the return of billions of euros to the EU's coffers and had yielded valuable leads implicating several other corporations in illegal tax evasion schemes.

She had just been talking to a useful contact at OLAF, Joost van Gassen. She had decided to call him because he was the most indiscreet of the people she had met and she was also pretty sure he fancied her. Her pretext for the call was to get an update on the misappropriation of European Regional Development (ERDF) funds in Calabria. He confirmed what she already knew – that OLAF had recommended to the European Commission the recovery of the full amount of €57 million in funding awarded from the ERDF for the 48 projects it had investigated. What she learnt, though, was that acting on OLAF's report, the regional authorities in Calabria were withdrawing a further 21 such "environmental projects" from EU funding to a total additional value of close to €50 million.

Joost insisted on repeating the local joke that she had heard many times before – that the only thing that can't be bribed in Calabria is the weather. She laughed politely and spent several more minutes chatting about Joost's favourite speed skating activity. She then casually asked him if he'd come across a Major Canepa from the *Guardia di Finanza*.

"Bruno Canepa? Yes I've actually met him several times. He was one of the officers providing intelligence to a big European customs operation last year called Operation Sirocco. We managed to seize millions of smuggled cigarettes and big consignments of counterfeit items such as clothes, toys and electronics. Bruno was invaluable in pinpointing exactly when containers loaded in the Far East were arriving in the Calabrian port of Gioia Tauro. Bruno's a great guy and from what I hear, he's one of the rising stars in the *Guardia*...why the interest in him by the way?"

"Oh, I'm thinking of doing a piece on the various European judicial and law enforcement agencies and I want to interview interesting people in the different organisations. I've heard Bruno's currently involved in some big trans-national investigation...have you heard anything Joost?"

"I shouldn't be telling you this but the gossip is that he's close to a really big bust. I happened to be with him in a meeting a couple of months ago when he had to leave the room twice to take calls from the Italian Finance Minister, *Signor* Tremonti. If he's working on something directly for Tremonti it has got to be a biggy. Oh yes, also one of our guys was over in London last month for a meeting at Scotland Yard. He saw Bruno there in very earnest conversation with a Commander in your Serious and Organised Crime Agency...anyway being nosy I then spoke to a pal in the *Guardia di Finanza* in Rome. I asked if he knew what Bruno was up to...talk about the door slamming in my face. My friend said the only thing he knew about his current assignment was that it was ultra sensitive and top, top secret. He said I'd do myself a favour if I didn't ask anyone about it."

"OK thanks Joost...Major Canepa certainly sounds like an interesting candidate for my article if I can get him to agree to talk to me."

Maurizia then spent a couple of minutes fending off Joost's rather clumsy attempts to arrange to take her to dinner when she was next in Brussels. She extricated herself finally with a non-committal, "I've no plans at the moment to come to the centre of the European universe...but I'll call you if I'm likely to be in town."

She put the phone down, sat back and wondered how long it would be before someone at OLAF cottoned on to the fact that Joost's loose tongue was a real liability. She felt a little guilty about shamelessly exploiting his professional laxness but, her guilt was immediately assuaged by the journalistic satisfaction of knowing she was on to something.

12 JANUARY 2011

PARIS

Luca Biagi sat in the bar of the Baltimore Hotel in Paris absorbed with a kaleidoscope of memories involving his best friend Bernardo. They had been inseparable and shared many memorable experiences. They had hurtled through the Puglian countryside on their scooters and each had scars following spills from these dangerous *motorini*. They had got drunk together to console each other over failed teenage romances; they had spent many magical summers sailing in the Adriatic; they had travelled to Amsterdam and London for fun-packed holidays and they had spent countless hours discussing the films they had seen and the books they had read. Indelibly imprinted on Luca's heart was the unstinting, sensitive support he had received from Bernardo following the tragic and senseless death of his parents all those years ago.

A little after 7.30 an old man entered the bar and Luca hardly gave him a second glance before returning to his engrossing store of memories. It was only when the man raised his hand in greeting and called his name that the hammer blow of recognition hit him. It was Bernardo. For once the expression *"he was a mere shadow of his former self"* rang heartbreakingly true. Bernardo had the sunken face and skeletal frame of a long-term Gulag prisoner. His hair had all but gone except for a few pure white wisps around his ears. In addition to his physical emaciation he had a look in his eyes which spoke of long-suffered pain.

Luca stood and embraced his friend with tears suddenly springing from his eyes.

Bernardo said, "My God Luca you look terrific. I would have recognised you anywhere."

Luca was too emotional to say anything sensible so blurted out, "Bernardo, what happened. Are you ill?"

"I'm so sorry Luca…I should have warned you when we spoke on the phone. Although I'm used to my appearance it must be a big shock for you to see me like this. The fact is I've got a very rare form of cancer. You know me...always trying to be different. You ever heard of heart cancer? No? Me either, but when I saw a specialist about nine months ago that's what was eventually diagnosed. I've had bags of chemo and radiotherapy but the tumours have not been blitzed and I'm afraid I'm not going to be around for much longer. That's why I was so happy to receive your call after so long...I can't wait to hear all about your life."

When the initial shock had abated and helped by a couple of glasses of an excellent champagne, Luca gave his friend a potted life history and showed him pictures of Rosalba and his two lovely daughters.

"I would have loved to have been an honorary uncle to your girls but, *c'est la vie*...it's wonderful to know you have carved out such a great life for yourself."

"And what about you Bernardo? Do you have a family?"

"Yes, I was married but we separated about ten years ago. My wife Valentina finally got fed-up with my workaholic lifestyle and left me. We are still on pretty good terms and get together for important family events. I have a son called Luca and a daughter Adriana...Yes, I did name my son after you and he has turned out to be a great guy. Here's a picture of them both at a friend's wedding a couple of years ago."

Luca took the photo and with a catch in his throat saw a mirror image of the Bernardo he remembered with his arm thrown casually over the shoulder of one of the most beautiful women he had ever seen.

"Yes, they are good looking kids," Bernardo responded to Luca's complimentary words. "Adriana is a bit spoiled...my fault entirely. Luca came into the family business and is doing well although he has no wish to take the helm when I'm gone. He saw what my totally unbalanced, work-obsessed lifestyle did to my marriage and doesn't want to repeat the sins of the father so to speak. He has a really sweet wife. They have two little kids and Luca is a great dad. He'll be happy to continue as Marketing Director of one of our food companies under a new CEO – or move outside the Group as he won't have any money worries. He and Adriana will be independently wealthy because of the trust funds I've built up for them over the years."

They had decamped from the Baltimore and were now in Bernardo's favourite restaurant, Le Butte de Chaillot. This was only a few yards from the hotel on the Avenue Kleber.

"This is the best *Poulet de Bresse* I have ever tasted Bernardo and accompanied by the creamiest pureed potato...it's fabulous."

"Yes...they laugh at me here because I have exactly the same thing every time I come here."

They were halfway through a bottle of Pouilly Fumé and Luca asked his friend whether it was advisable for him to be drinking several glasses of alcohol.

"Yes, the medics said no to any stimulants but this is an extra special occasion and I'm going to give myself a night off such restrictions and enjoy the company of my closest friend."

He underlined his point by ordering, despite Luca's protests, a second bottle of the superb Pouilly Fumé Ladoucette. For a while he became more animated, but their long conversation and too much alcohol had clearly taken their toll. He suddenly looked absolutely spent but said in a strained and hesitant voice, "Luca, there is something I must tell you and I've needed a few glasses of wine to build up the courage to do so."

He paused and then blurted out, "You have a son."

"A son…what do you mean?" stammered a dumbstruck Luca. "I've only my two girls."

"Remember Antonella? Before you had to get out of Italy you had a brief summer romance with her which resulted in her having your child…She came to see me several weeks after your disappearance in a desperate state. I had no idea where you'd gone so I just tried to be a shoulder to cry on and encouraged her to come clean with her parents."

"But where's the child now?" Luca asked quietly, still in a state of shock.

"Sadly, that I can't tell you. Antonella's father sent her away to stay with his sister in Le Marche region. She spent her confinement in virtual seclusion and as soon as the baby was born he was taken from her. Her father apparently arranged for an adoption by one of his business associates. Antonella never knew where her baby went. She was, of course, devastated and for a while suicidal but eventually decided to make a new life for herself in Australia."

Bernardo reached into his jacket pocket. "I kept this letter from her telling me about her plans…as you can see it's really heartbreaking."

Luca scanned the note with wildly discordant emotions. Had he stayed in Italy he knew he would have done the right thing and married Antonella – a woman he didn't love – but he would have had a son and probably other children to cherish.

He couldn't keep a hint of annoyance out of his voice. "Why are you telling me this now? She asked you not to, didn't she?"

Without saying a word Bernardo reached into his pocket again and gave Luca a creased newspaper clipping. It was an obituary from the Melbourne *Herald Sun*.

Antonella Zanca, much loved wife of Aldo, mother to Guido and Patricia and grandmother to Fabiana and Elisabetta, passed away peacefully at home on 14th September 2009 after a short illness.

Luca's eyes filled with tears and the rest of the notice about funeral arrangements and donations to a local hospice became a blur.

"You see Luca, Antonella kept in touch. She wrote periodically telling me about her career and life in Melbourne…and for the first few years asking whether anyone had heard from you. As you can see, she married a great guy of Italian stock and had a family. In fact, I arranged for her son, Guido, to do an internship in one of my companies in his pre-university gap year…must have been in the late 90s. He was a really nice kid and became great friends with my son, Luca. They stayed in touch and it was Guido who rang him to tell him his mum had had a massive heart attack and died without regaining consciousness. Luca, believe me, I've agonised about whether or not to tell you about your son…but as Antonella is now gone and I won't be long in following her, I thought you ought to know. I wanted you to have the right to choose what to do with this knowledge."

Luca wasn't sure whether his friend was right to give him this shattering news after so long but he knew that Bernardo had acted from the purest of motives and could not really be angry with him.

"Bernardo…please don't feel bad. It must have been hard for you to decide what to do."

As they strolled back to their hotel, Luca's head was reeling. Bernardo was exhausted and went straight to bed. Luca sat in the quiet hotel bar and sipped a cognac. He realised that this bombshell had completely sidetracked him from the prime purpose of his trip – to see what intelligence he could pick up on the contemporary Puglian mafia scene. He would talk to Bernardo about it over breakfast.

He slept extremely badly and got up at 6 a.m. He was still a keen jogger and always packed his running kit when he travelled anywhere. He loved the feel of a place when it was just waking up to a new day so he decided to go for a short run. He turned left at the Trocadéro and ran straight down towards the Eiffel Tower crossing the Seine at the Pont d'Iena. As he recrossed the river, he reached the underpass at Pont de l'Alma, where Princess Diana met her tragic end. He couldn't stop himself reflecting that she wasn't much older than his own daughter Gina when she died. This served to escalate his disquiet about the potential danger she was in because of her commitment to help Bruno.

He was even more determined to enlist Bernardo's help in gathering whatever useful intelligence he could. His friend was already in the hotel's breakfast room when Luca entered after quickly showering and changing. Luca could see his friend looked more than a little apprehensive but he simply embraced him and said, "You did the right thing in telling me about Antonella, but I can't deny it was a real shock."

Luca knew Bernardo had left the morning free but he wasted no time in apprising him of Gina's part in the *Guardia di Finanza* investigation into Sacra Corona Unita.

"I'll do some quiet digging for you with a very good friend of mine who is a *Generale di Brigata* in the *Carabinieri*. In fact, he helped me rid one of my companies of mafia infiltrators in a big anti-mafia operation several years ago. But Luca, I already know a good deal about the key players in SCU, the Santoros. Arturo is undoubtedly the most feared man in the whole of Puglia. Many stories I've heard testify to his brutality...maybe better described as his bestiality as he doesn't seem to have one iota of humanity in him. He has done things to people that have reached nightmarish levels of violence...and he has tried to mould his son Vittore into a better educated clone of himself."

Luca shuddered inwardly at his friend's disturbing words and he resolved to redouble his efforts to persuade Gina to extricate herself from her potentially dangerous involvement with these psychopaths.

Bernardo promised to call him as soon as he had anything useful to report. They hugged each other as they parted in front of the hotel, each with a heavy heart thinking that they would never meet again. On his return flight to Manchester, Luca could not extinguish a feeling of unbearable sadness at his imminent loss of a man who was more like a brother than a friend. This was coupled with an almost tangible fear that something terrible would befall his daughter because of her headstrong incursion into the darkest depths of vicious criminality.

15 JANUARY 2011

LONDON

Adam Palfrey was furious. He had been in his new role as CEO of Mondo Foods for less than a week and he was already beginning to regret his decision to take the job. At his first briefing meeting with the Chairman, Sir Roger Simmons, he had been told that he would not have responsibility for three companies in Italy, Hungary and Greece. These would continue to report directly to Sir Roger who said that he had built such a close personal relationship with the local Chairmen of these companies that imposing a different reporting line to a new CEO would create unnecessary friction. In any case, he had said, the companies were all pretty small so there was more than enough for Palfrey to do in managing the Group's major businesses. When Palfrey had said that he felt understandably aggrieved that this had not been disclosed during the recruitment process, Sir Roger said, "For heaven's sake don't make a mountain out of a molehill."

Palfrey had bitten his tongue but had very nearly told Sir Roger where to stick his job. After discussing this over dinner with Gaby, his astute wife, he was glad he had not acted hastily.

"Darling, if you were to leave the company after only a few days you would risk damaging your excellent reputation."

"You think so Gabs?"

"Yes I do. Business people would question your judgement…They would at least think you hadn't done enough due diligence before accepting the job. And I bet Sir Roger would mobilise the big PR guns at his disposal and put the best spin he could on Mondo's conduct in contrast no doubt to your alleged petulance."

He nodded ruefully.

"What I'd do, darling, is take action at a time of your own choosing. If you really don't think it's going to work out there why don't you arrange to have a confidential chat with a handful of top headhunters. You know you are one of the highest profile Chief Execs in the consumer products field and I'm sure you could unearth other more congenial rôles pretty quickly."

Not for the first time Adam Palfrey thanked his lucky stars he had married this lovely woman who had an amazing ability to understand the machinations which were an endemic feature of corporate life. Whenever they returned from an office party he was always staggered by her extensive insights into office politics, frictions and rivalries. She usually learned more in a few hours about what was going on under the surface than he had picked up in a whole year."

"You're right Gabs. I did speak to quite a few headhunters before taking the Mondo job. Much better to have something else in the bag before I burn my boats at Mondo."

One of the headhunters he knew well was the Managing Partner of Buckman Collins, John Campbell. He called him the following day and asked if he could see him for a confidential chat. John knew Gina was working for Mondo Foods so he called her to see if she knew why Adam Palfrey was keen to meet so soon after his appointment there.

"I have no idea John," she said, "but I think his chairman Sir Roger is a pretty difficult character to work with and maybe there's been an early falling out…Can you keep me in the loop as I'd really like to know what's going on there."

A few days later John briefed Gina on his conversation with Palfrey who had been very candid about his misgivings regarding Sir Roger's cavalier approach to redefining the scope of his job. Gina rang Commander Gibbs immediately.

"Remember, I said I'd ask my researcher, Tom Nyholm, to see if he could dig up anything useful about the sudden departure of Simon Ramsay, the previous CEO of Mondo? Well, for the very first time my tame bloodhound has failed to come up with the goods. None of Ramsay's Board colleagues to whom Tom has spoken know anything. All they had been told by Sir Roger was that Ramsay was stepping down for personal reasons and he had asked for his privacy to be respected. They were to a man surprised as everyone believed Ramsay had been doing a fine job at the helm…But, Commander, we may just have the opportunity of enlisting the help of his successor in progressing your case against Sir Roger and his mafia associates."

Commander Gibbs appreciated that the three ring-fenced companies on a direct reporting line to Sir Roger were all vital links in the clandestine pipeline for smuggling drugs, contraband and people. He already knew about the Hungarian company but the fact that there was also a Greek company implicated was news to him. He would follow this up with Bruno Canepa and get the Greek police to do some low key investigation of Eliades

Cargo, the company concerned, based in the port of Piraeus. It was highly likely that this was a conduit for narcotics coming in to Europe from several sources.

However the Commander was not immediately persuaded of the merits of Gina's argument that, if they told Palfrey of the malignancy polluting the company he had just joined, he would be an invaluable insider ally in prosecuting the case against the villains. He said he would check out Palfrey's credentials and reputation and talk things over with the Home Secretary and Major Canepa.

Gina was wrestling with another problem. She did not know how to square her own professional integrity with the need to continue to progress the candidates she had interviewed in Verona for the SSP job. Her clients at Mondo still wanted to see the three people she had shortlisted for other possible rôles in the Group. She was afraid that they would want to hire the front runner, Corrado Gori. She knew she would feel bad if he accepted a job with Mondo and then got caught up in the backwash of all the adverse publicity when the criminality at the heart of the Group was eventually exposed. She had spoken to Bruno about it and he had reassured her that the evidence against Sir Roger was approaching critical mass. It was very probable that he would be arrested before Gori had to make a decision whether to resign from his present post.

Commander Gibbs enlisted the help of MI5 in running the rule over Adam Palfrey. After a very rigorous check on his personal and financial affairs he was given an absolutely clean bill of health. Their exhaustive report concluded that he was a man of unimpeachable probity. In all his business dealings he had never sailed close to the wind and their soundings of competitors and colleagues produced a unanimous chorus of respect. He was regarded as a totally honourable man. The Commander also had a lengthy conversation with Bruno about these latest developments.

"What do you think we should do, Bruno, to follow up the lead on Eliades Cargo? I've never dealt with the Greek police but I thought you might have done."

"Not with the police as such but I have had a lot of contact with the Greek Coast Guard. The *Guardia di Finanza* has conducted several anti-smuggling operations with their specialist elite unit the OEA. I know the officer who heads up this unit very well. I can vouch for him as a very competent professional. In the first instance I suggest we ask him to do a bit of digging. This way we won't risk involving people we don't know and trust at this delicate stage of our investigation of Mondo."

"That sounds like an excellent idea and I think you agree on the merits of taking Adam Palfrey into our confidence."

"Yes I do George. I think the benefits of having someone with their eyes and ears open on the inside outweigh the risks. Also, in the light of what we believe happened to Carlo Giordano and Simon Ramsay we really owe it to Palfrey to tell him what a nest of vipers he has landed in so that he can watch his back."

They decided it was too risky to talk to Palfrey over the phone. Instead, George Gibbs would have a plain clothes officer call at his home address in West London. The officer would simply say that the Met Police needed his help in a highly confidential matter relating to the departure of his predecessor at Mondo Foods…and could he please keep this to himself until he had called Commander Gibbs on his private line.

Mid-evening on 21 January, the officer waited outside Palfrey's large house in Bedford Park, Chiswick until he saw him drive in. He had earlier checked with the switchboard at Mondo Foods in Mayfair that Palfrey was working in London that day and had confirmed his car registration number with DVLC. He was quick off the mark and managed to reach Palfrey whilst he was still searching for his house keys.

"Good evening, Sir. Sorry to disturb you but my name is Sergeant Cobham. I'm a police officer," he said, flashing his Warrant Card. "Could we have a quiet word please?"

"Yes…of course…was I speeding?"

"No…Nothing like that sir." And the sergeant gave him the agreed cryptic message and asked him if he would call Gibbs immediately. "Also, Sir, we would really appreciate it if you would not mention this to anyone."

Somewhat bemused, Palfrey entered his hallway and was about to shout to Gaby that he was home when he remembered that she'd taken their teenage kids to the cinema to see *The Kings Speech* which had just been released. He rang the number Sergeant Cobham had given him and Commander Gibbs picked up immediately.

"Adam Palfrey here…I'm a bit disconcerted about all this cloak and dagger stuff…can you tell me what's going on?"

"Yes, I'm sorry we had to approach you in this rather oblique way but when I explain why, I think you'll understand the reason for our discretion. I can't do that over the phone, though, so can we meet somewhere privately as soon as possible. I do assure you that this is a matter of the utmost urgency and seriousness."

"I'll have to take your word for that Commander…as it happens I'm free this evening or tomorrow morning, Saturday…"

"No…This evening would be fine. I can be in Chiswick by, say, eight o'clock. I'll meet you anywhere you want."

"Well you can come to my house as my wife and kids are out all evening."

At nine o'clock that night Palfrey sat back in his favourite chair in his study and looked with bewilderment at the senior police officer who had just told him the most amazing story he had ever heard.

"I now understand why you were so circumspect in making contact with me…but I can hardly credit that I am working for a degenerate who has sanctioned the murder of one of his own executives…"

"And has also been an active collaborator in flooding our country with hard drugs," interjected Commander Gibbs.

"I have to tell you, Commander that my wife, Gaby, persuaded me a couple of weeks ago not to resign from Mondo. After only a few days there I was very unhappy with Sir Roger's high-handed approach to redefining my job…obviously, I now see why he barred my involvement with those three companies."

"Mr Palfrey, I'm very glad you didn't quit because you may be able to help us bring these extremely nasty people to justice."

"I'm not sure how Commander…"

"Well, we have some pretty sizeable gaps in our understanding of what is going on in these three companies. I appreciate that you can't be seen to be poking around in their affairs…but we know that they do trade with other mainstream Mondo companies that come under your control. We believe that the Hungarian company provides a cover for heroin smuggling but we don't know how. We have no idea yet where the Greek logistics company fits in…and we don't know how SSP distributes cocaine…We have to have hard evidence of how the drugs are transported to build a cast-iron case."

"OK Commander…look, I'm just about to embark on a whistle stop tour of the fifteen companies that comprise my 'empire'. All I can do is keep my eyes and ears open for linkages between these three firms and other businesses within my portfolio. That may give you something to follow up but I think it's a real long shot. I suppose I can also see if I can pick up any clues in my regular review meetings with Sir Roger but, again, I think the chances are pretty slim."

"That's all we can ask Mr Palfrey…it's really a question of putting a huge jigsaw together so every little piece helps…but I have to stress that you must tread very carefully. These are extremely vicious people and they have no compunction in eliminating anyone or anything which is a potential risk to their operation."

After the Commander left he poured himself a big brandy and mused, "I know why I agreed to help so readily." He was not blind to the possible risks but he felt he owed it to his best friend at university who had died of a drug overdose.

"I'll do all I can to bring these people down, Brian, to honour your memory."

20 JANUARY 2011

LONDON

Gina was both excited and apprehensive. She had been asked by her Managing Partner, John Campbell, to give a courtesy interview to Simon Ramsay the former CEO of Mondo Foods who had left the company so suddenly and inexplicably. John said Ramsay was now back on the job market and wanted to discuss his next move. She rang Commander Gibbs who was predictably keen for her to meet Ramsay to see whether she could discover anything about the circumstances leading to his abrupt exit.

She arranged to meet Ramsay a few days later on 20 January. He arrived very early and Gina asked her shrewd PA to offer him a cup of coffee and say that Gina would be with him as soon as she could.

"What do you make of him, Veronica?" Gina asked when she came back.

"Well I'm a bit surprised really. For such a senior guy he seemed really, really nervous and when we shook hands, his hand was very clammy."

When she went to collect Ramsay about ten minutes later she saw exactly what her secretary had meant. Simon Ramsay was a fiftyish, well-dressed man of medium height with thinning, greying hair, and a distinct paunch which indicated too many rich business lunches. Tom's earlier attempts to find out anything he could on Ramsay had uncovered the fact that he was a real *bon viveur* who ate in top London restaurants at least four or five times a week and kept a wine cellar at home in Ascot which was reputed to be spectacular. As Veronica had said, he did seem ill at ease and his palm was really damp when they shook hands and he had a distinctly hang-dog demeanour. Once seated in her office in one of her easy chairs, he found it difficult to make eye contact. Gina was a past master at relaxing people but none of her ice-breaking pleasantries served to reduce his nervousness.

He startled her by suddenly blurting out, "Look Miss Biagi I just want to know how difficult it is likely to be for me to get another big Chief Executive job given the widespread speculation about my departure from Mondo."

"Well, Mr Ramsay, what will undoubtedly deter potential future employers is the fact that there has been absolutely no information whatsoever about why you left Mondo when you seemed to be doing such good things there. If you can tell me something about what caused you to quit I can then assess whether it might affect your candidacy for other positions."

Ramsay looked a little like a rabbit caught in the headlights.

"I'm afraid it is something very personal and I just can't talk about it."

"Mr Ramsay," Gina said quietly but firmly, "you must appreciate that we couldn't present you to any of our clients unless we could assure them that there was nothing suspicious about your departure from Mondo. I'd like to help you but you must see that the very first question we'd be asked is 'Why did he leave?'…Wouldn't you ask the same question if you were the client?"

Ramsay's shoulders slumped even further and for a moment Gina was convinced he was going to break down completely, but he seemed to rally, raised his head and nodded in stoical acknowledgement of this confirmation of what in his heart of hearts he already knew.

"Thanks for being straight with me. I'll have to think about how to deal with this situation…but I want you to know that the reason I resigned from Mondo had absolutely nothing to do with my performance as CEO. You'll find, if you check, that I left the company in a very profitable and healthy state. Furthermore there was no financial impropriety on my part."

"I already know that you did a first-class job there which makes it such a shame that you can't tell me in confidence why you resigned. One thing I also know is that your Chairman, Sir Roger, can be a pretty difficult guy to work with…"

Gina thought it was worth firing this particular shot across his bows but she could not have foreseen the immediacy or violence of Ramsay's reaction. He leapt to his feet and shouted, "You have no bloody idea what it was like…the man's a monster. He's completely destroyed my life."

He subsided as suddenly as he had erupted and sank back into his chair with a wild, despairing look on his face.

"I've said too much…I'm sorry I shouted at you. I know you are only trying to help but I think you should forget my outburst. It's been a very emotional time for me recently and I think I need a good long break before I re-enter the commercial world."

Gina knew she had pushed as far as she dared and offered a few conciliatory and sympathetic words, assuring Ramsay that if he thought she might be of help in the future she'd be pleased to hear from him. He gave her a rather quizzical look and said he didn't think that would be necessary.

About half an hour after he'd gone, Tom popped his head round Gina's office door. Gina felt a twinge of guilt about keeping him in the dark concerning the machinations of Sir Roger Simmons regarding the SSP assignment. All she had told Tom was that she had found herself in the middle of some intractable internal politics at Mondo. She had, plausibly she thought, explained that the Board was split on the calibre of person they needed to run this small company. Sir Roger wanted to hire a real heavyweight but had been thwarted by the rest of the Board who felt a less senior person was required.

Tom said, "I saw from the daily meeting sheet that you were seeing Simon Ramsay today. That was a short session. How did it go?"

"Not very well…The man's a wreck but I'm still none the wiser as to why he left Mondo. He completely clammed up on the subject."

"I may be able to help you there," Tom said a little shamefacedly. "I was out of the office first thing this morning so I didn't see the interview list until I got back a few minutes ago…otherwise I'd have briefed you."

"About what?"

"Yesterday I found out something interesting. One of the people I contacted a few weeks ago to try to get some idea of why Ramsay left so suddenly was a Finance Director who worked closely with him and was mystified as to why he decided to go. I've got a very good relationship with this chap and he's helped us identify useful candidates for a number of assignments…Anyway, Ramsay had a driver who was fired about a week ago and he contacted this Finance guy to see if he would give him a reference as he used to drive him around as well. This very disgruntled driver said that he thought Mr Ramsay had discovered something dodgy in Mondo's Hungarian company and he heard him relaying this on the phone to Sir Roger as he was chauffeuring him to a meeting. The driver was apparently flabbergasted at what happened next. Ramsay threw his phone down, ordered him to stop the car, jumped out and was violently sick on the grass verge. When the driver asked if he wanted to return home Ramsay just nodded mutely.

The driver said he was ashen and remained completely silent all the way back to Ascot...the next day it was announced that he had left the company."

"Wow...that's quite a story, Tom, but I'm not sure we can do any more for Ramsay at the moment as he's likely to take a long break from the business world. Our relationship with Mondo is very fragile right now so I'd appreciate it if you could leave it there. If I find out anything else, I'll fill you in."

Gina didn't like fobbing Tom off, but she felt she had to. After he left her office looking bemused she rang Commander Gibbs and briefed him on her short interview with Ramsay and then repeated Tom's input.

"Just as we thought Gina, Sir Roger must have something on Ramsay that is so potentially damaging as to guarantee his silence about whatever he discovered regarding that Hungarian company...Balog Oils, isn't it? I'll talk to Bruno about maybe pressing Ramsay on what he found out."

They left it at that but mid-afternoon the following day Gina had a call from the Commander.

"Gina, Simon Ramsay tried to kill himself last night."

"Oh my God," gasped Gina immediately acknowledging the appalling prospect that her meeting with him had pushed him over the edge.

"Yes, he took a large quantity of sleeping pills washed down with a half bottle of scotch. His wife was due to stay overnight with her sister in London after an evening at the theatre. But because her sister was not feeling well Mrs Ramsay took her home and put her to bed. As it was only about 10 o'clock, she decided to go back home to Ascot as she was worried about Simon and that's why she was able to call an ambulance around 11 o'clock. The medics said that if she'd been a couple of hours later he would have been a goner."

"But he's going to be alright?"

"Yes, he's at Wexham Park Hospital in Slough. I've put him under 24 hour police protection...just in case you know who tries to get at him."

He left a note to his wife apologising for living a lie as he put it. He really unburdened himself in the note and from this information and our additional checks we've been able to piece together what appears to be a very strange story."

"I'm all ears," said Gina.

"Yes, apparently, his real name is not Simon Ramsay but George Ramsay. He was the son of a very wealthy property developer who seems to have been a bit of a Rachman type. The father had young George set fire to one of his derelict properties so that he could make a substantial insurance claim.

George was caught and given three years in a young offenders' institution as the fire had spread to several adjacent properties and several people were injured. The seventeen-year-old George did not shop his father and when he got out his old man decided, maybe to assuage his own guilt, to 'buy' him a new identity so that he would not have a criminal record. I don't know yet exactly how he did this but one well-trodden path is to search the births and deaths records and find a baby or child who died in infancy and was born around the same year as the person who needs the identity swop. In this case it appears that the people who performed this service for his father struck lucky and found a deceased child with the same surname…We can fill in the gaps when we interview Ramsay. Clearly, somehow Sir Roger knew about this and when Ramsay rang him to report on what he'd discovered at Balog Oils, he was threatened with the exposure of his youthful detention at Her Majesty's pleasure and subsequent identity fraud."

"So now all that's in the open, there's no reason why you can't ask Ramsay what he discovered in the Hungarian company?"

"None whatsoever," the Commander said emphatically, "and what he can tell us could put one of the final pieces of the jigsaw in place. We still don't know exactly how Balog Oils fits into the drug distribution system."

A thought suddenly occurred to Gina. "You said the suicide attempt was at Ramsay's home in Ascot…how did you hear about it so quickly?"

"Oh yes…after our initial discussions about Ramsay's strange exit from Mondo I asked a senior colleague in Thames Valley Police to do a bit of quiet local digging to see if he could come up with any gossip or clues which might give us a lead. He was on duty last night when the call came in about Ramsay and he called me immediately. I asked him to lock down the scene until I could get there about midnight…it was only a few minutes from my home in Windsor. I actually found his note in his study…his wife hadn't seen it as she had gone with him to the hospital in the ambulance."

"Did he say anything in the note about Mondo or Sir Roger?"

"No…I initially thought that was a bit odd but on reflection I concluded that the omission was probably an attempt to protect his wife and family from any possible vengeful retaliatory action by Sir Roger or his cohorts."

The following day Ramsay was well enough to be interviewed and Commander Gibbs saw him on his own in his private room at the hospital. For one who had been teetering on the edge of life, Ramsay did not look in too bad shape. His opening remark when the Commander introduced himself was, "I'm strangely relieved my secret is out at last. I can't tell you what it's been like for thirty years or more living a lie…always worrying that someone would find out what I and my late father did to cover up my crime and detention."

"I would like to get a few more details on that later, but my main purpose today is to find out what you know about Balog Oils in Hungary."

This direct unexpected question hit Ramsay like a hammer. His earlier insouciance evaporated and he stammered, "I don't know what you mean…I can't talk about that…I have a confidentiality agreement with Mondo."

"That's bullshit Mr Ramsay…let me put my cards on the table. We know you discovered something pretty rotten going on in Hungary and when you reported it to Sir Roger Simmons he threatened to expose your false identity unless you kept quiet and left Mondo. He may have used more extreme threats against you and your family…you'll have to tell me if that's the case…I want you to know that your false identity is of no interest to me. As far as I've been able to ascertain you have not transgressed since your youthful offence, for which you served your sentence. I'd be prepared to forget about this if you help us with our enquiries into certain continental subsidiaries of Mondo Foods."

Commander Gibbs paused to let all this sink in and waited for Ramsay to respond.

"You really would let my assumption of a false identity go unpunished?"

"Yes. We have much bigger fish to fry here, Mr Ramsay. If you can help us bring to justice some very nasty people and, by the way, put a stop to a large-scale drug trafficking operation, I can guarantee your immunity from prosecution."

Ramsay remained quiet for a few moments and then said firmly, "What do you want to know, Commander?"

"Well you can start by explaining what you found out about Balog Oils?"

"OK…The company was not actually my responsibility. The MD report-ed directly to the chairman, Sir Roger, as did the MDs of a few other small companies in the group. This arrangement was justified on the basis that Sir Roger enjoyed a very close relationship with the chairmen or MDs of these companies, who were usually members of the founding families…I thought this was a bit odd, but I was running all the big companies in Mondo so I didn't give it much thought…that is until something happened to arouse my suspicions that all was not what it seemed."

"What was that Mr Ramsay?"

"Well…one of my Managing Directors, Vidor Bodnar, is Hungarian. On one of his trips home to see his elderly parents, he had paid an impromptu visit to Balog Oils to discuss a possible joint promotional campaign with his own division in France. This guy was my top MD and we had become very good friends. When we met after his trip, he said he'd had a very odd reaction from the MD of Balog Oils who obviously did not want him to spend any time in the production facility. Vidor said the Balog guy appeared to be very nervous, even frightened to have someone interested in his company. He said he was too busy to discuss any joint working arrangements and seemed mightily relieved when a rather bemused Vidor drove off."

"That does seem odd but I don't see why that would have led to anything."

"Commander, my ex-colleague Vidor is a very resourceful and determined guy. He asked around his extensive network of Hungarian contacts and discovered that there were strong suspicions that Balog was involved in some kind of clandestine activity possibly but not certainly involving drugs. One of Vidor's boyhood friends had joined the police and he was sure that Balog had been accorded special status by the local police colonel… meaning he had been bought off. He also found out that another possible link in the chain was a Greek transport company although he didn't get a name."

"Eliades Cargo," thought Commander Gibbs.

Ramsay continued, "Because the company reported directly in to Sir Roger himself, I thought I'd better get him to check all this out…so I called him and got the shock of my life…He went very quiet for a while and then said, "This won't do at all George…He actually used my real name! I went completely cold and he said, 'Yes I know all about your fire-raising exploits and your false identity. Listen to me very carefully. You will never talk about this to anyone. If you do, the police will be told you have been living a lie under falsified documents…your career will be ruined. You should also give some thought to the continued well-being of your family, particularly those cute grandkids down in Newbury.' My heart nearly stopped at that point, Commander. Simmons went on to say that I was to leave Mondo immediately, not go into the office and he'd arrange for a termination payment of two years' salary."

The Commander said quietly and sympathetically, "I know that you then asked your driver to stop the car and you threw up on the verge."

"How the hell do you know that?"

"Your driver has since been fired and he told someone we know what happened…just tell me what you said to Vidor after all this."

"When I got home I had another call but this time from that little creep Williamson, Sir Roger's HR guy. He simply confirmed that he'd arranged for the £800,000 payoff to be deposited in my bank account. He reiterated that I should tell no one, not even my wife, of my suspicions about Balog Oils. He told me to ring Vidor to say I'd resigned due to a major health problem. I should also say to Vidor that I'd talked to Sir Roger who had assured me that he had already addressed the problem at Balog and was going to remove the MD who was diverting, off the books, a proportion of the company's output to another firm owned by his brother-in-law. The slimy little sod closed by wishing me and my family well."

"How did Vidor react when you told him?"

"He was so shocked by my sudden resignation that he took what I told him about Balog at face value and said he was pleased that his suspicions had been well founded. I rang Williamson to tell him and he just grunted and put the phone down. I've been worried ever since that Vidor might be in danger but he's still in Lyons running his division."

"That's quite a story and I really appreciate your candour…Just clear up one other thing for me, would you? How do you think Sir Roger found out about your false identity?"

"Yes, I've given that a lot of thought too. Sir Roger is obviously involved in something crooked and must have extensive criminal connections. Somehow his criminal network and that of my late father's must have intersected. The people my dad used to establish my new identity may have been part of the same criminal group that Sir Roger is involved with. I can only think that he had compiled a dossier on all the senior people in Mondo covering anything that might be used to blackmail them in case any of them discovered what's going on in the company…which, by the way, I'm still not clear about."

"I can't tell you exactly what he's involved in but it's very big, very unsavoury and the subject of a massive effort by law enforcement agencies across Europe. We are closing in on the principal offenders and will be arresting a lot of people very shortly. Your input adds one more link in the detailed information chain which will very shortly underpin an impregnable case against these criminals."

"I'm glad I could help Commander and thanks for giving me my life back."

28 JANUARY 2011

L'AQUILA, ABRUZZO

Arturo Santoro did not like to admit to himself that he was feeling an emotion he had never felt in all his life – fear.

On 28 December 2010, Italian anti-mafia forces had arrested eighteen prominent members of Sacra Corona Unita in Brindisi. He had been tipped off about this so-called "Operation Last Minute" by a senior *Carabinieri* officer who was on his payroll. The day before the swoop he had hidden in a clan member's house but on the 28th his wife Serena sent a message that no one from the police had been to their house. Although surprised that the police did not pick him up as part of this cull, he decided things were getting too hot for him in Puglia. He had not the slightest inkling that he had been excluded from this operation on the express instruction of the *Direttore Generale* of the *Guardia* in order not to jeopardise the Mondo investigation. Santoro put into effect an escape plan which he had constructed some years earlier. The huge profits he had made from his illegal activities had enabled him to buy a number of secluded properties in Sicily and the Abruzzo region in Italy – and also in Montenegro and Albania. These had all been purchased by an ostensibly *bona fide* property company as villas to be rented to wealthy holidaymakers. All four properties were serviced regularly but kept vacant in case Santoro needed any of them as an urgent bolt-hole.

On 29 December he had been driven by Vittore to the house in the Apennines on the outskirts of the village of Aragno to the east of L'Aquila in the Abruzzo region. He did not tell his wife where he was going. He just said he would be away a long time and Vittore would deliver a large bag of cash to cover her day-to-day expenses. He had kept to his resolution not to tell her anything about these houses, or indeed about any of his criminal activities so she would never be able to incriminate him if she were to be interrogated by the police. Serena had been a great beauty but she was under endowed in the intelligence department. Santoro knew she would have been a risk if ever she was questioned by a skilled prosecutor.

In the few weeks since his getaway, he had liquidated most of his easily disposable assets and he and Vittore had stashed the enormous proceeds in oiled, waterproof sacks in various carefully chosen hiding places on the perimeter of the extensive grounds to the house near L'Aquila. The rest of the cash was left with the only person he trusted with the task of asset divestment, his long term associate, the businessman Ottavio Palumbo. He and Palumbo had been like brothers since their teenage delinquent days. Apart from his son Vittore and the indispensable lawyer Moscatelli, Palumbo was the only other person he trusted.

He had taken this extreme but prudent step because of the escalating programme of confiscation and redistribution of mafia goods and assets for the benefit of local communities and institutions – under the government policy of *Libera il Bene*. This had been gathering pace for years but had been given a tremendous boost by the establishment of a National Agency for the administration and appropriation of assets seized from criminal organisations. Silvio Berlusconi had set up this Agency in 2009 and symbolically had based it in the mafia heartland of Calabria.

On this particular late January day in 2011, Santoro had been waiting for a call from Vittore which came in the early evening.

"I start on 14 February," Vittore confirmed, "I've just heard from Sir Roger Simmons that the Mondo Board rubber stamped my appointment at SSP. I'm going up to Modena tomorrow to look for an apartment. I'll spend three days a week up there but I need to be in Brindisi for part of each week to make sure things are OK at this end of the pipeline."

For the past three years, since Sir Roger had been "persuaded" to work with them, the company SSP had become a key hub in the drug smuggling activities of Sacra Corona Unita. Cocaine from Latin America arrived in Brindisi by sea and passed under the "blind eyes" of heavily bribed customs officials. It was then taken by a constantly changing set of vehicles and couriers to SSP in Modena where Sacra Corona Unita had planted its own Operations Manager, just before the arrival of the new *Direttore Generale*, Carlo Giordano. The Operations Manager, Guido Guarini, had set up a six-man team of SCU people in a separate unit on the factory site. Their job was to process, bottle and pack a speciality product line – chilli-infused olive oil.

The olive oil was sourced in bulk from an SCU company in Puglia. Ninety per cent of this product was high quality *olio d'oliva extra vergine*. The remainder in a separate container was an olive oil and cocaine cocktail. A skilled chemist working for SCU had perfected a method of diluting cocaine in the olive oil and then having it separated and recovered in the country where it was to be sold.

The cocaine/olive oil cocktail was bottled in the self-contained unit at SSP and then transported in company vehicles to Distribution Centres in France, Germany and Spain for onward shipment to its drug dealer customers. The cargo manifest was prepared by the Operations Manager to show legitimate delivery addresses for the genuine product and a fictional customer location for the doctored consignment. The four truck drivers involved, who were well rewarded by their mafia paymasters, simply off-loaded the cases of cocaine/olive oil mixture at pre-determined drop-off points. The cocaine was then liberated from its liquid host and entered the drug distribution network in that particular country.

This drug transportation method had worked spectacularly well and Arturo Santoro was eager to ramp up the volume of cocaine shipments. He was about to introduce a new importation route. This would triple the volume of cocaine sourced from his existing suppliers in Columbia, Bolivia and Peru. The extra volume would be shipped across the Atlantic to *Côte d'Ivoire* in West Africa. It would then be taken by low-flying aircraft to Tunisia.

Through their links with one of the local criminal organisations, SCU had bought a small plastics moulding company. Among other products, this firm made plastic crates for carrying bottles of various sizes. These would be purchased by SSP's Operations Manager and delivered via the port of Livorno – but not before they had been given an extra ingredient in the Tunisian plant. The handful of workers on the night shift in a self-contained part of the factory would be criminals recruited and handsomely rewarded by SCU. For one full week a month they would work under the watchful eyes of two trusted SCU members. They would mix cocaine with molten plastic before moulding it into the crates which would be a different colour to the authentic ones. These superficially innocent looking items would be used by SSP to ship its bottles of specialised vinegars and oils to various European markets. When the products arrived in the country concerned they would be diverted to a warehouse where the crates would be emptied and the bottles repacked in undoctored crates stored there. The product would then be delivered to legitimate customers.

Meanwhile the cocaine crates would be broken up into smaller pieces and dissolved in acid. This would free the cocaine from its temporary convey-ance and the liquid would then be dried to obtain the powdered form of the drug. Vittore Santoro and one of his key lieutenants had been planning this new drug trafficking pipeline for two years. Now all the components were in place and Arturo Santoro had set the launch date for the end of February when Vittore would be at the helm of SSP. Vittore had already organised a dummy run and the first consignment of plastic crates had been delivered from Tunisia to SSP, clearing customs without any problem after paying the necessary duty. When in full flow, the combined volume of drugs channelled through SSP and the Hungarian company, Balog Oils, would be by far SCU's biggest profit earner.

"Vittore, you are sure that there are no loose ends…We can't afford any slip ups…To be even clearer you can't afford to fail. You may be my son but I have to be seen to treat you the same as anyone else in our clan. You know what the price of failure is, don't you…?"

"Yes *papà*," Vittore said nervously. "Don't worry, I've been over every-thing a thousand times and the operation will run like clockwork. The plastic camouflage will be fantastic."

Although he had checked every tiny detail of the new *modus operandi* for their drug trafficking, Vittore couldn't help thinking about the fate of his cousin, Vincenzo. He had been diverting heroin heading for Balog Oils, in Hungary to his own small storage unit near the Romanian border. The heroin from Afghanistan via Iran and Turkey was to be mixed with palm oil and bottled by an SCU team at Balog before shipment to several European markets. Vincenzo took about five per cent of each shipment before it was mixed and bottled and sold it to a contact in the Russian mafia.

Vincenzo had slept with the wife of one of his men who knew about this skimming activity. When this man discovered her infidelity he had shopped Vincenzo anonymously to Arturo. Vittore had watched Vincenzo being tortured over two full days by the killer Pozzi and several other SCU thugs.

By the end of the second day Vincenzo's mind had gone and he had become a gibbering, mewling sub-human creature. At this point Arturo was bored with the whole thing and told his men to apply the final horrific touch to the process. Vincenzo was strapped securely to a table and his stomach wall was cut open in several places. Three rats that had been caught and not fed for several days were then released onto his body and started to gnaw at his intestines. Amazingly, it still took Vicenzo four hours to die in unimagi-nable pain.

It had been a good few years since anyone had dared to muscle in on Arturo's business and this extreme punishment served as a chilling reminder to new and established members of his SCU clan just how sadistically ferocious he could be in extinguishing any threats.

20 JANUARY 2011

SKOPELOS, GREECE

Commander Andreas Speros of the Greek Coast Guard was in the wheel-house of a fast open sea-patrol boat off the island of Skopelos. His crew had just completed the all too familiar job of fishing several bodies from the Aegean Sea which in winter could be extremely inhospitable. From the few documents and personal items recovered, all the men appeared to be of Pakistani origin. Speros was pretty sure they were all would-be illegal immigrants trying to get into Greece. They represented a tiny fraction of the seemingly unstoppable flood of people from Africa and the Near and Far East heading for his country as a first stepping stone into the European Community.

Crossing by boat from Turkey was a very popular option. Frequently the vessels were old, leaky buckets and usually massively overcrowded – with predictably tragic results. This was the third time since Christmas that the Coast Guard had been called out on similar missions.

Commander Speros, as head of the Special Operations team or OEA, did not usually get involved in these routine tasks. But, on this occasion he had received intelligence that a terrorist cell with Al-Qaeda was on its way to Greece by sea. There was nothing in the personal effects of the four bodies so far recovered to suggest anything other than that the men were just ordinary folk. The National Identity Card for one man, Nayandeep Chaudry, showed he was from a small village near the town of Silanwali in the Punjab. Speros said a silent thankyou to the Pakistan Government for introducing multi-biometric information, including fingerprint and face recognition, for the vast majority of its citizens several years earlier. It would be easy to confirm whether Chaudry was the farmer he claimed to be from one of the most impoverished provinces of Pakistan. This would be reason enough for him to have sought a better life elsewhere. Speros was almost certain that further enquiries of the Pakistan authorities would show no terrorist or criminal links. Terrorists didn't tend to carry identity cards.

The Commander was musing on the sad state of affairs which led to poor people seeking a better life ending up in body bags, when his cellular phone rang.

"*Ciao* Andreas…Bruno Canepa here. How's the leg now?" Bruno was referring to their last joint operation when Andreas had broken his leg whilst chasing a gang of Albanian drug smugglers across a rocky promontory near Corfu.

"*Ciao* Bruno…it seems ages since I spoke Italian…good to hear from you. My leg is fine. Luckily it was a clean break so I was back on duty after a couple of months. So what can I do for you *amico mio*?"

"I need a favour Andreas. I wonder if you can do a bit of quiet digging into a company called Eliades Cargo in Piraeus. We think they may be a small cog in a very extensive criminal network. I'm sorry but I'm not authorised to tell you a lot more. We have a pan-European task force working on this and, if we succeed, we'll put away some very unpleasant people for a very long time…Andreas, this is by far the biggest operation I've ever headed up."

"Well, you know I owe you one Bruno. I think more than my leg would have been broken if you hadn't tackled that huge Albanian bastard who was firing at me when I had my leg trapped in that cleft in the rock."

"Always happy to help you brave boys in the Hellenic Coast Guard… Seriously though, I'd be really grateful if you could have a quiet look at this company to see if you can smell anything fishy…But, Andreas, it's really important that we don't give them any hint we're looking into them."

"Hang on Bruno…Eliades Cargo you say. That rings a bell. I'm sure I saw a bulletin from our police colleagues asking us to keep our eyes open for any dodgy activities in a number of shipping firms…and I think they were on the list. What I recall is that the police were suspicious about a number of ships docking at the dedicated berths of these particular companies…I'll double check when I'm back ashore and give you a call."

Bruno ended the call after a few more minutes of catching up chat. He finally asked Andreas to find out the name of the officer leading any enquiries into Eliades Cargo so that he could talk to him. He was worried he might jump the gun and jeopardise the total case against Mondo and SCU. He didn't want either party diving for cover or aborting any of their operations before the bigger investigation had been concluded.

A few hours later Andreas called back.

"The officer heading up the investigation is Major Yannis Kapouzis…but he doesn't speak Italian…so he's asked if you could call him around 10 a.m.

tomorrow when he'll have an Italian speaking colleague on hand to translate for you. His direct line is 30 for Greece then 210 4175449."

The next morning Bruno rang on the dot of 10 and the phone was picked up by a Lieutenant Liakos.

"*Buongiorno Maggiore Canepa*, I have Major Kapouzis here so I'll just put you on speakerphone."

Bruno explained that he was joint leader of a highly confidential multi-country investigation and stressed the importance of treading carefully *vis-à-vis* Eliades Cargo. Major Kapouzis said he would be happy to keep Bruno in the loop before any action was taken. He said that they had, in fact, only just started their investigation after receiving a tip-off from a reliable underworld informant. The Major said they were very hopeful of securing an early breakthrough as they had managed to get one of their own under-cover officers into the Port Authority's department responsible for logging cargo manifests. It was fortuitous that this particular young sergeant had worked at Thessaloniki docks before joining the police. One of Major Kapouzis's senior officers, a Brigadier General was in the same Masonic Lodge as a Board Member of the Port Authority. The Brigadier was primed with a falsified CV for the sergeant – allegedly his nephew. It disguised his last five years in the Hellenic Police by claiming he had been working at the port of Avonmouth in the UK. On returning to Greece, he was looking for a job.

Bruno had to smile at this oblique *modus operandi* and reflected on the fact that the Greeks and Italians were indistinguishable in their approach to such patronage – after all, the Italians had originally coined the word *nepotismo*.

6 FEBRUARY 2011

KRUŠEVO, MACEDONIA

Bruno had never been so frozen. Although he wore the best thermal clothing available, the cold seemed to have penetrated to the very marrow of his bones on this pre-dawn early-February morning. He had just spent the night in the mountains above the Macedonian town of Kruševo. He knew that Kruševo was the highest town in Macedonia at 1,350 metres above sea level and he guessed his reconnaissance post was at least another 300 metres higher. The temperature was tolerable during the day but at night it had dropped to between -10 and -15C. The camouflage sheet in front of his alpine sleeping bag offered scant protection from the icy wind cutting through the pine forest and blasting the surface patina of snow like so many tiny needles into his face.

Bruno had been given permission by his *Comandante Generale* to spend a few days in these inhospitable mountains with a specialist anti-terrorist group from the Macedonian police. The *Comandante* had thought the mission was of sufficient potential importance to the Mondo/SCU investigation to warrant his lead officer spending time on this undercover operation. One of the *Guardia's* undercover units in Italy had got wind of an arms smuggling gang of Albanians and Kosovans who were planning to ship a large arms consignment from Albania to Brindisi and then onward, with help from their SCU partners. Their final destination was probably Sunni militia groups in Iraq preparing themselves for the likely power vacuum following the planned withdrawal of American troops from their country later that year.

Bruno was familiar with this region of western Macedonia. He had been involved in the big operation, Mountain Stream, in November 2007 when the largest ever seizure of weapons by the Macedonian police took place in the village of Brodec near Tetovo. After a fierce firefight with the Albanian criminal group involved, six of the gang were killed and thirteen arrested with no casualties incurred by the police. One of their leaders, Lirim Jakupi, known as "Nazi" had managed to escape, although wounded. Bruno had been pleased to hear that he had been arrested in Kosovo in September the previous year.

What amazed Bruno was the size and mix of the arms cache they had found in houses in the village and in pits in the surrounding countryside. There were mortars, cannons, electronically guided anti-tank missiles, anti-aircraft missile systems, rocket propelled grenade launchers, land mines, anti-tank mines, sniper rifles, machine guns and plastic explosives. The head of the police operation had commented that the seized weapons were enough to arm a battalion.

Unfortunately such events were not a rarity in western Macedonia which bordered Albania. The population of largely ethnic Albanian and much of this region was virtually uncontrollable by the Macedonian police. It is considered a "home country" along with Kosovo by the fearsomely ruthless Albanian mafia. The criminal gangs are often indistinguishable from the various Albanian guerrilla groups that fought against Macedonian troops in 2001.

The operation in which Bruno was presently engaged was directed by the Regional Centre for Combating Cross-Border Crime in Bucharest and comprised specialised commando units from the Macedonian police force and Bruno's team of six *Guardia* officers. This forty-strong squad was perched in the forest on the hillside above an old quarry where there were a number of sheds and more substantial buildings plus cave-like apertures in the rock walls. The Macedonian police had solid intelligence that this was the main storage base for a huge stockpile of weapons left over from the recent widespread Balkans conflict. The *Guardia's* inside man on the Italian side had indicated that the weapons would be moved during the early part of the week of 7 February. There were only two gang members permanently stationed at the quarry as guards but the commander of the police operation had decided to wait for the whole gang to turn up in a convoy of trucks before triggering the arrest swoop.

That was why Bruno had been uncomfortably encamped on this freezing hillside since the previous Sunday and as dawn was breaking on Tuesday 8, he prayed that their vigil would not last much longer. His prayers were answered almost immediately when the interpreter assigned to his unit said they should get ready to move. One of the scouts positioned about a mile away, above the approach road to the quarry, had radioed that heavy vehicles were trundling towards them.

The order was given to wait until the vehicles were parked and their occupants had disembarked before advancing in a broad arc down the hill. The Macedonian interpreter relayed this message to Bruno and he was flexing his cramped muscles when all hell broke loose and one of his men went down as a hail of bullets rained down on them.

"Major, we are under fire from the ridge above the quarry," shouted his number two. This was a redundant communication as Bruno could clearly see in the dawn's half-light a stream of tracer shells traversing the intended line of the police attack. As far as he could tell, there were about a dozen people firing at them from well-coordinated positions with a heavy machine gun perfectly placed to put down a lethal wall of fire.

The cross-fire was so well directed that all the policemen could do was find cover and keep their heads down. Bruno also heard the unmistakeable whoosh of a rocket propelled grenade and the explosive splintering of pine trees as the missile struck the canopy above them. Obviously their operation had been compromised and this gang of criminals and paramilitaries had despatched an advance unit to pin them down whilst the trucks were loaded behind the protective walls of the various quarry buildings. The police commander had radioed for helicopter support, so the interpreter said, but was not confident reinforcements would arrive soon enough to prevent the fully loaded trucks from leaving.

Bruno signalled to two of his men to crawl over to his position. Like him, both were experienced mountaineers.

"I think we can get up onto that ridge via that fissure in the rock that will not be visible to the shooters on top. We can lob a couple of stun grenades into that machine gun emplacement and also make sure we take out the guy with the rocket launcher. Are you with me?"

Both men nodded in unison. "If we do that the rest of our force can then mount an attack on the guys down in the quarry and stop them driving those trucks away."

Bruno and his two officers, with the interpreter, wormed their way over to the police commander and told him what they planned to do. Bruno saw a relieved look on the commander's face. Bruno guessed the reason was that he was being presented with a possible way out of this impasse. There might be a way of extricating himself from a monumental failure which would look very bad on his record. Bruno also reflected that the police commander must have come to the same conclusion he had himself – that the leaked information to the criminal gang about this operation was most likely to have come from someone in the commander's own team.

Bruno and his men left in a fast crouched run through the trees. The firing from the ridge was now sporadic but with well-chosen bursts across the police lines aimed at ensuring they could not advance. Bruno reached the bottom of the fissure and was pleased to see it did extend like a chimney to the top of the ridge and was shielded by some fairly heavy vegetation. There were enough hand and foot holds to enable them to ascend the chimney without climbing aids but the rock was covered in a crust of ice which made it very treacherous. Bruno went first and managed to reach the top in a few minutes but one of his men slipped and fell about twenty feet to the base of the fissure. He signalled that he had broken his leg and was out of commission. Bruno waited until his other man had successfully made the ascent before peering over the lip of the fissure.

He saw that there were eight men on the ridge, the nearest being the machine gunner who was about thirty metres away. He was relieved to see that the gunmen had virtually no cover so their advantage in numbers over himself and Sergeant Bassoli, was nullified. They were both on a broad ledge a metre or so below the edge of the fissure, just behind a bush that offered some concealment but was not thick enough to hamper their firing arc. Bruno whispered to the sergeant to shoot the man with the rocket launcher as soon as his own stun grenade had disabled the machine gunner. His grenade was a perfect hit and both Bruno and Sergeant Bassoli put down a withering barrage of fire with their Beretta AR90 assault rifles. It was all over in seconds. All eight gunmen were killed or wounded. The two casualties were knocked off their feet and they both kicked away their weapons and raised their hands. Bruno could hear a fierce firefight in the quarry bottom and when he looked down he saw that the police unit had already taken out several of the loading gang who must have been caught by surprise as they were carrying heavy crates and took too long to deploy their own weapons. Bruno and Sergeant Bassoli also started firing at the remaining gang members who had taken up positions behind one of the larger buildings. Caught in this deadly cross-fire the skirmish ended very quickly, with the four gunmen left standing throwing their weapons down.

The support helicopter arrived about twenty minutes later and the six wounded gang members were loaded aboard together with a few injured policemen and flown to the hospital in the capital, Skopje. The inventory of the weapons they had seized was a remarkable illustration of how much military ordnance was left over from the most recent conflicts to afflict this war-torn region. In addition to two thousand brand new AK47s, there were hundreds of grenades, fifty heavy machine guns, fifty artillery pieces, one hundred kilos of plastic explosives and the largest haul of laser-guided anti-aircraft missile systems ever recorded by any law enforcement agency. Twenty gang members had been killed and six were wounded. The casualties on the police side were remarkably light thanks mainly to Bruno's courageous intervention. Two Macedonian policemen were injured, one seriously and two of Bruno's squad were casualties, one with a broken ankle and the other with a bullet in the shoulder. The police commander was effusive in his praise for Bruno's exploits and said he would be recommending him for Macedonia's highest award for bravery in the field. Clearly, the commander's heartfelt thankyous were in recognition of Bruno's singular contribution in turning a potential debacle into an exceptional triumph.

Bruno could now concentrate on the secondary purpose of this Macedonian episode. He had made a prior agreement with the regional command centre in Bucharest that he could interview any captured gang members to gather intelligence pertaining to the confidential investigation into SCU's activities. He knew that this particular gang was involved with SCU in gun running and people trafficking. He had also heard from his coastguard comrade Commander Speros that the Greek police believed that the gang was working with a Greek criminal group operating out of Piraeus docks. Bruno thought that an interrogation of one of the captured gang members could be a way of joining the dots regarding the drugs pipeline via Piraeus to Balog Oils then on to Western Europe.

He thought he might make most progress by interviewing one of the injured Albanians who had been flown to the military hospital in Skopje. They were likely to feel more vulnerable and may even be disoriented by the pain-killing drugs they would have been given. That evening, Bruno was permitted to interview the one gunman who was not in a critical condition with a flesh wound in his thigh. He had been identified as Azem Simaku, an ethnic Albanian from Kosovo. As soon as Bruno saw him he knew he had struck lucky. Simaku was an athletic, bushy haired young man in his late teens, with an open face and a diffident manner. Bruno had been told by the interpreter that they had identified him as the youngest brother of one of the gang leaders. It appeared that he was not a regular member of the gang but had been enlisted as an extra pair of hands to help shift the arms consignment. The police had used the latest Gunshot Residue Testing to establish that Simaku himself had not actually discharged a weapon during the gun battle. He had blurted out to the doctor removing the bullet from his leg that he had not even been carrying a weapon. He said he was simply helping his brother as one of the regular gang members had gone down with the flu. He did not know that his brother was one of the fatalities and seemed to be stupefied to find himself caught up in this horrifying vortex of circumstances, remorselessly driving him towards a lengthy sentence in a maximum security facility.

Bruno had agreed with the totally compliant Macedonian police commander that he could cut young Azem a fair amount of slack if he provided valuable input on the gang's *modus operandi*. Azem had been put in a private room to ensure none of the other hospitalized Albanians were privy to his police interviews. But, just in case, Bruno had asked the medical staff to say within earshot of the beds occupied by them that complications had arisen during Azem's surgery and he had been transferred to the Intensive Care unit.

Through the interpreter Bruno introduced himself to Azem and surprised him by asking if he was comfortable and up to answering a few questions.

"I'm OK…my leg feels numb but the doctor said the bullet went straight through, just grazing the bone so there should be no permanent damage."

"That's good…but you know you are in big, big trouble and I'm here to see if we can do anything about this mess. The doctor has told us you were not supposed to be with this gang at all." As the interpreter translated Bruno's words, Azem looked at Bruno with so much rekindled hope that Bruno knew he could extract whatever information Azem had about the gang's activities.

"That's right…I'm actually a student at Epoka University doing a degree in Computer Engineering but my brother has been the head of our family since *baba* died and we are all afraid of him. He forces all the family to help him in various ways and my brothers and sisters have told me they dare not say no because he is incredibly violent and capable of anything if he's crossed. So far, he's left me alone and let me get on with my studies. But one of my sisters has told me that he is merely waiting until I finish my IT course and then he's going to use me to help with some cyber-crime ideas he has."

Bruno stopped the young man in full spate and told him his brother Edon was dead. A look of sheer relief crossed Azem's handsome face and Bruno thought this was an opportune moment to press home the advantage.

"Look Azem, I really want to help you. If I can convince the Macedonian authorities that you were coerced into joining this ill-fated convoy you will get much more lenient treatment."

"What do you mean exactly?"

"Well…If the intelligence you provide is valuable, we may be able to get you a suspended sentence and you could avoid jail time altogether…But I don't know whether you can tell us much as you've already said that you were not really involved with the gang."

Having baited the hook, Bruno looked quizzically at Azem. As soon as the interpreter had relayed this, Azem became very agitated and insisted that his other brothers and sisters were always gossiping about Edon's activities and he therefore had a pretty good idea of what he had been doing.

Over the next hour or so Azem gave Bruno a rundown of the gang's illicit operations. Much of this was not news to Bruno, but there were two or three real nuggets in the mix. He learnt how opium and opium products such as morphine base and heroin from Afghanistan arrived via Iran and Turkey into the Balkans. Edon's group then moved them through the Albanian ports of Durrës and Vlorë under the blind eyes of two particular customs officials. One of his sisters had been forced to meet these men on a monthly basis to hand over their substantial bribes. She hated the job and complained constantly about how sleazy they were. She had asked Azem to accompany her on a number of these trips and he would arrive in the designated bars in the two ports before his sister and keep an eye on her whilst the money exchange took place. He was therefore able to give Bruno a detailed description of each man. As they appeared to be regulars in these bars it would be easy for the Albanian police to pick them up once he was able to release the information without compromising the SCU investigation.

Azem confirmed that the drugs were sent to various small ports in Southern Italy, several of which had not been picked up by the *Guardia* as links in the supply chain. There was also a regular delivery of drugs to Greece in high powered motor launches which drew near to several small ports like Galaxidi in the Gulf of Corinth. The motor boats never docked but the Albanians rang their Greek partners in crime with their exact coordinates when they were a few hundred metres offshore. A small Greek fishing boat then rendezvoused with them to pick up the drugs. Azem did not know where they went after that but he had heard his brother talking on the phone once or twice to someone in Greece and he was fairly sure that this person was some kind of dock worker in Piraeus. Azem had studied Greek for seven years at school and he was sure his brother had mentioned the name of a transport company that was used to move the drugs. He remembered the name Eliades because a couple of years earlier he had been very keen on a Greek girl called Dimitra Eliades.

****

The next day Bruno was back behind his desk in Rome. The first thing he did was call Gina.

"*Buongiorno cara*, I'm back in one piece from my undercover operation and I've had a real breakthrough on the Mondo/SCU connection. I just wanted to check whether you can back pedal on the interview arrangements for the spare candidates you identified for the SSP job. We are getting close to the end of our investigation but I didn't want you to suffer any professional embarrassment when all this goes public."

"Not really *caro*, the dates have already been set for the two best people to be interviewed in London…they are both coming here on 28 February… but it will still take several weeks before any job offers are finalised. After the initial interviews next week, the candidates will need to meet other senior people in the particular Mondo companies where there are openings. Even if that happens quickly there will then be contract negotiations on the details of the job offers which I can easily spin out for several days."

"*Va bene*, Gina and if necessary we can involve Adam Palfrey to help with any necessary delaying tactics…remember I told you he's now in the loop regarding this whole case."

"Yes, we should have enough time to avoid these candidates having to take irrevocable career decisions. I really couldn't look at myself in the mirror if this whole exercise jeopardised their relationship with their current employers."

"I know Gina, but I think we are so close to bringing this investigation to a close that you can rest easy. The last thing I want is for you to compromise your professional ethics. In fact, I'm coming to London in a few days to review all the evidence with Commander Gibbs. We will be drawing up a detailed plan to ensure we coordinate how we close the net on this widespread criminal operation…so no one gets away."

14 FEBRUARY 2011

BARI, PUGLIA

Bruno was sitting in the main office of the *Carabinieri* in Bari with *Colonnello* Fredo Sportelli, the officer leading one of the major investigations into the criminal activities of the Sacra Corona Unita. They were awaiting the arrival of Giuseppe Moscatelli, the former head of legal services for the province of Lecce to the south. Bruno had sent parts of Luca's original dossier to Sportelli whom he had worked with in the recent past on mafia crackdown operations. Sportelli told Bruno that he had been about to bring Moscatelli in for questioning although he didn't have any really cast-iron evidence on his corrupt activities. Although Moscatelli had retired around a decade earlier from his local government position, the *Colonnello* was sure he continued to provide legal advice to the mafia right up to the present day. Luca's dossier was, therefore, a Godsend and he said they could now really go to town on Moscatelli. Sportelli was very happy to accede to Bruno's request to be present when the ex-lawyer was interrogated to see whether he could provide any useful leads for his top secret investigation into links between SCU and Mondo.

Moscatelli was escorted into the sparsely furnished interview room and told to sit facing the two officers on the other side of the table. He had the shell-shocked look of a disaster survivor and his hands were shaking visibly. The years had not been kind to Giuseppe Moscatelli. Still only in his early seventies, he looked a good ten years older. He was obviously paying the price for a lifelong over-indulgence in food and wine. He was carrying at least thirty kilos of excess weight, most of it concentrated around his enormous midriff.

His nose was an unhealthy patchwork of broken veins and purple and red discolourations. His narrow shoulders and skinny legs were in grotesque contrast to his monstrous belly which hung down like a bulging sack seemingly disconnected from the body which had spawned it.

Bruno thought, "With that belly it's surprising he doesn't fall flat on his face when he stands up."

The two officers fixed Moscatelli with cold, hard stares and said nothing until Moscatelli broke the silence with a plaintive question.

"I must ask why I was picked up this morning and brought here with no explanation except that I may be able to help you with your enquiries. I am a respected citizen who has served this region in a professional capacity for many years and…"

Colonnello Sportelli stopped him in mid-flow. "*Signor* Moscatelli, you are certainly not a respectable citizen and the only person you have served is yourself. Do you remember the Graziani Winery project back in the seventies?"

The suddenness of the question shook Moscatelli to the core. It was as if every drop of blood had been forcibly drained from his face.

"The…the what project?…That was years ago and I don't really recall…"

"Let me refresh your memory," continued the *Colonnello*, "You awarded the contract to a mafia backed company, Vizzari Costruzioni, for a kickback that enabled you to buy an expensive Alfa Romeo. You approved payment of their massively inflated invoices. You knew Vizzari planned to declare bankruptcy after they had siphoned of the huge amounts of money you had approved for very little real activity…in fact, we have a complete dossier on this scam including copies off documents from your own office at the time."

Sportelli slammed the thick file he was holding onto the table and made Moscatelli nearly fall off his chair.

"But even if this were true," he stammered, "the Statute of Limitations applies and you can't bring an action against me now…"

"Ah, of course, you're a lawyer aren't you, *Signor* Moscatelli?" Sportelli said sardonically, "But I haven't said that we intend to arrest you, have I?"

"Then why am I here?" asked a cautious Moscatelli.

"My colleague *Maggiore* Canepa and I thought you might, in your declining years, want to give something back to our great country which has clearly bestowed its largesse on you in no uncertain manner."

A look of utter amazement appeared on Moscatelli's face but this was quickly followed by a flash of animal cunning in his eyes as he saw that there might be an exit route from this unpleasant situation.

"How might I do that?" he said with increasing confidence and a touch of haughtiness.

"By giving us chapter and verse on your dealings with senior members of the SCU and 'Ndrangheta clans, many of whom, as you know, are now in custody."

"What on earth gives you the impression that I'd be prepared to do that?"

"Well, we thought we'd try first to appeal to your better nature before we let our informant on your repellent abuse of public office release everything he has to both the national and local media. I'm sure your friends and family would like to know what you've been up to in your so-called career."

"You wouldn't...You couldn't do that...You would be colluding in a campaign to destroy my reputation and besmirch my family."

"No, *Signor* Moscatelli," interjected Bruno, "You've got that wrong. We can't stop the private citizen who has brought this dossier to our attention from doing what he thinks is right. We've managed to hold him off for now from contacting the media because we convinced him that the inside information you could supply could do real damage to the activities of the mafia. We said that that was much more important than nailing your miserable hide to the wall. He agreed to give us a few days to assess the value of your input, but he's a real crusader and he won't hold back if we fail to get you to supply really incriminating details on your erstwhile mafia comrades."

It was a bluff, of course, but it had certainly hit Moscatelli in a truly sensitive spot. A vain and pompous man, he relished the material trappings and visible standing in Puglian society which his decades of graft had given him. He could not bear the prospect of outright vilification in the press and probably worse, the insidious, behind his back, whispering of social contacts and family members once details of his corrupt dealings were disclosed.

The two officers were practised readers of human fallibility and body language and they exchanged almost imperceptible nods as if to say... "We've got him!"

His haughtiness of a couple of minutes earlier had now completely dissipated and Moscatelli lowered his head and mumbled so quietly that they had to crane forward to catch his words, "*Va bene*, I'll tell you all I know but you should recognise that I'm a dead man if any whiff of this gets back to SCU or 'Ndrangheta. What guarantees can you give me that my own and my family's safety will not be compromised?"

The two officers had known that this would be an issue and had worked out a game plan which they put to a now completely submissive Moscatelli. First, they underlined the massive crackdown which had resulted in the recent round-up of most of the *capos* in the SCU and the neighbouring 'Ndrangheta. News of this had reverberated throughout Puglian society and the *Colonnello* said Moscatelli should be in no doubt that the forces of law and order were well on the way to stamping out the mafia in Puglia once and for all. Secondly, they only wanted Moscatelli to provide corroborative details to the mass of evidence they had already collected. They didn't intend to identify him as a witness or ask him to give evidence in court. Thirdly, they would only meet with him at a secure location of his choosing when they were in plain clothes. And finally, they confirmed that from then on they would be the only people who would contact him on his mobile phone to maximise his security and they would simply identify themselves as either Fredo or Bruno. If anyone had heard about this trip to Brindisi for questioning, he could just say that the police had been on a fishing expedition which he was able to avoid with ease as they had nothing on him.

Moscatelli seemed resigned, if not happy, about this and said, "I'll pull some preliminary information together for you in the next few days." He went on with a hint of pride in his voice…"I have kept meticulous records which are in my safe at home and also in a safety deposit box at my bank so it would help to know what you are particularly interested in so I can prioritise accordingly."

The two officers had also predicted this issue and they had disguised their principal interest in Santoro by simply including him and his son Vittore in a list of about twenty SCU *capos*, local government officials and policemen they knew to have been corrupt during Moscatelli's tenure and who were still alive.

****

Three days later, back in his Rome office, Bruno got a very excited Sportelli on the phone,

"Bruno, this is unbelievable. Our man Moscatelli kept the most detailed records I've ever seen. He must have the mentality of a squirrel...Every illegal transaction...Every payment made...Every name...Every date... Every judge and juror who was got at...all meticulously noted. Incredibly, he kept a list of secret bank accounts under assumed names for dozens of SCU members and also property deeds for hundreds of farms and houses owned by the mafia through a web of front companies. These lists alone should enable us eventually to appropriate mafia assets worth tens if not hundreds of millions under the *Libera il Bene* policy. I have informed my commanding officer *Generale di Brigate* De Luca about this incredible find and he wants to add his heartfelt thanks to mine for enabling us to get Moscatelli to spill the beans.

"I'll be sure to pass that on, Fredo."

"You know, as he is still actively involved with the mafia, we could clearly prosecute Moscatelli as there would certainly be no applicable Statute of Limitations. But before he handed over his incredibly comprehensive archive he had the good sense to tell me what it contained and get me to agree to waive prosecution because of his age and also the death sentence he would be under if this all came to light. I have no doubt that my waiving prosecution in his case was the right thing to do to ensure we got our hands on this priceless data."

"I agree, Fredo. There are much bigger fish to fry than him and I'm sure my informant will be thrilled to learn that the dossier he put together all those years ago has finally borne more fruit than he could ever have dreamed of. I'm sorry I can't reveal his identity but, as I told you, he had to get out of Italy fast when the mob learnt what he was trying to expose. He's still understandably wary about stepping onto centre stage..."

"*Capisco.* No problem Bruno, but you must tell him he has rendered a great service to his region and his country and he should be proud of his contribution."

"I'll certainly tell him...But listen, how much info did he provide on the Santoros?"

"I think we've struck gold there. Loads of references to personal and business deals, many of which I'm sure are illegal. Also, Moscatelli appears to have acted as their family lawyer. There's one thing that's quite interesting. I don't know whether you know that Vittore is not Arturo's natural son. Moscatelli did all the paperwork regarding his adoption in 1975."

"No, I didn't know that. Not sure if it has any relevance but can you send me what you have on that together with everything else he's provided on his links with the Santoros so I can have a really good look at it all."

The next day a couriered package was brought to his desk. It contained photocopies of dozens of documents provided by Moscatelli, all fastidiously indexed and cross-referenced by him. Sportelli had added information on people and organisations in Puglia which would otherwise have meant nothing to Bruno.

Having told his *aide* that he did not want to be disturbed, Bruno spent the next three hours immersing himself in the sordid underworld inhabited by the Santoros, their mafia associates and their accomplices in supposedly respectable society.

Even though he thought he had seen it all in his eventful career in the *Guardia*, Bruno couldn't help emitting frequent audible exclamations of amazement as he scrutinised the documents. The sheer range and volume of the bribery, corruption and extreme criminality which was exhibited on every page was mind blowing. And he had in front of him only a fraction of the records so scrupulously maintained by Moscatelli. The Santoros seemed to have a finger in every illegal pie as well as an alarmingly extensive list of legitimate businesses. There were legions of public officials from senators down to local health inspectors who were on SCU's payroll. Added to these corrupt functionaries were scores of policemen, judges and business people who were either on the take voluntarily or whose silence and passivity were assured by threats. These were made either against their families or to disclose information prejudicial to their good name which the SCU had got hold of via its huge network of informers or, if they could not find any dirt, had simply fabricated to irreparably blacken the person's reputation. This was all made clear in the extensive supplementary notes provided by Sportelli. He had obviously had further discussions with Moscatelli to decipher the latter's often cryptic notations against the names of people on a list headed *Quelli in Pugno* – or those in SCU's pocket. Opposite each name there was a single letter – either a *V* or an *F* ndicating whether the individual was a *volontario* (voluntary) or *forzato* (forced) collaborator. Against the V-s were records of retainers and specific payments made but nothing against the F-s.

Moscatelli had also kept a list of the hundreds of firms, large and small who paid *pizzo* or protection money to Santoro's SCU clan. This had inevitably become one of the standard costs of doing business in his territory and even with growing grass roots anti-mafia campaigns such as *addiopizzo* (goodbye protection money) it looked as though he still had a stranglehold on local business activity. What surprised Bruno was the up-to-dateness of the information supplied by Moscatelli. He had retired from his local government job several years earlier but he was obviously still acting as a key manager for Santoro and was trusted with the most sensitive information. Santoro had clearly recognised Moscatelli's value as a punctilious administrator, but Bruno grimly reflected that had Santoro known about the incredibly detailed records he was keeping, he would have been killed after probably suffering the most painful death Santoro's warped sadistic mind could devise.

Most of the information contained in the thick file *Colonnello* Sportelli had sent him was of academic interest to Bruno. It was only when he got to a page headed "Sapore Senza Pari" that he clicked into full alert. Much of what he read confirmed what the investigating team had already established about the use of SSP as a vital conduit in the Sacra Corona Unita's drug trafficking supply chain. What he gleaned in addition, with a growing feeling of excitement, were singularly useful clues about the methods used to transport the drugs. It was clear that Moscatelli made regular generous payments to SSP's Operations Manager, Guido Guarini, and to six blue collar operatives who worked in a so-called "special" unit. This unit produced a premium chilli-infused olive oil but the factory workers were given monthly payments equivalent to four or five times the standard hourly rate for their counterparts in the food industry. It was likely that they were also paid a normal wage through the proper SSP books – so they were earning well over €100,000 a year, 80 per cent of which was tax free.

Clearly, the special unit was producing a very valuable commodity. Bruno was familiar with the ingenious ways in which illegal drugs were mixed with other innocuous materials to avoid detection by law enforcement agencies. He knew hard drugs could be diluted in liquids such as oils or orange juice and subsequently recovered by expert chemists. He had also read about a case in New York where a consignment of lollipops had been used. In each lolly a hard sugar confectionary shell had sheathed a large plug of high-grade heroin.

"So they must be using this bottled oil to ship the drugs out of Italy," Bruno mused. He immediately saw a way of getting an inside track on the operation. He had the names of the six production workers and he would send one of his best men to Modena to do a detailed background check on each of them. The aim would be to identify the one who would be the most likely to crack when they leaned on him to give them chapter and verse on the intricacies of the operation.

There was something else in the list of payments made by Moscatelli that seemed incongruous. Every month a large sum was transferred to an individual in Tunisia. Against this person's name Moscatelli had noted in his tiny spidery writing the name of a company. Bruno Googled the company and found it was a plastics moulding firm which made many different kinds of products for the food and other industries. He had a Eureka! moment. A few weeks earlier he had scanned an exhaustive report on the myriad inventive ways criminals were deploying to disguise drug shipments. He asked his assistant to find the report and he started to read through it carefully. He kept shaking his head in amazement as he went down the incredibly long list of methods. These included soaking pieces of fabric in liquid heroin then drying them and subsequently washing the heroin off with water and turning it back into powder. Another well-tried method was mixing cocaine with the clay used to cast sculptures or other pottery items, like a forty piece crockery set made entirely of compressed cocaine!

"There it is!" he finally murmured as he jabbed his finger on a particular entry which stated "…the cocaine is mixed with molten plastic before it is moulded into innocent items like dashboards for cars, cases for DVDs, plastic buckets etc. Once these specially treated products arrive at their final destination, they are broken into smaller pieces and dissolved in acid. The cocaine is thus freed of its bonds and the liquid is dried to obtain the powdered form."

"So this Tunisian firm must be incorporating drugs into a product they supply to SSP," Bruno reflected. One of his team checked with the Italian Customs, *Agenzia delle Dogane e dei Monopoli* and reported back that the Tunisian firm, *Société* Plasmorph was supplying SSP with customised plastic crates for transporting 500ml and 1lt sized bottles.

"So that confirms how they are shipping the drugs out of Italy to other European countries," thought Bruno.

A phone call the previous day from Commander Speros had also added another important piece to the intricate forensic pattern they were painstakingly piecing together.

"I've got some interesting news, Bruno. The inside man at Piraeus docks I told you about confirmed that a shipment of caustic soda destined for Balog Oils had been offloaded, checked by customs and left in a warehouse overnight. He saw the drums stacked and had the good sense to count them – 15 in all. These were due to be delivered the next day to Balog by Eliades Cargo. This undercover police sergeant took a smoke break when the truck arrived and counted 19 barrels hoisted onto the vehicle."

"Smart guy," interjected Bruno.

"Yes…He did a quick internet check on the physical properties of caustic soda and discovered that sure enough it was a material used in the refining of rapeseed oil, but more interestingly, in its white granular form was indistinguishable from cocaine powder. When he checked the shipping log he discovered that a few hours after the German vessel carrying the probably genuine Dow Chemical caustic soda product had arrived, a small cargo vessel from Marseille had docked right outside the warehouse where the drums of soda were stored. Unusually, this ship had no cargo to offload but was due to pick up several tons of lemons for its return leg. Our man made the reasonable assumption that in the middle of the night the four extra drums probably containing drugs had been quietly transferred from ship to warehouse."

"Great work," exclaimed Bruno.

"One other thing…he was also pretty certain that one of the customs officer's was in on the subterfuge because when the sergeant checked the goods inward sheet he saw that the customs officer had specified 19 rather than 15 barrels so there would be no query if the number was checked again when they were loaded onto the Eliades Cargo truck."

So Bruno was now almost certain that Balog Oils was also using some shipments of its bottled rape oil to conceal an extra ingredient of diluted cocaine. He rang Lieutenant Liakos and asked him to congratulate the undercover policeman for his excellent work. He also asked if he would get his superior, Major Kapouzis to confirm that the Greek police would take no immediate action. He should tell the Major that they were only weeks away from pressing the button on a total coordinated crackdown to arrest all those implicated in this massive international trafficking operation.

18 FEBRUARY 2011

LECCE, PUGLIA

Moscatelli sat staring at the wall in his home office. Since meeting the *Carabinieri* officer and his colleague from the *Guardia* he had been trying to find a way of putting himself and his family out of harm's way. He knew that he had been placed in this hazardous position by a ghost from his past. "It's all down to that young bastard Vento…that 'whiter than white' squealer," he thought to himself. "For all these years I've lived with the possibility that he'd kept a copy of that damned dossier I managed to retrieve before it got to that interfering magistrate Fontana."

The man he had planted in Fontana's office had, by pure chance, been able to open the envelope delivered by Luca Vento that early morning in August all those years ago, before Fontana arrived in the office. Moscatelli knew that he himself would have been brutally disposed of by his Camorra paymasters for allowing Vento to piece together this incriminating document. His inside man, Umberto Fagioli – who was in fact his nephew on his wife's side – had happened to be parking his *motorino* outside the magistrate's Brindisi office just as Vento was delivering his bulky envelope to the security guard. It was much earlier than Fagioli's normal start time but he had been reprimanded the previous day for sloppy work on an important case and the magistrate had told him he wanted a complete rewrite of the submission he had been working on by nine that morning. Fagioli recognised Vento having seen him in Moscatelli's Lecce office several times. Vento had passed him without a sideways glance and as he climbed the steps to the building's imposing front entrance, Fagioli's curiosity was aroused. He stopped at the guard's cubicle and asked what his "friend" had wanted. Discovering that he had left an envelope for *Dottore* Fontana alarm bells started ringing as he knew Fontana had suspicions that his uncle was on the take and he also knew that Vento had worked with the magistrate previously.

Fagioli told the guard that he would put the envelope on Fontana's desk himself and when he got to his own little office he opened the envelope, knowing that he could always readdress a new envelope if the contents were innocuous. He had removed the document and read it with a certain amount of admiration for the forensic work undertaken by Vento. He noticed that there were some other unopened envelopes in the magistrate's in-tray so he took out a fairly large one with a local postmark, extracted the papers inside and reinserted them in another envelope which he sealed and addressed to the magistrate and wrote "By Hand". This was to provide cover in the unlikely event that the security guard might mention to the magistrate that he had received a hand delivered missive. After work, Fagioli took the dossier to Moscatelli who was on holiday near Bari.

Moscatelli reflected grimly, "My life would have been snuffed out if my nephew had not arrived at the office two hours earlier than usual."

He could not very well tell his mafia paymasters that Vento had uncovered such a web of incriminating information as that would still leave him in a perilous position. His solution was to feed in to the mafia *capo* with whom he had the most contact that he had discovered that Vento was a grass. He had been specifically placed in the *Giunta Regionale's* offices by magistrate Fontana who had "recruited him" during Vento's internship in his office. Moscatelli told the *capo* that his own inside man on the magistrate's staff had intercepted a report from Vento on a scam in the garbage collection department. This was apparently his first report to Fontana. Moscatelli was careful to pick a minor infraction which involved a few supervisors and which he knew had only low level mafia involvement. He impressed on the *capo* that Vento was a very clever and determined young man and that he would, in due course, inevitably uncover more serious illegalities which would implicate the higher echelons of the mafia.

****

While Moscatelli was musing on the vagaries of fate, in his Rome office Bruno was still poring over the minutiae in the files provided by the old lawyer. He was reviewing some of the ostensibly more peripheral details supplied. He had put a question mark against the item concerning the adoption of Vittore Santoro. In Moscatelli's crabbed hand there was a brief note that on April 20th 1975, Arturo and Serena Santoro had adopted a baby boy supplied by one Franco Perugini. Driven by his usual pedantic need to include as much detail as possible, Moscatelli had underlined, "The mother was his unmarried daughter."

The name Perugini rang a bell and when Bruno cross-checked it with the list of those in the SCU's pocket – *Quelli in Pugno* – sure enough there was Franco Perugini with a "V" against his name and a note of the three companies he owned. These, from their names, appeared to be haulage firms. As there were no cash payments to Perugini indicated, Bruno surmised that Perugini was actually a business partner of Santoro's, maybe providing cover for smuggling of people, drugs or contraband.

His musing was interrupted by the insistent buzzing of his cell phone. He saw from the screen that it was Luca Biagi.

"*Ciao*, Bruno…You left a message earlier…What can I do for you?"

"Oh, hi Luca, thanks for phoning back. I wanted to let you know that your dossier has yielded some spectacular results. It has enabled us to confront your old boss Moscatelli with chapter and verse on his mafia involvement.

To save his own neck he's giving us the most amazing info on the activities of the mafia in Puglia for whom he was their main "Banker"...Still is as a matter of fact. I'm going through the data right now so you called at an opportune moment as you may be able to fill in a few gaps. I know it's a long time ago but did you ever come across a man called Franco Perugini? It appears that he was a businessman in the mafia's pocket but his connection with Arturo Santoro went a lot further than that...He seems to have provided the Santoros with a child to adopt."

Bruno had to move the phone away from his ear as Luca responded with a loud, strangled cry.

"What was the child?"

"What do you mean?" stammered a startled Bruno.

"Was it a boy or a girl?"

"It was a boy, Vittore, the Santoros' only child"

"Oh my God...oh my God," came the response from a stunned Luca, "He's my son."

"What do you mean your son...how can that be?"

"Bruno you've got to promise me that whatever happens you will never ever tell Gina or her mother what I'm about to tell you or it will break their hearts,as surely as it's shattering mine at this moment."

"Of course, I promise. I'd never do anything to hurt Gina."

Luca then explained his youthful fling, Antonella's subsequent secret confinement and her being forced to give up the baby.

"I only learned about this a couple of weeks ago from an old friend, Bernardo Colangelo, who is dying and felt I should know the truth...Oh sweet Jesus, Santoro has reared our son to be a vicious gangster."

Bruno tried to calm Luca down by saying that this was all conjecture and needed to be substantiated. But when Bruno told him the date of the adoption Luca had all the proof he needed. Vittore Santoro was indeed his son and both he and his beloved daughter were helping to construct a case which would put him away for the rest of his natural life.

"Bruno, you've got to stop involving Gina with these people...It's too awful to contemplate her ever finding out that she has a half-brother who is a vile criminal"

"OK, Luca. I promise I will. I won't ask her to do anything else except schedule the interviews of the candidates she has already identified."

After putting the phone down, he remembered that Sportelli had sent him a set of police mugshots or other photos of the main suspects. He dug this out and found one obviously taken at a business convention with Vittore

Santoro circled in red ink. Bruno felt a chill up his spine. Looking out at him was the handsome face of a younger Luca Biagi. If Bruno had had any residual doubts about the startling connection Luca had just made, these were now totally obliterated.

18 FEBRUARY 2011

SUNNINGDALE, BERKSHIRE

Maurizia Biagi was in a particularly good mood. She had received a phone call from Joost van Gassen who was, as usual, angling for a date. As possible bait, he said he had some very interesting information on Major Canepa. Joost was playing a bit hard to get so she had to promise to have dinner with him when he was next in London. As she had her fingers crossed when she made the promise, she didn't feel too bad about her resolution never to meet him socially.

"I was in my office at Eurojust in The Hague, working on my own in a small meeting room when I overheard a tele-conference in the adjacent room. The three participants were a senior Eurojust official, Bruno Canepa in Rome and a police Commander in London whose name I didn't catch."

Maurizia could picture the scene vividly. Joost, the inveterate nosy parker with his ear glued to the partition picking up every word of this tripartite dialogue.

"Listen Maurizia, you've got to keep this to yourself but they were discussing the raising of European Arrest Warrants for a lot of people. I heard that one was for the top guy in a company called Mondo Foods. I think his name was Simmons...but there were many others in Italy, Greece, Hungary, France and Spain. It sounded like a really massive case and it could give you a tremendous scoop if you could discover what's going on."

Maurizia thanked him profusely and marvelled again at the lack of professional discretion and also the sheer stupidity of this high ranking eurocrat. But, on the other hand he had given her a lead that was absolute dynamite and she immediately started to dig out what she could on Mondo Foods and the man Simmons, who she quickly discovered was its Chairman.

She also put a call in to George Mellon at the giant financial services firm, Fidelity. George was one of their top consumer sector analysts. His job was to keep a close eye on the performance and strategies of major companies like Mondo. His input was key in determining whether his firm's investment managers bought, sold or held a particular company's stock. She and George had shared intelligence several times in the past and, as usual, he was only too pleased to help. They met for lunch the following day and she said she was doing some research for an article on the chairmen of several international groups. She first asked him what he knew about three other prominent business figures before introducing Sir Roger Simmons into the conversation. She felt this subterfuge was a necessary corrective to Joost's loose cannon approach.

"I've seen him a few times at their AGMs and he's also well known in the City. He's undoubtedly a hard nut and a rather cold fish…He takes no prisoners and I don't think you'd want him as an enemy. The general view is that Mondo Foods has performed better than most over recent years, although most people think that this has more to do with the outstanding stewardship of the previous long-serving Chief Executive, Simon Ramsay than to any distinctive contribution from Simmons…In fact there's an unsolved mystery surrounding Ramsay's sudden departure last autumn. He appeared to be flying high but then out of the blue his resignation was announced. No reason was given at that time or since and no one has been able to get to the bottom of why he left. One of my contacts is a non-executive director on the Mondo Board and he was as much in the dark as anyone as to why Ramsay left so abruptly.

"This is really interesting stuff George, please go on…"

"OK, well this particular bloke and I are members of the same club and we happened to have a late night drink together when he'd already had a few. He said Sir Roger had told the Board that Ramsay was stepping down for personal reasons and that he'd given his word that he would not disclose what these were. What I found a bit odd was that this chap also let slip that he and the other board members were surprised at the size of the termination package awarded to Ramsay. As he had resigned it would not have been unusual for him to have received twelve month's salary to pay off his contract – but he got twice that as well as a big chunk of cash when he exercised his share options. Reading between the lines, this guy was hinting that something fishy was going on."

During their somewhat elongated lunch Maurizia realized that although she had always found George attractive, she had now moved his rating to highly fanciable. He was clearly extremely astute but she had discovered a rich vein of fun under his urbane exterior and the priceless ability not to take himself too seriously. She could tell from the way he looked at her that he liked her a lot and this was reinforced by the prolonged parting hug he gave her and the promise to call soon to fix a dinner date.

Reflecting on the lunchtime conversation on the walk back to her office, she had a journalist's hunch that the unexpected exit of Simon Ramsay had something to do with whatever it was that Sir Roger Simmons was embroiled in.

"I've got to contact Ramsay to see whether I can shake loose any potential leads," she thought to herself.

His phone was ex-directory but she found out that he lived near Ascot and with a bit of further digging managed to get his address and also a fairly recent photo from a previous Mondo Annual Report. She was massively on the credit side regarding her holiday entitlement and as she had just finished a big series of articles, she decided to take a couple of days off to do a bit of private sleuthing. She logged on to her laptop and had a look at Google Earth. She found the street on which Ramsay's house was located, off Bagshot Road in Sunningdale. She moved her cursor this way and that so as to view the whole length of the street and discovered it was a typical stockbroker-belt wide, leafy avenue with well-spaced, imposing houses, usually behind substantial walls or hedges. She thought it would not be too difficult to park on the street and see if she could spot Ramsay leaving his house and then approach him as he was opening the gate from his long driveway to exit to the street.

Maurizia got to her chosen spot at 7.15 on this chilly but dry late-February morning just as the sun was beginning to lighten the dark grey sky. She did not have long to wait as fifteen minutes later the porch light went on in Ramsay's house. Out came a figure bundled up in a quilted jacket and as he stood on the front step looking up at the sky for a few seconds Maurizia could see through her high resolution binoculars that it was the businessman.

She then heard the garage doors whirr open and shortly after an executive saloon emerged and headed towards the large curlicued iron gates which were just beginning to open automatically. She shot out of her car and stationed herself in the centre of the gateway as the Mercedes rolled towards her. Ramsay had to stop otherwise he would have hit her.

The driver's window slid down and as Maurizia approached Ramsay said rather tartly, "Can I help you?"

"Mr Ramsay, my name is Maurizia Biagi and I'm a journalist with the *Financial Times*. Sorry to approach you in this way but there are some questions I'd like to ask you about your exit from Mondo Foods. My paper is investigating some disturbing aspects of the company's governance. Can you spare me a few minutes?"

Ramsay looked startled but then blustered, "What the hell do you think you're doing camping outside my house and ambushing me like this…it's totally unprofessional and not what I'd expect from the *FT*."

He was about to wind up his window when Maurizia decided to use her trump card. "Mr Ramsay, I know Mondo's chairman is being investigated by the police and I simply want to ensure that your reputation is not sullied in any way…I've only heard good things about you."

Ramsay stared at her with an expression flitting between fight and flight. After a few seconds he seemed to gather himself and said in a strained voice, "Before I say anything I need to know what you think you know about Mondo or whether this is just a fishing expedition. I won't do anything right now except go and get the morning papers and then make my wife some breakfast as she's in bed with a cold…But I'll meet you for a drink later in the Berystede Hotel just up the road, say at noon, to hear what you have to say."

Without waiting for Maurizia's reply, his car window slid up and he pulled away.

Maurizia was a little shaken as this was far from her normal methodology, but on the whole she was pretty satisfied with her dawn raid. Ramsay would hardly have agreed to meet her unless there was something going on at Mondo. As she would have hit the peak rush hour traffic, she decided not to drive back to her flat in Primrose Hill but instead go into nearby Windsor, have some breakfast and then go to the library there for a couple of hours. This would give her the opportunity to plan what she was going to say to Ramsay to get him to open up to her about the goings on at Mondo.

By the time she pulled in to the Berystede Hotel car park just before noon, she had decided on a full frontal attack. She would say that she knew that Sir Roger Simmons was suspected of criminal activity and that his arrest was imminent. That was all she had except for the unusual size of Ramsay's exit payment which she thought was hush money but had no proof. At hotel reception she asked if Mr Ramsay had arrived. She was directed to a meeting room and when she entered she was surprised to see that Ramsay was not alone. With him was a stocky man of medium height with a cool, authoritative look about him.

This man held out his hand and said, "Miss Biagi, I'm Commander Gibbs from the Serious and Organised Crime Agency and I have to ask you why you confronted Mr Ramsay this morning."

Although somewhat startled by this turn of events, Maurizia regained her composure and said, " I'm an accredited journalist and I was following up a lead…incidentally I would like to see some identification to establish you are who you say you are."

Gibbs gave her an appraising look, nodded with what seemed to her to be a grudging respect for her rejoinder and produced his warrant card which she took a few moments to inspect carefully. This gave her time to gather her thoughts. With mounting excitement, she realised that she had the makings of a real scoop if a high ranking police officer had jumped in so quickly after her brief conversation with Ramsay, then there must be some really big story here.

"Ms Biagi, please sit down," Commander Gibbs said matter of factly, "I need to ask you to stop probing into Mondo Foods. If you continue to do so you will put at risk a huge police operation and possibly allow some very nasty people to escape justice."

"But I'm a journalist and I have a right to follow up some leads I have."

"I know you are an excellent journalist and I also appreciate that you were instrumental in uncovering corporate tax evasion on a grand scale which enabled my European colleagues to prosecute a range of senior business people. If you hold off on this, I promise you that you will be the first reporter I will brief when we have put this massive police operation to bed. You will definitely have a very big scoop."

"And if I don't comply with your request?"

"I will then have no option but to get a judicial restraining order to prohibit you from any further work on this…and you will certainly not be first in the queue when the case goes public."

Maurizia digested this and then blurted out, "Is Major Bruno Canepa involved in this investigation?"

Commander Gibbs lost his *sang froid* momentarily but quickly recomposed his features and asked quietly, "Why do you ask?"

"Because a source indicated that he might be…"

"Would that source be your sister?"

It was Maurizia's turn to be wrong footed. "Gina?…How could she tell me?…Is she involved in this?"

From her obvious genuine surprise, Commander Gibbs immediately realised that he had jumped to the wrong conclusion. He tried to soft pedal.

"No…it's just that I know she and Major Canepa are close and I thought you and she may have been speculating about what he was working on."

"So is he or isn't he involved in this?" asked Maurizia.

At this point Commander Gibbs seemed to decide to adopt a totally non-committal stance.

"Ms Biagi, I can't discuss any aspect of this case with you. All I can do is call upon your sense of justice and good citizenship and ask you to accede to my request to back off. I repeat that if you do that I will guarantee that very soon you will get a mammoth exclusive story out of this."

Maurizia decided not to press any further and simply said that she'd noted Commander Gibb's request and would consider her position. Although far from satisfied with this neutral response, he realised that he'd better not push her for a more definitive commitment. He knew she was a very determined and resourceful woman and he did not want to risk antagonising her. He stood up and held out his hand. "Thankyou for listening and I'm sure you'll think very seriously about what I've told you."

Maurizia nodded and shook his proffered hand. "Thankyou Commander and good afternoon to you and to you too, Mr Ramsay."

She sat in her car in the hotel car park for a good fifteen minutes mulling over this strange encounter. There was clearly a very big operation under-way. Why else would a top policeman drop everything and hurry out to Ascot to warn her off. She was conflicted as to the right course of action. She was more public spirited than most but her journalistic instincts were deeply entrenched – and she had also inherited the Biagi stubbornness gene. She wanted to be proactive rather than wait for the promised exclusive. But she did not wish to do anything that could rebound adversely on Bruno and therefore indirectly on her sister.

In the end, her journalistic curiosity won a partial victory. She decided that she would not do anything too overtly regarding Sir Roger Simmons but she would continue to do some desk research. She would also have another chat with her financial analyst friend, George Mellon. She wanted to stay ahead of the game. She had a strong inkling that her sister Gina knew something about this intriguing situation. When she got home she rang Gina to see if she fancied a drink that evening. Gina was free so they met in their favourite pub, The Prince Albert in Primrose Hill. Never one to beat about the bush, as soon as they were seated with their drinks, Maurizia said, "Do you know anything about Mondo Foods and in particular its chairman, Sir Roger Simmons?"

Gina almost gagged on her gin and tonic and gave her sister a pointedly quizzical look. "What…Why do you ask?"

"Well, I have a source who seems to think that something illegal is going on there and Simmons may be involved."

Gina took a reflective sip of her drink and putting her glass down a little more firmly than she had intended she leaned towards her sister and said, very quietly but firmly, "Maurizia I know you are a damned good journalist but I have to ask you to back off from digging any further into this. If you continue to do so you might jeopardise my relationship with Mondo, one of my key clients."

"I'm sure you know something…"

"No, I don't and that's all I'm going to say about it…Now, let's talk about something else." Maurizia knew she would not get any more out of Gina so they continued to chat about family matters over another round of drinks. But clearly neither of their hearts were in it. Maurizia was itching to get back to her computer. Far from warning her off, Gina had whetted her sister's appetite even more to get under the skin of Mondo. For her part, Gina wanted to phone Bruno to alert him to the worrying news that his investigation was not as watertight as he thought.

Before parting Gina said as forcefully as she could, "Maurizia please hold off looking into Mondo Foods. I promise you, you could do a lot of harm."

Maurizia smiled sweetly at her sister, nodded vaguely and strode off to her flat just round the corner. When Gina got home she immediately phoned Bruno and told him about her strained conversation with her sister. His response was unexpected. "Yes I know, *cara*. Maurizia has picked up some leads on Sir Roger Simmons and Commander Gibbs tried to warn her off earlier today…Obviously that didn't work so we may have to get her editor to put a stop to whatever she's up to."

Gina was very annoyed that her sister had not told her what had happened earlier with Commander Gibbs. She and Maurizia had always been highly competitive but they were really close. Mingled with Gina's irritation was a sense of hurt that her sister had not come clean with her.

For her part, Maurizia felt a bit guilty about keeping her cards close to her chest but she overrode this by reminding herself that there was a real scoop to be had here and the end justified the means. Later that evening she had an idea about how she might do some more digging without getting into trouble with Commander Gibbs.

A couple of years earlier she had passed on some valuable information to the Fraud Squad about a major UK company breaching UN sanctions by trading with Iran. She had dealt with a super-bright young Detective Sergeant called Mark Lord who had joined the police as a graduate entrant. Maurizia's input was of material help in the Squad's successful prosecution of the company. She and Mark had met up a few times since for a drink and she thought he would be happy to do a bit of quiet checking for her if she told him it was ultra-sensitive.

She picked up the phone and dialled his number…

18 FEBRUARY 2011

MODENA, EMILIA-ROMAGNA

Sergeant Bassoli left the apartment on the outskirts of Modena feeling very pleased with himself. After two days of careful surveillance he had finally interviewed a production worker from the Sacra Corona Unita team at Sapore Senza Pari and tapped in to a rich vein of intelligence on the plans to ramp up the illegal drug smuggling operation.

Matteo Michelini was in fact the foreman of the team working in the self-contained unit adding cocaine to bottles of olive oil. After carefully researching the backgrounds of all six members of the team, the *Guardia* had picked him out as the most likely to spill the beans in exchange for immunity from prosecution. By a serendipitous coincidence Michelini was one of the people on the long list, provided by the lawyer Moscatelli, of forced or voluntary people working with Sacra Corona Unita. Bruno had sent an email to Luca thanking him for his dossier and, as concrete proof of its usefulness, had appended the Moscatelli list. Luca had obviously run his eye over the names and alerted Bruno to the fact that he was worried about one particular individual called Michelini marked as a "forced" recruit.

Luca phoned Bruno, "My father had a manager in his olive oil business called Ernesto Michelini and other members of the same family worked in our winery. Ernesto was a man of unimpeachable integrity. He had three young sons and I'm pretty sure one of them was called Matteo, who would be in his mid-forties now. You should follow up on this to ascertain what hold the mafia had over him, assuming he's the person I think he is."

When one of his officers showed Bruno the list of the six men working on the SCU olive oil line at Sapore Senza Pari, Matteo Michelini's name jumped out at him. Further background checks confirmed that he was from Puglia and his father's name was indeed Ernesto. Michelini lived on his own during the week in a rented apartment in Modena but drove down to Lecce every Friday where he had a wife and a grown-up son. He had no criminal record but his son Giacomo had a fairly lengthy sheet of petty theft offences probably committed to finance his drug habit.

Bruno had told Sergeant Bassoli, "Observe Michelini's movements to map his daily routine and then confront him when you're sure he's alone in his apartment."

The sergeant had spent two hours with a totally acquiescent Michelini and reported back immediately to Bruno with chapter and verse on the current status and future direction of the drug trafficking operation at SSP.

"As soon as I told him that we knew he had been pressed into service by the mafia, he capitulated and told me that he had been planning to take flight with his family the following week. They were going to stay with a relative in the mountains above Trieste in an attempt to escape retribution from Sacra Corona Unita."

"Lucky we got to him in time then," said a relieved Bruno.

"Yes, apparently, a year or so earlier when he had been running a small olive oil bottling plant in Manduria, he had been approached by a local mafioso who had offered him a lot of money to take a job in a company in Modena. He knew there was something shady about the offer and he kicked the guy out of his office. The next day his wife received a chilling phone call from someone saying her son had murdered a local politician the previous month. This was a *cause celebre* in the press and was widely assumed to have been a mafia hit. The absence of any leads was yet another example of the code of silence we know so well in the mafia strongholds."

Bruno remembered the old Sicilian adage, "*Cu è surdu, orbu e toci, campa cent'anni 'mpaci*" or, He who is deaf, blind and silent will live a hundred years in peace.

Sergeant Bassoli continued, "The caller said there were three witnesses who would swear her son was the killer unless she could persuade her husband to accept the generous offer of employment they had made. When his terrified wife asked her son if he had been involved he swore his innocence. But because he had been on the fringes of the Puglian under-world he had no doubt that the mafia would follow through with their threat. His pitiful entreaties to his father that evening bore fruit. Their son was finally clean and well on the way to recovery from his drug problem and Matteo's paternal instinct was to protect him at all costs. He rang the number his wife had been given and said he would take the job at the company in Emilia Romagna. He had been at SSP since the previous January, taking over from a foreman who had been seriously injured in a bar brawl. Matteo knew they had picked him because he had the skills to increase output dramatically on the clandestine production line."

The sergeant confirmed that Michelini had spent a miserable year producing the cocaine in olive oil product that he knew would wreak untold damage on the lives of many people. He had seen at first-hand the disastrous impact drugs could have, not just on the addict, but on those closest to him or her. As he told Sergeant Bassoli, he had finally decided he could not continue to be involved in this filthy trade no matter what the risks might befor his family. If the Sergeant had arrived a week later than he did, he would have missed him. Michelini said when he had made it to Trieste, he planned to tip off the authorities about what was going on at SSP.

The Sergeant clearly believed him and when Bruno heard his report he was relieved that Michelini had not had the chance to alert the police to the SSP operation. Any unilateral action by local law enforcement could have ruined Operation Achilles, the coordinated masterplan of arrests in several countries to which Bruno and Commander Gibbs were putting the final touches.

On Friday, 18 February, Bruno and Sergeant Bassoli were burning the midnight oil in the *Guardia's* offices in Viale Piersanti Mattarella in Modena. Adriano Bassoli was Bruno's most trusted officer and he was the only one of his unit to know the full story of the Mondo and SCU connection. Adriano had just finished the first part of his report on his meeting with Michelini.

"OK, Adriano, I see that you think this man is a good guy forced to do a bad thing but did you get anything tangible on the SSP operation that we didn't already know or suspect."

"Yes Sir. I got some concrete details on the timetable for a big increase in the volume of drugs shipped to France, Spain and Germany. They have already had a dummy run with the plastic crates, which as you surmised, had heroin implants and this went off without a hitch. In a couple of weeks – in fact on Tuesday 1st March – they will press the button on a tripling of their drug volumes with a combination of the crates and the specially doctored chilli oil bottles. Michelini told me that the new *Direttore Generale,* Vittore Santoro, had just started and that everyone in the clandestine production team, even hardened mafiosi, were very wary of him. They knew he was the son of the biggest cheese in the SCU and he seemed to be on a hair trigger, erupting into a violent rage at the smallest hiccup in the operation. One of the older bottling machines needed a spare part and when Michelini told the Operations Manager, Guerini, that it would be inoperative for at least 72 hours he said the man went white. Within ten minutes an incandescent Santoro was literally frothing at the mouth as he screamed at Michelini that unless he had the machine up and running by the next day he would be dead meat. Michelini said that Santoro himself seemed terrified at the prospect of anything going wrong with the big hike in production volumes."

"So what happened, Adriano?"

"Well, luckily Michelini managed to cannibalise another spare, even older machine and get the part he needed. But, Major, that was the incident which accelerated the decision Michelini had already made to get the hell out of there and take his family as far away as he could get from these maniacs."

"Great work, Adriano…but you need to go back to Michelini and tell him to grit his teeth and stick it out for a little longer. Tell him we need someone on the inside to make sure we have accurate intel on the production and shipping schedules. Get him to report in to you on a daily basis."

"OK, Sir. I think he will welcome the chance to do anything to help nail these bastards who have threatened his family."

"Good. You can tell him that we will do everything we can to make sure he will not face prosecution for his involvement in the bottling operation as he clearly had a gun held to his head to force him to do it."

22 FEBRUARY 2011

SILVERDALE, LANCASHIRE

Luca Biagi's mind was in turmoil. His normally upbeat personality was so muted following his phone conversation with Bruno a few days earlier that Rosalba was seriously concerned about him.

"Are you ill *caro*?" she asked anxiously as, for the umpteenth time, he did not respond to her attempts at conversation.

"What?"…He replied abstractedly, "Yes, I do feel a bit under the weather but it's probably a touch of flu. Don't fret…I'll be fine in a day or two."

But a few days went by and he became even more distant and depressed with no sign of any physical ailment. One evening, as she walked into his study with a cup of coffee for him, she saw him slumped at his desk with tears streaming down his face. Alarmed, she rushed over and hugged him tightly. "Come on *carissimo* this won't do…You'll have to tell me what on earth's going on…Is the business in trouble or what?"

Luca composed himself, sat up straight, held her hands and looked through moist eyes at this beautiful woman he loved more with each passing year.

"It's nothing to do with the business but something from my past has come to haunt me…I really can't talk about it."

"Of course, you can. You can tell me anything. I love you and I simply can't bear to see you so unhappy. It's breaking my heart."

Luca swallowed and suddenly the floodgates opened and the whole story poured out of him…His one night stand with Antonella, the shattering recent disclosure by his terminally ill friend that he had a son. The nightmare discovery about what his son had become. But he couldn't bring himself to tell Rosalba about Gina's involvement with Vittore Santoro. He hadn't fully processed the implications of this himself and he was tormented by the thought of Gina discovering the part she was playing in the destruction of her half-brother.

When he had finished his incredible story, he looked rather anxiously at his wife not knowing quite what reaction to expect. But spontaneously she pulled him towards her and kissed him tenderly.

"Oh my poor darling, you've been bottling all this up for days. Why didn't you tell me earlier? I'm so sorry to hear about your son. He has been formed into what he is by the vicious environment he has grown up in. It has absolutely nothing to do with you. You have fathered two wonderful daughters and taught them to live good and honourable lives. If Vittore Santoro had had your guiding fatherly hand, he would have turned out just as well."

To Luca's great relief she said. "Let's keep this to ourselves…No point in upsetting Gina and Maurizia."

The next morning Luca woke up with a start. He had slept so soundly after unburdening himself to Rosalba that he woke an hour later than his customary 6.30. It was the insistent buzzing of his mobile phone that had woken him. He got out of bed, padded over to the dressing table and picked up the phone.

"Hello, Luca Biagi." A familiar voice replied in Italian. "*Buongiorno* Signor Biagi, I hope I didn't wake you. It's Luca Colangelo here. I'm afraid I have some bad news. My *papà* died last night having gone downhill very fast in the last few days."

"Oh my God Luca...I'm so sorry. I've been dreading this since I met your dad in Paris last month."

"Yes...We are all very upset here. He was a great dad and a wonderful granddad...But you should know *Signor* Biagi that meeting you again after so many years gave my father an enormous amount of pleasure. I can't tell you how many times he mentioned you when I was growing up. Shortly before he died he gave me your number and asked me to ring you personally to let you know of his passing."

"Thankyou, Luca. I've missed his companionship since I left Puglia but nothing can erase the wonderful store of memories about the times we had in our younger days."

The tears were now coursing down Luca's cheeks and he had difficulty pulling himself together to ask when the funeral would be held.

"It's scheduled for Friday 25th February at the Basilica di Santa Croce in Lecce and after the interment in the *Cimitero* everyone will come back to our house for food and drink."

Without a moment's hesitation, Luca said. "I'll be there...I must pay my respects to my oldest friend."

"It will be a great pleasure to meet you and it would be a comfort to me to share some of your memories of my father as a young man. You must, of course, stay with us when you are here, so please let me know your travel plans."

Both of them were too upset to engage in further conversation so they said their goodbyes having exchanged email addresses.

****

So it was that the following Thursday lunchtime, for the first time in close to forty years, Luca Biagi stepped on to home soil – or more precisely via an air bridge into the Arrivals hall at the *Aeroporto Internazionale di Napoli*. He had researched various flight options to Bari and Brindisi, the two closest airports to Lecce but none of these were ideal. He therefore opted to fly British Airways from Gatwick to Naples, pick up a hire car and drive the 400 plus kilometres to Lecce. Luca Colangelo had insisted he stay with them on the Thursday and Friday nights and fly back to London on Saturday. The

Colangelo's house was in a village called Acaya, not far from his *nonna*'s house in San Cataldo. After nearly five hours at the wheel Luca pulled into the drive of a very imposing, white, modern split-level house with huge floor to ceiling windows set in a lovely olive grove. Before he had opened the car door an exact replica of his friend Bernardo bounded down the exterior stone staircase and stood with his arms open wide in welcome. The poignancy of seeing his old friend reincarnated in this way brought a tear to Luca's eye. As they embraced he knew with cast iron certainty that he wanted this young man to be part of his life from now on.

Ushered into the unusual house's cavernous open plan living space, Luca marque 2 introduced his stunningly beautiful wife Fabiola, who looked uncannily like a young Gina Lollobrigida, and their two children, Nico and Ariana. After freshening up, Luca joined the family for a pre-dinner drink. At the start, the atmosphere was muted in anticipation of the events of the following day but Luca's recounting of some of his and Bernardo's more amusing youthful escapades helped to lighten the mood. Young Nico was particularly tickled to hear about when his much loved *nonno* had crashed his scooter into a tree whilst wildly distracted by a bee which had somehow buzzed into his ear. Nico's father was very taken with Luca's accounts of their many trips on *Il Delfino*.

"Yes, *papà* really loved that boat and some of my happiest times were spent pottering about on it…It's still fully seaworthy and he has bequeathed it to me and Nico to continue to enjoy."

Whilst Fabiola was putting the kids to bed, Luca Colangelo ran through the funeral arrangements. "*Papà* was a very important and popular figure in Puglian society so, although he was not particularly religious I thought it fitting to have the service in the Basilica di Santa Croce. There will be a very big turnout and, as you know this is one of the largest and also, in my view the most beautiful of the churches in Lecce."

"Yes, I know it well…that sounds very fitting."

"Signor Biagi, it would please me greatly if you would agree to be one of the pall bearers…"

"Please…call me Luca and of course I will. It will be an honour."

"*Grazie mille*. You will know that it's customary to have an open casket so mourners can kiss the deceased but I've decided not to do this. *Papà*, was so debilitated at the end that I don't want people to remember him like that. Instead on the casket there will be a large photo of him at the helm of *Il Delfino* before he was taken ill."

Luca nodded, reflecting on how shocked he'd been when he saw Bernardo in Paris. He was pleased at his son's sensitivity in defying convention.

"After the church service, a motor cortege will travel the short distance to the *Cimiterio* in Lecce, near the Porta di Napoli, where my dad will be laid to rest in the family mausoleum. After that close friends and family will come back here for some refreshments."

That night Luca slept badly and woke with a very heavy heart. The day's events proceeded with a solemn grandeur. He marvelled at the huge throng who crammed themselves into the vast interior of the Basilica. He knew that Bernardo had been a popular figure but the size of the congregation staggered him. He had also forgotten how truly beautiful was this famous church with its richly decorated baroque façade and its ceiling of gilded wood.

The interment in the Colangelo family tomb was a much more intimate affair with about thirty people there and afterwards the mourners set off for the Colangelo house. Luca had agreed with Luca marque 2 that he would not socialise with the other mourners at the evening reception. He had confided in the young man the reasons for his forced departure from Italy. He had explained that it was likely someone had recognised him at the funeral and he did not want to run the risk of them asking about his new life and whereabouts. If anyone asked, they should be told that he was unwell.

As Luca had predicted, his prominent role as a pall bearer had caused one member of the congregation to question the flash of recognition he had just experienced. The old lawyer Moscatelli had not been sure it was the man he knew as Luca Vento as his view was partly obscured. But as the pallbearers paused by the main entrance to the Basilica, he manoeuvred himself to get a clear view and his initial suspicion was confirmed. It was indeed the bastard who had blighted the final years of his comfortable life. When he got home, Moscatelli sat quietly in his home office hell bent on finding a way to exact vengeance on that man. He knew he would have to tread carefully. He wanted to alert his mafia contacts to Luca's re-emergence, but he had to be sure that there was no risk that it would rebound negatively on him given his recent involuntary relationship with the forces of law and order. In the end, he decided that the least risky route would be to have a quiet drink with Ottavio Palumbo, the businessman who was closest to Arturo Santoro, the most powerful mafia *capo* he knew. Santoro had gone to ground but the lawyer knew that Palumbo would be able to contact him as he had already acted as a conduit for some information Santoro had demanded of Moscatelli. He was sure Santoro was the man to give him the revenge he craved. He had heard many times of his pathological hatred of informers and he knew Santoro had disposed of, in the most brutal way possible, anyone he suspected of being a "grass".

Palumbo would simply have to tell Santoro that this was the guy who had escaped their clutches all those years ago and Santoro would ruthlessly ensure this omission was rectified. But first, Moscatelli needed to find out where Luca Vento was living now. It was widely believed that he had fled Italy but apart from some rumours that he had gone to Argentina no one had seen hide nor hair of him for nearly forty years.

As he had not been invited to the post-funeral reception he couldn't do any digging himself. But he suddenly remembered that one of his younger cousins was on the board of Transmeridionale, Bernardo Colangelo's company and he was probably on the invitation list. He called him on his mobile and discovered that he was just parking outside Luca Colangelo's house. Moscatelli told his cousin that he thought he had seen someone in the church, one of the pall bearers, who used to be a close friend. If he was right, he was keen to reconnect with him but wanted to keep it a surprise. He asked his cousin to see if he could quietly ascertain whether Luca Vento had been carrying Bernardo's casket and where he was living now.

Later that evening Moscatelli received a call.

"Hello Giuseppe, I think you must be mistaken. I spoke to Fabiola, Bernardo's daughter-in-law and she said that the old family friend who had agreed to be one of the pall bearers was called Luca Biagi. She was not sure where he was living now but she knew he had flown in to Naples the previous day and driven down to Lecce."

Moscatelli knew then that Luca Vento had assumed a new identity since his flight from Puglia. He also felt sure that his mafia associates would have their own contacts in the airline business who could unearth passenger details for incoming flights to Naples within the past twenty-four hours.

Moscatelli called Ottavio Palumbo and asked if they could meet for a drink as he had some tickets to give him for the next match of the local football team, *Unione Sportiva* Lecce. This was a pre-agreed signal that he had a message to pass on to Santoro and did not want to risk saying more on the phone in case the police were listening in.

They agreed to meet in the cocktail bar of the Patria Palace Hotel in Lecce at nine that evening.

24 FEBRUARY 2011

LONDON

"'Ello Roger, eez me." Sir Roger Simmons had picked up the phone in his riverside penthouse near Chelsea Harbour. The ex-directory number was known only to a tiny group of his underworld contacts and was, in effect, his emergency hotline.

Simmons recognised immediately the heavily accented, coarse voice of Elio Doronzo who was the *capo* of the London offshoot of Sacra Corona Unita. He was a direct beneficiary of the Italian Government's misguided policy of *Soggiorno Obbligato*. Under the aegis of this social experiment his family had been relocated to Turin from Calabria in the late nineteen sixties following his father's release from jail for extortion. Far from going straight, his father had founded the Turin branch of the 'Ndrangheta and the young Elio had followed in his footsteps eventually moving to London and acting as the UK "agent" for the combined criminal operations of the 'Ndrangheta and SCU.

It was Doronzo who had, through his big investment in male and female prostitution, discovered Sir Roger's predilection for brutalising young rent boys. On one occasion, in a brothel run by Doronzo's clan, Sir Roger was caught on film viciously beating a small, defenceless youth, little more than a boy. He died a few hours later and was casually dumped in the Thames in a heavily weighted sack by one of Doronzo's men.

The totally unemotional way in which he had responded when Doronzo had shown him the video gave the mafia *capo* a great idea. He recognised that Simmons had an evil core and he persuaded his cousin Arturo Santoro that his company Mondo Foods could furnish them with an unparalleled supply chain infrastructure for their fast developing drug trafficking business. This was a much better strategy than the original plan to blackmail him for a large amount of money.

Sir Roger's enforced collaboration had proved to be of inestimable bene-fit. He had shown a remarkable aptitude for criminality. He seemed able effortlessly to compartmentalise his ongoing high visibility corporate career from his ruthless prosecution of SCU's agenda. Doronzo realised that Simmons and Santoro were cut from the same cloth except Simmons had a better tailor to camouflage his psychopathic inclinations. With Simmons' help Santoro was able to ramp up SCU's drug trafficking operation at a staggering rate and also lay the foundations for explosive future growth.

Simmons knew that the call he had just received must be urgent as Doronzo had never phoned him at home before and he was jolted by what he heard next.

"One of the senior peegs on our payroll just called to tella me something that we need to sort out *immediatamente*. He's a Detective Inspector in the Fraud Squad. 'E was acting as Duty Officer today and was monitoring all incoming calls and information received from the public. One of 'is team got a call from a journalist asking if 'e had heard anything not quite kosher goin' on at Mondo Foods. Thees copper *ovviamente* knew the journalist and seemed keen to 'elp…so he did a file search and came up with *niente*. Our man saw thees on the log and got the name of the journalist. The slag is called Maurizia Biagi and apparently she's made quite a name for herself as a successful investigator of corporate fraud. Our tame peeg thinks she's just sniffing around without anything concrete on us but we can't afford to let 'er do any more deeging."

Sir Roger almost choked when he heard the name Biagi. "Christ, I bet that's a relative of the consultant we hired to put a gloss on the SSP recruitment before we shoehorned Vittore into the job there. She's called Gina Biagi…it's too much of a coincidence. She must have smelled a rat when we pushed Vittore forward ahead of the other candidates she had found. Shit!…We need to confirm that they are related and then we need to eliminate them as a potential threat. Understood?"

"*D'accordo*," said Doronzo with cold-blooded finality.

∗∗∗∗

Later in Rome, Bruno picked up his mobile phone which was bleeping insistently on the bedside table. He blearily registered that it was 1 a.m.

"Oh *ciao* George, what's up?"

"Bruno, I think we have a problem and may need to press the button on the Mondo operation pretty damn quick."

The Commander explained that their tapping of Sir Roger's phones had produced a disturbing new angle.

"Listen to this Bruno. It's a recording of a conversation last evening between an unidentified man and Sir Roger." He pressed a button and Bruno heard the chilling interchange starting with, "'Ello Roger, it's me…"

His blood ran cold as he listened to the rasping tones of the caller identifying both Maurizia and Gina as potential threats who must be eliminated. Bruno was now wide awake with adrenaline pumping through his body.

"George, we have to protect both of them for a few days while we finalise the multiple arrest operation."

"Already in hand Bruno…don't worry, I've already posted experienced armed officers outside their flats. First thing in the morning I'm going to have them both brought to one of the safe houses we use for our witness protection programme. I'll impress on them that they need to be sequestered for a few days until we can execute all our arrest warrants across Europe in one fell swoop."

"George, I'll come to London tomorrow to coordinate everything with you…by the way, any idea who the caller to Sir Roger was…he seemed to have a strong Italian accent."

"We are sure it's SCU's senior henchman in London, Elio Doronzo. We've been investigating him for some time but he's a pretty canny character. So far we've got nothing concrete on him because he always puts himself at one remove from any thuggery he's initiated. Also, you well know the problem of getting anyone in the criminal fraternity to give us useful info.

"What are you going to do about the bent copper he mentioned in the Fraud Squad…?"

"Well, that's given us a possible way of trapping Doronzo into doing something visibly criminal. We are going to feed this bent Inspector whose name is Nailsworth with some information about a potentially dangerous development affecting Mondo which should bring Doronzo into our net."

"George, I'm really sorry that Maurizia has jumped into this with both feet. I know Gina has told her nothing, so she must have picked up something from her extensive contacts in the business world and European law enforcement. But I don't think she has compromised our operation or has got anything concrete about Mondo as Simmons and his caller seem to think she was just on a fishing expedition."

"I agree Bruno and we are so close to pulling the trigger on the whole exercise that as long as we keep the girls safe and incommunicado we can still go for our planned 'D Day' of next Tuesday 1st March."

26 FEBRUARY 2011
ARAGNO, ABRUZZO

"What news?" Santoro wheezed into the phone. He had a bad cold and his arthritis was playing up. His mood was very dark after several secluded weeks in the rainy Apennines. His trusted associate Ottavio Palumbo was calling him. Before bolting from Puglia Santoro had arranged for Palumbo to call him at 7 p.m. every other day on a pre-paid disposable burner phone. Santoro also had a stock of pre-paid phones and had given the number of the first one he intended to use to Palumbo before he left. At the end of each call he would give his associate the number of a new phone and two days later Magarelli would call that number also using a new burner phone. In addition to these elaborate precautions to avoid police intercepts, Santoro would drive at least 50 kilometres from his hideout near L'Aquila in a different direction each time to a secluded spot to take these calls.

"Arturo, I saw Moscatelli last night and he thought you'd like to know something. Remember back in the seventies you tried to snuff out a young lawyer working in Moscatelli's office in Lecce who was planted by that bastard magistrate in Brindisi who you managed to kill."

"You mean the guy who got away to Argentina...yeah...I do remember. I was the *capo* who was asked to find him and whack him. It really pissed me off that he somehow got away. What was his name...Venturi or something...?"

"No it was Vento...Luca Vento, but not anymore. According to that old woman Moscatelli who saw him at a funeral, he's changed his name to Biagi. We know he flew in from London last week and one of your guys put the strong arm on a girl in the BA ticket sales department at Naples Airport to find out more. We know he lives in the UK and we now have his home address."

"Just a minute...did you say Biagi...that's odd because my cousin in London who handles our business over there called Simmons at Mondo and told him he'd heard that a female reporter called Biagi had been sniffing around his business. Elio rang Vittore to tell him to pass this on to me and my son thought it important enough to motor down here from Modena to talk about it. It seems we have a problem because what my cousin Elio and Simmons have been able to piece together is that there are two Biagi sisters and these *puttane* could spell trouble for us."

"How do you mean?"

"Well, one of them, was a consultant hired by Mondo who had a run in with Vittore when he was being slotted into the SSP job. The other bitch, Maurizia, is an experienced journalist with the *Financial Times* who has uncovered some big cases of corporate fraud in the past. We can't risk anyone poking around in our business so Doronzo will arrange for these two bitches to be eliminated. But before killing them I've told him via Vittore to extract whatever info they have on Mondo."

"OK, I understand."

"And another thing Ottavio, you also need to contact Elio on the number I gave you and get him to check with one of our tame coppers in the UK whether this Luca Biagi is related to these slags…though it doesn't really matter one way or the other because I want him killed anyway. I wasted a lot of time and manpower trying to track down that fucking grass in the seventies."

After the call, Santoro had the grim satisfaction of knowing he could tidy up a loose end that had nagged away at him over the years. When, in the seventies he had agreed with Franco Perugini to take his daughter's illegitimate baby, he had discovered that the child's father was none other than that young lawyer Vento who had simply vanished. Arturo and his men had spent many days in a fruitless search for him. They had even tapped into criminal contacts in Argentina to see if there had been any sightings of him there. The failure to locate Luca had not gone down well with Arturo's bosses in the Camorra. Even now Arturo still seethed at the vivid recollection of the humiliating public bollocking he had received. The corrosive impact of this had fuelled his hatred of Luca to a pathological level. In a weird way, knowing Luca was Vittore's father had intensified this implacable loathing. Somewhere in Arturo's twisted psyche was the feeling that the elimination of Luca would somehow expunge the connection between him and Vittore and reinforce Arturo's own undisputed "ownership" of his son. The fact that Luca's two daughters could be rubbed out as well was, in Arturo's warped mind, an unexpected bonus.

****

A little later that Friday evening, George Gibbs and Bruno Canepa were deep in discussion in the Commander's capacious kitchen in Windsor. They were putting the final touches to Operation Achilles, one of the biggest multi-country criminal dragnets ever attempted. They had decided to meet away from Scotland Yard to avoid even the remotest possibility of their conversation being overheard at this critical final stage.

In the twenty hours or so since their nocturnal phone call they had both been exceedingly busy. Bruno had arrived by taxi directly from Heathrow and after supper the Commander's wife Grace left them alone to work.

"Bruno, I'll brief you first on what I've set in motion to flush out Doronzo so that we can arrest him. The bent Inspector who tipped Doronzo off is called Glenn Nailsworth and on Monday I'm going to copy him in on a limited circulation top priority bulletin I've fabricated. This purports to inform a rota of four Inspectors that they will head a close protection unit guarding two females who are at serious risk from unspecified criminals. Each Inspector will be expected to spend a six-hour shift in the safe house where the women are being held. A note of the address of the safe house will be delivered by hand to each man and I'm sure that Nailsworth will be on the blower immediately to Doronzo to give him the location. By then Doronzo will have realised that Maurizia and Gina have gone to ground. In his attempts to nab them he'll discover that they have not been seen since this morning and no one in their respective organisations has any clue as to their whereabouts."

"But George," interjected an apprehensive Bruno, "you can't put the girls at risk in that way…"

"Come on, Bruno, you know me better than that surely. Your Gina and her sister won't be at that address. I'm going to put a couple of youngish female detectives in the house who are specialist undercover operators with the Mersyside force so Nailsworth won't recognise them. What I anticipate will happen is that Doronzo's men, or maybe even Doronzo himself, will extract the women during Nailsworth's shift and take them somewhere else to interrogate them. I'll schedule his shift to start at 6 a.m. on Tuesday morning so that Doronzo's arrest is synchronised with our big swoop and doesn't risk tipping off Simmons. We will have the house surrounded and will also have mobile surveillance teams on motorbikes and in unmarked vehicles to follow the two detectives once they are extracted. They will be wearing wires so we can hear if they need immediate help. As soon as they arrive at their destination we'll swoop and nab the kidnappers, hopefully including Doronzo…What do you think?"

"Not sure I can come up with a better option but we need a big team to ensure these villains don't get the chance to hurt your undercover officers. Also we need to brief the teams as close as possible to Nailsworth's shift so that he doesn't get wind of the operation. But what if they don't go for the girls during his first shift? That will increase the chances of Nailsworth sussing something's going on."

"Good point. So what we could do is stress that this safe house will only be used for 24 hours and after that other steps will be taken to transfer the women to a location a long way from London."

"OK...that's better. What else is new?"

"Well, we now have some concrete evidence to use against that creepy Mondo HR guy, Williamson. When we briefed Mondo's new CEO Adam Palfrey on our investigation into Ramsay, we mentioned that Williamson was also bent and Palfrey has come up with something that implicates him in a serious criminal act. Like all the big companies, Mondo has an internal audit department and the head of this reports directly to the CEO. Palfrey's Director of Internal Audit alerted him to the fact that Williamson probably profited from insider dealing in Mondo shares."

"That's great!"

"Yes, last summer when Simon Ramsay was still CEO, the Mondo Group reported a big hike in pre-tax profits which triggered a substantial rise in the share price. Three weeks before the public announcement and in the closed period for company directors to trade in company stock, £500,000 worth of stock was purchased in the name of Geoffrey Hepworth."

"OK, why's that significant?"

"I'll tell you...Two weeks after the annual results were announced this holding was sold at a profit of £80,000. When the internal audit guy spotted this transaction on the share register it prompted him to do a bit of digging. By a flukey coincidence he discovered that Hepworth was well known in London gay circles and was frequently featured in photos taken in gay clubs. In one photo he found on Hepworth's Facebook site he was startled to see this man with his arms clamped around the neck of Charles Williamson. The gossip in Mondo was that Williamson was gay and that he had a long-term gay partner. This was the point at which the audit guy told Palfrey of his suspicions that this instance of what was technically "outsider trading" looked dodgy and he didn't want to go any further because of the extreme sensitivity of the situation given Williamson's senior position. When Palfrey told us,we were able to get a court order to examine Hepworth's bank account and, bingo, what did we discover? On 1st August last year £80,000 was transferred to the account of our man Charles Williamson."

"Is that enough to get him, do you think?" Bruno asked.

"Probably, but my expectation is that when we arrest Simmons and Williamson sees the writing is on the wall, he'll be keen to reduce his own vulnerability by spilling the beans on a lot of the illicit stuff that Simmons was engaged in."

"*Va bene*. He will be able to corroborate a lot of what we already know or suspect...Now, I need to fill you in on what I've been up to."

Bruno then ran through the finalisation of all the European and Interpol Arrest Warrants for the coordinated police swoop, timed for 0700 GMT on Tuesday 1 March. There were in all 293 Warrants encompassing people in Italy, Greece, Hungary, Albania, France, Tunisia and the UK. These covered everyone from Simmons and the Santoros to SCU *capos* and soldiers, corrupt customs officers in various ports and production workers and drivers in several locations. Thanks to Moscatelli's meticulous records the list also included local and national politicians, businessmen and police officers in Puglia and elsewhere.

"The only thing we can't do yet is net the biggest fish of all, Arturo Santoro. An intensive search operation by my own men and the *Carabinieri* has failed to locate him. He seems to have vanished into thin air. We don't even know if he's still in Italy and we've picked up absolutely nothing from our most sophisticated satellite phone monitoring efforts."

"Well Bruno he's bound to surface sooner or later and in any case we are dismantling his entire extended criminal network so he won't be able to regenerate anything...He'll be marked as the most wanted man in Europe."

"I know, but I can't help feeling gutted that we've let this ultra-dangerous thug slip through our fingers."

Bruno paused and looked quizzically at Commander Gibbs before continuing.

"OK, George, I'm going to share with you an idea I've had to nab him. Next Tuesday morning at 0730 continental time, before we carry out the multiple arrests, we can arrange for Moscatelli to call one or two of his SCU contacts. He'll say that one of his senior *Carabinieri* 'friends' has got wind of a big police operation focussed on Sapore Senza Pari and that Vittore is on the list of people to be arrested later that morning...so he needs to be told to get the hell out of there immediately. I'll have my Sergeant Bassoli sit with Moscatelli when he makes these calls to make sure he sticks to the script...and to make sure that these calls don't cause any ripples outwards to any of the people on our full arrest sheet, I'll get all the arrest squads on the continent to be in position well before we press the button. I will lead the surveillance team tracking Vittore myself. What I will also do is get one of our specialists to attach a couple of small transmitters to Vittore's car on either Sunday or Monday. Sergeant Bassoli has confirmed that, during his recent reconnaissance in Modena, he inspected the block of flats where Vittore is living during the week. He discovered that for the last two weeks he had driven up there from Puglia each Sunday evening. My assumption is that when he scarpers he will head for his father's hideout to work out an escape plan – so we can then collar both of them."

Bruno paused for breath after rattling through this plan, "What do you think, George?"

"It's risky Bruno. What if you lose Vittore? We'll then have failed to grab two of the three major criminals we've been pursuing."

"I accept that there are risks but I can't think of any other way of catching the biggest prize of all, Arturo Santoro, and cutting off the head of one of the largest mafia tribes in Italy. If I get my *Comandante Generale* to back me, I'll take full personal responsibility for this course of action."

28 FEBRUARY 2011

SILVERDALE, LANCASHIRE

In a layby close to the M6 north of Lancaster, an Albanian man was asleep in the fully reclined front seat of a stolen BMW. It was 6 a.m. on Monday 28 February and he had driven up the M1 and M6 late the previous evening after one of Elio Doronzo's men had delivered the car to him in Islington with its newly switched number plates.

The Albanian was Doronzo's hit-man and had already snuffed out five people on the Italian *capo's* orders, although he had never met his employer. Careful as ever, Doronzo always used his most trusted lieutenant to contact the assassin with instructions for the hit and a down payment of £10,000. The balance of £10,000 was paid when the hit was confirmed. The Albanian's name was Leka Dragusha and he had been in the UK for three years on false papers. He had to leave Tirana in a hurry after he was fingered for the killing of the head of a rival mafia clan. Arturo Santoro had collaborated with Dragusha's clan in drug and people smuggling activities and he arranged for this cold-blooded executioner to be transplanted to London to become a valuable asset for his cousin Doronzo. Santoro had sent instructions for this particular hit via his friend Palumbo. Dragusha had set his mobile phone alarm for 0700 and when it peeped he immediately raised his seat and turned the key in the ignition of the powerful saloon.

Within five minutes he was cruising past Luca and Rosalba Biagi's house on the outskirts of the village of Silverdale. It was still quite dark and it was drizzling. He had decided to do a quick recce and then enter the house and kill Luca and if necessary his wife if she got in the way. The road was deserted and he was about to park and put on his grotesque face mask when he saw in his rear view mirror the Biagi's porch light go on. The front door opened and Luca emerged in running gear and a bobble hat and started to do some stretching exercises. Dragusha smiled and knew he would not now have to break into the house which was always a risky manoeuvre. He could simply use his car as a weapon and then drive away. Luca took a few minutes to complete his warm-up routine and then ran purposefully into the road. He passed Dragusha's car giving it a curious glance as he jogged by. The Albanian let him run on for about two hundred yards and then gunned the V6 engine and rocketed towards him. The car hit Luca with a sickening crunch and threw him into the air and over the roof of the vehicle until he landed on the grass verge. Dragusha screeched to a halt and was about to get out to ensure Luca was dead when he saw a truck coming towards him. He was sure no one could have survived the impact of such a collision so he slammed the car door and took off with tyres screeching.

****

Three hours later there was a knock on Gina's door at the safe house in Cockfosters where she and Maurizia had been deposited the previous day. It was one of the police officers guarding them who said. "Can you come downstairs please, we need to talk to you and your sister."

Gina was already dressed and went down to the kitchen where she saw a very apprehensive looking Maurizia and a grim-faced plain clothes policeman in a heavy overcoat who had clearly come specially to talk to them.

"I'm afraid I have some bad news to give you," he said without preamble. "Your father has been involved in a hit and run incident and is in hospital in Lancaster in a critical condition. Your mother tried to call you but obviously couldn't reach you as we have kept both your mobiles switched off. She found Major Canepa's number in your father's phone log and called him instead."

"What…How did it happen?" Both sisters started talking simultaneously.

"That's all the information we have at the moment but Commander Gibbs has said you can talk to your mother on a secure line from here."

Stunned, the sisters looked at each other with tears welling up in their eyes. Since arriving at the house they had not spoken. Gina had been too angry with her sister to say anything and Maurizia had decided to keep a low profile until her sister had simmered down. Now all that was forgotten as they clung to each other.

"Which phone can we use?" Gina asked quietly.

One of the officers handed her a nondescript Nokia cell phone. Gina keyed in her mother's mobile number and tried to compose herself but as soon as she heard her *mamma's* voice her own voice cracked and she blurted out, "How is *papà*?"

"Not good, I'm afraid," Her mother replied in a weary, strained voice. "We don't really know what happened but it looks like your father was deliberately run down by a man in a stolen BMW. He sped off when Joe Higham, one of the local farmers drove up in his milk wagon."

"Is…will *papà* recover?"

"He has multiple external and internal injuries and they are operating on him at the moment to relieve some pressure on his brain. Joe got the ambulance very quickly and he had the good sense not to move your dad but just keep him warm with some blankets he had in his cab. The good thing is your *papa* landed on the grass verge after being thrown up in the air and we've had a lot of rain lately so the soft ground cushioned the impact."

Maurizia beckoned to Gina to give her the phone. "Hi *mamma*, I heard most of that and we are going to come up to Lancaster to be with you as soon as we can catch a train…"

She was stopped by the police officer in the overcoat waving his hand vigorously and saying, "Not possible I'm afraid, you must stay here for another couple of days."

Rosalba Biagi heard this interjection and Maurizia's loud, indignant reply, "You can't do that…we have to go?"

"Maurizia…Maurizia," her mother's insistent voice echoed from the mobile. "You must do as the officer says. Bruno has told me that both you and Gina are in danger and it will do no good at all to have me worrying about you two as well as your father if you break cover. Please darling, don't make a fuss. I promise I'll call you the moment I have any news. Please put that police officer back on the phone."

Maurizia knew better than to argue with her very strong-willed mother so she meekly passed the phone back to the policeman. He nodded in response to a request from Rosalba and said, "Yes, I'll leave this mobile phone here so that you can call anytime. The number is 07803 225295. OK...Thankyou Professor Biagi."

1 MARCH 2011

LONDON

Inspector Nailsworth was extremely edgy. It was 6.15 a.m. on Tuesday 1 March and he was sitting in the front room of a terraced house in Acton. He was asking himself why he had ever allowed himself to get involved with the murderous gangster Elio Doronzo, although he had to accept that he had been a bent copper for most of his career. He had been persuaded to take his first cash bung when he started out on the beat twenty years earlier. His sergeant at the time was in with a South London mob running an extensive protection racket and a big prostitution ring. The sergeant had been a father figure to the young constable whose wife had just had two kiddies in quick succession. The sergeant knew Nailsworth was desperately short of money and it was a doddle to get him to turn a blind eye to the rampant street hustling of the toms on his patch in exchange for a sizeable monthly wedge of cash.

Nailsworth thought initially that this was relatively harmless as no one was being hurt by it. It was simply a "live and let live" approach. But inexorably, as the years went by he became more and more entangled with the criminal fraternity and the blind-eye turning escalated to more active perversions of justice such as falsifying evidence and contaminating forensic samples.

When Doronzo appeared on the scene in 2005 the "services" expected of Nailsworth ramped up considerably, as did the size of his regular cash bungs. Nailsworth wanted out but he knew he was in too deep and had to dance to Doronzo's tune.

The previous evening, Nailsworth had been told the address of this safe house in Acton, West London where the Biagi sisters had been placed temporarily. He was told his six-hour shift would start at 6 a.m. the following morning. He immediately contacted Doronzo, who said, "OK, my guys will hit the house at exactly 6.30 and take the women."

There would be one other armed officer at the house, and Nailsworth's job was to distract him so that the kidnap squad could overpower him without risking a shootout. At 6.28 Nailsworth said to the junior officer, "Why don't you make us a brew?"

After he left for the kitchen at the rear of the house Nailsworth slipped to the front door and put it on the latch. A minute later three masked men crept in and, as pre-agreed, one of them hit Nailsworth hard in the face. When the other policeman came in carrying two mugs of tea he saw Nailsworth on the floor with a gun to his head, blood flowing from his nose and lips. Both policemen were disarmed and bound and gagged with masking tape.

Upstairs DS Rona Cartwright and DC Pippa Kerr were pretending to be in bed asleep and when an armed hooded man appeared in each of their bedrooms they put on a convincing act of being terrified. They were strong-armed downstairs and told to put on a coat over their night clothes before being shoved into the back of a transit van parked just outside with the engine running. The kidnappers had not thought to frisk the women for weapons or communication devices so Commander Gibbs and his team had caught all the exchanges between the intruders and his officers. The police-women were wearing watches which had micro-voice transmitters in them and a number of tiny GPS trackers had also been sewn into various items of their clothing. Those in their pyjama tops and overcoat lapels were working perfectly. In the control room Commander Gibbs was able to direct the following unmarked motor cycle and car police posse, maintaining a healthy distance between them and the transit. The van only drove a few miles northward, crossing the A40 and heading deep into the huge warren of light industrial buildings on the Park Royal estate. It stopped in the forecourt of a nondescript warehouse and the police listeners heard the warehouse doors being wheeled back, the van then being driven into the building and the large doors being slid shut.

"Bring those bitches over here." It was clearly the rasping voice of Elio Doronzo and Commander Gibbs breathed a sigh of relief that the plan to draw him into the open had worked.

Gibbs had heard enough and ordered the Inspector from CO19, The Met's Special Crime and Firearms unit, to have his men surround the building and ascertain alternative points of entry. Three minutes later he knew the building had two normal rear doors and two side doors. He ordered a synchronised hit with battering rams on all four doors and as the officers burst in he heard the Inspector scream, "Armed Police! Drop your weapons and get on the floor with your hands behind your head." A brief silence then Gibbs heard a single shot followed by a rapid fire fusillade from what sounded like the standard police weapon, the Heckler and Koch semi-automatic carbine.

"Inspector Hawes, status report please."

"OK, Commander, all secure. The two girls were being tied to chairs as we entered so that left only Doronzo and two others with their hands free. One silly sod tried to shoot it out with us. He's dead and one of my boys will have a bloody big bruise on his chest tomorrow. He was hit dead centre of his Kevlar vest, lucky bugger. We have Doronzo and three of his gang in custody."

"What about DS Cartwright and DC Kerr?"

"Both fine Sir…a couple of bruises on their wrists and arms but these Liverpudlians are made of tough stuff and I think they actually enjoyed the operation judging by the smiles on their faces."

1 MARCH 2011

MODENA, EMILIA-ROMAGNA

Shortly before 0800 on Tuesday 1 March, Bruno's radio phone crackled and Sergeant Bussoli said, "Major, Moscatelli made the scripted call to the two most senior *capos* left in Santoro's clan. They should be in contact with Vittore any minute now, Sir."

Bruno was in a battered looking but souped up Fiat Punto outside the building in Modena where Vittore Santoro had his rented apartment.

"*Va bene.* We fitted the tracker to his car last night so I'm ready to tail him." Bruno had also deployed unmarked back-up vehicles on the major exit routes from the city. He did not have long to wait. About fifteen minutes later, Vittore walked quickly out to his car, threw a large bag into the boot and joined the rush hour traffic on this grey, drizzly morning. Bruno radioed his men in the back-up cars to confirm their target was on the move and followed Vittore's grey Audi TT at a distance of a few hundred metres. Exiting the city, Vittore headed south-westward and Bruno realised he was not taking the *autostrada*, presumably to avoid being stopped at one of the toll stations if his number plate had already been widely circulated.

At around 0930, on the outskirts of Imola, the blip on Bruno's screen stopped moving forward. Vittore had obviously parked and after a few minutes Bruno, who had been hanging back about a kilometre, decided he had to get close enough for visual confirmation that Vittore was still in the vehicle. He got to the perimeter of a large factory car park and spotted the grey Audi. Vittore was clearly not in the car and Bruno's heart-rate rocketed upwards. Out of the corner of his eye he saw a car moving slowly along one of the long parallel lanes of the otherwise totally quiet car park. He could see a single male occupant but was still too far away to make a positive identification. "It must be Vittore," he thought to himself. "He's hotwired a replacement car in case we have put out an all-points bulletin on his Audi." Bruno realised also that Vittore had made a smart move in stealing a vehicle relatively early in the working day from a factory car park. The owner was unlikely to discover the theft until the lunch break or even the end of the working day thus buying Vittore valuable hours. He had also picked a totally innocuous small, old Fiat 500 as his escape car. There were many thousands of these cars on Italy's roads and compared to Vittore's up-market Audi TT, this vehicle would be virtually invisible.

Bruno radioed his men with the new target car's make, colour and registration number and set off in pursuit. After Imola, Vittore headed towards Forli and then on towards Arezzo, criss-crossing the central spine of Italy and skirting Lake Trasimeno near Perugia. As there was a fair bit of traffic on the road it was not too difficult to follow the little green Fiat whilst keeping two or three vehicles between his car and Vittore's. He realised though that, as they got further away from any sizeable population centres, the traffic was thinning alarmingly and the risk of Vittore spotting he was being followed was escalating unacceptably. Bruno radioed one of his men in the small convoy behind him and told him to overtake both himself and Vittore and get ahead a few hundred metres so he could keep Vittore in his rear view mirror. Bruno would then pull back several hundred metres. If the lead driver saw Vittore take a right or left turn he would radio Bruno and then back up and revert to a position behind the last of the following four police vehicles once the convoy had made the same turn as Vittore. Between Todi and Spoleto this manoeuvre was repeated twice with the second and then third vehicles in the pursuing group overtaking Bruno and then Vittore. It was now after 1 p.m and Vittore was passing through the city of Cittaducale in Lazio about 70 kilometres north-east of Rome.

Bruno still had no idea of Vittore's ultimate destination but he sensed that they were getting closer to it as Vittore was intensifying his efforts to confuse any would be pursuers by taking the most minor roads possible where the traffic flow was infinitesimal. "Christ, he must have spotted us," muttered Bruno to himself and the words had barely left his lips when his officer in the lead car radioed to say that he'd lost Vittore.

"Sir, there were two or three roads off to the left and right and as this road has so many blind bends I must have missed him turning off a while back. Did you spot him?"

"*Merda!* No I didn't and I can see we are approaching your position now. OK, all units turn round and we'll each take one of the side roads to see whether we can catch up with him. Go! Go! Go!"

Twenty minutes later Bruno had to admit that they had lost Vittore. They were near a village called Arischia about fifteen kilometres north west of L'Aquila, the regional capital so tragically devastated by the earthquake the previous year. As soon as he realised they had lost Vittore, Bruno had asked his command centre to put out an all points alert to the State, Provincial and Municipal Police forces, the *Carabinieri* and the *Guardia's* officers in the area. "I want road blocks to be set up on all roads at a radius of thirty kilometres from Vittore's last known position."

As they were in an area where there were a number of national parks, Bruno had made sure that the *Corpo Forestale*, the Park Ranger group, were also put on high alert. It was possible that Vittore might move off the road network and try to drive along some of the forest tracks. But because of the rugged wooded, hilly terrain it was unlikely that Vittore would make much headway if he took this option, particularly in a small, clapped out Fiat.

It was scant consolation to Bruno that Vittore would probably be contained within a circle with a sixty kilometre diameter. A quick mental calculation told him that this represented a surface area of over 2,800 square kilometres. But at least, he told himself grimly, there were no big centres of population except for L'Aquila with its 70,000 inhabitants. He called the drivers of the other three cars in his pursuit convoy and told them to rendezvous with him at the *Guardia di Finanza* Office in Via Raffaele Paolucci in L'Aquila. He needed urgent access to the office's sophisticated communications network to coordinate the hunt for Vittore and plug back into Operation Achilles to see whether the many other arrests had gone according to plan.

Had Bruno known exactly where Vittore was at that precise moment he would have taken some comfort from the fact that he was still well within the cordoned off area. During the last leg of his drive, before he turned off abruptly onto an unnamed track, Vittore had become unsettled by the fear that he was being followed. He couldn't really believe it was possible but he was almost certain that a car that had passed him once had overtaken him again about an hour later. Although he was not a hundred per cent convinced it was the same car he decided that, as he was getting close to his father's hideaway, he couldn't risk leading anyone to the house near Aragno. He had therefore taken evasive action by driving along a forest track towards the village of Collebrincioni. When he was about six or seven kilometres from Aragno he turned off the track and ran the Fiat into a dense thicket. He spent fifteen minutes covering the vehicle as best he could with fallen branches and foliage so it couldn't be easily spotted from the track or from the air. In the glove compartment he had found a number of detailed ordnance survey maps from the *Istituto Geografico Militare*. The owner of the car was clearly a keen rambler and had obviously walked in this particular part of the Abruzzo as one of the maps covered the L'Aquila area. In the car boot Vittore found a pair of old hiking boots and an anorak. The boots were a touch too big for him but he pulled on a couple of extra pairs of socks from his overnight bag and that helped to make them fit more snugly. This footwear would certainly be more suitable for a cross-country hike than the dress shoes he had on when he left Modena in such a rush.

It was now about three o'clock and he decided to stay put until nightfall which would be in about three hours' time. It wasn't particularly cold and it was dry so Vittore hunkered down with his back against the trunk of an old beech tree and waited for dark. He had decided not to use his mobile phone to ring Palumbo, his father's contact man, because he was afraid that his phone might be tapped. He did not have a contact number for his father as, when Arturo went into hiding, they had agreed that he would only have contact with Palumbo on burner phones at pre-agreed times and dates. In retrospect this had not been the most sensible arrangement and certainly made their current tricky situation even more fraught.

Vittore cursed his luck and was chilled not only by the rapidly cooling temperature as night fell but also by the terrifying prospect of his father's reaction when he realised that their lucrative drug trafficking operation had been blown to smithereens. At around 17.45 he stood up and did a few stretching exercises to relieve the stiffness in his legs. He was on the heavily wooded south side of the track he had driven up. On the other side there was just a bare rocky hillside with very little cover. He set off through the woods in an easterly direction keeping the track about twenty metres to his left. Having studied the detailed map he had found in the stolen car, he reckoned that he should cover the six or seven kilometres to Aragno by about 19.30. After two kilometres, near Collebrincioni, the woods petered out and he had to be much more circumspect, skirting round the village and climbing over a number of walls and fences. At 19.40 he was approaching the large, isolated house on the outskirts of Aragno and was dismayed to see there were no lights on and his father's BMW with the false plates was not in the driveway. Vittore panicked and let out a string of obscenities. "What the fuck do I do now?" he thought.

What he hadn't realised was that his father had gone to take the scheduled phone call from Palumbo and at that precise moment was sitting in his car about thirty kilometres away. He was digesting the devastating news he had just heard from his henchman. Santoro had left the house mid-afternoon, much earlier than usual as he felt cooped up there and needed to spend a few hours outside. Unbeknown to him he had missed the road block being set up on his exit route by ten minutes or so although he had been alarmed when a convoy of police vehicles passed him at high speed with sirens wailing.

He replayed the terrible news from Palumbo over and over in his head. It was obvious that a massive international police swoop had led to the arrest of most of the people involved in his drug trafficking operation from London down to Piraeus and across to Tunisia. Palumbo had also picked up that not only Simmons and Williamson had been arrested but also Elio Doronzo. Santoro knew that his cousin's arrest indicated that either his or Simmons' phone had been tapped and the multiple arrests in several countries confirmed that this must have been the result of a long-standing coordinated police operation.

He decided to head back towards Aragno and ten minutes later the burner phone he had just used to receive the call from Palumbo rang again startling him. "Where are you, *papà*?" The voice of Vittore was at an almost hysterical pitch.

"Why…What the hell's going on?…You shouldn't be calling me on this phone…"

"For God's sake, listen to me *papà*. How far are you from the house?"

"I'm about fifteen minutes away, why?"

"Pull off the road, I need to talk to you."

Vittore told his father about the early morning warning call he had received, his subsequent swift departure from Modena and his ditching of the stolen car in the forest after he thought he was being followed.

"When I got to the house and you weren't there I had to call Palumbo to see if he knew where you were and he told me our whole operation is in the shit."

"How the fuck did you allow yourself to be tailed you stupid bastard… You've blown my location…I'll have to come back to the house to plan how we get away from here…"

"No, *papà*, don't do that. I suspect the cops will have put road blocks on all the roads in the area a good distance from where they lost me."

"Yeah, when I was driving to take the call from Palumbo I did see a convoy of police cars speeding past me in the other direction. OK…Let me think…We have to get out of here…We'll need to meet somewhere and we need to recover some of the stash of cash we buried outside the house."

"But I can't risk nicking another car and driving out of here *papà*…"

"No, you'll need to lie low tonight in the house…You'll have to break in through one of the downstairs windows. But first dig up those three bags of cash and see how much you can carry…there's a big rucksack in the cupboard under the stairs that should hold a fair amount."

"What do I do then?"

"In the bathroom you'll find some peroxide. Dye your hair blond and wear my glasses that I left on the bedside table to change your appearance a bit…Have you got a map?"

"Yeah, I found a really detailed one in the car I dumped together with some walking boots and an anorak."

"OK, good. Tomorrow morning wear the outdoor gear and one of the woolly hats that are in the hall and plot a route across country heading south, off the beaten track. With the rucksack on your back it'll look as as if you are a rambler. You'll have to suss out where the cops have put their road blocks and bypass them. Once clear of the police perimeter you'll have to flag down a motorist on a quiet road and take their car at gunpoint…You'll find a spare gun and some ammo clips in the cupboard under the sink in the downstairs toilet. Don't leave any witnesses."

"OK, where do we hook up after that?"

"I think it's too risky to head back to Puglia…I'll have to talk to some of our friends in Calabria to see whether we can be smuggled out of Italy and go to one of our other houses to lie low for a bit…I'll keep this phone open but don't call me unless you have to. I'll give you a call as soon as I've figured out where we should meet up…No, that's no good…We don't want to use your own mobile phone again. What you need to do is use a disposable cell phone…there's a box of them in my bedroom…As soon as you've found one, ring this number…just let it ring three times and then end the call. I'll know then it's you and I'll have the new number in my phone log."

Vittore thought long and hard about his father's suggested plan. In the end, he decided to use this golden opportunity to free himself from the clutches of the psychopath he had to call *papà*. He thought back to the conversation he had with his mother a few years earlier when she had been rather tipsy and maudlin at the baptism of Vittore's second child. Arturo had left the party early to attend to some business and Vittore and his mother were having a nightcap when she suddenly burst into tears. "I must tell you something *caro*. Arturo is not your real father…We adopted you when you were a little baby and I think you should know that you do not have any of his blood in your veins. The truth is that he terrifies me, Vittore…He has since shortly after we were married when he dropped the charming façade he had adopted during our courtship. He wanted me as a trophy because I was very beautiful but he tired of me pretty quickly when it was obvious that I was not going to be able to give him any children. His macho image would have been dented if we remained childless so he arranged for us to adopt you."

Vittore sat in stupefied silence as his mother continued, "He thinks I'm stupid but I only pretend to be so he doesn't get worried I might know too much about his business…But I do know that he arranged for us to get you through one of his cronies, a local businessman called Perugini. This man's unmarried daughter had got herself pregnant and the father of her child had mysteriously disappeared. The girl was sent away to have her baby and I was also sent to a mountain village in Calabria. As soon as she had delivered you into the world, you were taken from her and given to me and I then returned to Lecce with 'my' baby. I overheard Arturo talking on the phone to that man Perugini and I know your real mother was called Antonella. I also picked up the name of the young man they thought was the baby's father…He was called Luca Vento and ironically he had fled Italy because the Camorra were going to kill him as he was trying to expose some of their activities…*Caro* Vittore, I felt incredibly sorry for Antonella and have never lost the horrible feeling of guilt at taking another woman's child. After we got you, I heard she had emigrated to Australia to start a new life so I accepted the precious gift of you and I've tried to be a good mother…"

Vittore was stunned by his mother's disclosure but the truth was that he had become increasingly sickened by Arturo's seemingly inexhaustible craving for the infliction of extreme pain on anyone who opposed him. Since his cousin Vincenzo had been tortured to death he had found it difficult to sleep. He had a recurring nightmare in which he was being attacked in a dark cellar by a scrabbling mass of bloodthirsty rats. He had tried to think of ways of escaping with his family but he knew that Arturo would not rest until he had found him and killed him for what he would regard as the ultimate betrayal.

But now, with Arturo's clan decimated and his whole operation being closed down, Vittore knew he had the chance finally to cut himself loose. To minimise the risk of violent retribution, Vittore resolved to have his father arrested. As soon as Arturo called to give him the address where they were to meet, he would make an anonymous call to the police…in fact, even better, he'd get the number of the local Anti-Mafia Directorate and call them with the location.

Vittore then got busy. After finding one of the 'burner' phones and using it to log it into Arturo's phone he retrieved the three oiled sacks of money from the grounds. One bag contained only high denomination notes and Vittore was able to separate out several large wads of €500 and €100 notes. He packed these into the rucksack. He reckoned that they weighed six or seven kilos and totalled about two million euro. He still had space in the rucksack for a couple of sweaters from his overnight bag and the Berretta pistol he'd retrieved from the downstairs toilet. He decided to hide the remaining money sacks in case he might have an opportunity to retrieve them at a later date when things had quietened down. Beyond the high walls surrounding the house there was a wood and Vittore threw the bags over the wall and clambered after them carrying a small shovel he'd found in a shed in the garden. He walked about a hundred metres into the wood, dug a hole near a large holly bush, dumped the bags and replaced the soil on top. He carried several armfuls of loose branches and leaves and thoroughly camouflaged the evidence of his digging.

It was now just after 10 p.m. and when he returned to the house his new cell phone bleeped and Arturo gave him an address including GPS coordinates in Calabria, the toe of Italy, near the village of San Luca. Arturo said, "You need to get down there as soon as you can and we can pay Silvio, the 'Ndrangheta *padrino*, who has agreed to let us stay there for a few days, with some of the money you are bringing. How much do you reckon you can get in the rucksack?"

Vittore told him he would have a couple of million euro and Arturo snorted, "No way Vittore…That's nowhere near enough…There must be at least twenty million in those bags. You'll just have to make two or three trips on foot dodging any police cordon with as much as you can carry and hide the bags somewhere while you steal some wheels. You can then motor down to Calabria on minor roads. I'll give you a couple of days but do as I say or you will make me very angry…Don't fuck up again."

If he needed any further encouragement to push on with his own plan, Arturo's final threatening words cemented his resolve. He had brought his laptop with him and after logging on he searched on Pronto.it, the on-line phone directory. He found the number for the office of the DNA, the Anti-Mafia Directorate in Reggio Calabria, the largest city in the region. First thing the next morning he planned to ring to shop his father but for the moment he needed to work out how he was going to effect his own getaway. He turned the TV on to see if he could get useful leads on any police activity and as the picture crystallised he jumped in his seat as side-by-side appeared full face photos of himself and Arturo. The news anchor was saying that the police were hunting two criminals from the Sacra Corona Unita and the public should under no circumstances approach them as they were extremely dangerous. If anyone caught sight of them they should ring the number shown on the screen. The newsman continued, "Within the past twenty-four hours there has been a massive roundup of criminals involved in one of the biggest drug trafficking operations ever seen. Close to three hundred arrests had been made in several countries in Europe and North Africa. Among those arrested, in addition to career criminals, were national and local politicians, policemen and businessmen. The most high profile arrest, was of a top UK businessman, Sir Roger Simmons, who had been remanded in custody pending further enquiries."

Although not super-intelligent Vittore was clear-thinking and pragmatic. He knew that there would be a nationwide hunt for him and his father and that he had to get out of Italy to let the dust settle. He needed to come up with some smart moves if he was to extricate himself and his family from this mess. But he realised he was ravenous, having not eaten anything since dinner the previous evening. So he found some bread, cheese and salami in the kitchen and attacked his cold supper with a vengeance.

He then started to jot down a few notes. He first listed the resources he had at his disposal. He had €2 million euro cash in hand and many millions more to retrieve from the wood next door at a future date. He and his father had also salted away another €20 million in top quality diamonds and one ounce gold krugerrands. These were in a secret compartment in a yacht moored in the port of Monopoli, south of Bari, together with false passports for each of them. Arturo had arranged for the boat to be purchased through a shell company and it was registered in the name of one of his *bona fide* business associates. The mooring fees had been paid for several years ahead so Vittore knew that the valuables could be recovered at any time. He had contacts with smugglers operating from a smaller port near Bari. He had no doubt that he could get them to take him across to Albania where he could lie low for a bit. Both he and his father had attached keys to the boat to their respective key rings so they would be immediately accessible if they had to go on the run.

Firmly in the asset list was his wife, Renata. She was the daughter of a top 'Ndrangheta boss and although their union had been arranged to cement ties between the Calabrian and Puglian mafia clans, Renata and Vittore had made it much more than a marriage of convenience. Unlike his father, Vittore told Renata everything and they had, in fact, together worked out a contingency plan in the event that he was ever on the run or arrested. The need for this was reinforced by the massive increase in anti-mafia operations in the recent past. They knew they would have to change their identity so they had organised false passports and identity cards for themselves and their two small children, Elisa and Tommaso. They had also obtained bogus driving licences and they had worked on an elaborate escape plan to put into effect when the time was right.

So, he had substantial assets but there was still the big problem of his appearance now that his photo had been broadcast on every TV channel. He knew he would have to change how he looked but he did not think his father's suggestion to dye his hair would do the trick. He opted for a more radical solution. He spent a good hour clipping his hair down to a fuzz and then very carefully using several disposable razors and copious amounts of shaving foam to shave his head completely without leaving any tell-tale cuts. He was naturally very dark shaven and it would only be another day or two before he would have the makings of a reasonable beard. He had some sunglasses with him and he would wear those together with the anorak and hiking boots he had found in the car he had stolen. It wasn't perfect but it was the best he could do and he went to bed in a more composed frame of mind to snatch a few hours' sleep before embarking on his hazardous expedition the following morning.

2 MARCH 2011

L'AQUILA, ABRUZZO

Bruno Canepa was not in the sunniest of moods. Since losing Vittore Santoro the previous afternoon he had been at the *Guardia's* office in L'Aquila until late into the night. He had spent fruitless hours coordinating the search effort across several law enforcement agencies. He had also had a heart-rending conversation with Gina who was on her way north to see her father having been able to leave the safe house once Doronzo had been taken into custody. Luca was still in Intensive Care in a medically induced coma to control pressure on his brain.

It was now 10 a.m. on Wednesday 2 March and he had just had a blistering ear bashing from his *Comandante Generale*. He had been forcibly reminded that his plan to flush out Arturo Santoro had clearly failed and not only that but he had in Vittore lost another key player in the drug trafficking operation. The *Comandante's* anger was somewhat mollified by the outstanding success of the total multi-country swoop which had netted upwards of three hundred villains without a shot being fired. There were also dozens of strong leads to other people involved in nefarious activities who had not been snared in this particular cull. Several of those arrested had been only too willing to grass up associates to try to improve their own situation. "So much for honour among thieves," had concluded the *Comandante* before exhorting Bruno to pull out all the stops to find the missing Santoros.

Within minutes of this uncomfortable call, Bruno's phone rang again. "*Ciao* Bruno, it's Fredo here. I've just been asked to mobilise a unit to head across to San Luca in Calabria to nab your friend Arturo Santoro."

"What!...You know where he is?"

"We know where he's heading. The *Direzione Investigativa Antimafia* in Reggio Calabria received a call an hour and a half ago from an informer who convinced them that he was genuine. He said Santoro had been hiding out in the Abruzzo but had been spooked by the huge cross-border police action which had shut down the many tentacles of his trafficking operation. He is now making for a house in the 'Ndragheta stronghold of San Luca. We even know what car he is driving…a seven series black BMW, although we don't have the reg. *Carabinieri* road blocks are already in place on the approach roads to San Luca and we may be able to intercept Santoro before he reaches the safe house. Otherwise, we'll surround the house after dark tonight and flush him out then."

"Are you sure this info is legit, Fredo?"

"Yes, we are. I talked to the senior magistrate at the DIA who had spoken to the informer and he is absolutely convinced the caller was genuine… What happened was that the DIA office received a very cryptic call at 8.30 this morning…the man simply said he had information as to the where-abouts of Arturo Santoro and would call back in exactly thirty minutes when it was imperative that he be put through to the most senior DIA officer. The guy who picked up this first call was an experienced officer and he made sure that the top investigating magistrate was on standby to take the second call. The magistrate told me the caller knew things about Santoro and his criminal activities that only a close insider would know. The magistrate was aware that I was leading the police push against SCU so he called me."

"Christ, Fredo…I hope to hell this is true and we can finally nail this vicious bastard…How are you getting over to Calabria?"

"I've got a helicopter on standby and me and a few of my best men will be there by lunchtime to support the local officers."

"*Va bene*, I'll move mountains to be there too…I wouldn't want to miss this."

From his *Comandante Generale*, Bruno got top priority authorisation to commandeer a helicopter from the *Guardia's* air base at Pratica di Mare, south of Rome. The 'chopper would pick him up at around 11.30 and he reckoned that, with one refuelling stop, he could be in the vicinity of San Luca by about four o'clock.

On the way down to Calabria, Bruno heard several encouraging bits of news. He was told that the Park Rangers had found the car Vittore had stolen just off a track in the woods a few miles from L'Aquila. In the car were several items of clothing belonging to the fugitive, including a pair of shoes. By midday tracker dogs had been deployed and were following a meandering trail in the direction of the village of Aragno. At 2 o'clock an excited *Guardia* officer radioed Bruno to confirm that they had found an isolated house near Aragno where initial forensics confirmed that both Arturo and Vittore Santoro had been in the recent past.

169

'So my plan did work after all," Bruno thought with a combined sense of relief and satisfaction. Following Vittore had been successful in flushing out Santoro senior.

Now both were out in the open and on the run.

2 MARCH 2011

LONDON

Commander Gibbs had his feet up on his desk, sipping an excellent single malt and reflecting on a very productive couple of days. It was late evening 2 March and he couldn't help smiling when he recalled the look of incredulity on the face of Sir Roger Simmons when he had arrested him at nine o'clock on the dot the previous morning.

By then Commander Gibbs had had an hour or so to interrogate Elio Doronzo after the latter's arrest and he turned out to be the very antithesis of the stereotypical, hardened, tight-lipped mafia boss. He capitulated immediately when he listened to the tape recording of his call to Simmons a few days earlier and tried to buy some preferential treatment by disclosing that he had a video tape of Sir Roger's savage and prolonged beating of a young male prostitute.

Doronzo was angling for a witness protection deal and given the range and depth of his contacts across most of the major mafia clans, Gibbs was thinking he might well be a valid contender for this programme. He and his immediate family would be given immunity in exchange for the priceless ammunition he could supply to help bring down many leading mafia figures and their associates in wider civil society.

If Doronzo was a willing informant, Charles Williamson was the chirpiest canary George Gibbs had ever encountered in his three decades of policing. He was a typical bully and when confronted with the evidence of his illegal "outsider trading" he collapsed into a snivelling, weeping heap. He then spewed out a mind-blowing catalogue of all the unsavoury things he had done at Sir Roger's bidding. Not all of this was illegal but much of it was and lifted the lid on the breadth of his boss's criminality. Since being blackmailed into joining forces with Santoro and Doronzo, Simmons had established his own highly lucrative offshoots in the fields of people smuggling, extortion and male prostitution. It was as if, Williamson said, Sir Roger ran two contiguous business empires – one in the public corporate world and the other deep in the shadows.

The Commander had also taken a grim pleasure in arresting his bent officer Nailsworth. Like Doronzo and Williamson, he was also eager to spill the beans. He gave up the names of a small corrupt cell of policemen in The Met who were quickly relieved of their duties. Gibbs almost felt sorry for Nailsworth who had done some very courageous things in his police career but had got himself seduced by his criminal paymasters and then sucked deeper and deeper into their world without any possibility of extricating himself.

****

At the same time as the Commander was reflecting on his successes, Bruno Canepa was in the village of San Luca in Calabria crouching behind a low rough-hewn stone wall. It was a few yards from the house the informant had given as Arturo Santoro's new hiding place. *Colonnello* Sportelli had ascertained that this was the home of an important 'Ndrangheta *capo* so he had waited until nearly midnight before deploying his crack team of about twenty officers around the house. They were all in black combat fatigues and with blackened faces and had moved very quietly in the deserted village to get into position.

Road blocks had been in place around San Luca since about midday but they had not caught Arturo Santoro. Since leaving the Abruzzo, he had, in fact, driven for most of the night to put as much distance as possible between him and any police dragnet in that area. He had snatched a couple of hours' sleep near the town of Cosenza before resuming his drive and arriving at the imposing house on the edge of San Luca at around 9 a.m. His host, Silvio Cenadi, was obviously not best pleased to see him but he had to pay a debt of honour to Santoro because of past services rendered by the SCU boss. Cenadi was aware that Santoro was the most wanted man in Italy having seen the TV coverage the previous evening. He wanted shot of his unwelcome visitor before the huge police hunt got fully underway. He coldly told Santoro over breakfast that he had to get out of Italy and they agreed that arrangements would be made for a fast boat to take him across the Adriatic to Albania the following day. Santoro argued vehemently that he needed more time to be sure that his son came first with the cash he needed.

For once Santoro's intimidating ranting cut no ice. Cenadi, backed by his two sons armed with shotguns said a car would take him to the chosen embarkation point on the Gulf of Squillace at dawn the next day.

In the darkness outside the house, Fredo Sportelli raised the loud hailer to his mouth and the somnolent night was lacerated by the eerily echoing command, "Arturo Santoro, I am *Colonnello* Sportelli of the *Carabinieri*. I have a warrant for your arrest. Come out with your hands behind your head. Resistance would be futile as we have the house surrounded."

One of his officers shone a portable searchlight at the front door. Sportelli let the second hand of his watch sweep round for a full minute. He was just about to use the megaphone again when the door opened and Santoro literally staggered down the steps with his arms flailing and crashed to the ground. He had obviously been forcibly ejected from the house and once he was outside the front door had been slammed shut behind him. Santoro was dressed only in a singlet and boxer shorts with an unbuttoned overcoat and two *carabinieri* darted out from cover and whilst one pointed his Beretta Assault Rifle at Santoro's head his colleague pulled Santos's huge arms behind his back and hand cuffed him.

Two more officers helped to haul Santoro's huge bulk upright and he was frogmarched down the street and bundled into the back of a police van firing a broadside of profanities into the night air.

Colonnello Sportelli used the loud hailer again. "Silvio Cenadi. Come outside with your hands behind your head or my men will come in to get you." The portable searchlight again picked out the front door and within a minute a diminutive figure emerged with his hands held high in the air. Cenadi was a tiny man and the booming voice which came from his mouth was totally incongruous.

"What the hell do you want with me? I'm a law abiding citizen."

"You have been harbouring a wanted criminal and we need you to accompany us to the *Carabinieri* Station in Bovalino to answer some questions."

"What are you talking about? If you mean Santoro, I didn't know he was a wanted man. He's a distant cousin who just pitched up out of the blue this morning and asked if he could stay the night…Am I under arrest?"

"No, but we do need to ask you a few questions with your lawyer present if you wish, as is your right…"

"OK, I'll call my lawyer and get him to meet us in town so we can clear all this crap up…Can I go inside and do that?"

"Yes…I'll give you five minutes."

After re-emerging Cenadi was led to a police car. Bruno joined *Colonnello* Sportelli in his unmarked Fiat Grande Punto and they followed the convoy of police vans and cars the twelve or so kilometres down to the coastal town of Bovalino. Bruno was cock-a-hoop and couldn't help thinking that but for the anonymous tip received that morning his future career prospects would have gone up in smoke. He and Sportelli would interrogate Cenadi as soon as they arrived at the station and they would make arrangements for Santoro to be transferred, accompanied by a sizeable police escort, to the principal Puglian *Carabinieri* station in Bari. There, no later than ninety-six hours after his detention, Santoro would be questioned by an examining magistrate as required by the Italian inquisitorial system, with his lawyer present.

"Fredo, we are really going to have to burn the midnight oil for the next few days to prepare a detailed evidential dossier for the magistrate."

"I know…bang goes my wedding anniversary trip to Palermo. You can stay at my place for a few days if you want while we work on this…In fact, I'll have to take you with me as protection when I tell my wife our little Sicilian break is off for a bit!"

2 MARCH 2011

ARAGNO, ABRUZZO

Vittore Santoro had left the house in Aragno immediately after making the second call to the *Direzione Nazionale Antimafia*. He had tried to make himself look like a serious hiker with his trousers tucked into his socks, his scruffy anorak and his battered hiking boots. With his shaved head and a hefty growth of facial stubble he was very different from the police mugshot that had been shown on TV.

With the heavy rucksack on his back it was difficult to make speedy progress. His pace was slowed further by his decision to cut across the challenging terrain of the southern edge of the Gran Sasso National Park away from any road traffic. He had spent a couple of hours since dawn studying the detailed map he had found in the stolen Fiat 500. He had decided his best bet was to head for the Adriatic coast. His wife Renata had a twin brother in Pescara and Vittore was pretty sure he could get some help from him as he was a prominent member of a 'Ndrangheta satellite unit. At least Maso would get word to his sister that Vittore was on the run and that she should be ready to put their escape plan into action at the appropriate time.

Given the inevitability of her and Vittore's bank accounts being frozen, they had asked Renata's sister, Patrizia, to keep a large bag of cash for them together with their new documents. She lived in the seaside town of Trebisacce on the Gulf of Taranto which was a good two hours' drive from Lecce. When Vittore and Renata were ready to take off, they would rendezvous with Patrizia, pick up their passports and cash and then head for one of the international airports in Sicily to fly out to Buenos Aires where Renata had family connections.

Vittore was sure that by now Renata would know that he was a fugitive but he was confident that she would not do anything precipitate. Their house would be put under surveillance so they knew it might be several weeks or even months before they could trigger their joint escape plan to Latin America. Renata was to wait for word from him and they had followed his father's lead in buying a few burner phones. Vittore had memorised the number of one of them and whilst he was in hiding Renata was going to keep this on and fully charged. All Vittore had to do was ring this number with a one word message, "*Vacanza.*" This was the signal that she should meet him with the children at 5 p.m. the following day in a café in Trebisacce.

Renata could only do this if she could somehow slip away from the police who would undoubtedly be watching her and tracking her movements. This is where they had a brainwave and enlisted the help of Patrizia, who was very similar to Renata in height, colouring and build. Once Renata had got the signal from Vittore she would call her sister and chat about this and that. But she would ask Patrizia what her holiday plans were and that would be the signal for her sister to drive over to Lecce early the next morning to meet her at the childrens' kindergarten.

Patrizia would be inside the nursery before Renata and her children arrived. She and Renata would both be wearing white baseball caps, sunglasses and the same colour sweaters and jeans. Renata would take her kids inside, retrieve the money and passports Patrizia would have with her and exchange car keys. Patrizia would then dash out and jump into Renata's car as if she'd just dropped off the kids. In Patrizia's own car would be a couple of suitcases with clothes and travel accessories that she would have carried home after her regular visits to her sister's home in Lecce.

Renata would be able to see if any police surveillance vehicles had swallowed the bait and followed Patrizia. If so, she would then bundle the kids into her sister's car and head off for the *rendezvous* with Vittore. Patrizia would drive towards Brindisi in the opposite direction to Renata and keep going for a couple of hours before stopping for lunch. She would then head back to Lecce arriving at Renata's house mid-afternoon.

In thinking this plan through, the Santoros knew the police would become suspicious a couple of hours after that when she did not go to collect the kids. On the assumption that Renata's phone would be tapped, she would, during their pre "D-Day" phone conversation tell her sister that her kids would be going for a play date with some friends after kindergarten the following evening so she would not have to pick them up herself. If the police bought this, it could buy a few more precious hours for Renata and Vittore to put as much distance as they could between themselves and any organised pursuit. At best they could have ten or twelve hours before the police realised they had been outmanoeuvred. They thought their best immediate objective would be to get to Villa San Giovanni on the west coast of Calabria and take the car on the short ferry trip over to Messina in Sicily.

But right now Vittore was contemplating a long hike before he reached the coastal resort of Pescara. He reckoned he would have to cover about seventy kilometres. With the very detailed maps he had "inherited" he felt that he could plot a good route without a compass, given that the hilly topography he would be traversing had many stand-out features. His first target destination, heading in a south-easterly direction was the hilltop town of Santo Stefano di Sessanio. He would then dog-leg north-east towards Pescara. He had packed as much food as he could carry so he felt confident he could reach Pescara without breaking cover to buy more supplies. The main dilemma he faced was how to stay under the radar once he left the mountains and entered the flatter, more highly populated strip between the Gran Sasso Park and the coast. He knew he would not be able to navigate after nightfall and he did not relish the prospect of sleeping rough with the temperature in the hills hovering around zero. He realised eventually that he could not risk walking all the way to Pescara so the only option was to steal and hotwire another car after dark.

He estimated it would take him four or five hours to cover the fifteen or so kilometres from Aragno to Santo Stefano di Sessanio, given the difficulty of the terrain and the need to avoid human contact. He should arrive there by mid-afternoon and could find somewhere sheltered to lie low until the town settled down for the night. Then he would do a careful recce to find and break into an old car not fitted with an alarm system. For once he was thankful for the apprenticeship he had served in the SCU where he was taught how to steal a car. He would pick one parked as far away as possible from the nearest house to minimise the risk of anyone hearing him drive off.

With this plan firmly embedded in his mind, Vittore set off on a bright but chilly morning. In a strange way he felt elated by the recent turn of events. For years he had wanted to find a way of leaving his life of crime. From an early age he had felt a real repugnance towards the vicious world his father had exposed him to. His happiest years had been those spent at university away from his father's overpowering influence. He even harboured the faint hope that he might, after graduating, pursue a legitimate career in business. That glimmer of hope was quickly dashed. When he got his degree his father left him in no doubt that, whilst any company he was asked to run might have a façade of legitimacy, it was merely a front for criminal activity.

He had to adopt a persona of overweening arrogance and callous disregard for people to show that he was his father's son. In any dealings with people who might oppose him, this persona became his default position. Any sign of weakness would have brought violent paternal retribution down on him. But in his heart of hearts he knew it was a sham and his true nature was very different. His mother's revelation about his real paternity had simply confirmed why he felt such a disconnect between himself and the way of life he had been forced to adopt.

Vittore resolved that when the time was right he would hire somebody to track down both his natural parents.

Now with his feared *papà* behind bars, this became a real possibility. If he could find an escape route for himself and his family, he would be free and clear to start a new life. His escape plan nearly came to nothing within an hour of leaving his father's villa. After wending his way carefully through a lightly wooded area south-east of Aragno he came into the open on top of the raised embankment alongside the A14 *autostrada*. Just below him was a *carabinieri* checkpoint and he had to drop to the ground very quickly to avoid detection and then move out of sight of the officers who were clearly stopping every vehicle heading in both directions. After about half a kilometre he scuttled down the embankment and across the motorway between a number of large trucks in the northbound queue to the checkpoint. The southbound lanes were relatively free of traffic so he was able to run across, climb the opposite embankment and continue on his way to Santo Stefano. The rest of the day passed without incident and at about three o'clock in the afternoon, somewhat footsore and weary, he found himself on the outskirts of this small hill town. Ahead of him was a derelict barn with half its roof missing and Vittore decided to lay up inside until nightfall. Once inside, he removed his ill-fitting boots and washed the bloody blisters on his heels with some of the bottled water from his rucksack. He had not slept much the previous night and a combination of sleep deprivation and physical exertion took its inevitable toll.

He woke with a start and realised it was after nine o'clock and pitch black outside. He still waited until midnight before venturing out. The low cloud cover and limited light pollution provided ideal conditions for a surreptitious scouting of the nearest outlying houses. He found a battered pick-up truck parked at the bottom of a long flight of stone steps leading to a detached house which was in darkness. He tried the driver's door handle and was not really surprised that it was unlocked. Car theft was probably a rare event in these mountain villages. He eased himself into the driver's seat, released the hand brake and coasted down a steep incline before pulling up. He quickly hot-wired the truck which belied its age by ticking over very smoothly. He was out of Santo Stefano almost immediately and after an uneventful hour's drive along minor roads he was about five kilometres from Pescara. He was on *Strada Provinciale* 12 near a little place called Caprara D'Abruzzo. He thought it would be safer to ditch the car and make the rest of the journey to his brother-in-law's house on foot but the area was mostly covered by olive groves and he was worried that these open plantations would not provide adequate cover to hide the vehicle. He looked again at the detailed map he had found in the first car he had stolen and saw that there were one or two more densely wooded areas. The nearest was easily accessible along an overgrown farm track and Vittore drove the pick-up into the centre of this wood which was about three hundred metres off Sp12.

He decided to wait until dawn before walking to Maso's house which was fortunately on this side of the coastal resort. At first light, he prised the number plates off the vehicle with a hefty screwdriver he found in a toolbox in the pick-up's flat bed. He took these with him and hid them under a hedge after putting a few hundred metres between himself and the truck. It was worth the effort, he thought, as it could buy him a little more time by delaying the identification of the truck and the possible connection to him and his escape route.

By eight o'clock he was approaching Maso's house at the end of a quiet *cul-de-sac*. As he was opening the front gate, Maso himself came out of the house, suited and booted, obviously on his way to work. He looked askance as this shaven-headed man in a shabby anorak, raised a hand in greeting and said, "*Ciao*, Maso." It took a while for Maso to respond hesitantly, "Vittore? What the hell…Quick, let's go inside before anyone spots you."

As soon as they were in the hallway, Maso blurted out, "Christ Vittore you must know that the cops are looking everywhere for you. I just saw on the breakfast news on TV that your dad was arrested last night down in Calabria…and dozens of people in your mob have been rounded up. It looks like your whole operation has gone to shit."

Vittore pretended to be shocked at his father's arrest in order not to arouse Maso's suspicions. "I don't know how they tracked Arturo to Calabria…but can you give me something to eat and I'll tell you what's been happening."

A few minutes later sitting in the kitchen with a couple of brioche and a large cup of coffee in front of him, Vittore quickly filled his brother-in-law in on the events of the past twenty-four hours and how he had slipped through the police dragnet. In his account, he omitted to mention his telephone conversations with his father to avoid any possible trace of his involvement in Arturo's arrest.

"It looks certain that we were hit by a well-coordinated international police operation. I got away from Modena in the nick of time after one of our men in Puglia called to tip me off about an imminent raid on our bottling plant at our company SSP. The same man obviously called my dad as well and he decided to make a run for it from his hideout near L'Aquila…He'd already scarpered by the time I got there."

"Christ you were bloody lucky," whistled Maso.

"Yeah, but I was followed from Modena by the police on my way to dad's hideout…They must have put a tracker on my car, but I managed to lose them a good distance from the house. It's pretty clear in retrospect that the cops let me run in the hope that I'd lead them to dad. In fact they were right. I needed to get there to warn him that our operation had been compromised and I couldn't call him because he was only contactable through his old mate Palumbo in Puglia via an elaborate burner phone system we'd set up."

Vittore paused for breath and Maso said, "How do you think the cops found your dad? He'd put a hell of a lot of distance between himself and the Abruzzo house…the news report this morning said that he'd been arrested in a house in a village called San Luca, hundreds of kilometres away."

Thinking quickly Vittore saw a way of deflecting any suspicion away from himself. "Yeah…I've been wondering about that myself since you told me about Dad…the only person he would have contacted would have been

Palumbo…I can't really believe he shopped him but he would have been the only one Dad would have told about his intended destination in Calabria."

With this seed of suspicion duly sown, Vittore asked Maso to get a message to Renata to let her know that he was OK. This would have to be done in person as her phones would certainly be tapped. Maso was close to his twin sister and agreed to drive down to Lecce that coming weekend to tell her that Vittore was safe. Maso's own wife had left to take their kids to school just before Vittore's arrival. She was then going to one of the *Enotecas* that Maso owned to discuss plans with a local architect for extending this wine shop. She would not be back until lunchtime so Vittore and Maso had plenty of time to decide how to get Vittore out of the country.

They agreed that the best idea was to get him to Croatia where Maso had solid contacts with people who would hide him for as long as necessary, provided there was a healthy profit in it for them. "I trust them more than I do those vicious bastards in the Albanian mafia," he said. "And Croatia's a hell of a lot more attractive a place to park yourself for a spell…certainly a thousand times better than that dump, Albania."

Vittore did not tell Maso about the huge stash of cash in his rucksack but in order to reinforce his brother-in-law's continuing commitment to helping him, he did mention the cache of krugerrands in Monopoli although again he kept quiet about the many times more valuable and transportable bag of diamonds. If Maso helped him recover the krugerrands from the boat moored there, Vittore promised to split the gold with him.

"I reckon at today's gold price the 800 krugerrands are worth at least three quarters of a million euro."

Maso was clearly pretty affluent but the thought of getting his hands on a readily disposal asset worth several hundred thousand was magnetically attractive and he was quick to say, "Count me in."

So, Vittore had a shower and a change of clothes provided by Maso. He did not shave as the combination of his heavy stubble and hairless head really did transform his usual appearance. Meanwhile, Maso called his closest associate in Croatia, as well as the Italian skipper of an ultra-fast speedboat that was used for drug runs from the other side of the Adriatic to small ports on the Puglian coast.

"OK, Vittore, it's all fixed. We'll drive down to Monopoli and when it's dark this evening we'll recover the gold and then *rendezvous* with the speedboat in Torre Canne about 25 kilometres south of there. This is a much smaller port and the preferred departure point for your skipper."

"Yeah, I know it…It's a small seaside place with a tiny marina. We've stayed there with the kids a few times."

"*Va bene*…That's the good news…plus our friend in Croatia will find you a place to hole up…but it's gonna cost you. He wants a hundred grand up front and another twenty thousand euro for every month that you are enjoying his hospitality."

"Greedy bastard…but he knows I'm on the run so he's got me over a barrel. Guess I'd do the same in his position."

Vittore thought to himself that the money he'd have to pay, although extortionate, wouldn't make much of a dent in the twenty plus million he would have to hand and the roughly similar amount he hoped one day to recover from the wood in Aragno.

Maso left a note for his wife saying that he had been called away on urgent business, a not unusual occurrence and he would probably not be back until the following day. They set off at about 11 o'clock and decided not to risk taking the A14 *autostrada* to Monopoli with its plethora of toll booths and cameras. Instead they took the *Strada Statale*16 which hugged the coast for about a hundred and fifty kilometres before cutting inland to the east of the *Parco Nazionale del Gargano* and then resuming its coastal track around Barletta and continuing all the way to Monopoli. If they had taken the A14 they reckoned they could have made the 350-kilometre drive from Pescara in about three and a half hours. Choosing the much slower SS16 would add a few hours to the journey and with a stop for refreshments they estimated they would be there mid to late evening. Maso had arranged for the speed-boat to be ready to leave Torre Canne by midnight so they planned to get into the yacht's cabin in the harbour at Monopoli a little earlier to recover and split the krugerrands and then drive south for twenty minutes to meet the waiting escape boat.

They got to Monopoli at about eight o'clock and Maso left Vittore in the car, bought some *panini* from a bar on the outskirts and they settled down to wait until it was time to go to the harbour. They arrived at the deserted port at around 11.30. While Maso kept watch Vittore unlocked the big padlock on the cabin door of the yacht and disappeared inside. Within ten minutes he reappeared carrying the two holdalls that Maso had bought in one of the little towns they had driven through earlier in the day. He'd also bought Vittore a fleece lined jacket, gloves and a woollen beanie for his trip across the Adriatic.

Vittore had already split the krugerrands into the two bags and he told Maso to take whichever one he liked as there were 400 coins in each bag. In the side pockets of his new heavy jacket Vittore had concealed two cloth bags of diamonds weighing about half a pound each so they didn't pull down the shape of the bulky jacket too much. He'd also pocketed the false passport he had stashed in the hidden compartment.

Anyway, Maso was not observing him too closely as he was hypnotised by the beautiful dull gold coins trickling through his fingers. He picked one up and turned it over in his hand to see the striking image of a leaping African springbok. On the "heads" side was the stern profile of the heavily bearded Boer statesman, Paul Kruger.

He said, "They are pure gold, aren't they? They look more coppery than gold in colour."

"Yeah, I know and when we bought them I had the same thought but I found out that they are in fact an alloy with about 92 per cent gold and the rest copper...so they weigh a bit more than a Troy ounce but contain exactly one ounce of pure 22 carat gold. Last time I checked they were being sold for over one thousand euro each so the twelve or thirteen kilos you are hefting in that bag should certainly cover your fuel costs in getting me here!"

Maso clapped his brother-in-law on the back and said he would have helped him regardless of this nice little windfall. But Vittore still thought to himself that he had needed to secure Maso's wholehearted commitment to his escape plan with some tangible recompense rather than rely on familial loyalty.

By ten past midnight Vittore was boarding the powerful speedboat moored by the harbour wall in Torre Canne. Maso's final comment was, "Don't worry about paying the skipper. I've already sorted it and I'll see Renata in a couple of days to let her know you're OK...*Buona fortuna.*"

4 MARCH 2011

BOVALINO, CALABRIA

"Contact Palumbo," Arturo Santoro instructed his tame lawyer who had travelled from Lecce to see him in an interview room in the *Carabinieri* station in Bovalino. "Tell him to make sure our 'mutual friend' in Bari keeps his ear to the ground. Tell him I expect to be moved from this shithole to

Bari in the next couple of days to be interviewed by a magistrate at the *Uffici Giudiziari.*"

Palumbo would know that "our mutual friend" referred to Ettore Pignatelli, a top *Carabinieri* officer, a *Generale di Divisione* who had been providing Santoro with vital intelligence for many years. Santoro had discovered that this man had staged an elaborate cover up after causing a fatal accident driving whilst very drunk. The junior officer with him in the car at the time had claimed he was driving and took the breathalyser test which was negative. The two officers colluded in their report of the incident saying that the woman killed had suddenly stepped into the road and it was impossible to avoid hitting her. But, the junior officer had a big gambling problem and got into serious hock to one of Santoro's betting operations. In an attempt to reduce his debt, he had told one of Santoro's enforcers that he had some useful info on one of the most senior police officials in the region. This gave Santoro the opportunity to put the bite on Pignatelli and make him an involuntary informant.

When the lawyer left, Santoro was escorted back to his cell to resume his murderous reflections on the violent revenge he would take for his adopted son's treachery. After his capture it did not take him long to realise that Vittore had betrayed him. He was the only one he had told about the intended safe house in Calabria. There was no way the burner phone call could have been intercepted and it was equally inconceivable that his host, Cenadi would have tipped off the *carabinieri*.

"No…It must have been that little shit," he thought to himself. "He has grassed me up so he can get his fucking mitts on all that dough we've stashed away. If it's the last thing I do, I'll make him pay in pain and blood." In a blind rage Santoro slammed his huge balled fist into the concrete cell wall and watched, impervious to the pain as the blood seeped from his mangled knuckles.

The next morning his lawyer was back with confirmation from Pignatelli that Santoro was to be moved to Bari the following day, Saturday 5 March. The route had also been disclosed. He would be in a prisoner transport van which would be in the middle of the convoy of three vehicles. The two support vehicles would be Nyalas – armoured personnel carriers – with half a dozen officers in each. This heavy duty escort reflected the importance of the prisoner in transit.

Santoro told his lawyer to get Palumbo to contact his main enforcer, Enrico Pozzi, and get him to assemble a team to attack the convoy and free him. The lawyer was fully implicated in many of Santoro's criminal activities but this was a massive escalation of his direct personal involvement and he tried to tell Santoro that he couldn't be a party to it. Santoro reached across the desk, grabbed his hand and with the tendons in his neck bulging squeezed until there was an audible crack and tears squirted out of the lawyer's eyes.

"Listen you fucking prick…you'll do as I ask or I'll arrange for your wife, your mother and your kids to be killed …Understand?"

The lawyer nodded mutely and scuttled out of the interview room clutching his broken hand. Santoro was ultra-confident that Pozzi would be able to intercept the convoy and extricate him. He spent the rest of the day imagining the prolonged inventive torture he would inflict on Vittore when he eventually caught up with him.

Early the next morning Santoro was hustled out of his cell and after being allowed ten minutes for his ablutions was surrounded by half a dozen *carabinieri* and bundled into the rear compartment of a prisoner transport vehicle which was sandwiched between two huge armoured personnel carriers with heavy grilles over their side windows and a hinged grille over the windscreen.

One of Santoro's wrists was handcuffed and the other cuff was snapped onto a heavy vertical metal stanchion. His ankles were also shackled. Santoro said not a word as the officers were securing him but just as they were backing out of the van's side door he said, "What happens if I need a piss?"

"You'll have wet trousers," was the laconic, unsympathetic response.

The convoy moved off on the first leg of its journey to Bari which Santoro estimated would take five or six hours. For half an hour the convoy went fairly slowly but then clearly joined an *autostrada*, picked up speed and apart from toll station stoppages kept going for what seemed to Santoro a very long time. His watch had been confiscated so he was unaware that it was nearly five hours since they had left Bovalino. He was sure they couldn't be very far from Bari now and he was getting increasingly edgy, cursing his men for not having the balls to rescue him.

They slowed down for another toll station. Santoro's van edged forward once the lead vehicle pulled away after the barrier had lifted. Suddenly all hell broke loose. He could hear the crackle of many automatic weapons and then two dull crumps which rocked the police van. Through the small porthole style window between him and the driver's compartment he could see that the two officers in there had been hit and one of them was screaming like a wounded animal. Against the backdrop of noise from the continuing fire-fight he could hear grinding metallic sounds and suddenly the side door of the police van burst open and two men in ski masks climbed in, one wielding a large crowbar and the other carrying heavy-duty bolt cutters. The bolt cutters made light work of the handcuff chain attached to the stanchion and then chopped through Santoro's ankle shackles. The two men half-carried half dragged Santoro from the van and moved quickly past the toll booths to the other side of the *autostrada* where a car was waiting with the engine running in a layby just past the toll gates. Santoro was shoved into the backseat and one of his rescuers jumped in the front as the car sped off in the opposite direction to the police convoy. The other guy headed for a four by four that was parked in the layby.

Everything had happened very quickly but Santoro had time to register that the lead armoured personnel carrier was through the toll barrier and his police van and the other heavy vehicle were in the entry lane behind the barrier. The three vehicles were being fired on by about a dozen men in balaclavas. It was obvious they had all sustained damage to their wheels and tyres, presumably from hand grenades. All the *carabinieri* were penned in their vehicles and there was no returning fire as far as Santoro could see. There was only one other vehicle waiting at the toll and the driver of this big truck had clearly jumped out of his cab and sought cover because the door was hanging open.

"Where the fuck are we?" were Santoro's first words.

The man in the front passenger seat pulled off his ski mask and Santoro saw it was Enrico Pozzi.

"We are on the A14 near Taranto and we are heading for Brindisi where we have a boat waiting to get you out of the country."

"Fuck that…I have to get to Monopoli first to get something I need."

"But boss, the whole region will soon be swarming with cops and there'll be roadblocks everywhere…"

"Are you fucking deaf you imbecile…just get me to Monopoli then we can arrange for a boat to pick me up there rather than Brindisi."

Pozzi knew better than to provoke his boss any further so he simply said, "We are going to swap cars in a few minutes so that will make it more difficult for the cops to track us."

Santoro realised that they had left the motorway at the first junction after the toll station, a distance of only a few hundred metres. He was grudgingly accepting that this whole operation had been well thought out and he decided to adopt a more emollient tone with his key attack dog.

"Hey Rico…Sorry I blew up a minute ago but being all cramped up in that van for several hours has really buggered up my knees. It's clear you put together a fucking smart plan and when we get going in the next car you can fill me in on the details."

After a few minutes they were driving through a light industrial estate that, mid-afternoon on a Saturday, was very quiet. They parked next to a large van with the logo of a well-known Puglian food cooperative on the side. Pozzi helped Santoro into the rear of the van which was almost full with sacks of vegetables and cases of wine and olive oil. Santoro made himself comfortable in a space which had been left in the middle. After Pozzi had spent a couple of minutes looking at a road map with the driver, he joined Santoro in the back.

As the van moved off, Pozzi told Santoro that he'd plotted a route to Monopoli mainly on minor roads. He reckoned they could cover the sixty odd kilometres in just over an hour. He then briefed Santoro on the guts of the plan to extricate him from the *carabinieri* convoy.

"We decided to hit the convoy as near as we could to the Adriatic coast to give us the shortest possible car trip to Brindisi where your old *amico* Giorgio has friends in the harbourmaster's office and can get his boat in and out without being challenged. We had a man outside the *carabinieri* station in Bovalino who called with your time of departure. We had two more men along the convoy's planned route and a third lookout near Palagiano where the convoy joined the A14, a few hundred metres from the toll station. I had already put a dozen men behind a wall on the northbound carriageway near the toll barrier. They were wearing high viz jackets like a road maintenance crew and carrying their weapons in innocuous looking sacks. As soon as the final lookout gave us the nod that the convoy was approaching, the men I'd stationed in the layby on the southbound side of the motorway took up their positions. Immediately after the first armoured transport got through the barrier, we lobbed a grenade at its front wheels and another at the last vehicle and opened fire with automatic weapons keeping all the cops penned in their vehicles. We had parked half a dozen cars and vans in the layby and I told our guys to keep firing for a couple of minutes after we'd got you away and then do a staged withdrawal to the cars in the layby and make tracks. Both the cops' heavy vehicles were immobilised by the grenades and we shot up the police van pretty bad so I don't think the cops inside were in any fit state to try to chase us…in any case they were facing in the wrong direction. Within a couple of minutes, all our mob would have been off the motorway and heading in different directions on side roads…Oh yeah, there was an office for the *Polizia Autostradale* close to the toll station so I put a few men there and as soon as the cops emerged to check on what the hell was happening my men were told to fire at their vehicles and shred their tyres so they couldn't come after us.

"Christ Rico, you are a revelation...I couldn't have planned it better myself and you managed to set it all up in less than twenty-four hours."

The journey to Monopoli took about fifty minutes and their van was not stopped although they did see a lot of police cars with sirens wailing speeding in the opposite direction. Pozzi had phoned ahead and arranged a safe house on the outskirts of town where Santoro could wait until well after dark before heading for the marina. Giorgio, the skipper of the escape boat had also been redirected to pick up his passenger in Monopoli at midnight.

5 MARCH 2011

BARI, PUGLIA

Bruno and *Colonello* Sportelli were just pulling into the *carabinieri* barracks in Bari when the police jeep's radio squawked and the *Colonello* picked up the handset. A crackly, breathless voice came over the airwaves. "Santoro's escaped, Sir. The escort convoy was hijacked about twenty minutes ago north of Taranto."

The two officers leapt out of the jeep and raced into the barracks. They found the Major in charge in the Comms room and he quickly brought them up to speed on the audacious attack.

"Ok, so what have you done since you got the news?"

"*Colonello*, we've put out an all-points bulletin to all enforcement agencies and organized road blocks on all roads at a radius of thirty kilometres from the hit on the autostrada. Also, Sir, I reckoned that the time lag between the hijack and us mobilising the response might have allowed the perpetrators to get beyond the first cordon of road blocks so I'm arranging check points at fifty kilometres as well."

"What about ports and airports?"

"In hand, Sir. We are in the process of arranging for all regional sea and air embarkation points to provide more intensive passenger screening and within the next half hour or so that will be extended nationally. As Santoro is such a huge man we should have a good chance of spotting him."

"And what if he's gone to ground locally?"

"Yes Sir, I've factored in that possibility. I have Captain Gagliardi coordinating a blanket search pattern including rounding up for questioning as many known or suspected *mafiosi* as we can in Puglia, Calabria and Basilicata."

"Well done Major"...Before Sportelli could make any further comments, one of the officers sitting at a communications console turned round and said, "Sir, there's been an exchange of gunfire at one of the thirty kilometre checkpoints. The report I've just received indicates that there were four men in an off-road vehicle who refused to stop when challenged and just started shooting, wounding one of our officers. In the ensuing firefight the vehicle was immobilised and two of the occupants were killed and two others wounded. None of these was Santoro. It is assumed they were members of the hijack gang as ski masks and other evidence was found in their vehicle."

Sportelli told the officer to find out where the wounded men were to be taken and said to Bruno, "You and I need to get to whichever hospital to see what we can get out of these men."

On the way to the hospital in Policoro, a small town about 70 kilometres south-west of Taranto, Bruno got a call from Gina. "Hi darling, I just wanted to tell you how dad's doing."

"OK...Great to hear your voice and you sound a lot more cheerful than when we spoke yesterday...you must have good news."

"Yes, he's out of Intensive Care. They put him into a medically induced coma and this has eased the pressure on his brain so they were able to bring him out of it this morning. So...he's out of Intensive Care and being treated for a broken pelvis and a fractured wrist...But thank God there are no serious internal injuries. The doctors say that sometimes it's incredible how some people survive being hit by a speeding car. It's something to do with the physics of exactly where the point of impact was. In Dad's case a helpful contributory factor was that he was thrown onto a grass verge which greatly cushioned his fall."

"That's really fantastic news darling...I can't wait to see him and fill him in on the massive number of arrests we've made...his dossier gave us invaluable help in compiling a huge list of criminals and their associates."

"Bruno, your operation has been widely covered on all the European news channels. It's being hailed as one of the biggest criminal round-ups ever...I saw Commander Gibbs on *Sky News* last night and he was very explicit in giving you and your men the lion's share of the credit for putting hundreds of crooks and fellow travellers behind bars."

"That was good of him, but I have to tell you that we've had a big setback. Arturo Santoro has been busted out of a police convoy and we are mounting another big manhunt for him and his son, Vittore. Can't talk more now…will call you when I can…*Ti amo*…and it's wonderful news about Luca."

It was late afternoon when they arrived at the *Ospedale Civile* in Policoro and found a squad of *carabinieri* in reception. "Status report please," was the terse request fired at a sergeant by Sportelli.

"Sir, two of the men who opened fire on our checkpoint are dead, one of the men arrested is in the operating theatre and the prognosis is not good. He took a couple of bullets to the stomach and chest and the odds are massively stacked against him surviving. The fourth man was only slightly injured with a flesh wound to his leg and he's being treated in the cubicle over there. Bruno and the *Colonello* strode over to the treatment room where a doctor and a nurse were attending to a swarthy youngish man with shaved head and a huge Viva Zapata style moustache. The doctor protested that they were in the middle of stitching up the hole in their patient's lower leg and that the officers should wait until they'd finished before questioning the man.

"Sorry doctor," was Sportelli's brusque response. "Time is of the essence here so you need to leave him to us for five minutes and then come back in to finish what you are doing."

After the doctor and nurse had left the cubicle, Sportelli moved close to the bed and without preamble said, "I'll give you a once only opportunity to shave a good few years off your inevitably lengthy prison sentence."

Sportelli's words provoked a grunt from the prone man and a calculating look in his eyes which confirmed that this was not an entirely unattractive prospect. His response, though, seemed to be at odds with his body language. "I'm no grass so you can go to hell."

Unfazed by this negative reply, Sportelli continued, "There's no need for anyone to know that you gave us information…but I guarantee that if you don't, I'll push so hard for you to get the maximum jail term that you'll be lucky to walk out of prison eventually without the help of a zimmer frame."

The man's bravado vanished in a puff of smoke and for the next quarter of an hour they were able to get some valuable leads. After they had climbed back into the rear of their jeep, Bruno summarised what they'd got. "The hijack was planned and led by Enrico Pozzi who we know is one of Santoro's enforcers. We've had him on our radar for ages. He's a stone cold killer but after many attempts to tie him to a series of murders we've been defeated by the power of the *omerta* code. Secondly, there's a leak from within the senior ranks of the *carabinieri* although this guy was too junior to know who tipped them off about the route the police convoy would take. Thirdly, the likelihood is that Santoro will try to make for Albania to find somewhere to hole up…He'll go by sea, probably from an embarkation point around Brindisi."

"OK, Bruno, so we need to intensify our surveillance at all ports and marinas along the Adriatic although that's a hell of a lot of coastline to cover given the huge number of places where a boat could pick someone up. We'll alert the Albanian police to the likelihood of Santoro making for their shores…But we both know that they are not the most reliable law enforcement agency on the planet so we need to find a way to put a bit of muscle into their effort. How do you fancy going over there to help coordinate things? If you go by helicopter you could be on the ground before Santoro is likely to make landfall."

"Good idea, I've got a high-level contact, the head of the Albanian Prosecution Office…He's a seriously good guy and we've worked together on a couple of joint operations against their and our mafia."

****

A few hours later, approaching midnight, Santoro was back in the delivery van and in ten minutes he was on the deserted quayside in Monopoli. With Pozzi's help he lowered himself onto the deck of his medium-sized yacht and told Pozzi to keep a look-out. As the *carabinieri* had confiscated his keys when they arrested him, he used bolt cutters to slice through the padlock on the cabin door.

A minute later Pozzi heard a stream of obscenities and his boss levered himself out of the cabin, waving something that looked like a passport. His face was suffused with a look of such venomous rage that even the battle-hardened enforcer stepped back in alarm. "What the hell's up boss?"

"My son Vittore has betrayed me. That treacherous snake has not only grassed me up but he has made off with something very valuable that we stashed on this fucking boat. All he's left is my fucking false passport." Santoro stood on the deck with fists clenched and his face changing to an incredible, apoplectic shade of red. Pozzi thought his terrifying boss could have a stroke any minute but he didn't dare say or do anything in case Santoro turned on him and released some of the pent up violence running through his enormous frame.

They stood like statues for what seemed to Pozzi like an age but, suddenly Santoro seemed to snap back to life. He grabbed Pozzi by the arm and shoved him to the side of the boat. "Help me get off this fucking thing," he said through gritted teeth, "We need to get hold of Ottavio Palumbo."

Santoro had been relying on the gold and diamonds secreted on the yacht to support him during what might be his permanent exile from Italy. His plan had been to lie low in the house he had bought in Montenegro and after the dust had settled a bit, to move to his other house in Sicily in a heavily mafia controlled area where he might be able to spend his final years undetected. He had to rejig this plan now because he needed to muster enough cash to see him through many years on the run. Palumbo would be able to liquidate a number of his remaining concealed investments but that would not generate enough to sustain him. Most of his investments had already been converted to ready money or valuables and hidden at the house near L'Aquila or on the yacht but both these sources had now been cut off. Santoro quickly realised that his only option was to get Palumbo to sell the large houses in Albania and Sicily as well as the yacht and channel the eventual proceeds to him in Montenegro.

Right now, though, he needed to find the boat skippered by Giorgio and head across the Adriatic. Pozzi would have to drive down to Lecce to knock Palumbo up and arrange for him to call Giorgio's phone when they were at sea, still using one of the burner phones. It would take several hours, even in Giorgio's fast launch, to cover the three hundred or so kilometres to the Montenegrin coast, so Santoro would be able to brief Palumbo comprehensively on what he needed him to do. First and foremost, he had to get picked up as soon as he landed by one of their trusted Balkan contacts, probably from the Albanian mafia. Whoever it was would have time to drive up the coast, cross into Montenegro and meet him near one of the small ports just over the border, probably Ulcinj which Santoro knew was virtually an Albanian ethnic enclave anyway. Palumbo would also have to arrange some way to pay the Albanians for their help and set up a conduit to get cash to him. With all this settled in his mind, he gave Pozzi his instructions and walked towards the launch on the other side of the quay where he could see Giorgio waving to him. As the boat headed out to sea, he rained curses on his adopted son for putting him in this predicament and swore to find him and make him pay.

Santoro did not realise that as the boat drew away from the shore, two officers from the *Polizia Municipale* had resumed their patrol of this particular part of the port of Monopoli. A minute before Santoro and Pozzi had arrived, the officers had left the marina where Santoro's boat was moored and driven across to the other side of the harbour to check on the *Porto Antico*. They missed their quarry by the narrowest of margins.

5 MARCH 2011

PASHALIMAN NAVAL BASE, ALBANIA

Bruno's helicopter touched down at the Albanian naval base of Pashaliman near Vlorë at eleven o'clock on the evening of Saturday 5 March. Before he left Brindisi, he and *Colonello* Sportelli had spent several frenetic hours mobilising law enforcement agencies on the other side of the Adriatic to help nab Santoro.

Fortunately, Bruno had been involved in previous joint operations against organised crime syndicates with both the Albanian and Montenegrin authorities. In 2009, he had participated in operation Domino with the Montenegrin police which had led to the arrest of eighty-three people including a Sacra Corona Unita boss, Savino Parisi. He also had an excellent relationship with the head of the Albanian Prosecution Service, Loran Vrioni. Bruno had provided him with cast-iron intelligence which had enabled Vrioni to secure lengthy jail time for two top Albanian mafia figures. A few months earlier Bruno and Vrioni had collaborated on another international anti-mafia operation codenamed Kalipso which resulted in the arrest of Albino Prudentino, another one of the top men in the Sacra Corona Unita. Following his arrest in south-western Albania the previous September, Prudentino had been extradited to Italy a few months later to face charges of drug trafficking, extortion and money laundering.

Due to Bruno's excellent reputation in these Balkan states, Prosecutor Vrioni had pulled out all the stops to get a top priority classification for the Santoro reception committee. With commendable speed he had pulled together Naval, Coastguard, surface Police and Special Forces resources across both Montenegro and Albania. He had stipulated that Bruno should be in joint command with a high ranking Albanian Naval Officer who was a fluent Italian speaker. Radar tracking stations were on full alert to monitor all vessels crossing from southern Italy to the Balkan coast from the Greek border to Croatia. At this time of year and given that it was night-time, the traffic volume was not huge, but it was still too large a sample to intercept. Bruno decided that as police units would be deployed at all the recognised ports to check the occupants of all incoming vessels, he could apply two additional filters which would narrow the search down dramatically.

He believed Santoro would be on one of the high speed launches the SCU used for their smuggling runs. He would also avoid docking at any of the established ports in favour of a disembarkation at a more secluded spot. The Prosecutor had secured the full support of the Albanian Naval Force, including its special Delta Police Force. Each of their fast coastal patrol craft would be allocated an area to watch and the radar stations would alert them to any vessels approaching at speed the less populous parts of the coastline.

It was not by any means a perfect plan but Bruno thought it was as much as they could have done in the limited time they had. Having relayed all his instructions, Bruno was sitting in the Officers' Mess at the Pashaliman naval base with Rear Admiral Nikolla enjoying his first food and drink for many hours. The Rear Admiral had been extremely efficient in translating Bruno's outline plan into concrete action and Bruno had made a mental note to send him a case of Brunello di Montalcino as a mark of appreciation for his help. Just then Bruno's mobile bleeped and when he looked at the time signal he saw that it was 0100 hours. He recognised the caller as Fredo Sportelli.

"Bruno, I think we may have had a lucky break, I've just had a report that a local cop in Monopoli may have seen Santoro leaving from there about half an hour ago. He was patrolling the whole of the port area and he had just driven back to the marina section when he saw a large, fast launch speeding away from the harbour. He ran over to the outer harbour wall with a pair of high resolution binoculars and he reported to his station commander that he saw a huge figure standing in the stern looking back to shore who matched the photo and description that had been circulated a few hours earlier. The young cop had the presence of mind to take a photo on his phone camera and our technicians are trying to upgrade the indistinct image and identify the type of craft he saw. The Municipal Police commander said his officer was a very bright young man and coupled with the fact that it was an exceptionally clear night, we should take his observation very seriously. I'll call you when we have more details."

After closing the call, Bruno asked Admiral Nikolla if he could work out the probable range of crossing times for a fast boat from Monopoli to the Albanian or Montenegrin coasts. Within ten minutes the Admiral was back.

"Our calculations show that the maximum distance from Monopoli to the northernmost point on the Montenegrin coast is around one hundred and ten nautical miles and to the southernmost point on the Albanian coast around five fewer nautical miles. We know that the people and drug smugglers often use ultra-high speed boats that can do up to 60 knots so they can cross the southern Adriatic in a couple of hours. If we knew what kind of boat Santoro's on we could get a more accurate fix on the crossing time."

Bruno rang *Colonello* Sportelli back and asked him to get any information from his tech guys to him as soon as possible. Within half an hour he got a call from the *Raggruppamento Carabinieri Investigazioni Scientifiche* in Rome. RaCIS was their Forensic Science Department and *Colonello* Sportelli had obviously sent them the fuzzy image from the officer's phone to see what they could do with it.

The technician said, "Major, we have been able to confirm that the man looking shoreward is Arturo Santoro. We believe he is on a Mochi Craft Dolphin 51 cruiser."

"That's great! How fast can that go?"

"According to its technical spec, it can hit 35 knots and has a cruising speed of 30.5 knots."

Bruno passed the information on to Admiral Nikolla and they recalibrated their calculations on Santoro's likely crossing time.

The Admiral said, "It's highly unlikely that the vessel would maintain top speed for the whole journey, but if it did it would make our shores in about two and three-quarter hours...at 0245 hours. I think it more probable that it will be close to shore by 0330 to 0400."

"OK, Admiral, so can you put all our teams on sea and land on red alert from 0200 and brief the radar stations on the likely speed of the vessel."

Bruno looked at his watch. It was 0115 and he felt a tangible buzz of excitement at the greatly increased probability of Santoro being captured again so soon after he'd been sprung from the police convoy. He paced restlessly up and down the Mess drinking copious amounts of the excellent coffee provided by the steward. At 0215, Admiral Nikolla received a call from the main coastal radar station. They had been monitoring one particular vessel which was travelling at around 32 knots, appreciably faster than any of the few other boats that were on their screens at this time of night. If it maintained its present course, it would hit the Montenegrin coast, just over the border with Albania, at around 0345. The Admiral turned to Bruno, "Major, the closest town is Ulcinj but north of there is very sparsely populated and that seems to be where they are headed."

"What's the coastline like, Admiral?"

"There are lots of rocky inlets where a launch could easily moor and transfer a passenger to shore by dinghy. The hinterland is quite hilly and heavily forested and there aren't all that many roads."

"OK, we need to deploy a sizeable team to that area whilst not relaxing our efforts across the rest of the coastline. Admiral, can you also patch in the nearest naval or coastguard patrol vessels so that they can keep track of this suspect boat and make sure any escape route seaward is blocked. But tell them to keep their distance…We don't want to risk scaring them off."

The Admiral and Bruno continued to get reports on the suspect vessel. It did not deviate from its earlier trajectory and the handful of other vessels which had been detected were travelling at less than half its speed.

They had a map of Montenegro spread out on the table and Bruno could see that north of Ulcinj there seemed to be a stretch of coastline with few settlements that would be ideal for a clandestine landing. But something was nagging at the back of his mind that he felt could be crucial in identifying likely points of disembarkation. "That's it!" He muttered to himself, "Admiral, I think we can narrow things down now. I've just remembered that Arturo Santoro is pretty much crippled with arthritis and can't move far on foot. That means the landing must be very close to a road so that a vehicle can get to him. He certainly can't make any distance off road on foot."

They looked at the map more closely and ringed the places with the closest road access. At 0300 the target vessel was still on course for the area just north of Ulcinj. "Looks like they're making for Valdanos Beach," said the Admiral stabbing his finger at a tooth shaped bay. "If I were the captain, I'd drop Santoro off on the southern headland. There's a road right down to the shore. They could easily get a car down there to pick him up."

Instructions were given to the closest police team to get to the Valdanos Bay area and stay undercover until Santoro's landing point was absolutely confirmed. The nearest patrol boats were told to stay on watch and once Santoro had been put ashore to intercept the vessel which had carried him as it started its homeward run.

An anxious thirty minutes elapsed before the Montenegrin police radioed in to the Pashaliman base's control room where Admiral Nikolla and Bruno were now located. The Admiral listened to the rapid-fire report before translating the gist of it for Bruno.

"That was an officer of the Special Police Unit of Montenegro, their elite team dealing with serious crime and terrorism. He's had the latest radar tracking report that the suspect vessel is about ten minutes away from

Valdanos Beach. He has a six-man squad near the headland and another squad near the main beach. He told me that the headland is deserted and because of its steep rocky nature he thinks it extremely unlikely that anyone could be dropped off there…But that they have observed a large SUV with Albanian plates parked under some pine trees near the centre of the beach. He believes the vehicle has three occupants…Major, do you want to say anything to this police commander?"

"Only to stress that the man they are going to arrest is one of the most dangerous, vicious individuals on the planet so approach him with extreme caution."

The Admiral relayed Bruno's warning and then looked at Bruno with a smile. "The officer said thank you for the advice but as this was his fifteenth big anti-mafia operation, he thinks he's got the hang of things by now."

About three hundred kilometres north of Bruno's position, Petar Borozan Platoon Commander of the Montenegrin Special Police Unit replaced the radio handset shaking his head at what he considered to be the patronising advice he'd just received. "Bloody Italians," he muttered, "They think they are the only ones who know anything about dealing with the mafia."

His unit was deployed just behind a line of trees about one hundred metres from the beach and the suspect SUV. One of his men passed over a pair of night vision binoculars and simultaneously pointed out to sea. Just as he raised the binoculars to his eyes he heard the faint sound of an engine breaking the otherwise deathly calm of the inky night and immediately spotted a motor launch rounding the headland. In the middle of the beach there was the metal skeleton of a ruined pier and it quickly became clear that the boat was making for this structure to tie up and offload its passenger. Borozan signalled his five-man squad to get ready to move out just as two men got out of the SUV carrying what looked like AK47s. They walked across the narrow beach towards the derelict pier and stood there waiting. Nothing happened for a couple of minutes and then the police commander heard what sounded like a very heated argument coming from the boat. "What the hell is going on?" he thought.

What was happening was that Santoro had point blank refused to drop over the side of the boat and wade the last few metres to dry land. Through the binoculars the commander could see that a massive man was bludgeoning another man before throwing him over the side. He then unhitched the mooring rope and started the engine. The commander assumed that the boat was about to head out to sea again but just as he was about to race across the beach to fire on it, the engine revs increased and the boat circled round and headed back to shore. It rammed itself aground with a gravelly screech with the prow ending up in only a few centimetres of water. The man in the water started floundering through the waves towards the beached craft as the man still aboard clambered with great difficulty towards the prow gesticulating to the two Albanians to help him as he climbed over the wire guard rail.

The Albanians had slung their Kalashnikovs over their shoulders and were supporting Santoro's enormous bulk across the sand when the police commander and three of his men emerged from cover and shouted at the ungainly trio to halt. One of the Albanians dropped to his knees and tried to reach round for his assault rifle but a rapid burst into the sand just in front of him from the commander's Heckler and Koch MP5 convinced him of the error of his ways. As commander Borozan was discharging his burst of warning fire his eyes were on the man threatening to go for his AK47. In the split second it took him to refocus on the other two men, Santoro had pulled a small Beretta pistol from his capacious parka and started shooting. Borozan felt a heavy thump to his Kevlar vest and fell backwards onto the sand. As he was going down he managed to get off a burst from his MP5. He was instinctively aiming for the centre of Santoro's body mass as had been drummed into him countless times during his intensive training. The angle he was shooting from meant that his bullets hit Santoro just above the knees causing him to crash to the ground with a scream of agony. One of the policemen kicked the pistol away from where it had landed a metre or so away from Santoro's outstretched hand. The two Albanians quickly hoisted their hands in the air to signal their lack of interest in any further resistance.

The commander's men quickly disarmed and handcuffed the two Albanians and frisked Santoro, who was screaming in agony, removing another small Beretta from his parka, before cuffing him too. The man wading laboriously ashore was also apprehended, searched and manacled.

In the meantime the SUV had been approached by the other two police officers but before they could yank the doors open the driver had rammed the vehicle into reverse and then fishtailed through the pines towards the road with the officers firing long bursts at it with many hits but without stopping the vehicle. But, as the SUV hit the tarmac of the only road away from the beach it suddenly slewed violently to the left and smashed into a large pine tree with a horrendous crump.

Petar Borozan congratulated himself on his foresight in having had his men lay "stingers", tyre shredding traffic spikes, at two or three points along the only exit route from Valdanos Beach. He was the first to reach the crashed SUV and realised immediately that the driver's time on earth had come to an abrupt end. He had obviously not been wearing a seat belt and although the air bag had been activated the severity of the whiplash effect had broken his neck.

Borozan's sergeant dealt with the badly injured Santoro as best he could. Santoro initially tried to headbutt him and unleashed a stream of obscenities. He had to be restrained by two other policemen whilst the sergeant stemmed the blood flow from his shattered legs with tourniquets to both of the huge man's thighs. He also gave Santoro a morphine shot from the medical pack the unit always carried on its missions.

He radioed the control centre at Pashaliman and reported "mission accomplished" to Admiral Nikolla. He told the Admiral that he would take his prisoners to the Special Police Unit's HQ in Zlatica close to the Montenegrin capital Podgorica. The Admiral said that Major Canepa would be helicoptered there to serve Santoro with a European Arrest Warrant and to interrogate the captain of the motor launch whose name had been confirmed as Giorgio Saponaro.

EARLY HOURS, 6 MARCH 2011

MONOPOLI, PUGLIA

Enrico Pozzi drove away from the port of Monopoli with his mind working overtime on what he needed to do to make the rest of his life as comfortable as it had been for his two decades as Santoro's main man. Although not the recipient of much formal education, Pozzi was cunning and extremely street smart. He was thinking through the impact of recent events on his own future options. He realised that he had been very lucky not to have been picked up in the extensive police operation a few days earlier. When, on the morning of 1 March the police smashed down the door of the apartment in Lecce he shared with his girlfriend, he was not there. He had been at an all-night poker game organised by one of his men and he had crashed out on the man's sofa at 5 a.m. He was shaken awake a few hours later with the news that dozens of SCU members and their associates had been rounded up by the police.

Pozzi had been well rewarded by Santoro for his many brutal acts elimi-nating or maiming those on Santoro's hit list. He had used some of his money to establish his own contingency plan in the event that things went sour. He had bought an isolated cottage from a trusted cousin and laid up enough provisions there to last him several weeks if necessary. Immediately after the police swoop he went to this bolt hole in the mountains near Matera in the neighbouring region of Basilicata. This put him about two hundred kilometres from Lecce but within easy reach of the Adriatic coast. He quickly established what was left of SCU's infrastructure. Almost all of the top men had been arrested. In fact, he was now the most senior gang member still free but there were still a hefty number of lower level soldiers who had not been picked up in the police dragnet. This group had provided the necessary manpower to spring Santoro from the police convoy.

Pozzi had thought long and hard about whether to mount this tricky and risky operation after receiving the order from Santoro via Palumbo. Pozzi knew his own days in Puglia were numbered. He had to move on to pastures new and probably get out of Italy altogether. For that, he would need help. He knew Santoro had international connections that could be of great use to him and he concluded that the potential benefits of rescuing Santoro outweighed the negatives.

Whilst they were waiting in the house in Monopoli before the rendezvous with the escape boat, Pozzi had talked to Santoro about his need to start somewhere fresh. Although Santoro had not an ounce of personal loyalty towards Pozzi or any gratitude for being rescued, he had a high regard for his enforcer's brutal repertoire of skills. He thought he might need Pozzi in the future so he told him, "Rico, as soon as I get settled somewhere I'll find a way to bring you on board again."

He also gave Pozzi contact details for several people in criminal organisa-tions in other parts of Italy, Albania and Greece. Once he'd seen Santoro safely aboard Giorgio's boat, he'd shot back to his hideaway to lie low for a few days before tapping some of the contacts Santoro had given him. He did not risk driving down to Lecce to brief Palumbo as ordered by Santoro. Instead, he phoned one of his trusted guys and got him to make the trip. Two days later the news channels were buzzing with reports of Santoro's re-arrest in Montenegro and Pozzi's hopes of a continuing fruitful relation-ship with his *capo* disappeared instantly. What was also troubling was that his own mugshot was prominently featured in all the bulletins together with those of half a dozen other wanted men who had not been swept up in the police swoop. This confirmed a course of action that Pozzi had been contemplating since the massive intensification of police operations against SCU. He had to change his appearance significantly and undergo extensive plastic surgery.

He had already planned for this eventuality and had a link to an eminent surgeon in Naples who was a world authority on facial reconstruction. This man had a predilection for nubile under-age girls and had come to the attention of the Camorra. They had forced him to perform plastic surgery procedures on several of their clan members under the threat of his expo-sure as a paedophile and the consequent jail time and professional ruin. One of Pozzi's close contacts in the Camorra had told him about this doctor and Pozzi knew it would be easy to put the squeeze on him to perform a transformative operation on his face. He could then easily arrange for a new passport and identity.

The other issue that had been preying on his mind was how the hell he was going to get the hefty funds together to support him for many years somewhere far away from his well-trodden patch in southern Italy. The image that kept shooting into his mind's eye was that of Arturo standing on the deck in Monopoli apoplectic with rage at his son's betrayal. Pozzi knew that there must have been something very valuable on that boat – valuable enough for Santoro to take the big risk of heading to the port rather than putting a lot more kilometres between himself and the intense police effort after the convoy ambush. This led him to the inescapable conclusion that he simply had to find Vittore and relieve him of whatever was hidden on that boat. From what he could gather though, Vittore had disappeared off the face of the earth. From the few bent policemen still in SCU's pocket the word came back that all efforts to trace Vittore had drawn a blank. Still, Pozzi thought grimly, "I'm sure I can tap underworld sources of information unavailable to the police. I back myself to find him eventually and I have enough cash to see me through for many months."

****

On the other side of the Adriatic in his hideaway in Croatia, Vittore Santoro was thanking his lucky stars that Arturo's escape from police custody had been short-lived. Had his father remained on the loose Vittore knew that he would never have been able to sleep easily at night. Santoro senior would without doubt have mounted a relentless crusade to track him down and would also have vented his fury on his wife and kids. The news reports confirming Arturo's re-capture on a Montenegrin beach had removed the terror he felt when he heard that he had been sprung from the police convoy.

Vittore had been at the safe house near the small Croatian town of Gospić for a few days. His "host", Kristofor Pribislav, was the man his brother-in-law Maso had contacted. Vittore paid €160,000 upfront for a three month stay including a move to a different property each month. Before leaving Italy he had agreed to set up a safe communication link with Maso. On the way to the small port of Torre Canne, Maso had bought a couple of burner phones and given one to Vittore. As soon as Maso had told his sister Renata that her husband had got away, he would call Vittore so he would have an untraceable emergency contact number on his call log. This would provide a back-up communication loop in case the arrangement he had made to call Renata direct on another mobile phone did not work.

In the early days of his self-imposed exile in Croatia, Vittore had all the time in the world to mull over what he wanted to do with the rest of his life. Free from the malign influence of his adoptive father he realised that it was very important for him to find his real mother and father. He couldn't fathom exactly why he felt this need so acutely. He was not given to deep introspection but he concluded that it was a critical first step towards normalising his life and perhaps returning to a life path denied him by his adoption. The search for his true identity became an all-consuming obsession and Vittore decided to pursue the leads his adoptive mother had given him on the evening of his son's christening. Burned into Vittore's brain were the names of Antonella Perugini and Luca Vento. He believed that Antonella had emigrated to Australia and that was at least something concrete to go on as opposed to the disappearance without trace of his father Luca.

Vittore decided to press the button first on a search for his mother. If he found her she may be able to shed light on the likely whereabouts of his father. He had in the past used a private investigator in Brindisi to undertake some sensitive undercover work for him. He obviously couldn't risk contacting this man under his real name but he had the new documentation he had collected from the yacht in Monopoli. In addition to a passport, a driving licence and an identity card or *Carta d'Identità Elettronica* in his new name of Sergio Greco, he had created a new email account. He had chosen Greco because it was one of the most common names in Puglia and therefore pretty anonymous.

He contacted the private investigator, Elia Lorusso, via email using his new name. He explained that Lorusso had been recommended to him but as he was currently living abroad he would not be able to brief him in person. As a demonstration of his *bona fides,* if Lorusso accepted the assignment, he would arrange a non-refundable bank transfer of €5,000 for a month's work. The email Vittore concocted read,

"I need to trace a young woman called Antonella Perugini who left the Lecce area probably in the summer of 1975 bound for Australia. I must find her because she could be the beneficiary of a valuable legacy from a distant relative. The matter is highly sensitive and it is imperative that any remaining members of Antonella's family in Italy are not made aware of this possibility. All I require is a current address for Antonella."

As Vittore anticipated, knowing Lorusso's venal nature, the assignment was accepted without demur and he immediately deposited the initial fee in Lorusso's bank account from the account he had opened in Croatia with the help of his "landlord", Pribislav.

A fortnight later, Lorusso reported back with the disquieting news that Antonella Zanca neé Perugini had died a couple of years earlier in Melbourne. Lorusso supplied her family address as 51 Victoria Avenue in Canterbury, an upmarket suburb of Australia's second city. He also confirmed that Antonella was survived by her husband, Aldo and two grown-up children, Guido and Martina. Vittore received this news as a hammer blow as it seemed to extinguish the faint glimmer of hope he had of getting any leads on the identity and whereabouts of his father. He stewed on this for a couple of days but finally concluded that he should go to Australia to see if he could ferret out any useful information from Antonella's husband or from his half-brother or sister. In any case, he thought it might be a good idea to go to the other side of the world for a while until the intensive manhunt across the Adriatic died down a bit.

As a first step he contacted Lorusso again and asked him to find the addresses of his half-siblings, transferring a further fee of €2,000. Lorusso took only twenty-four hours to confirm a Melbourne address for Guido and an address in Sydney for Martina whose married name was Graham. With the eye-wateringly expensive help of Pribislav, Vittore obtained a genuine Croatian passport in the name of Ivano Horvat with a photo reflecting his present appearance – crewcut and goatee beard. If anyone spoke to him in Serbo-Croat he would say that his parents moved to Italy when he was little but he had decided to retain his Croatian identity even though he didn't speak the language. He also had with him the other Italian passport in the name of Sergio Greco.

4 APRIL 2011

SYDNEY, AUSTRALIA

On a blustery day in early April Vittore arrived in Sydney on a flight from Zagreb. He had thought long and hard about how to initiate contact with the Zanca family. In the end, he had decided to contact his half-sister Martina first. He thought that there was invariably a special bond between mother and daughter and Antonella may have shared more details of her past with Martina than with Aldo or Guido.

After a day spent strolling around Sydney and getting over his jet lag, the following morning Vittore took a cab out to the suburb of Mossman. He knew Martina had a couple of school-age kids and that she was a stay-at-home mum so he arrived at her house in a street close to Balmoral Bay at 9.30, when he thought she would probably be on her own. He found himself outside a sprawling single storey house and saw a tanned young woman with black hair tied back in a short pony tail and wearing shorts and a t-shirt. She was kneeling on a mat by a flower bed with a garden fork in her gloved hand. She looked up quizzically and sat back on her heels as this handsome well-dressed man approached. In halting English Vittore said, "Hello, my name is Sergio Greco and I have come from Europe in an attempt to find my family." He then said hopefully, "Do you speak Italian?"

"*Certo.*" Martina said, "*Come posso auitarla?*" How can I help you?

Vittore then explained that he had been adopted as a baby and had a compulsion to find out who his real parents were. His investigation had led him along a trail that, "Conclusively indicates that Antonella Perugini, your mother, is also my mother…and I am so sorry that she passed away a couple of years ago."

Martina's hand flew to her mouth in an involuntary shock reflex. She stammered, "So…you're saying that you are my half-brother…oh my God…that's a lot to take in…let's go and sit on the verandah and I'll make some coffee."

When she returned with the coffee she handed him a photo without saying anything but he could see there were tears welling in her eyes. He took the rather dog-eared print and at first the image of a smiling young man did not register with him. He looked at Martina in surprise and she said, "Don't you see…that could be a slightly younger version of you without your beard and with longer hair."

He looked again and then did see a really strong resemblance to himself.

"Where did you get this…is this my father?"

"I'm sure it is. Let me explain. When my son Peter was born about six years ago my mum was so happy for me but my giving birth to a boy brought it all back to her. She confided in me that she never really got over the fact that she had to give up her own baby all those years ago. She said she had had a brief fling with a young man called Luca Vento, the father of the child, but that he had mysteriously disappeared before she had the chance to tell him she was pregnant. My dad knew of this and they had a really happy marriage but I think the terrible sadness of this loss of a child lasted all her life. I'm pretty sure it contributed to her dying before her time. After Mum died I was going through her things and decided to keep the photo…maybe it was a premonition that this particular circle would be closed one day."

Martina was crying now but she wiped away her tears and said, "Sergio I'm sure you are my brother."

"So am I but we can have our DNA tested to prove it if you want."

Martina shook her head, "No, I have no doubt whatsoever and I'm sure Mum would be so pleased that you made the effort to find us."

After this encounter, things moved on quickly and Martina flew to Melbourne with her newly acquired brother the next day. Meetings with her father and brother were equally positive and Vittore really clicked with his half-brother Guido. Vittore had invented a simple back story for his new identity of Sergio Greco. He said he had lost both his adoptive parents within six months of each other the previous year. On her deathbed, his mother had told him he had been adopted and given him the names of his real mother and father. He had been unable to trace Luca Vento but had managed to get someone in the Perugini family to confirm that his mother had emigrated to Australia, got married and stayed. He said he himself was married with a couple of young kids but he obviously couldn't give his real address in Puglia so said that they had just moved to Croatia where he was CEO of a food company.

Vittore had quizzed Martina about Luca Vento but she clearly had no idea what had happened to him. The only useful information he gleaned from her was that her mother had kept in touch with Bernardo Colangelo, Luca's closest friend and he was also totally in the dark about Luca's disappearance.

After she had flown back to Sydney, he and Guido went out on the town to celebrate their newly forged fraternal relationship and had a lot to drink. Vittore learnt that Guido had spent a fair bit of time in Puglia with the Colangelo family and it was when he mentioned that his last visit a few weeks earlier had been to attend Bernardo Colangelo's funeral that Vittore finally hit pay dirt. Out of the blue Guido said, "This may be completely off the wall but there was a mysterious guy at the funeral. He was a pall bearer but he didn't show up for the reception at Bernardo's son's house…funnily enough he was also called Luca. I thought it was a bit odd as he was actually staying with them. My mate Luca told me that this other Luca was a close friend of his father's but that they had only recently met up again after an interval of nearly forty years. Apparently this guy was living abroad…I think he said in the UK…but Sergio, he wasn't called Vento…his name was Luca Biagi. It just seems a weird coincidence that we know your dad was a friend of Bernardo's who vanished in the seventies…and he was called Luca…It may be a lead."

Vittore felt sure that this was a vital link in the chain. His mother had told him that Luca Vento had fallen foul of the mafia. In that case it was highly feasible that he had assumed a new identity having left Italy in a hurry.

A couple of days later Vittore flew back to Croatia having given his new siblings his temporary address there, his new email address and the number of the burner phone Maso had given him before he left for Croatia. He did not want to risk them getting too close in case they discovered that he was not who he claimed to be. But he knew that it would be suspicious if he did not leave his contact details with them.

He immediately contacted the private investigator again and said he would transfer a further €3,000. He wanted to locate a Luca Biagi who lived somewhere in the UK and was around sixty years old. A few days later, Lorusso emailed details of three men he had found – in Cardiff, London and the north of England. For the Luca Biagi in the north he had attached several press photos as he was a well-known restaurateur. As soon as Vittore saw the photo of Luca shaking hands with some local dignitary at the opening of a new restaurant in Manchester he knew his quest was over.

Two days later, he flew from Zagreb to Manchester using his Sergio Greco passport and driver's licence, picked up a rental car with satnav and set off for the village of Silverdale in Lancashire. He could not really explain to himself this compulsion to connect with his father. Deep down he felt that if Luca acknowledged his paternity it would somehow expunge the dreadful years of terrified subservience to his adoptive father.

Late afternoon he parked outside the Biagi's house and without any concrete idea of what he was going to say or do he strode up to the front door and rang the bell. He was totally unaware that his true identity would be known to the Biagis. Rosalba opened the door to see a well- dressed, good looking young man with a neatly trimmed goatee beard.

"Can I help you."

"*Si*...er, yes...I come from Italy...*mi dispiace*...sorry my English not good."

"That's OK, I speak Italian."

"*Va bene*. I am Sergio Greco and I need urgently to speak to Luca Biagi on a personal matter."

Something about the timbre of his voice triggered a flash of recognition. "My God," thought Rosalba, "He sounds just like Luca...Could he be the son he fathered before he fled Italy?...Without that beard he would look just like Luca did at his age." She decided to buy a little time.

"*Signor* Greco, you are probably not aware that my husband was involved in a serious road accident and has only just returned home after several weeks in hospital. In fact, he is out at the moment having physiotherapy in Lancaster. Do you think you could come back this evening around eight o'clock? I'm sure Luca will be happy to talk to you then. Perhaps you can tell me why you are here."

"I'm sorry *Signora* Biagi but I think your husband would prefer for me to speak to him first about this sensitive matter...I will come back this evening as you suggested...*Ciao*."

As Rosalba closed the door and turned round, Luca emerged from his study walking very gingerly with the help of a stick. "Who was that?"

"Shush! *Caro*, I think it was your son Vittore masquerading under a false name."

"Vittore!" spluttered Luca. "What did he say?"

Rosalba explained that he had been non-committal about why he had come and she thought it best to say Luca was out so that they had time to decide what to do.

"Luca, you should ring Bruno so that he can arrange for Vittore to be arrested when he gets here in a few hours."

"No *cara*, I don't think I can do that. I want to hear what he has to say first." Although she was very uneasy about this, Rosalba reluctantly agreed and they spent the rest of the afternoon in nervous anticipation.

Vittore mooched around nearby Grange-over-Sands and drove right round Lake Windermere until the allotted time. When he rang the doorbell

Luca himself opened the door, ushered him in and invited him to take a seat in his study.

Luca had no doubt about who sat facing him and without preamble said, "Vittore, I know who you are so you can stop this Sergio Greco nonsense. Why are you here?"

"What the hell! How did you know?"

"We'll get to that later but I repeat, why are you here?"

It was as if a dam had burst and the words poured out of Vittore in an unbroken flow. He explained that he had long felt imprisoned in a life not of his choosing. How he had come to hate his chillingly sadistic brute of a father. How the revelation by his mother of his true paternity had suddenly made everything clear. His life had been hijacked by Arturo Santoro who had made him pursue a criminal career. Luca listened attentively without interrupting him but when Vittore paused eventually he said, "Vittore, I believe in free will and whilst I accept that you were trapped in a horrible situation, I don't understand why you didn't break away and forge a different path?"

Vittore looked at Luca despairingly, "You don't know Arturo Santoro… he is the most thoroughly evil and brutal human being you could imagine. Any attempt by me to escape would have driven him to hunt me down wherever I went and almost certainly kill me for what he would see as an act of betrayal. When I got married and had kids it was even more impossible as he would not have had the slightest compunction in punishing them as well."

Luca could hardly disagree with Vittore's stark assessment of the lethal risks involved in going against the monster he had called *papà* for so many years. He himself could have been eliminated by the mafia and he had to admit that with no family ties to bind him it had been easier for him to escape and re-invent himself.

Vittore continued, "You need to know *Signor* Biagi that I have made some recompense for my years in crime. I tipped off the police about my father's location and it's down to me that he was captured. You also need to know that I never killed anybody. My father wanted to keep me away from any violent criminality so that I would have a clean record when he needed someone to front his legitimate business interests."

Luca was torn. He sensed genuine remorse in Vittore but he knew that his lost son had been party to criminal activities, particularly drug trafficking, which had blighted the lives of so many people. He thought that Vittore had only one option.

"You must give yourself up Vittore. I'm sure that your role in delivering Santoro to the police and the information you can provide on him and Sacra Corona Unita will be taken into account and will lighten your sentence. You can probably also help the police to grab some of the ill-gotten gains which Santoro salted away. I'm sure you can unearth substantial assets which can be used for the public good. Am I right in that?"

Vittore nodded and grunted assent. Luca continued, "Look Vittore you are a young man and once you have served your time you will be able to live the rest of your life as a normal member of society. I promise you that I will help your family in every way I can and will also ensure you get the best defence lawyer there is to argue your case for mitigation. What do you say?"

Vittore looked his newly found father directly in the eyes and knew he was a thousand per cent sincere in his promises.

Luca went on. "You know also that in addition to your relatives in Australia, you have two new half-sisters here who will want to help."

Luca told him about Maurizia and Gina, obviously proud of their career achievements. When he mentioned that Gina was a headhunter, Vittore immediately made the connection to the feisty woman who had interviewed him in Verona. With all that had happened in the intervening months he had forgotten the surname of the headhunter who had insisted that he allow sufficient time for an extensive interview. When it became obvious that she would not be fobbed off with a cursory account of his career, Vittore had been worried that her input to Mondo Foods might jeopardise the plan to put him into the SSP company. His paranoia about Arturo's reaction to any hiccups in their plan had translated itself into a thinly disguised belligerence towards Gina. Vittore told Luca that he had already met Gina and was surprised when Luca said he knew about this encounter.

That led on to Luca telling Vittore about Major Canepa and his involvement of Gina in the ongoing investigation into SCU/Mondo and the close call the two sisters had had with the foiled kidnapping attempt. Their conversation had by now lasted about an hour and had moved into a more relaxed phase. Vittore had shown Luca photos of Renata and his Italian grandkids, Elisa and Tommaso. Luca had reciprocated with photos of his parents and *nonna* Valentina. At about 9.30 Rosalba came in with a quizzical look on her face and Luca said, "*Cara*, let me introduce you to my son Vittore."

Vittore rose and approached Rosalba. After a momentary hesitation she clasped his outstretched hand and said, "You need to know that your father is one of the finest men I know and if you do anything to hurt him you will have me to answer to." To the surprise of both Biagis, Vittore sank back down into his chair with tears streaming down his face as the years of camouflaging his identity melted away. The realisation hit him that his life could have been so different if he had been within the orbit of these good people.

After composing himself he stood up and said that he would take a day or two to mull over Luca's advice to give himself up and he hoped that his *papà*-using that word for the first time – would allow him that window before alerting the police about his visit. Vittore left with his mind in turmoil. On the doorstep Luca had embraced him and said he knew Vittore would do the right thing and that he would give him forty-eight hours before telling the police he had been there. Luca had already given Vittore his email address and mobile number. Vittore had not told Luca that he was in hiding in Croatia but he knew he had left a trail by using his false passport that the police would be able to pick up fairly easily. He desperately wanted to talk to Renata before he made his decision and resolved to find a way to contact her securely when he got back to his safe house.

20 APRIL 2011

GOSPIÉ, CROATIA

As Vittore was boarding his flight back to Croatia, Enrico Pozzi was driving up to the house Vittore had "rented". A lucky break had enabled him to discover where Vittore was hiding. One of Pozzi's crew knew that Maso was Vittore's brother-in-law and that he was also involved in some cross-Adriatic smuggling. Pozzi paid Maso a visit after dark one evening with a concocted tale. He said that Arturo Santoro had got a message to him that he needed to contact Vittore urgently to get him to unlock some substantial financial holdings not yet discovered by the police.

Maso did not know that Vittore had shopped Arturo and when he was approached by Arturo's right-hand man with this credible story he had no hesitation in disclosing the name of his contact in Croatia. Maso arranged for Pozzi to make a night crossing in a boat skippered by the same man who had transported Vittore. This skipper would be on standby to pick Pozzi up the following night or the one after that for the return trip to Italy. Maso also contacted Pribislav to let him know that Pozzi was on his way and asked him to provide the Italian with Vittore's address and a car to get him there. Pozzi had nearly lost his cool when he met Pribislav who had demanded a fee of €1,000 for the car he provided. But he managed to rein in the strong inclination to smash his fist into the face of the greedy Croat and keep himself focused on the main prize. Pozzi arrived at the second house Vittore had moved to, also near the town of Gospić in the early afternoon. A quick recce indicated that the house was shuttered and seemed to be uninhabited. After parking his car a couple of hundred metres away, Pozzi jemmied open the kitchen door at the rear of the property and cursed as a thorough search with his gun in his hand confirmed that Vittore was out.

There was nothing for it but to make himself comfortable, raid the refrigerator for the makings of a meal and wait for Vittore's return. He knew that Vittore had taken something valuable from the yacht in Monopoli and caused Santoro's furious outburst so he decided to search the house from top to bottom. After a couple of hours of fruitless effort he literally struck gold when he found a bag of krugerrands under a pile of logs in a lean-to next to the house. The gold coins sat on top of several wads of high denomination euro notes. Pozzi was very pleased with his haul but he said to himself, "I bet there's a lot more somewhere and I'll make sure Vittore coughs up the lot before I'm done."

Around five o'clock Pozzi heard a car pull up outside and a quick look through a crack in the shutters confirmed it was Vittore. As Vittore entered he got the shock of his life as the bulky ominous figure of Pozzi emerged from the shadows pointing a pistol at his chest.

"*Buongiorno* Vittore…I've been waiting for you and thanks for the gold and dosh I found outside. Let's go and sit down so you can tell me what else you have stashed away."

Vittore's brain was in overdrive. On the flight back he had decided to take Luca's advice and hand himself in. He believed that he had other bargaining chips he could use. He could hand over the diamonds he had with him and tell the police where he had buried the bags of cash near the house in Aragno. The sudden appearance of Pozzi potentially scuppered this plan although he had clearly not found the diamonds. Vittore had sealed these in a small plastic bag and taped it under the rim of a full water tank in the loft. Vittore knew that he had to offer Pozzi something otherwise he was all too well aware that this merciless enforcer would torture and then kill him. He couldn't risk giving him the diamonds. He would be a dead man immediately after Pozzi had them in his large mitts. The only option was to tell him about the buried cash in the Abruzzo.

"OK Rico…What you've found is all I could carry when I got out of Italy in a hurry. There is a lot more but it's not here. You know my father went into hiding when the cops were getting too close. He had a house near L'Aquila and in a nearby wood I buried close to €20 million in some bags. I need to take you there to show you exactly where it is…and maybe you could leave me with a couple of million and take the rest."

Pozzi gave Vittore a hard look as he weighed up the possibility that he was being taken for a ride. In the end though he thought, "What the hell…I've already got a lot of dough and if he's telling the truth I'll be rolling in it. If he's lying and trying to buy himself some time, I'll kill him…I'll kill him anyway…He's no soldier…He's just a flabby businessman."

"*Va bene* Vittore…We'll go back to Italy together tonight and find the money…But I warn you don't piss me off or I'll cut you into little pieces."

The trip back over the Adriatic went without a hitch. Pozzi had left a car at Torre Cane and just before dawn Vittore led Pozzi to the spot near the holly bush in the copse next to the house on the outskirts of Aragno. He knelt down and started to dig with the tyre lever Pozzi had taken from his car boot until he dropped the tool and felt for the oiled sacks with his bare hands. Pozzi was standing a little way away with a hand on the gun in the pocket of his bomber jacket but as soon as Vittore started to haul up the first sack he edged closer as if magnetically drawn to the money. As Vittore was pulling out the second bag Pozzi leant down to grab the first one and Vittore threw two big handfuls of soil and grit into his face.

"You stupid bastard," bellowed Pozzi as he tried to wipe his eyes and free the pistol that had snagged in his coat pocket. By the time he had blinked away the soil in his eyes and raised his weapon, Vittore had put several yards between them and was racing through the woods zigzagging wildly to try to dodge the bullets spitting from Pozzi's Beretta. Just as Vittore was about to burst out of the wood onto a lane he was hit in the shoulder and staggered on drunkenly before crumpling and sinking to his knees. Pozzi was on him in seconds and having emptied his gun took out the outsize flick knife he always carried and thrust it into Vittores side, jerking it viciously from side to side to cause maximum pain. Vittore screamed as Pozzi said, "You stupid fucker. Did you think you could get away?"

Just then Pozzi looked down the lane and saw the lights come on in a house about a hundred metres away and heard the unholy racket made by what seemed like a whole pack of dogs. The gunshots followed by Vittore's ear-splitting scream had obviously alerted the whole household. Pozzi yanked the blade out, stood up and looked down at the nearly comatose Vittore who was bleeding profusely. "OK, you can bleed out here while I go and get my millions."

Vittore knew he had been grievously wounded but as Pozzi disappeared into the trees he managed with a superhuman effort to get back to his feet holding his side with the blood pulsing through his fingers and tottered toward the nearby house. He collapsed a few yards from the front gate and moments later an elderly man in his undershirt and trousers came out to see what was going on. "*Gesucristo*," he blurted out when he saw Vittore covered in blood, "What the hell's happened to you?"

Vittore grabbed his hand and whispered hoarsely to the mystified old man, "I am Vittore Santoro. Tell Luca I was going to hand myself in."

5 YEARS LATER, 10 MAY 2016

ROME

Bruno and Gina were having a late dinner in their apartment having just managed to get their son Stefano off to sleep. He was just two years old and had been the most placid baby until well into his teething phase. Now he wailed constantly and none of the teething remedies they had tried came close to placating him. As was the case this evening, he finally fell asleep through sheer exhaustion brought on by his constant lusty crying. Gina had baulked at the suggestion of Bruno's mother to rub a little brandy or whisky on his gums although she thought she might have to give this a go if his heart-rending crying persisted for much longer. *Nonna* Canepa had insisted this was the only thing that worked when Bruno and Marco were toddlers. Gina and Livia Canepa had bonded from that first spring day in 2011 when Bruno had taken his intended to meet his mother at her home in Frascati to the south of Rome. Livia had been an absolute rock in supporting her daughter-in-law during Stefano's early months and Gina genuinely saw her as a second mum.

On this balmy May evening, Bruno and Gina had been planning to go out for dinner to celebrate Bruno's forty-second birthday. *Nonna* Canepa had willingly agreed to babysit as she had done countless times before but Bruno had called to cancel when it was clear Stefano was inconsolable and Gina was herself tired out. The past few years had been eventful ones for the Canepas. They had married on 8 December 2011, exactly one year from the date they met and a month after he had been promoted to Colonel in the *Guardia*. It was a double celebration for the Biagi family as Maurizia also got married to George Mellon on the same day at St Mary's, the small Catholic Church in Yealand Conyers close to the family home in North Lancashire.

Luca Biagi had proudly walked both his daughters down the aisle. He had made a remarkable recovery since the horrific hit-and-run accident and apart from a slight limp was back to his old, ebullient self. He had spent six weeks in hospital but since his release he had worked with his usual tenacity to get himself back into top physical shape. He had substituted cycling for running but other than that minor adjustment to his exercise regime his life was completely back to normal. He knew that his survival after having been hit so hard was a rare piece of luck. The car had struck him in exactly the right spot to flip him end over end to land on his back on the soft grass verge. His surgeon said he had only once before seen such limited damage to a human frame from so violent an impact.

In the autumn of 2011, Luca was surprised to get a call directly from the Italian Minister of Finance thanking him personally for the dossier he had put together all those years earlier. The Minister said that this had been, in effect, the master-key which had been used to unlock the voluminous database of Giuseppe Moscatelli and led to the biggest ever anti-mafia clean up. The Minister acknowledged that Luca had suffered significant financial losses when he had to flee Italy and he was happy to tell him that, with the approval of Prime Minister Berlusconi, the Italian State was granting a special award from assets confiscated from the mafia. Luca was to receive the sum of €250,000 in recognition of his courageous and unique contribution.

Bruno had called Luca in April that year to tell him that Vittore had been killed. After Pozzi left him to die, Vittore had been taken by ambulance to the hospital in L'Aquila. But he had lost so much blood that after an hour of intensive but futile attempts to save him he was declared dead. The police had interviewed the old man who had found Vittore. Because of his lead role in the hunt for the Santoros a copy of their report had been forwarded to Bruno. He was able to give Luca the small comfort that Vittore's last words showed that he had decided to face the music for his life of crime.

Luca went to the funeral in Lecce and he was able to assure the heart-broken Renata that he would be there for her and his new grandchildren. He had immediately set up a trust fund for Elisa and Tommaso and when the Italian government gave him the award, without hesitation he transferred the entire amount into the Trust. In the years following Vittore's death Elisa and Tommaso spent many holidays in the UK with the Biagis and Luca and Rosalba became very close to them. It was somewhat different with Renata. Whilst she was clearly grateful for their unstinting help and support, she never really connected with them on an emotional level.

Arturo Santoro did not escape again. He was extradited from Montenegro to a top security prison in Parma. After he was convicted of numerous murders and other serious crimes he was placed under Article 41-bis of the penal code which involved almost total isolation from the outside world to avoid any communication with his previous criminal associates. He was kept in isolation for twenty-two hours a day except for one hour in the open air and one hour with three other selected prisoners. Escape would have been virtually impossible in any event as he had to have both legs amputated above the knee after the burst from Borozan's machine pistol did irreparable damage to his legs. The latest news Bruno had on Santoro was that he had descended into a demented, feral state and no one was able to reach him.

Renata's brother-in-law, Maso had tried to make amends for unwittingly leading Pozzi to Vittore in Croatia. As soon as the circumstances of Vittore's death were publicised, he made an anonymous call to the police tipping them off that Pozzi was the killer. In spite of a massive police manhunt Pozzi was not picked up immediately. But a year later at Naples airport a vigilant passport officer suspected that the document handed to him by a cold-eyed tough looking man was a fake. Pozzi was taken out of the line and escorted to an interview room to wait whilst his passport was checked. Ironically, his passport under the assumed name he was using passed these further checks and he would have been allowed to board his flight. But his violent refusal to accompany officers to the interview room led to him being handcuffed and then fingerprinted. Although the cosmetic surgery he had undertaken had altered Pozzi's facial structure substantially, his fingerprints were on the system following several previous arrests. Once his identity was confirmed and he was arrested and charged, he went berserk. It took six policemen to subdue him and even though he was manacled he put four of them in hospital. He was tried and given several life sentences to be served concurrently for the attack on Santoro's prison transfer convoy, Vittore's murder – his DNA was found around the stab wound – and several other murders which were confirmed by revisiting the forensics of a number of homicides in Puglia.

The arrest and subsequent trial of Sir Roger Simmons gave the British Press an absolute field day with a depth and breadth of coverage unseen since the Robert Maxwell affair. Simmons was sentenced to life with a recommended minimum term of twenty years. He was also stripped of his knighthood.

Luca's nemesis Moscatelli did not see the end of 2011. That November Bruno received a call from Fredo Sportelli with the chilling news that Moscatelli had been found in his car with his throat slashed and his tongue cut out. This classic mafia punishment of an informer had caused Bruno to wonder whether his friend the *Colonello* had decided to let slip Moscatelli's role as a supergrass. He decided that the *Colonello's* code of honour precluded his involvement but that it was perfectly possible that someone in his team with links to the mafia had shopped the lawyer. The long arm and longer memory of the mafia had closed his mouth for ever.